A Gazillion Little Bits

CLAUDIA BREVIS

Cover Art & Design and Map by Sam Tsui

For Skip, Casey, and Dylan

ACKNOWLEDGMENTS

Much love and thanks to my husband, Skip, for taking this journey with me. For stopping the car whenever I needed to explore a park, climb a rock, or peer down a New York City alley. For standing next to me at the top of the Palisades and down along the water's edge, and for scouting every chapter's hills and valleys beside me. This trip wouldn't have been any fun without you and I love you and loved every minute! Thank you, also, for being the first to read my completed draft, and for not being afraid to ask the hard questions.

To my son, Casey, thank you for your deep insight, for reading and re-reading, for discussing and questioning my story in ways and in light of events and ideas beyond my vision. Thank you for bringing history and context and an overview to my equation. Your curiosity and spirit inspire me.

To my son, Dylan, thank you for challenging my words, for finding my loopholes and errors. Thank you for your keen debate and sharp eyes. For scrutinizing all my choices. Thank you for showing me Aja was hairless. You keep me honest and on my toes.

Thank you to Reddit's /r/climbing. I asked and you answered and I could not have scaled the Palisades without your advice.

Thank you, Joe, for your conversations on nanos and satellites.

Thank you, Kathy and Jean. Your input was invaluable.

Many, many thanks to you, Sam, for your brilliant art and cover and map design. I'm so grateful for your talent and time.

And thank you, especially to my parents, Mike & Juliette, for reading, proofreading, consulting, advising and supporting my every effort, always.

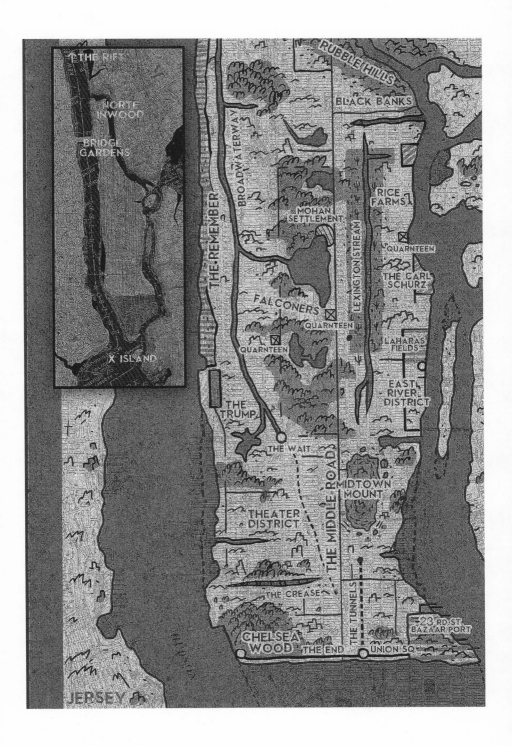

PROLOGUE

SHE WAS DREAMING of her boys—they were much younger—and they were running ahead through a lush and sweet-smelling Central Park. She called out to them but her voice was lost in the temperament of the dream and they ran around a twist in a path without looking back. Her father walked with her, and her mother, and her husband, Melly, oddly—she hadn't dreamt of him in years—but soon, they too pulled ahead out of sight. Slow motion, like molasses, feet stuck on the path, she struggled to move, but her leg burned now, and the cold breeze that caught her clothes and whipped her hair did little to ease the fire.

She woke, confused, and stared blankly out at the dark gray waters, and when she remembered, her head split and her heart broke and her arms flew out to clutch at hunks of fallen cement on the forty-seventh floor of the tower that was her home.

The earthquake—or were they explosions?—had blown out the southern floor-to-ceiling windows, and the building had collapsed into itself, somehow leaving her loft intact. The streets sunk in odd angles and rushing water flooded in carrying swirling debris.

Aftershocks jolted the city and with each shudder even more of the neighborhood disappeared. Whole blocks—the school, the clinic, the government complex, the finance cubes—crumbled and drowned, and now only churning ocean surrounded the remnants of this tower on Bleecker Street and Sixth Avenue.

A falling beam crushed her leg. She felt little pain, but the exposed bone distressed her and she covered the gore with her sweater. Later, shivering where she lay, she tried to take her cardigan from the wound but found the wool stuck to the flesh.

It stormed the first night, and she turned her face to the puddles of rainwater on the floor, opening her mouth to the ashy streams. Still thirsty, she sucked the water from her wet shirt, but that was the last she had to drink.

She thought continually about her sons as the days passed, lips moving in prayer even as she slept, though she knew they must be dead. She threw up nothing and wept without tears, desperate in her sadness. She'd learned not to think of Elizabeth—Elizabeth who'd left with Melly when he came back for them. She'd learned not to think of Melly either. The decades spent without her husband made that easy. Not thinking of Elizabeth was harder. That wound was fresher.

The SolSat kept her company. She watched the numbers in the sky change from 09.09.2078 to 09.10.2078 to 09.11.2078. One night, a helicopter buzzed overhead but flew off again before she could shout.

After a while, the hunger and thirst left. According to the SolSat she'd been laying on the floor for five days and except for the occasional smell of smoke and a thick ash blowing in when the wind shifted, the hours were uneventful.

On her last morning, during her last few minutes, the sky was clear and the sun warmed her skin. Deep in a daydream, she was watching a flock of birds cross the water to the south when a twisting thrust bent her tower to the sea and threw her broken body toward the blown out windows. She flailed and grabbed a dangling cable.

Complete sorrow, almost unrecognizable in its depth, washed over her. I will die here now, alone, she thought. No one to mourn or remember me. All gone.

"I'm sorry," she said to herself, to her sons, and then, somewhat relieved, she let go of the cable to slide out the window and into the cold, dark water.

SUMMER

THE RUNNER

JANELLE DUYVIL lifted her face to the morning light, the sun searing just moments after its rise. The numbers in the southern sky shimmered a silver 07.04.2256 against the dawn, but she paid little attention to the flickering pattern.

She padded lightly, calloused feet wrapped in tar cloth, along the quiet of the overgrown road south from the jagged tip of Manhattan, singing—chanting, really—the dispatches she'd accumulated, in order to keep the words fresh in her mind.

In less than a mile along the Hudson, weaving her relay around misty rubbled inlets and detours, Janelle had collected word that Skyson's raft was unmoored at Two-hundred-tenth—please flag and tether if found—that the Boro children were hot with a rash, and that Jared Hopes of her own Norte Inwood was gone missing.

That news frightened her, as the simple young man who hummed songs of gold and lead wouldn't have wandered from the dead-end canal. All he was driven to do found expression right there at the mud channel, where, every day, he traced and retraced onto the rocks the endless words and images—the *whispers*—in his mind.

He was a *Touched One*, and although his aunt would find him home each evening just a short climb southeast along the wooded path, the light-eyed man had not returned in two changes of the numbers. A search of the area located his chalks, scattered, his meal pail untouched, and no clue where he'd gone.

Janelle rubbed her eyes. The winds were stirring up the fumes and threatened to slow her pace. She wrinkled her nose against the smell, lowered the veil of her visor, and lengthened her stride. Two Runners waited inland for her at One-hundred-fifty-eighth to take the relay, and Janelle's hand-off needed be timely. Runners connected the city, and news sharing depended on those carrying the words. Delay was no option. She would power through.

She centered the rhythm of her breathing, keeping her mind clear for the information gathered as she did every morning. She loved the run, setting out through a dark city framed by the orange glow of the burning lands west of the Hudson, and stars in a black sky that would fade to indigo, to steel and gray and blue as the sun came up in the east.

She loved the discipline of the memorization of words, and the solitude of this stretch of shore, mostly deserted but for an oyster digger or fisherman who more often than not waved her off without asking for the news. She loved the sound of the birds over the river—gulls and terns—the cries of the peregrine falcons, and the cooing of the pigeons in the towering stone salvage of the westernmost avenues and the trees blanketing those ruins. And she loved the grindings and rumblings of the city itself, as it stretched every morning, shifting its backbone and underpinnings.

Janelle would run this route forever, but it was difficult and getting more so to leave the elders alone. The forest and water crossings were dangerous enough for the sturdy, and fewer in her camp were available in the earliest hours to oversee the great and greater grandparents. Grandfather was forever wandering, his blind eyes searching for what he remembered of his boy days, and Janelle would often find him sitting on the ridge, feet dangling, mind empty as he waited her return, or chasing the geese on the flatland below the forest to the east, near the ruins. Those were good days. Other times it might take half a night to locate him in the thick woods.

She cleared the distractions from her mind and concentrated on the breathtaking view before her. The River Bridge, a structure particularly untouched by cataclysm, was just emerging from the morning fog. This construction of the old city stretched from the western shore of Manhattan across the water to Jersey where it terminated abruptly—without explanation—in a massive brick and steel wall built into the crumbling, scorched cliffs.

Janelle was too far from the Bridge to see the corn, but she looked anyway, hungrily, toward the mid-span of the upper level where green and yellow rows were open for harvest. She'd visit the gardens after her run, and with her vouchers earned, collect a sack full of the long ears before returning home.

The Norte Inwood crop this year was suffering the fungus. Fort Tryon, too, had a diseased harvest, and the supplies Janelle traded for daily—oil, or beans, or roots, or fresh or pressed fruits or whatever the Gardeners offered to share—helped feed the Norte's nineteen elders, two children, and five young men and women—four, with Jared Hopes gone missing.

Not far from the Bridge now, Janelle focused on the giant sunflowers high above as she ran, meditative and sure-footed under the protective shade of an old wall that bordered the irregular road.

An unexpected movement caught her eye, rousing Janelle from her reflection. Without breaking stride, she squinted for a better look. Something disrupted the morning stillness on the Upper Level, maneuvering through the raised gardens. Deer were a problem in every community, as were larger, invasive creatures, but except for ever-circling birds, the gardens remained mostly immune to animal incursion. Every now and again, though, a beast made its way onto the Bridge, endangering the crops as well as the Gardeners asleep on the Lower Level. Such movement at this early hour was reason enough for Janelle to change direction and sprint inland.

She gained entrance to the complex system of approaches at One-hundred-seventy-eighth and followed the ramps. At the patina-covered eastern tower Janelle stopped to catch her breath and survey the gardens. Flat pebble paths ran along either side of the roadway. Vines twisted and climbed skyward around steel cables. Flowers of every color and variety bloomed, and beyond the sunflower fields, mid-span, corn and beans and tomatoes and squash grew tall. Further west, tobacco and other smoking greens were ripe for barter.

For a moment Janelle thought she must have imagined the movements, her concern unfounded, but then the oddest thing happened. A sleek, hairless horse, muscles clear and rippling, emerged from the sunflowers. On its back, a man wrapped in silver—the metal cloth both reflecting and absorbing the sunlight—urged the animal east.

Janelle's heart skipped a beat. The last of the uptown horses, one carrying her father, had left the city five summers earlier. If this bald horse was returned from that group, perhaps her Da might also return, a hope long faded.

She stepped forward to whistle a greeting, but the horse began a canter, and the next was so unexpected, so foreign to Janelle's world-view she would later wonder if she had seen it at all. A black pod—long and sleek in the sun, but with no apparent puller or pusher—shot out from the sunflower fields after the horse to slide over the soft earth, rolling over crops beneath and leaving deep trails in its wake. A hideous bulbous-eyed figure stood atop the—was it a wagon?—shouting as he closed the gap and pulled alongside the silver man.

They sped east, side-by-side. The man-like creature with the dark, shiny head thrust a stick at the silver man. Sparks and what looked like fire flew with each jab. One sharp turn of the black wagon and he cut the horse off, causing the animal to rear and throw its rider to the ground.

Unbelieving—and confused—Janelle watched the man scramble to avoid being crushed. The figure forced him up onto the Bridge's outer railing, where the silver man wrapped his hands around the thick cables and swung his legs in wide defensive kicks. Undeterred, his aggressor moved in. After a few moments, the man on the railing held an arm up in surrender.

The two exchanged words but then just as it seemed he would submit, the man in silver looked over his shoulder to the river below, and with only the slightest hesitation, he leapt off.

Janelle gasped. The bug-eyed figure leaned over the barrier to stare, six hundred feet down, to the river. The horse darted back and forth. On the other side, across the plantings, the ten Gardeners scooted up over the railing from the Lower Level.

They shouted and tripped on each other in their haste, but before they could reach him, the man abandoned the horse and jumped on his black pod wagon to disappear west into the sunflowers. The Gardeners stopped, and after brief discussion, split up—some to follow the man, others the horse.

Janelle had little time to wonder what was going on. The horse zigzagged east toward her. She flattened against the steel frame tower, unsure which way to run, then climbed over a stone impediment to dodge the huge beast. The rough concrete offered her fingers traction and she hung a moment before dropping to the ramp below, repeating the action again and again until she reached street level.

Below the tower, Janelle dashed across a trail to the water's edge and peered through the mist. The man who had leapt from the Bridge was gone, no sign of him on the water or shore. A lone paddler mid-river waved to her, and the two looked up at a whistling high above. The long, wooshy sound increased in volume until the wail seemed to split her head. She clamped her hands over her ears but the shriek persisted. Suddenly, the noise stopped, and the sky turned white, and green, and pink like a summer storm through a sunrise, but even that did not describe the sky-paint colors.

The mane-less, tail-less horse bolted down the old concrete highway south, then east over grass and rubble hills to disappear beyond a series of ancient green signs hanging on steel scaffolds.

Janelle hesitated. Although her first inclination was to raise a drum for a raft to locate the horseman, and her second to give chase to the horse heading inland, she knew any further detour would create an unmanageable delay in her route.

In the end, the thought of the monster in the wagon cinched her decision. She would continue her run and warn the city.

LAHARA

LAHARA 12 WAYLIN beat back thorny brambles along the shore of the East River, her long blade dull after a morning's work, her muscular arms burning from the effort. The brush always grew quickly, but this year the growth seemed determined to overrun the fields and choke the crop. Lahara worked daily to clear the land, yet on each return she'd find renewed invasion from the fibrous, sprawling hedges. It was endless work, but there was only her to do it, and she didn't complain.

She kicked through the spiked thicket. Sharp, tiny thorns raked her arms etching thin lines that filled with blood but didn't drip. The sea wall was collapsed here, and the tidal river rose and fell in charted patterns. Now the beach was narrow. The waters lapped close to the planked walkway that led north and south on the other side of the brambles and vines, and small waves splashed her toes.

Black-streaked ice boulders drifted on the river's currents. Lahara expected last year's cycle of seasons to repeat. The heat of the summer waters would melt the ice, and the river would overflow its banks—crops destroyed by the salt water, homes flooded. Neighbors along the river spoke of sandbagging the embankments, and Lahara had begun to stitch large canvas cases in preparation.

A breeze cooled by the river's ice dried the sweat on her bare legs, and she stopped a moment to savor the chill. Mack McKay's ferry was making careful journey south against the tide. His passengers paddled with their arms to help negotiate the tricky passage and Mack thrust a pole into water and mud to avoid being pulled onto the mid-river island. Late start, Lahara thought. Most days Mack would be half the way to his downtown by now.

A battered rowboat drifted uptown to the north. Lahara recognized the fisherman Leo from Carl Schurz. The man stood precariously in the dinghy, testing a long piece of rope he'd looped around a boulder of floating ice. Lasso attached, he sat back down to allow the river to pull him and his cargo upriver.

Lahara wondered idly if she could do the same. She would find many uses for such a boulder of ice. Her husband's apprentice had come to them in a wide, wooden outrigger and taught Lahara how to paddle the heavy boat and raise the sail. She could trap an ice rock in no time if she followed the current, but, no, not today. The nets needed emptying and the catch set to vinegar.

She walked along the concrete jetty into the river and crouched at the flag, feeling for the hook attached to the cement. She yanked the net above the water. Empty. She wiped her cold hands on her hot face, maneuvering back over the rocks to the fields.

They'd been lucky this season with the corn. No sign of the black rot, and although the plants were thirsty—would the rain ever come?—they were tall with rounded stalks and full ears. If they survived the heat of summer and the river stayed between its banks, there would be corn enough to trade through next season.

There was promise in all the yields. Her neighbors below the Watch expected a successful potato crop, and further south, greenhouses had been harvesting vegetables all season. There was even talk this district-wide abundance would reflect in the census.

The past three years had returned diminishing numbers, but Lahara knew the census did not accurately describe the state of the island. Often years the people below Crease were left out of the tally, the Tunnelers downtown at the east would refuse to participate, and the Inwood settlement at the far north was a difficult group to find in the woods. Families who moved seasonally from below to above ground were sometimes counted multiple times, and, of course the Disconnects, secluded and inaccessible, did not engage at all. How many Disconnects breathed? Fifty or five hundred? Lahara didn't know.

Although the count was mostly tradition, almost every neighbor could recite the figure—the last census recorded 12,419 people—even if that sum was too big to comprehend. Same with the numbers in the sky, each day unique. In fact, many people included part of the daily number in their birth name. On the thickly clouded day Lahara was born, the numbers were shining 12.08.2238. In recognition, her father called her Lahara 12.

Lahara missed her parents—Da, a quiet man, quick to anger,

and Mother, fearless even after her eyes went dark. Corn in these hand-turned fields had been her mother's idea. Her greater grandparents had cultivated a variety of grasses here, but over time the wheat refused to grow in the salty soil so Mother gambled on the corn, and the yellow and orange crop had thrived in their fields for as long as Lahara could remember.

The work was difficult but the land sometimes surprised her. Last fall the river had washed out a section of the farm, and at the bottom of the mudslide Lahara discovered a rusted box. Inside the case, shiny red balls, gold ropes and bells, a silver star and strips of glitter sparkled together like sunrise on the river. She'd never seen such things, not in bazaars or salvage or trade. And that wasn't the only gift the dirt had surprised her with. One time she'd uncovered a plastic doll the size of her own self on a hill she'd explored a thousand times before.

Lahara walked between the bramble and the field, tracking a rabbit in the crop ahead. An unwelcome buzz began deep inside. Waves of nausea pulled the air from her lungs. Not again. She closed her eyes to brace against the familiar flood—*whispers* the people called them, for want of a better term—and as they always did, the *whispers* grabbed her with bone-crushing pressure.

The land fell away. Where a moment ago Lahara's feet found traction on the soft narrow path, they burned now, through her thin sandals, with the heat of a paved tar road. She breathed deeply. Mixed with the odor of sulfur and tar, Lahara smelled rotten garbage in the heat shimmering up and over the pavement.

She focused on the new world laid before her. A click in her head—maybe the sound came from outside—aligned the view, sharpened the focus. A series of stacked parallel roads hugged the shoreline, disappearing beneath a spider web of concrete and asphalt to the south. A roar came upon her like a sudden storm, a blast of metal and siren louder than the shriek of a thousand gulls. Lahara instinctively dove from the screaming vehicles, though they could not touch her, then turned to watch them barrel north.

She had barely dragged herself from the road when the *whispers* swamped her again. This new crush pulled Lahara from the highway, from the sky-touching buildings that loomed over the river, away from the incredible noise and dirt to a quiet rocky bluff overlooking the water in the very same spot.

She gasped at the small brown face that veered so close to her own. A woman, naked but for a cloth wrapped around her hips, led the black-haired child to the cliff's edge. They climbed to the riverbank below, hanging onto strong vines and roots for support.

The water lapped against the shore and the air smelled of sweet grasses and salt. The boy ran into the water and after a brief half-submerged tussle, pulled a silver fish out with a splash, raising it in both hands to the sun.

Whispers had brought Lahara to this place before. She'd seen forests and lakes on the very land now covered by civilized ruins and rubble, but this was the first she'd seen people here. She wondered who they were. Almost before the question was formed the word *Lenape* echoed in her mind, and she understood, with no further guidance, these primeval people of the east.

The pressure in her chest dropped and released her. She gulped familiar air to remind herself the *whispers* weren't real. They were memories or dreams of different times. Dreams forced on her because she was Touched, one of a group of people, random people all over the island, who had begun to know things, see things, hear things—unbelievable, fantastic, unknowable things.

She shook her head. The rabbit still scampered ahead in the corn. Mere seconds had passed in the space the *whispers* had begun and ended, though the time gone felt much longer. It would take a few more moments to shake the sadness *whispers* always left. The knowledge that everything disclosed and every secret shared was long dead and forgotten. Her head hurt from trying to make sense of the *whispers*, an impossible undertaking.

She pushed the damp hair from her neck, irritated by the hot muddle. She'd been up before dawn to help prepare her husband's cart for the journey crosstown and to oversee the dying of cloth her niece insisted on. In the earliest hours the girl had the gray weavings from the loom to soak in a blueberry mash, adding beetroot and blackberry until the fabric turned a certain color she wouldn't explain the need for. So distracted by her niece's mystery, Lahara had left for her chores without a veil. The bridge of her nose, burnt in the sun as a result, stung in retaliation.

As they often did when she walked the field, Lahara's thoughts turned to her sister, Keisha. She had her grandfather's gift, they said, and it was true. Beasts stayed clear, plants grew tall, and the fields flourished in Keisha's hands. It was all different since they'd lost her in the birth and death of her only daughter. All different. In her failed pregnancy, she'd left more than untended fields. She'd left her husband, Switch, and a young son.

Faint in the heat, Lahara pushed her way through a thinning of the bramble and stepped carefully into a sheltered shallow. Broken pieces of a ruined city had settled into the river, changing the channel's course and depth, and while the people well enjoyed the bathing shallows, keeping watch for beasts that occasionally attempted the crossing, encounters with sharp fragments and shards in the mud were common. Lahara tossed her rough robe onto the shore but kept her slippers on.

The sun was relentless. A blister rose on her face and she splashed water to soothe it. The combination of ice and swelter helped quiet the *whispers*. Lately they had become more insistent. Sometimes *whispers* seemed to pull her to a place where others waited. Hard to describe, the notion was odd yet comforting.

Lahara closed her eyes, submerged to her shoulders. The water numbed her skin and unburdened her mind. She drifted, thoughts full of family, of home.

"La-haa-raaaaa," her six year-old stepson shouted from inland. "La-haa-raaaaa, it's the drums from the west."

She stood in the water, the dust of the city in streaks down her bare skin. Marly, her sister's son, ran waving toward the shore. Small for his age, brown from long days outdoors, he wore his head shaved, as was the fashion of the young. Lahara would have liked to shave her own head, but at seventeen she was too old, and besides, Switch preferred her hair long.

In the two years since Keisha's death, when, as was the people's custom, she had married Switch and taken Marly as her own, Lahara had not once cut her hair. She, like many other longhaired women and men of the island, styled her tresses by weaving bits of glass and wire into the strands. Blue pieces of salvaged tile and slivers of hammered silver dangled from the twisted curls. Sometimes she dreamed of piles of long black hair at her feet, and upon waking didn't know if the hair she dreamt was her own, or *whispers* of another age.

The boy ran through the field, his head appearing and disappearing in the corn. He emerged to run along the side of a fallen tower, its top deep in the waters of the East River. The *whispers* had revealed images of this smokestack that stretched skyward from the building just west of her field. That substantial ruin, an ancient power station long stripped of its machinery and relevance, still retained thirty-foot high arched and gated facades visible from the windows of Lahara's home across the street.

"Why don't you answer?" Marly called, scrambling through the brush, oblivious to the thorns and spikes against his skin.

Lahara shook the *whispers* from her head. "The water hypnotizes under the sun's heat," she said. "Ya, to see you here, you must be finished with the soapings."

"Almost, but there was the drum. Reko sent me to find you."

"What drum?" Lahara puzzled, drying her skin with her robe.

"Call to Tent," Marly whispered. "The Group that Left has come back across the River Bridge."

Her heart caught at the mention of The Group. "Do you and Reko invent stories?" Her husband's apprentice Reko—that was a nickname, his given name difficult to pronounce—hadn't been back to Chelsea Wood in a long while and missed his brothers. To ease his homesick, he often engaged Marly in games.

"It's the true," Marly insisted. "Well, not all come back. One come with his horse, and the horse has no hair, over the Bridge. A message bird flyed home from the west tells a monster threw the man in the river. Everyone's to Tent."

"Threw what man in the River? And what do you mean the horse has no hair?" Lahara asked. "Where's Beatrice?"

"My cousin's ahead to save a place for us."

None of his news made sense. The River Bridge, one of the only intact from the old times, spanned the Hudson to the great wall of New Jersey, where the last settlement had died or its survivors departed in a time too long ago to remember. The Bridge was not crossable for the wall. Beyond the wall the underground burned as it had for generations. There were no people to the west. The land was uninhabitable, the air not breathable. And what monsters did the drums describe? Surely such creatures existed only in the *whispers* of the Touched.

The people's world was a gentle one. A verdant, watery island disturbed only by fumes from the west and creature crossings from the east and north, crossings that had become less frequent. That much Lahara knew to be true.

Lahara led Marly by his small, sticky hand through the narrow street toward the York, a wide, flat promenade bordered by tall trees on grassy hills. Reko waited at the crossing for them, one foot on the triple-wheeled scooter-board he'd designed and built with Switch. The Chelsea crest—a spiral of arms and legs surrounded by trees inked in muted colors—was visible beneath the stubble of Reko's shaved head, and he scratched the tattoo absentmindedly as they approached.

"Flag your wheels and leave them." Lahara said to the apprentice. "You'll sit with us, yeah?"

Reko shook his head. "Nah, canna. I'm to help cart rubber."

"But all are called," Lahara said. He shouldn't ignore a call to Tent. It was the way of the East River district.

"The man expects me," he said, holding her gaze.

Lahara took in the set of the boy's mouth and the tapping of his foot. She hesitated, and then nodded. She felt a warmth for this fourteen-year-old who had journeyed uptown for opportunities not available in his own isolated community and who had such loyalty to his mentor.

"Will your wheels make the journey across the park?"

Reko grinned. "Ball bearings, they're called. Inserted them myself according to a schematic I found at bazaar. Gave the Touched One my hard shoes in barter."

Lahara looked at his feet. They were wrapped in canvas. Hard shoes would be worth more to most, but to Reko, the schematics were more valuable.

"I'ma test them now," he said. "I'm confident of a perfect job."

Lahara didn't understand what Reko worked on, but didn't need to. He had a blazing comprehension of whatever the Touched shared, which was more than most Touched could claim.

Whispers often languished, unused, untranslated, thrust upon unwilling recipients.

Some *whispers*, misunderstood, ended disastrously. The Group that Left had been seduced by such. But that was history. Lahara trusted Reko. Switch depended on him.

Marly crouched to pat the rubber wrapped around the wooden wheels of Reko's scooter. "I want to go, too."

Lahara pulled her stepson up and waved Reko away. "Safe journey. Work well."

He tugged Marly's ear and pushed off. The scooter-board rolled slowly past the jumble of lean-to's, carts, and fires crowding the Tent plaza, picking up speed in the open space to the uptown.

From all along the York, neighbors streamed into Tent, the sun-bleached structure stretching north from Seventy-sixth to Seventy-seventh and west to the First Avenue Stones. Lahara held tight to Marly as they maneuvered through the market. Tables were piled with textiles, wagons offered sweets and savories, dealers hawked herbs, and stands displayed salvaged stone and glass for barter. Neighborhood dogs lurked by the food stalls, hungry for scraps vendors might toss into ditches behind them.

Lahara's mouth watered at the smell of sizzling bread—she had eaten only an apple at sunrise—but a sharp stomach cramp forced her to turn away.

The drum repeated the pattern of warnings, and the people hurried to its renewed sound. The commanding beat sent a flock of pigeons skyward over the press of arriving neighbors. It was the most urgent of the community rhythms. The pattern announced, simply—TENT NOW—repeated at intervals, and all who heard the drum came right away to gather in the public enclosure.

The rhythm guided Lahara and Marly through the open flaps. A frame of recovered metals and wood supported the spacious, canvas structure of the East River district's great meeting place. Inside, rising benches circled a center dais from which the Drummer Petro struck hardwood mallets on a standing drum he'd hollowed from the trunk of an ancient tree.

Lahara sniffed the familiar mildew of the arena. She knew all the neighbors filing in, called from chores to this meeting, some carrying children, others carrying work—tools, or textiles, or baskets of forage. Those who arrived from farms or salvage left hand wagons outside. Even with the exceptional turnout of the drum call—Lahara guessed there to be over a hundred people—the Tent was mostly empty and voices echoed in the amphitheater. Lahara had no memory of a Tent filled to capacity. That age had slipped away with the grandparents of her grandparents.

Lahara directed Marly down the center aisle and they took seats next to Beatrice. She was surprised at the fresh red ink ringing the edge of her niece's veil. Some sort of fruit painted along the hem. Marly climbed onto his cousin's lap and touched the decorative trim but Beatrice swatted his fingers. Behind them, the young widow Tooma sat with her Da, face creased with worry.

"Hallo, sister friend," Lahara said gently, turning to the anxious woman she'd known her whole life.

"What do you make of it, Lahara? The rumors are thick. A monster on the Bridge?" The widow spun her yellow hair around her fingers. "I'm frightened."

Lahara's eyes clouded as she thought what to answer. Tooma's husband had been found sliced by beasts on the shore just a single season after their union. She, and other neighbors, had accompanied the young Touched One's body across and over the city, by foot, to the Remember. Under a simple stone, Tooma had buried her husband before leading the procession slowly back east.

"I don't know what to think." She took Tooma's plump, inked hand in her own. "We can't worry about what mightn't be real."

Marly bounced in excitement. "Remember Reynaud's story? George and the fire breathing dragon?"

"Stop," Beatrice complained, shoving the boy off her lap. "I didn't like that story. I don't like the dragon."

"I think a dragon come on the River Bridge today," Marly said.

"Or something worse," Beatrice said softly.

Speculation spread like a brush fire through the arena. Voices escalated as rumors boomeranged across benches, around the stands and up to the height of the tent.

"The Runner was trampled by a beast."

"A monster drowned a visitor in a whirlpool."

"The western reach has crumbled."

"The flames are spreading along the Bridge gardens."

On and on the words circled, younger neighbors afraid and close to tears, older ones wondering where in these embellished stories the true was to be found. Lahara wished Switch were there to deflect some of the confusion.

"Why hasn't my Uncle come back from the subway salvage?" Beatrice asked. "Because of the dragon?"

"Nonsense," Lahara began, but as she tried to reassure her niece, *whispers* crushed her words. Powerless against the vibrations, she found herself in a dim space. Hot air scorched her throat. Pressed against a throng of people, assaulted by the smell of a thousand bodies, her heart quickened at the screech of the arriving train. Panels opened in each car and people pushed out even as those on the platform forced their way into the cars.

Lahara struggled to breathe. Despite the fierce hold of the *whispers* she could hear her niece cry out and almost feel the pressure of Beatrice's long fingers on her arm.

"The subways ran day and night." Lahara spoke into the direction she knew her own world was to be found, using words her neighbors might not understand. "Millions traveled through tunnels illuminated by a light not of the sun."

Unable to shake the *whispers*, Lahara watched with horror as crowded subway platforms cracked. Water raced through the tunnels ahead of orange fireballs. The cries of trapped people mixed with thick smoke and steam. Lahara fell to her knees, her face pushed against the cool, sticky tile of the subway walls.

She shouted over the mayhem. "Water mains broke, passages flooded, the sidewalks disintegrated and gave way. Many tunnels collapsed, and the tidal ocean flowed into those that remained."

"My uncle is trapped in the underground," Beatrice sobbed.

At her niece's cry, the *whispers* released Lahara. She blinked, back in Tent, the air clear, the light natural, neighbors regarding her with interest and concern.

"No, no," Lahara said. "It was *whispers* had me. Your uncle is only beyond the reach of the drums."

The drum boomed again and the neighbors grew quiet at its instruction. Petro lowered his mallets. "Many greetings, people."

Lahara whistled and clapped with the crowd, trying to leave her *whispers* behind. She focused on the drummer, a heavyset, muscular man who was older now than her own grandparents would have been.

"Just after daybreak," Petro said, "a Runner observed strangers on the River Bridge, one on horseback. Since most horses departed with The Group that Left, and none remain in the uptown, she assumed this man to be a survivor of the same."

A voice from the crowd interrupted. "If this is true, if they're returned, why aren't we west to greet them? Why the waste of time to Tent?"

"And why in dangum would one of the Group be on the River Bridge?" a second voice challenged. "To barter tomatoes?"

"There's no reason," a third interjected. "It's nonsense."

"And what of the horse? No hair? Have you ever heard such?"

Petro waved his mallet for attention. "We all have questions," he agreed. "I don't know that we'll find answers today." He gestured to his neighbors. "Perhaps *whispers* will help. More than common sense is needed to unravel this next."

Lahara shrugged and looked to see scattered others—Touched, each one—acknowledge Petro's words. There was Reynaud, the dark-skinned young man who braided his hair against his scalp, *Touched with Story whispers*. Old Jasbro, one of the triplets from Sixty-fifth, was *Touched with Law whispers*. Lahara saw Neal, a Touched One who didn't understand his *whispers*, but who carefully copied the images and spellings on cloth and carried them in his turban for barter. Above him, in a top bleacher, Martina Belle, a six-year-old *Touched with Music*, sprawled in her mother's arms.

Petro waited for all eyes back on him before he continued. "There was an altercation between the man on horseback and a second, likely a man as well. There is some confusion as to what, if anything, covered his face. The Runner named him monster. He journeyed on a heavy wagon low to the ground."

Lahara's *whispers* had shown strange and varied vehicles that drank thick gasoline, vehicles later powered by light fuels, and batteries, and hydrogen powders created from refuse, vehicles that at one time clogged city streets and were later restricted to brightly lit multiple stacked highways that outlined the island to connect with wider arteries and bridges, vehicles whose exposed shells decomposed in the highest layers of remaining road and lay forever buried in the salvage of lower collapsed layers.

"Gardeners followed the wagon as best they could but lost sight of it in the western plantings. Examination of the horse tracks and the wheel marks show they begin abruptly at the western wall." He rested his hands on his drum and leaned forward. "The wheel marks return to the same spot. The tracks end at the wall."

"Did the wagon drop from the sky?" a neighbor called. "Or take off again like a bird?"

"Perhaps they come through the wall," another added.

Petro shook his head. "The track assessment is difficult to reconcile with what we know of the sealed western reach. Touched Ones, do your *whispers* inform?"

"My *whispers* are telling the tale of a little red lighthouse under the Bridge," Reynaud said. "A story loved by children in their time."

Marly poked Beatrice. "What's a lighthouse?"

"Any others to share?" Petro asked, disrupting *whispers* in Lahara's mind as pebbles disrupt a reflection in a pond.

Martina Belle stood in the top tier. Her mother placed a protective arm around her as the girl's clear voice sang out.

> *Sur le pont D'avignon*
> *L'on y danse, l'on y danse*

The ancient melody raised a deep sadness in Lahara, though the words were in a language long gone. She wasn't the only one affected. Tears ran freely down faces of the neighbors around her, and their arms reached out in support. Martina's voice faltered a moment, and when she began to sing again, the words were ones they could understand.

> *On the bridge of Avignon*
> *We all dance there, we all dance there*
> *On the bridge of Avignon*
> *We all dance there, round and round*

"Where is the man now?" Martina's mother called down when her daughter finished. "Surely somebody will recognize this one returned as I would yet know my husband after five years."

Petro shook his head. "He was pushed, or fell, from the Bridge. Unless the waters give him up to the shore there will be no chance to recognize him."

"Who would do such a thing?" a neighbor shouted.

"What barbarism comes this way?" said another. "And what of the horse?"

The Drummer held up his hand. "As more news is received," he promised, "it will be relayed. In the meanwhile, this morning's events have a practical consequence. A portion of the sunflower trade harvest is destroyed, so we expect oil to be short. Word is relayed Midtown Mount will offer sunflowers into the barter pool."

Lahara had rare occasion to travel up the wide steps of the Midtown Mount, a highland over one-hundred feet in elevation, originating, Lahara's *whispers* had described, with subterranean flooding of the burning skyscrapers, the erosion and crumbling of the bedrock that anchored them, the toppling of the compromised structures and the subsequent overgrowth and settlement throughout the ruins.

She hoped her oil reserves would last the season, but would not mind another opportunity to visit and barter for additional. Besides the trade, she'd love to hear again the piano housed deep in the Under Mount and the many mixed voices that sang with it. The climb into the interior was difficult for an outsider, but she'd done it with her mother years before and had dreamed of the music ever since.

Petro hit the drum and as Lahara and the children followed their neighbors into the sun, Martina shared her *whispers* again.

On the bridge of Avignon
We all dance there, we all dance there
On the bridge of Avignon
We all dance there, round and round

THE STRANGER

AT FIRST, HE could only recall the drop from the Bridge, the startling, abrasive rush of the free fall and the seconds it took to straighten his body, arms up, feet pointed, praying that he enter the water like a knife and avoid any debris in the river below.

That must have been hours ago, for from his position on the Hudson River's eastern shore, he calculated the sun at noon, and his escape to the city had begun before dawn. Escape from where?

He rubbed his legs, numbed by the waters that lapped over him to his thighs, and dragged himself from below the remnants of a pier, nauseated by the exertion. Had he been drinking?

Somehow, after jumping, he had gotten himself onto the shore. He didn't remember how. He assessed the damage to his body—raised welts on his arms and chest, a sprained ankle, a gash above his eye. His fingers explored the blood dried in his brow and sticky on his cheek. He blinked, trying, unsuccessfully, to clear his vision. Likely he had a concussion.

He sat up slowly, the sun on his bare shoulders, and examined the landscape. To the west, the Hudson and the Palisades. Beyond the cliffs, heat from New Jersey's burning caverns made the air shimmer. Somewhere below or beyond would be the Vault. The Vault? So hard to remember.

He squinted north. A mile or more away the steel towers of the George Washington Bridge rose over the wooded landscape. To the east, a rubbled hillside, the cupola of Grant's Tomb visible over the trees, and to the south, no recognizable landmark, just parkland continuing into the distance.

He placed a careful finger on his blistered red shoulder. "Shit."

A quick scan of the shoreline yielded nothing. He beat at the marsh grass, kicking up pungent mud. His protective jacket was gone. He reached into the wet dirt, and, grabbing dark handfuls from between the wild reeds, smeared the paste over his bare arms, his torso, his face—over his smooth head—letting the thick sediment drip down his unprotected back. He didn't know how well the mud would safeguard him, but it had to be better than exposure.

His tongue stuck to cracked, dry lips, and he realized, with distress, that along with his jacket, his provisions—his water—had also vanished. Vertigo threatened to topple him so he sat back down and the world stopped spinning.

Just up the incline a tree beckoned, and he crawled toward its shade on bruised knees, through the stone and boulder-covered hillside. As he crawled, he began to remember.

He'd waited until the scheduled power down. The generators were recharging, and Vault was brown, all personnel to their assigned wait-duties. Vault engaged multiple power systems— solar, thermal, wind, steam, and others more complex—and he knew that although the horizontal-vertical elevators would be disabled, the Freights would be operational.

He'd opened the steam elevator, and inputted the stolen codes, each number forcing hot water through a pipe. The lift was supposed to bring him to a cruiser cloaked on the Hudson. He was on a horse. An unconnected memory of horses dead in whale-sized capsules flickered. He'd been riding Vault's last horse.

"Aja," he shouted, startling a wild turkey hidden in the stippled grass. Did he really desert Aja on the George Washington Bridge?

So many mistakes. The first, thinking power down wouldn't affect the alarms. He didn't know the sirens bypassed the grid, powered by steam, not electricity. His second mistake was in the codes. When the chamber opened he rode Aja through the long tube as expected, but at the end no water cruiser waited. The codes had deposited him not at Level Eight, but up at Level One, and the tube had opened on the Bridge, not the river.

His third mistake, against all training, was to indulge in culture shock those first moments outside. He shouldn't have stopped to wonder at the cornfield where eight lanes of traffic once sped, or at the wall that rose a thousand feet from the river. The air was so different. Thick and hot and yes, acrid, but he breathed deeply, not caring that without a mask he risked the gasses.

In response to the alarm, Racine came up and through the tube in an armored transport. Fourth mistake. Waiting to defend himself to his colleague. His friend.

"Melly wouldn't have allowed it to play out this way," he'd told Racine. "It's insane. Admin would never have sanctioned such actions."

"We have one mission," the masked Vaulter countered from the transport. "None of it is my call or your call. Melly's dead. We answer to Seth. You took an oath and you know the penalty."

He'd hesitated at that reminder. The Project was his life—he'd left everything behind for it. They all had. But nobody could have foreseen the breach. Those remaining had been divided into the knows and the know-nots and he'd been one left in the dark. The work was all consuming, he rationalized, but he'd ignored awful hints. God only knew how he came to stop pretending, but once he did, he had no choice but to try and stop the Recovery.

"How can you live with yourself?" he challenged Racine.

They'd worked side by side when the Project began. Patriots of civilization. Four phases passed without incident until they'd been awakened, five years earlier, to a disaster that had no contingency. They took different paths then. He stayed inside to repair, recode, reconstruct, and Racine went out to reclaim what had been lost.

"We can figure a better way," he begged, unable to see Racine's expression behind his mask. And then his friend had leveled against him the thin photonic laser they carried for protection.

Too much to remember. He crawled the last few feet up the hill, palms raw from the rough soil. With his head throbbing and his own name just out of reach, he rested a bloody check on the wide oak's gnarled roots.

Some time later, he opened his swollen eyes. He climbed to his feet, bruised body stiff, and ran his hands over his peeling scalp. His fingers caught a thin wire wrapped around his head and he pulled free a tiny silver sphere. He looked at it curiously, and then remembered—the Connex-Link.

He twisted the core. Nothing happened, and he feared the river had rendered it inactive. But the bead came out of sleep mode with a vibration, and he saw a hill covered with white and yellow flowers under a steel arch, one of a series of arches that stretched north.

It took a moment to recognize the view transmitted from Aja's Connex-Link. Below Riverside Drive, somewhere above One-hundred-twenty-fifth. If not for the filigreed arches rising from low hills, he might not have identified the horse's location. Centuries had camouflaged the city, the only other clues to her location the shell of a sky tram and graffiti covered billboards.

The Connex was supposed to work in reverse as well. He turned the bead on its wire to transmit his own face and spoke a few words to get the horse's attention, but she didn't react and the connection faded. He twisted the sphere—a failed reboot—and finally threaded the bead back on the wire in hopes of a recharge.

Much as he wanted to find his horse, it would be risky traveling back to the Bridge. He'd seen the flare from the river. Messages between cruisers in the field. They'd be looking for him.

He needed water and shelter and a place to heal. He'd head south, away from the Bridge. Aja would fend for herself until he was certain he wasn't putting her in danger. He'd figure out how to rejoin her and how to begin warning the people of Manhattan.

The secluded waterside park gave good cover as he traveled, and he stayed away from the darker, more ominous hills obstructing the roads inland. He stumbled south, disoriented in the heat. After so much time in the Vault, open areas made him uncomfortable and his anxiety spiraled when a dry thunderstorm crossed overhead.

At the first boom he fell to his knees, forehead pressed against a standing stone, hands behind his head in brace position. Neon cracks split the sky and thunder echoed across the river and through the corridor of ruins to the west.

The storm passed quickly but his heart continued to race. As he waited for the panic to subside, he looked more closely at the smooth engraved stone he'd leaned against. *Remember David.*

He moved through nearby similarly scratched or chiseled stones and ran his fingers along the etchings and read them out loud. "Remember Gregory." And another, "Remember Sharon."

From stone to stone, he continued, "Remember Lawrence ... Remember Renee ... Remember John."

It was a cemetery. The whole of Riverside Park a cemetery. He followed the markers further south. The stones here were older, with more elaborate inscriptions. "Beloved Brother," he read. "In God's Hands. Heaven Bound."

At the sound of rough wheels on the uneven road above, he dove for cover, afraid to be found, damning the tracer embedded in his body. The wheels drew closer and he stretched his neck to peer through the trees. A woman pulled a heavy cart, head down. He waited until she was out of view and resumed his hike.

He was exhausted. Dehydrated. By the time he reached Eighty-ninth Street he was hearing music—drums and voices—and he suspected he might be hallucinating. He sipped carefully from a thin, milky stream flowing across the park. His own reflection in the waters startled him. It was nobody he knew.

The stones were broken here, crumbling, some blank, erased by time and weather, or marked with stark notation he wept while reading. "Unknown Person ... Children in Taxi ... Family Together ... Lost One ... Burnt Man ... From the Water."

On and on and on, he read the epitaphs on the stones crushed together, impossibly crammed into this park by the river, on both sides of the collapsed West Side Highway.

"Girl in Hole ... Person ... Bodies ... Man and Dog ... Boy..."

His voice faded. He stretched his arms out and spun slowly to witness the graves upon graves. A piece of fallen highway lay across the field. Hammered into the concrete ruin, and painted over with a thick tar were the words "Gone to fire, gone to flood, gone to earth. Have mercy on those we could not claim."

He'd been safe in the Vault—Cocooned—four and a half years into their second phase, when the collapse began. He'd later seen every available satellite image and transmitting news feed, but the feeds and histories were a lifetime from this necropolis. He stood for a long, long while as the sky darkened, and only when a summer lightning lit the sky, did he remember who he was.

He was Anthony Steele, born in Brooklyn, New York, in 2015, a Restoration Specialist in the *Global Data Management Project*.

LAHARA

LAHARA SLID THE crate from under the stairway and sifted through pieces of metal signage and scraps of marked wood. The sun was far across the sky, and though the Carl Schurz boats might have already traded the whole of their day's catch, with her own nets empty, she needed find dinner elsewhere. She slipped a few painted scraps into her robe—a gift for her cousin—and stood, knees dusty from the floorboards.

"Children," Lahara called. "Fill my flask."

The sound of wood on brick outside told Lahara she'd been heard, and just a moment later Beatrice came in to hand her a container. "The cistern is low, Auntie."

Lahara sipped and spit out the dregs without swallowing. "You'll need bring six buckets from the river," she said, wondering when the rains would come. "After you've filled the distillery, pour the tub water on the vegetables. Leave the latrine. We can get another day from it."

Beatrice made a face. "Only if we void on the rocks instead."

"The letter box is out," Lahara said. "You need practice spellings when water chores are finished."

She looped her pack over her shoulder and headed out past the compost hill through the rubble alleys, to emerge from a gray brick tunnel at Seventy-ninth, one of the few roads that crossed unobstructed—except where the First Avenue Stones and the Lex Stream slowed passage—from the East River to the Central Park, and west of the Park over the Broadwaterway to the Hudson.

Lahara walked north under the mossy shade of East End Avenue, quiet fields on one side, blocks of wet half-buildings on the other. Her mind drifted as she hiked and she felt, beneath her *whispers*, the deep undercurrent that called her name.

What exactly were *whispers*? Why did they rise in some and not in others? All Lahara or anyone knew for certain is they referenced old times, though in the short period before this was sorted, during the illnesses—oh, the headaches—the mania they caused had been ruinous. How many had, in hallucinations and pain, believed the *whispers* directed them to leave everything behind? The loss of those Gone cut deep. Had any recovered?

Lahara was *Touched with the City*. Her *whispers*, random and non-linear, were memories and dreams—a confusing history—of the constructions and streets she lived in.

As a treasury of practical information, her *whispers* were a currency of barter. For most anything else, they were often a burden of little use.

Vine-covered stone walls surrounded the Carl Schurz. The walls had been in place forever, the vines renewed themselves every spring. Lahara passed through the gate under the cover of sprawling trees. Tiny flowers grew in cracks in the paths, and low fences were barely visible for the foliage.

Crossing the field that stretched to the promenade, Lahara smelled cured eel and cook fires come from the longhouses facing the river, and she felt hungry at the smoky scent.

The fish trade was below the wide, railed walkway, and Lahara climbed down to the cooler, lower paths where a dark-inked woman rinsed cloth in a small fountain in the plaza. Lahara waved.

"When's that niece to come north for lessons?" the woman Barti asked, wringing water with strong hands from a man's tunic. "We're to build a shed for the light boats."

Of the twenty-one lived in the Carl Schurz, three were children and a good many elderly or infirm. Chores outnumbered able bodies so the community welcomed young, strong neighbors to help, swapping lessons for their time.

"We're almost to harvest," Lahara said, "But Beatrice can for sure trade a morning's work."

Barti smiled. "I'll tell the husbands."

Lahara continued along the dandelion-covered trail, the path spongy beneath her feet. Small boats drained upside down in the sandy dirt, the remains of their haul set in nets that hung from the pier. Dogs lurked in a half-hearted pack nearby, chasing the occasional squirrel while the children played on a huge hunk of melting ice drug onto the concrete beach.

"I'm the king of the salvage, you pay me for your passage," chanted a girl Lahara didn't recognize. The twins, Mario and Roosevelt, scrambled to slap the girl's waiting hand as the smaller boy, Mario, sang in response, "Watch the wolves in the water, they'll take away your daughter." His brother shrieked as he slid down.

Ross, one of Barti's husbands, was up to his knees in the river to sort the catch. "What's good?" Lahara called. "The birds left my own net empty."

He lifted a mesh. "These perch'll fill your pot."

Lahara nodded. "Marly's got his father's appetite."

"His cleverness, too. Might he be interested in the *Chinese*?"

"What's that?"

"Leo's second wife, Nina, shares the chinese every morning. The Touched One and her daughter Rieni come from the west side to make a new start."

"*Kuai yi dianr*," he said to the girl on top of the ice, and she laughed at him.

"The chinese," he explained.

Lahara puzzled the chinese, and tried the strange words in her own mouth.

"News spreads of the horse returned and the monster on the Bridge," Ross said. "It makes no sense."

"About as much as the chinese," she admitted.

Old Martin with the flyaway white hair pulled his dinghy ashore. His light blue eyes were sharp in wrinkled lids. "Were you at Tent? I missed the call for river work."

"Yes," she said. "But it's more questions than answers we got."

"Is my cousin arrived?" a familiar voice called from behind. "I hope you're come to gossip." Lahara turned to the gray-haired Sue-Bee, the woman descended from the brother of her own great-grandfather.

"Barti told you were here," Sue-Bee said, pulling Lahara close. "I'm up from my stitchings to say hallo. Our net caught on some dangum new metalwork this morning. I swear there was no debris yesterday. The river's spitting up bones."

"It's a moody water," Lahara agreed.

"What of the monster on the Bridge, Touched One?" Old Martin interrupted.

She shrugged. "The Runner seemed certain what happened. According to the Drummer, anyway."

"I've seen such a monster to the north. On the water," Martin said. "Under sky-paint in the night."

"Always monsters. *Ni zenme zheme ben a*?" Sue-Bee chided.

Lahara looked at her with surprise. "The chinese," Sue-Bee offered. "I can teach you what I have."

Lahara was sure she had no room for anyone else's *whispers*— her own took enough of her time. "I've brung you a present," she said, to change the subject. "Give me your hand."

Sue-Bee opened her palm to the sky, and Lahara lay each of the scrap letters in her hand. "S-O-O-B-E-E."

"Name spellings," her cousin laughed. "I'll copy the letters on the side of my boat so the fish know who's to catch them."

Martin waved Sue-Bee away. "Gossip says the monster drove a wagon of fire."

"It's not for us to worry on," Sue-Bee said. "These stories clear themselves after a time. We'll find it's just the Runner breathing fumes."

The fumes. Lahara caught her breath as the vibration rose. A high-pitched hum filled her head and she squeezed her eyes against the sound. *Whispers* pushed her through a tiny spot in her mind ... to where?

She opened her eyes again and a clicking sharpened the scene around her. She could barely move for the press of people holding rags over their faces. Boxy, flashing vehicles blocked the road. A man in a strange, dark mask shouted instructions through some mechanism that allowed his words to carry over the noise.

"Proceed to the Lexington Avenue entrance."

Lahara joined the crush, glancing at the sign—*26th St*—as they rounded the corner. Endless waves of people pushed through the arched entryway of—click—the *Sixty-Ninth Regiment Armory*.

She crinkled her nose in the sour air. A roaring mammoth metal bird hung in the sky—*helicopter*, her *whispers* shared—and now, wooden crates with undecipherable letterings were lowered from the bird on thick twine to disappear onto the roof.

A shot of white squeezed her. In the flash Lahara found herself in a large arena inside the Armory. Men and women in black hooded masks were lifting more of the same from the crates. The people replaced rags against their faces with the masks, and screwed canisters to the hoods.

"This gas mask doesn't work," a woman cried, pulling the attachment from her young child's head. "Give me another." But the toddler was taken from her arms and placed in a truck with many other bodies.

Lahara grabbed phrases from the mayhem—*toxins, evacuation, withdrawal*—and as she tried to make sense of the words—*gas masks, ammonia, thermal*—the pinhole in her mind expanded, knocking the *whispers* from her.

She sucked the salt air of the Carl Schurz Marina. Old Martin, Sue-Bee, Ross, the children on the ice all where she had left them, as if just seconds had passed, for in the true, only seconds had.

"Are you back?" Sue-Bee asked, offering a drink from her flask. Lahara sipped, trying to remember the *whispers* as she might recall a dream.

"The air was unbreathable. Gas masks kept them alive." The neighbors leaned in so not to miss a word. "With the masks on, the people looked like insects. Or beasts," Lahara added slowly. "Like monsters."

"How scary," Sue-Bee said.

"What the Runner saw this morning," Lahara said, recalling the description. "Maybe it was a man in a gas mask."

"If a man come from the fires at the Bridge," Sue-Bee said, "he might need such a thing. The smokes are unbreathable."

"How can a man come from the fires?" Martin argued. "What does that mean? Have you forgotten the wall on the Bridge?"

"My guess," Ross said, handing the wrapped fish to Lahara. "The monster is a beast found his way across to the island and wandered up to the Bridge."

Martin's voice rose in frustration. "A beast in a wagon without a pusher or puller? How can it be a beast?"

"In the north," Sue-Bee said, "they hear beasts across the dead end canal."

"Disconnects," Ross corrected. "They make a strange noise in their privacy. Some say they sing, but it's an odd song if that."

The conversation went round and round without resolution. Lahara's *whispers* had retreated and her fish needed be put in the fire. "I appreciate the perch," she said. "What can I offer in return?"

Ross calculated. "The catch are heavy for the pot, and would be a voucher each, but you've exchanged *whispers*, and I thank you for what no one else can give."

Sue-Bee took a small bag of smoky, dried oysters from her pack and passed them to Lahara. Martin offered a piece of chewy honey gum. The barter served each well. The *whispers* would fuel conversations through the night and into the next, to be swapped with others they encountered.

Lahara made her good byes and started back on the path to East End. She slipped a salty oyster chip into her mouth with hopes her husband would be home by the time she arrived. Old Martin shuffled up from behind. "I've seen things," he said. "Things dismissed as elder babble."

Lahara stopped. "Have you been Touched, Martin? Do you speak of *whispers*?"

"It doesn't take a Touched One. My eyes and ears do well enough." He shook his head. "There's a stranger been near. I've seen what he means to hide and we won't share further words."

Lahara wrinkled her brow. "Perhaps you've met the census man?" she offered.

Martin threw his hands in the air. "I don't have a name for him and your *whispers* have none either." He scurried into the trees, and Lahara watched until shadows covered his movements. He never once looked back.

Lahara smelled charred flesh as she turned onto Seventy-fifth. Switch was not yet home—the street was empty of his wagon—so it would be Reko returned alone. The boy from Chelsea Wood ate animal, as the people from the southern tip did, and although Lahara didn't find the practice kind, she was curious.

She whistled her approach and peeked straightaway into the wide, open hut Reko had built next to the workshop. Inside, stripped to shorts and vest, he turned a skinless—cat?—on the center fire grate. The meat sizzled and popped, and smoke from the burning fat pulled up through a hole in the composite roof.

Lahara averted her eyes. There was something disturbing about animal in that condition. "What's the word on your journey west?"

"Failure. The ball bearings aren't stable," he said, displaying long, raw scrapes on his side. "By the time I arrived at salvage, the man had departed." He poked the meat with a finger. "He's not yet returned?"

"No," Lahara said, ill from the fatty smoke.

"Would you share my grill?" Reko asked politely.

"Thank you, no." Lahara backed away with haste, and Reko laughed out loud at the expression on her face.

In Lahara's absence, Marly and Beatrice had set their scrap letters through the kitchen and around the storeroom. Marly guided Lahara along the trail that circled a barrel of pickled vegetables.

"Thare waz wons a velveteeeen rabbit, and in the baginning he was rilly splendid," he recited, pointing at each letter and ending with, "He waz fat and bunchy as a rabbit shood beee."

"Reynaud's *whispers* from the moon past," Lahara said.

"Beatrice knew the spellings, but I remembered the story."

Lahara clapped her approval. "Now copy the spellings with chalk."

"I don't know where my board is," Beatrice said.

"Your uncle's made replacement twice," Lahara said, thinking of the slate Switch had framed, and of the thin bars of light stone he'd cut and wrapped for writing.

"You drawed pictures last night," Marly told his cousin. "Your board is up the stairs."

"I don't want to make letters," Beatrice cried. "My head hurts."

Lahara put her hand on Beatrice's face, afraid for the fever, but her skin was cool. The girl's complaints came frequent of late, and the mint wrapped in a wet towel set above her eyes offered no relief. Lahara sighed and checked the length of the shadows.

"Never mind." She grabbed a piece of wood from the pile, and with the fish and flour bucket in her hands and the plank under her arm, she led the children out to the yard kitchen. The scrap sparked and caught almost immediately, filling the brick with salvage smoke, and Lahara removed the capstone to vent the offending burn-off.

She dropped the fish onto the hot surface where it spit and crackled. Beatrice shaped the dough, and the flatbreads turned brown as the last light faded and darkness came again.

Lahara pinned up the cloths that had kept the house cool during the day, and lit the lamps. Her consumption of oil might seem excessive with the looming shortages, but she was anxious and the multiple pools of pale yellow light were her attempt to cheer the children and summon Switch, who still hadn't returned.

A late homecoming was rare, though at times trade did keep Switch away long hours, especially if he made a far journey. But the morning's rubber salvage was at One-hundred-twenty-eighth near the Broadwaterway. Switch should have been east before sunset. He carried a message bird and would have sent word to the Watch if he'd found danger, but even so, the delay concerned Lahara.

The relief she felt when the glass tinkled at the gate was short, for a moment later, Reynaud's voice called, "Halloo?" and Switch was still not returned. "Tonight's story is The Little Red Lighthouse," the Touched said, and Lahara invited him in.

Marly and Beatrice dragged flat cushions to the bench. Reynaud visited all the homes to share *whispers* when he had them, and he did not disappoint this night in the telling, with his funny voices and dances. By the time he finished, her stepson and niece were able to recite the story back. Lahara was cheered the girl felt better. They'd even learned some of the new spellings.

"To hammock, children," she said, breaking the enchantment.

"The moon is already high, so make your good nights."

Lahara ladled cupfuls of a cool, thick beer from the ferment barrel for Reynaud, and he drank deeply, thirsty from the stories. "I have glad news," he said between draughts. "The Tweet's come with word of my sister Celina at Central Park."

"Is it happened?"

Reynaud nodded. "A boy. Tomorrow night is the Meet."

"We'll be there," Lahara said. She'd bring the soft cloth saved since Keisha passed. The cloth meant to dress the baby never come.

"At Tent, my *whispers* rose more than once," Reynaud confided, "but I left some unshared. I'm to gift the unspoken *whispers*—a nursery rhyme—to my new nephew, Nared vay Moham. Will you have the first listen?"

> *Humpty Dumpty sat on the wall.*
> *Humpty Dumpty had a great fall.*
> *All the king's horses and all the king's men*
> *Couldn't put Humpty together again.*

He clapped his hands, expecting Lahara's response, but vibrations began within and her own *whispers* grabbed hold. A flash. A pull. A pressing weight.

Lahara recoiled from the screams and covered her head with her arms against the fists and bricks and long nail-studded boards, gagging at the stench of death and decomposition along a torn up roadway. Young people ran past in tattered clothes, their dirty faces shiny with fresh blood and black with dried.

Seagulls circled overhead. She was on the Bridge. The River Bridge. But where were the gardens? There was only chaos and the awful smell. Gray smoke poured from a wall that stood, half built, at the Bridge's western reach. Fires burned on the water's surface and a long boat negotiated the smoking debris. Light-robed figures—Disconnects?—were pulling people from the river.

With a thrust, the *whispers* released their hold. Lahara covered her mouth and stumbled, retching, to her pail.

"What is it?" Reynaud cried.

She wiped her face, unwilling to share the horror. "It's not anything. See, the spell has already passed."

"Your *whispers*—"

"Many thanks for the nursery rhyme," she interrupted. "Please, from my bag, enjoy the honey gum."

"That's not necessary."

"In appreciation, Touched friend."

Reynaud smiled and slid the candy from her basket. "You're sure to be fine?"

Lahara nodded. Would he never leave?

"Until a cooler hour, then," he said as the glass tinkled his exit.

Lahara fell again to the bucket. Drained, she lay on the floor, listening to crickets and owls in the night. After a bit, she pulled herself up to check the children.

The air was damp and Beatrice and Marly were slick with sweat. Asleep in his hammock, Marly clutched a cloth his mother had quilted at his birth, stitched from dyed scraps and decorated with shell and sanded glass. He loved this blanket, and Lahara often took the cloth from his sleeping hands to mend and clean before he woke.

Beatrice owned no such talisman. Her belongings were lost in the slide that left her father a widower, stranded in the unstable place they'd Gone, where underground forces rose without warning to remold the landscape, and where night was often bright as day. Beatrice and her father were two of the very few to return, against the severest of odds, after the Leaving.

Lahara listened to her niece's breathing. Her face was calm on the flannel, no sign of the nightmares that often woke her to scream for her father.

She climbed to the third floor and leaned against the cool wall of the room once belonged to her parents. Mother would be glad Lahara still lived here. At the start of their union, her parents had built a wood house behind the fields near Lahara's grandmother's own home. The hungry beasts came frequently in those days and the elders stayed close to guard the crops.

When the houses collapsed during winter quakes, the families did not rebuild. Instead, they chose this sturdy old-world space to restore. In the dangerous years before Lahara was born, the larger family lived together, separated by door and stair—aunts and uncles and cousins and children of cousins, a clan united for safety and warmth—but one by one the others had passed on or moved on for new starts, so just this small family—Lahara, her husband, stepson and niece—lived here now in this building by the river.

She loved her home. *Whispers* named it *tenement*. It had survived a distant past that left similar buildings razed, withstood the rippling tremors and floods that pulled the city to its knees, and had remained upright through the fires and Bad times. This tenement had sheltered the people and their ancestors for longer than anyone could know and Lahara found comfort in its endurance.

She opened the window and leaned out to the street below. An oil lantern burned at her door, a beacon for her husband, as dawn was still hours away. On either side of the front stoop, low fences enclosed yards that led to the rear of the house. Through moonlight reflected in the glass, she could just make out, across the street, the open gate of Switch's workshop.

If Lahara stretched her neck a certain way she could see past the dark trees to the York, where torches burned all night on the main road, but other than the flickering of those orange and yellow points, the street and avenue were still.

Later, much later—she must have dozed in the double hammock at the window—she was awakened by the sound of dogs in the distance. The air had cooled slightly and Lahara smelled the tide shifting on the river, a sign the sun would soon rise, and indeed, even as she peered into the shadowed street, the sky was lightening and she could hear Marly and Beatrice stirring below.

The barking intensified. The dogs were agitated, on the move. As their howls drew closer, Lahara wondered what had set them off. She slid out of the hammock to check on Marly and Beatrice.

A wild cacophony rose in the street—a pounding, and a snorting, and a shouting.

"To the roof," Lahara whispered to the children, a drill they hadn't reviewed in ages, as the shore had been quiet for so many seasons. "Slide the bar behind you."

Her stepson and niece fled up the stairs, the girl sobbing, "Are the beasts come?"

Lahara went quickly to the downstairs. She grabbed a rough plank from the woodpile, and opened the front door, ready to strike. A thunderous pounding neared, and Switch, reddish yellow braid flying behind him, galloped past on what must be the very horse come over the Bridge, its hairless body smooth and dark. A moment later, from behind, an excited, vocal hound pack flew past, their howls inviting responses from dogs throughout the neighborhood.

Lahara darted into the street as her husband turned the horse around at the end of the block. Framed by the rising sun in the east, he rode back towards her and through the open gate of his workshop.

An instant later the dogs caught up and followed him inside, their barks muffled by the thick walls, and before Lahara could even guess what was going on, Switch galloped back out, sliding the gate shut behind him. The dogs slammed against the bars, distressed at their confinement.

The horse spun in the street. Switch pulled the reins and gently pushed the horse's head down, a motion that seemed to calm her as she slowed and stopped.

Lahara peeked from between fingers she hadn't realized were covering her eyes, dizzy with relief to see Switch dismount. "Husband?"

"Go on then, Horsey, say hello to my wife."

Lahara put her hand out, and as Marly and Beatrice watched, transfixed, from the tenement's roof, the hairless black horse snickered and came to her.

ONE TOUCHED WITH MEDICINE

AS IT ALWAYS did, the sun rose in cherry blossom and salmon splendor over the East River, but Marjorie Jane knew only that she had missed the retreat of night by hours in her Midtown Mount workroom.

The woman *Touched with Medicine* wiped a corner of cloth along the inside of the baby's mouth then dabbed the wetness on a pane of glass washed in boiling water. She'd created slides from the children died this season on the Mount and collected samples from as many others possible, but she couldn't be all places at once and had exhausted herself in the trying.

She took one last look at the infant's drawn and dehydrated body before wrapping the girl in cloth and placing her cooling form in a dark bucket for removal. Was it just this midnight the mother brought the child to Marjorie, begging for help?

She pulled the thin gauze from her face to reveal a tired, lined mouth, and tossed the mask into the center fire. She dipped her hands and arms, up to her elbows, into a tall barrel of vinegar, then shook them to dry in the stale air. Her eyes, red from the sharp tang of the fermented wash and hours under the uneven cast of oil lamps, looked at the ladder to the surface, twenty feet above. If she hurried, she would just make the Runner, though Marjorie's weary body felt incapable of such a fifteen-block hike south.

She slung her satchel across her back, grabbed a cane, and climbed, hand over hand, reviewing what the *whispers* had revealed of childhood illnesses—some preventable by vaccine, of which none existed, most highly contagious, and very few life threatening, although she supposed the people might be more susceptible to these forgotten sicknesses than *whispers* suggested.

The neighbors labeled her *Touched with Medicine*, but it was a narrower *whisper* visited her, one called *Microbiology*. Many Touched found a crossover of disciplines, and despite her targeted specialty, Marjorie was able to help with day-to-day healing, her extensive clinic informed by the virus and bacteria and microbes flooding her thoughts and dreams. In five years of *whispers*, she and other *Touched with Medicine* had made neighbors all over the city stronger, healthier and more comfortable, a cooperative effort that brought learning to them all.

Marjorie pulled herself from the shaft, eyes adjusting to the daylight. The Mount was bustling, its people emerging from hatches and passageways, containers in hand for dumping in the waste channel that wound through the settlement.

She walked briskly along the well-worn Madison Heights trail on the western side of the Mount, the tip of her cane sinking in the soft ground. She enjoyed the view to the right, across the trees and rusted remains that jutted from cement foundations and all the way west. Beyond the descent platform where a man waited in queue to rappel down, the trail detoured around water towers and cornices poking through the surface, many opening to interiors still in use.

"Touched One," an old woman said, poking her head from a steepled hatch.

"Good morning, Pel," Marjorie said. "I'm late for the Runner." She noted the bacterial biofilms in the crone's mouth. *Whispers* rose, and though she would have dismissed them in her haste, they compelled her to speak.

"Dissolve a pinch of salt in water and rinse your mouth at sunrise and sundown," she advised. "Then take a thread from your robe to pull between each tooth."

"Thank you," Pel said, her voice gravelly from years of Calling—the job of shouting down shafts to announce the sun's position. She smiled, bloody gums swollen over her teeth, and disappeared back into her hole.

Marjorie had grown up in the dark, muted Under Mount, her childhood spent exploring its tunnels and descents. Doorways marked with red X's were off limits, but Marjorie would venture in regardless to examine the contents. Skeletons didn't interest her. She opened doors hoping to find paper. Every now and again she'd discover drawers full of sheets covered with the spellings, or even better, whole stacks of dry, clean unmarked pages to draw on. Her uncle taught her to fold paper birds to toss from the Mount, and sometimes their creations flew all the way to the bottom.

Younger neighbors still salvaged in the Under Mount, unconcerned with the skeletons their grandparents had warned against. Marjorie's cousin Drake—*Touched with Genealogy*—who needed only brush his fingers on another to read a complete lineage, had visited the bones a single time since the *whispers* come upon him, touching skull after skull to learn their history until he'd found his own aunt, broken and died many generations back. After that first sorrowed night he never again spoke of the aunt and never again ventured near an X.

Marjorie understood now—her *whispers* insisted—the X's weren't about skeletons, but rather about diseases. The ancestors had painted the marks in an effort to stem the effects of multiple, spiraling disasters. She had gone down often since, to collect samples of skin and bone, but in this world, with no equipment—even with her advanced knowledge—there was no story she could coax from the tissues.

Marjorie whistled her approach to a group of children who blocked the trail at Forty-fourth. At the sound of her call, a white bird—one with the strange black bars on its head—launched into the sky from their midst, and they fell back with screeches and giggles. Marjorie watched the bird—they usually weren't seen this far inland—circle overhead, its deep honks echoing long after it disappeared.

She gasped as she neared the children. A second river bird lay dead in the sun and the boys and girls were grabbing its white feathers with bare hands and feet.

"Leave that carrion," Marjorie scolded.

"It's mine," a little girl revealed. "I found the slimy and I'm to bring it inside down the ladders to my Da."

Marjorie lifted the carcass with the tip of her cane. The underside was ripe with maggots. These large birds with the striped heads and orange beaks had first appeared in late winter with other migrating flocks and they didn't stray from their nesting areas on the rivers. Marjorie knew a girl who hiked to steal their eggs—they bartered for a good price. How had the bird ended here?

"We'll leave the mess for the dogs," Marjorie said. "Your Da doesn't want blood smeared on the piano. And aren't the voices making song this morning? You're not to disturb, you know. All of you, go wash your hands in wine." She covered the dead bird with weeds. Later, she'd retrieve a specimen to examine.

The children dispersed, the little girl in tears for the loss of her prize. Marjorie put the bird out of her mind and joined the crowd gathered to hear the relay and contribute news at the southern steps. Tweets also waited by the linen flag. For a voucher or barter, these high-speed, short distance messengers dispatched news off the regular route. Marjorie squeezed past them into the press of neighbors. The flag was more a tradition than necessity here, for the Runner never bypassed the Grand Central.

Down at street level, Runner Thomas Flower U jogged across Fortieth, sidestepping debris to travel the most efficient path. He sprinted up the one hundred and ninety concrete, brick and granite stairs that began on Forty-first and climbed, for the next block and a half, one hundred fifty feet before reaching the plaza.

His run seemed effortless, painless and beautiful, up stairs bordered on both sides by sunflowers that covered the entire southern slope, but Marjorie's *whispers* told the running took great effort. Blood and oxygen and muscles and heart worked together to create his grace and speed. There was pain, as well. Strained legs, blistered lips, parched throat. Marjorie smiled as the young man completed the final stretch to the flag.

The Runner began to speak immediately, almost before he reached the crowd, and Marjorie suppressed her *whispers* so as not to interrupt his words.

"At Central Park, born a boy, Moham family. Meet this night."

Marjorie stretched. Almost fifty-years-old, her body suffered the effects of a sleepless night. She shifted from foot to foot as Thomas continued, her thoughts drifting during the Runner's update.

She opened her satchel and rifled through instruments she'd located at bazaars over the years—a stethoscope, a speculum, a broken blood pressure cuff, the microscope she made work with the stub of a lit beeswax candle. At the bottom of her bag she found the small tin filled with a peppermint salve she'd prepared.

She looked up again when the Runner began the personalized news. He called out names, took vouchers, repeated private messages and collected the same for dispatch.

"Marjorie Jane 09?"

"Yes," she said. "A gift for you. Thank you for the news."

The Runner applied the balm and smacked his lips with cool relief. "Touched One, there is news from the Central Park. A father sends word his son, a teen of healthy history, has fallen ill with a rash and fever. From the Norte Inwood. The younger Boro child has died. High fevers have enflamed two others."

"Is skin sent for my exam?"

"No skin, but more relay from the Norte. Jared Hopes is disappeared. His aunt warns, *Beware the Touched Curse.*"

Marjorie shook her head. The people had, since the onset, determined that Touched were alternately drunk, lucky, crazy or liars. This belief in a Touched Curse spoke to fear. Fear of becoming Touched, of the confusion arrived with the *whispers.*

Touched did often disappear, yes, it was true. The pressure was difficult, and some of them, in an attempt to outrun the *whispers*, probably did relocate for a new start. People made new starts all the time for much less. Marjorie sighed. "Send thanks for the warning."

"Also missing," the Runner continued. "From the East River curve. A girl, thirteen-years-old. *Newly Touched.* She answers to *Pliny*, a name come upon her in the dementia."

Marjorie ran her hands through her gray hair. There had been, over the last few months, a second series of people become Touched, and word had spread the *whispers* affected them in an awful way. They forgot their language, their histories, became confused with a dementia or retreated into the *whispers* not to come out again. The reports were unsettling and yes, it seemed that more than should be of these *Newly Touched* were disappearing.

"There is one last for you," Thomas said. "A salvage woman relays that a stranger to the settlement is found last night, incoherent, at Eighty-ninth in the Remember. The woman calls for a *Touched with Medicine* to attend the man."

"Why Touched? Surely the West is familiar with sunstroke."

"There was no further detail. You are the first I've connected with. Should I hold the news for the next?"

Marjorie considered. The fact it was a stranger needed treatment complicated the situation, as she would need remove him to his home, perhaps at some distance, or to a Wait. It promised to be a lengthy process. A long day's work.

"I'll go," she said, and waved a Tweet over. "Run ahead to the Remember. Find a pallet. I need a push and pull with strong arms to assist. Neighbors on Eighty-ninth or the Riverside Drive can direct you."

The Tweet, a young woman of about sixteen years, stretched her arms up then dipped to touch the ground. Refusing Marjorie's voucher—just yesterday the Touched One had stitched a gash in her brother's leg—the Tweet started down the cascading steps.

Marjorie Jane adjusted her bag and turned to retrace her path along the length of the Mount. From the bottom of the northern stairs at Fifty-sixth, she'd hike overland to where the stranger lay. The journey would take the better part of four hours.

Marjorie hoped the man could wait.

LAHARA

LAHARA MOVED WIDE jars and empty baskets on the shelves of the low-ceilinged cellar, wondering what to feed a horse. The scent of the wine barrels, a smell she usually enjoyed, this morning turned her stomach, and she covered her mouth, desperate to keep her breakfast of bread and bitter acorn jam down.

When the flush subsided, Lahara considered the slim inventory stacked on the dirt floor and rough shelves. There remained a barrel of dried whole corn, stalks of rice awaiting the mill, various flours, a half-crate of apples—soft now in the heat—and a dwindling supply of nuts. Empty sacks lay limp on the floor—no carrots, no potatoes, no wheat kernels—those would come in later, rolling harvests. Even the black radishes, stored over two seasons, were gone.

Lahara took a bruised apple and, rejecting containers of honey, dried beans, and salt, picked a mouse-nibbled sack of ground corn. Would the horse eat mush?

She toted the supplies up the ladder through the ceiling to the kitchen. "Put water in a pail," she told Beatrice, who was busy scraping morning mold from the still.

Marly's excited voice carried into the house from the yard, along with the deep rumble of Switch's responses and the gentle snorts of the horse her husband had found on a hill at One-hundred-twenty-ninth the night before. Beatrice siphoned water from the distillery with a strange expression, eyes on Marly through the window as he climbed a stool to reach the horse.

Lahara poured the cornmeal into the water and stirred until a thick soup formed. Her niece had barely spoken since Switch's return at dawn with this crazy tale how he'd abandoned his wagon to spend hours convincing the horse to let him approach. Lahara didn't know exactly what was going on with Beatrice, only that when she was in such a mood, she required space, not questions.

The horse was tethered to the end of an old link fence along the side of the yard. Calmer now, *Horsey*, as her husband called her, was undetected by the dogs freed from their temporary confines to vanish back into nooks and crannies of the city. Switch brushed dirt from the horse with a broom of tied twigs and straw.

"She likes a scratch of the head," Marly said to Lahara from the top of the stool.

"Be careful," she cautioned. "Her head piece looks broken." She straightened the thin band wrapped in and around the horse's ears. A small, faceted sphere rolled off the crumpled wire and into her hand. "Is this glass? Or metal? See how the jewel sparkles."

"Such a tiny ornament," Switch said, "is better suited for your own head, wife."

Lahara twisted the bead into a length of hair pulled from the back, and the bit of silver dangled with the clay and glass and metal pieces already woven into her long curls.

"I want to give Horsey the apple." Marly said.

Lahara could still remember the East River district's barren plough horses, though she had been just a child when old age took the last of them. Marly, however, was too young to know the workhorses, and had been just a baby when the wild Central Park horses were corralled and conscripted by the Group that Left. He'd not ever seen one up close. Horses still lived to the south, but they weren't often ridden uptown as the hilly roads did not make easy travel.

"Watch your fingers," she said, handing Marly the fruit.

"She's like a people," Marly said, as the horse took delicate bites. "A bald people."

"She's nothing like a people," Beatrice said, a flush rising on her pale cheeks.

Lahara winced. At age six Beatrice had left the city on horseback. She'd looked so small, sandwiched between her mother and father. What did she remember of the horse that carried her from Manhattan?

She took her niece by the arm. "Let's give her the mush." Beatrice dropped the bucket and the food sloshed onto the grass.

"The Egyptians pursued them, all Pharaoh's horses and chariots and his horsemen and his army, and overtook them," the girl said.

"What are you on about?" Switch asked.

Beatrice looked at her uncle. "For when the horses of Pharaoh with his chariots and his horsemen went into the sea, the Lord brought back the waters of the sea upon them, but the people of Israel walked on dry ground in the midst of the sea."

"It's a story," Marly said.

Beatrice pulled her cousin from the stool and hissed in his ear. "What he did to the army of Egypt, to their horses and to their chariots, how he made the water of the Red Sea flow over them as they pursued after you."

"Are you gone barking mad?" Switch asked his niece.

Lahara's stomach lurched. What was this? The girl's tone frightened her. Beatrice's mother, in a similar tone five years earlier, had commanded Lahara join them—a call to follow hard to resist but for her sister's strong arms. Keisha kept her from following as the Group that Left set out for the edge of the city, the edge of the world.

Lahara placed her hands over her eyes, the darkness a refuge quickly laid bare by her husband's strong fingers pulling them apart again. "What do you hide from, wife?"

"For all the words, the *whispers* offer few answers," Lahara said, and as she spoke, she stumbled, and Switch caught and held her upright against him.

"Damn all the *whispers*," he said. "Begone, them."

Lahara shook her head. "Not *whispers*," she said. "A faint come on suddenly."

A sweet whistle trilled from the street. Lahara recognized the song of Garrison Landry, a neighbor who lived just inside the Stones near Fifty-ninth.

"At the back," Switch shouted. Word of the horse had spread, and neighbors were gathering. At Switch's invitation, the crowd filed into the backyard, kicking up the dirt.

"Halloo, hallo," Garrison said. "They've returned. Tell me everything."

"There isn't much to tell," Switch said. He held a hand up to stop the man rushing the animal. "When I left my trade at the subway," he said, "I saw fresh tracks in the mud. I followed the trail west beyond Amsterdam, up the hill under the arches. The horse was drinking from the spring at the falls."

"The Group that Left returns and you don't search for the rider?" Garrison accused, in disbelief and tears. "Why didn't you?"

"I didn't know anything about what you say." Switch's face was red with defense. "Here was a horse had no flag, no tether. And I don't remember a horse having no hair Gone with the Group. I called and whistled. Nobody came."

Garrison clenched the link fence, for support or in anger Lahara didn't know. "You could have searched," he said softly.

"I thought maybe the horse come across the dead canal in the night," Switch said. "I've heard of hairless beasts at the Norte."

"Danny rode this horse when he left," Garrison said. "He promised to return. I don't know what happened these years to make no hair, but she is true his horse."

"There was a black horse with the Group," a woman said from the crowd. "Her mane was white. This isn't the same one."

"How can you say?" Garrison argued. "There's no mane to compare."

Beatrice's opened her eyes wide. "Dan shall be a serpent in the way, a viper by the path that bites the horse's heels so that his rider falls backward."

"What about Dan?" Garrison asked.

"Touched Ones fill their heads," Switch apologized.

The horse whinnied, and the neighbors drew back, but she was only acknowledging the woman who approached carrying a basket of roots and hard biscuits. Lahara didn't know how Alicia Starr's *whispers* gave her such skills, but neighbors told she was *Touched with Animals*, and that birds and beasts shared thoughts with her.

"Beautiful girl," Alicia said. The horse blew gently through her nose onto Alicia's face and the Touched One closed her eyes to blow back. Lahara wondered if the older woman felt transported, as she did, or if *whispers* rose in her ears, as Reynaud's did, or if they moved her differently yet.

Alicia continued, "The horses worked with New York's Finest."

Lahara braced herself. Alicia's *whispers* would prompt her own. Rooms opening onto rooms, roads leading to further, unexplored roads. An unexplainable connection between Touched linked them, and in just a short moment, responding vibrations flashed screaming white in her eyes, the flash an emergency vehicle, the scream a siren wailing.

"Police," Lahara said.

"The Mounted Unit," Alicia added. The neighbors observed, eager for the *whispered* words. Even Beatrice, who pretended indifference, paid careful attention.

Lahara doubled over from the pressure. When she straightened again, she was at a Hudson River stable beside piles of pungent manure. A man in dark pants—a single yellow stripe on each leg—led a horse down a ramp. Lahara followed them into the perfect, cloudless day to join a host of men and women in blue helmets and high boots assembled on horses at the riverfront.

A banner flew at the head of the procession, the spellings unfamiliar. The clip clop of the horses hypnotized, and as the parade headed north toward the glass towers on the river, Lahara relaxed in the *whispers*, thoughts of her own world far away.

Perhaps only seconds had passed when Alicia's voice startled her. "Broken skin. Salves applied. Fire stomach. Bitter tonics. Torn muscles ... cold ... relief."

Another flash pierced the space behind Lahara's eyes, and in the next instant she was under the East River Bridge at Fifty-ninth, looking up at the roadway that stretched to the mid-river island and the Queensland.

Electro-carts and buses zipped across. The movements made her dizzy. Layered roads followed the eastern shore and tall glass and mirrored buildings extended west. The towering stone wall enclosing her district at its southernmost edge at Fifty-seventh did not exist. A policeman was leading his horse into the building just north, through a wide bay at the back of the structure.

"There's a hospital on the hill where Garrison's crop grows. An animal medical center," Lahara said through her *whispers*. "The doctors keep the horses healthy so they can protect the people."

"Protect the people from what?" Beatrice asked.

The sound of her niece's voice ripped Lahara from the unfinished *whispers*. Displaced, she ran her fingers back and forth noisily along the chain link fence until Switch stopped her.

Alicia, still in her *whispers*, stood motionless. "The horses are content this familiar day. They parade. The air is clear. The sun warms. Stretching muscles. Step together in time. Synchronized.

Dance, count, hypnotizing. They carry friends, no effort. Smooth. Walk. Warmth. Oh." Her voice changed. "Deep tones far beneath the earth. Discomfort. Reflexes. Tremors. Heat."

Lahara held her breath. Her skin tingled as she listened to Alicia, and she felt at the edge of a precipice. For a long moment nobody spoke. Switch held Marly by the arm. Beatrice, behind her uncle, peeked her head around at Alicia. The one *Touched with Animals* blinked several times.

"The horses smell sulfur and steam and the scent of catastrophe. Before anyone else, they and other animals know."

At this, Lahara's mind imploded and sent her into a smoke that darkened the sky. For all the horror, the air was hushed, and the people who streamed past, silent.

"The horses have innate knowledge of prior land shifts and gas releases. There is no fear," Alicia said. "Many died within the first moments. Sucked below, trapped or chased by the sea."

Lahara recognized the Central Park's crossing at Seventy-ninth. Flood waters swept through, obliterating gardens and fields—whole trees uprooted in the wash. And the people. Arms and legs and faces smashed against stone that had collapsed into scum-filled ponds.

Alicia's voice reached Lahara again. "Birds dropped from the skies, blistered by scalding, shooting gasses."

A long moment passed. Alicia continued. "The police horses were trained in disaster relief, but training saved none. The surviving horses regrouped, as taught, in the Central Park."

Alicia spoke directly to Lahara. "You see it, yeah?"

Lahara looked through the black smoke over the Great Lawn. Alicia, high atop a white steed, grabbed her hand. The horse pawed reared up, snorted, but Lahara held on, knuckles white with the effort. Beyond Alicia, a column of riderless horses waded through water churning halfway up their legs.

Another flash. Lahara let go of Alicia's hand and tripped through tents and barracks erected on mud left by the surges. Dirty children and hopeless adults. Fear. Disbelief. Heartbreak. Disease. Putrid water. Confusion. Red X's. Hunger. Thirst. Starvation. Absolute isolation.

"Over time," Alicia said, "the horses lost their chokes, their bits, their harnesses."

The herd ran free. Ravaged survivors carried their dead west. Lahara dove to avoid a galloping wild horse, and the motion threw her not only onto the ground, but from the *whispers*.

She clung to Alicia in the bright sun of her own backyard. How much had the neighbors understood, Lahara wondered. To what end did she need share this nightmare?

The mare nickered, and Alicia fed her a biscuit, making small noises in response. Garrison spoke first. Lahara focused on his words, grounding herself in the moment.

"You see," Garrison said, tears in his eyes. "It's true. Our horses descend from the police horses, as we descend from the ancient people. This black horse is one of them. Danny's horse. My son will be returned."

"No," Alicia said. "This horse is something else entirely."

"But you had *whispers*. They told you. You told us."

Alicia fingered the horse's saddle. "The design is unfamiliar. And look." She lifted the horse's foot. "Shoes. She can't she ours."

"Then where did the mare come from?" Lahara asked.

"I don't know," Alicia admitted as Beatrice ran into the house.

Beatrice had climbed to her room by the time Lahara caught up. Huddled on the window bench her niece sobbed.

Lahara pulled her close, frightened by the strength of her shudders. She hummed the beginnings of an old lullaby, one her grandmother had chanted, and before long she remembered the words and sang in a soft voice that quieted Beatrice's cries.

A million little bits
waiting in the night
A billion little bits, a gazillion little bits
will make things right
forever saved, forever saved

She rubbed Beatrice's back. From the yard, conversations carried up to the quiet room, passing easily through thin window cloths that hung limp in the still air. Lahara watched, without seeing, and listened to, without hearing, the activity below.

"I've something should work in back of the shop," Reko was saying, and Marly was shouting, "I want to ride Horsey," and the neighbors were taking their leave, dazed, unsettled, with words to each other that did little to ease their bewilderment.

Beatrice fell asleep in Lahara's arms. Lahara watched her niece's eyelashes flutter. Tears escaped the closed eyelids, balancing heavy before rolling down flushed cheeks, and Lahara knew the girl's torment had pursued her into sleep.

The sounds from the backyard faded, replaced by hammer on metal reverberating from Switch's workshop across the street. Her husband came up the stairs, his angular face questioning in the doorway. Lahara motioned to the sleeping girl.

"I'm west to retrieve my wagon," he said.

Lahara looked out at the purple haze low in the afternoon sky. "What of the horse?"

"Reko's outfitting a rig. Marly's to come as well."

"Darsh it," Lahara burst out, almost waking Beatrice. "I forgot we're to the Central Park tonight to meet Reynaud's nephew."

Switch shook his head. "Are you well enough?"

It was a long hike to the Reservoir, but Lahara needed see and greet the new baby. They'd sing and dance and swim, and the people would reminisce and rejoice. When the children went to hammock they would gamble. The baby Meets were so few and far between and she didn't want to miss the celebration.

"It's strange days," Lahara agreed. "But the distraction will be welcome. The girl and I will start our trip at sundown."

"The horse will make swifter journey," Switch said. "We'll take the flat roads and be arrived before you." He touched his fingers to his lips and left quietly.

She smiled at the gesture, for Lahara understood, though they never spoke of his first marriage, that he missed the bond he'd shared with her sister. He was no doubt a kind husband to Lahara, but their couplings were simply acts of hope for the future as their marriage was designed to be.

Her arm tingled under her niece's shoulder, and she shifted to relieve the pressure. Beatrice opened her eyes, clear blue eyes that looked straight through Lahara, beyond her even, and when she spoke, it was a whisper.

"Mother named our horse Australia."

Lahara's heart caught in her throat. Beatrice never spoke of her mother. She held perfectly still, fearful her very pulse would shatter the fragile moment between them, and the girl pushed a length of flyaway hair from her face. The scars on her cheek and under the band of her veil reminded Lahara of all she didn't know about the time her niece had been gone. More than a year.

Beatrice stood and stretched her long, lanky body, pacing the small room—like a caged animal, Lahara thought, though the door was open giving freedom to leave, and stairs led up and down.

"Mother told us there was a whole world out there and that her *whispers* would find it," Beatrice said. "She kept us moving. We were safer moving." Beatrice chewed her lip. "She told me to remember the others never got the chance."

"Never got the chance?"

"We hid in the Queensland," Beatrice continued. "A crack split the field during the night, but I didn't know. I followed Australia into the Flushing Meadow."

A pressure in her chest and clicks in her mind gave face to Beatrice's words. The Flushing Meadow lay to the east, in the other land. Click—a festival, a *World's Fair*. Click—an immense metal ball, higher than twenty men, on display. Click——the orb is fallen, crushed.

"The unisphere," Lahara said.

Beatrice hesitated. "The steam was loud and hurt my head."

The girl stared away into the yard. A cat chased a squirrel along a branch of one of the trees closest to the house, and Beatrice held out her lightly freckled arm, as if to give the bushy tailed animal a bridge through the window.

"What happened in the meadow?" Lahara asked, fearful to break the tenuous connection, but compelled to know.

"The crack in the earth was deep. I don't know if Australia ever hit bottom." She rubbed her arm absentmindedly. "Did you ever hear a horse scream?"

Lahara flinched, dreading what her niece might next say.

"By sundown the mud came, and Mother was taken. The mud

broke Father, and took everything else. I lay in wet dirt for two changes of the numbers," Beatrice said, standing to take a deep breath, one that fueled a long, wordless howl.

Her knees buckled and the girl grabbed a wall fabric as she went down, dragging the musty quilt with her. From where she fell, Beatrice screamed and kicked at the hard seat of the bench until her ankles were raw and the wood splintered, and when nothing remained of her storm, she curled motionless on the floor.

In the aftermath, Lahara spoke calmly to her of things ordinary. Of picking peaches in the orchard behind Third Avenue and of the sacks to be mended before the outing, of the dry grasses caught fire to the south and of the drought that left turtles and frogs bloated in the field, of the evening's Meet and of the gifts to be prepared. And as they spoke not of the broken furniture or horses lost in bottomless holes, Lahara quietly disassembled the remainder of the window seat for repair.

She lifted the bench's frame, puzzled to find two boards beneath, one her niece had complained of losing, the other a replacement with Beatrice's name stenciled across the top and a white pencil hanging from a strap.

The first board was covered with sketches. A tent, lamps, a fire and hearth, numbers and words scribbled in thick chalk streaks. Untranslatable spellings. *Cherubim. Tabernacle. Testimony.*

The second slate was filled with Beatrice's small, flowery handwriting. A riot of words spiraled around the board's edges in four-sided rows until no room remained in the center. Lahara located the cramped beginning at the top left corner and read the words, a chore made more difficult for the smudges.

"They shall make an ark of acacia wood."

Beatrice turned to her aunt's voice. "Stop."

Undeterred, Lahara rotated the board, unsure how to pronounce the spellings. "Two cubits and a half shall be its length, a cubit and a half its breadth, and a cubit and a half its height."

"It's mine."

Lahara turned the board again. "You shall overlay it with pure gold, inside and outside shall you overlay it, and you shall make on it a molding of gold around it."

"Please," Beatrice begged.

One final turn of the slate. "You shall cast four rings of gold for it and put them on its four feet, two rings on the one side of it, and two rings on the other side of it."

"I don't understand," Lahara said as Beatrice took the slates, head turned against the questions. "What do the spellings mean? Did you make the words yourself?"

"No."

"What are the pictures?" Lahara waited. "Beatrice?"

"The words and images come. My eyes ache and I see as someone else, more each morning."

Lahara stopped, stunned, and held the wall for support as the gravity of her niece's situation sunk in. "You're *Newly Touched*?" she asked, unable to mask the fear in her voice. Along with new *whispers* came confusion. The forgetting. Dementia.

Her niece shrugged. "I don't know if I am."

"They seem to be story *whispers*," Lahara suggested.

"They aren't stories."

"What then? What are you hearing?"

"I hear nothing," she said. "You don't know who I am."

"You're Beatrice. My niece."

Beatrice shoved her long hair under her bandana and pulled the veil over her face. "You shall not uncover the nakedness of your father's brother," she said through the rough lace. "That is, you shall not approach his wife; she is your aunt."

"Your aunt?" Lahara asked, trying to understand. "I'm your aunt." She shook her head. "If *whispers* have caught you, I'll surely not let them take you."

But Beatrice no longer listened, instead drawing feverishly with the stone on her slate.

THE BOY

CALLUM SPENCER raised his arms above his head, skin exposed to the light of the Central Park's late afternoon sun, and turned slowly for Frannie. Her fingers tickled, trailing down his back and over his chest as he revealed himself for the Touched One's inspection.

Wagon wheels clacked against the cobbled surface of the road that led north to the reservoir—a wheelbarrow passing through the trees. To the east, above the treetops, a yellow kite bobbed over the museum at Fifth, the spellings welcoming the new baby born.

"Watcha doing naked?"

The twelve-year-old blushed. His friend, Vella, red hair tucked under a veil, a falcon on her shoulder, stood behind him.

"Getting checked for the rash," he squeaked, embarrassed at the sound his voice made.

"You weren't at school."

"My brother's sick," he said, gesturing to the steam rising from the longhouse's smoke slit—an herbal vapor Frannie created to help his brother breathe.

Vella nodded. "Ya missing chores, too?"

"Yeah," Callum said. "I guess."

"Whadda ya got?"

"Beehives." He grimaced as the Touched One combed his scalp, pulling his hair up and to the side to check his skin.

"Beehives is better than latrine," Vella said. "I got that 'til the rain is come." The falcon stretched its wings.

"All done," Frannie said, patting Callum's head and scratching a blue mark on his shoulder with a small quill. "No sign of the rash. And no fever."

"Are you to Meet tonight?" Vella asked.

Callum stepped into his shorts. "Yah. The babe's my cousin."

"Until then," Vella said, starting across the lawn.

Callum watched his friend head into the thick pines to the north. He wrapped his half cape around his shoulders and turned to the tall woman who was putting a square bottle of ink back into a wooden box.

"Jan's gonna be good, too?"

Frannie rearranged the quill points, wiping a drop of ink from one of the tips with the corner of her bandana. "Your brother has age in his favor."

Callum reached for the net hanging across his longhouse entryway.

"Don't go in."

"But I need my roller," he said, wondering why she would care.

"I'll find it." She slipped behind the curtain and reappeared after a moment with Callum's long polished board, but before handing the roller to him she uncorked a flask and poured a sour-smelling liquid over the wooden base and wheels.

"Why'd you go and do that?" Callum complained. "It's a stinker."

The Touched One's response was lost in the sound of a strangled keening more bird than human. "Stay here," she said, ducking back through the hanging net.

Ignoring her, Callum followed, drawing the curtain up with a force that tore the mesh from its rod above. The sweet spice of steam combined with the dark smell of feces hit Callum and he covered his mouth. At first he didn't see his brother on the dirt floor, but as Callum moved from the doorway he saw the tangle of Jan's braids and the stained sheet pulled over his chest.

His brother's eyes were fearful and he was unable to catch his breath. Frannie rolled him to his side and held his head as he spewed thick bile.

"Get out," his father said as Callum stared.

"Now," his father growled, and there was no disobeying.

He tripped over the fallen curtain as he stumbled out backwards, fleeing south across the Great Lawn through jagged rows of longhouses, past high domed wire cages and around the pond and rocky elevation that shimmered with silver flecks.

Stopping for a brief moment to look back over the Lawn, he climbed down to the Seventy-ninth crossing, where he dropped his roller to the pavement and shoved off.

Callum navigated the board to the Broadwaterway and over

the scaffold bridge, jumping off only once to let a pack of feral dogs pass. He leaned his body to the left, gaining momentum as he adjusted his balance and cruised west on Eighty-sixth. The hardwood wheels picked up speed along the well-packed trail, vibrating and whining as he negotiated curves around the rubble piles of the old city.

With the speed came the wind through his hair, and Callum felt he was flying, all worries left at the lawn. At the foot of Eighty-sixth he dodged a gray-haired woman talking to a big man in a thick, knotted tunic who wore the longest and widest beard Callum had ever seen, and he nearly collided with an empty cart for staring as he sped by.

He skated onto the Riverside Drive, jumping off at the Soldiers' and Sailors' Monument, where weeds grew in the cracked plaza, crumbling, granite benches were unoccupied, and brown vines covered the columns that overlooked the Remember.

He leaned over the railing and looked uptown to where his mother's stone would be, but it was too far to see from here. The memorials in this section were older, much older, and there wasn't anyone left to remember them. He was surprised then at the bearded man heading downhill, a stretcher in his arms, the gray-haired woman beside him poking the ground with her cane as she descended.

Callum tried to politely mind his own business, but curiosity tempted him and he tied his crest to the roller, leaving it on the plaza, and ducked under the railing to drop to the field. Wildflowers tickled as they brushed against his legs and the scent of climbing roses relieved the fumes from across the river.

The man and woman were visible through the trees. Callum followed a series of crumbling markers toward them, working his way through the maze of weathered stones to find the two in a clearing at the shore.

A man lay on the ground. He tried to get up, but couldn't make it past his knees before falling back down. The woman manipulated him onto the hard stretcher and tied long lengths of cloth around his waist and ankles. The man fought his loose restraints.

"It's just to keep you safe. Stay still," the woman was saying.

Callum whistled a tentative greeting and the bearded man turned to him and called, "You, little man, come help."

He slogged through the mud and knelt beside the pallet, positioning his hands carefully on the man's dirt-covered, scraped shoulders. The stranger was bald, and bare-chested. Dried bits of muck flaked off his chest. He wore odd silver knee-length pants.

"Anthony Steele," the man whispered.

"Is Anthony your name?" the woman asked, and he nodded.

"Anthony, I'm called Marjorie. I've come to help you. Do you know this place?" He shook his head. "Tinny, check his pockets."

The bearded man searched Anthony's strange pants. "No crest. No nothing."

"What's wrong with him?" Callum asked.

"He's sunburned," Marjorie said. "I need to cover him."

Callum unwrapped his short cape and Marjorie laid the cloth over Anthony's chest and arms. The man nodded, eyes still closed.

"Anthony, can you tell me how you were injured," Marjorie asked, examining the gash on his face and the swollen bloody leg.

"They may be following."

Marjorie ran her hands over his scalp. "Who?"

"He makes nonsense," Callum said.

Marjorie nodded. "What are you called, son?"

"Callum Spencer, mz'm. Central Park."

"Callum, will you fill this container with river water for me?"

He tramped through swamp grass to the walkway along the Hudson, careful not to step through broken sections where water sloshed. He filled the bottle—his father had a similar jug traded from the plastic man—and skipped the short distance back.

He returned the canteen to Marjorie who had wrapped strips of oiled fabric around Anthony's ankle. She dipped a length of gauze into the salty river water and swabbed the wound above the man's eye. The rest of the cold water she poured over the injured man's knee, flushing the cuts still oozing blood.

Anthony jerked. "I have to disable the trace."

"Shhh," Marjorie said. She uncorked a beaker and tipped a clear liquid into his mouth. He sputtered and spit out the draught without swallowing. "The drink will make quieter journey," Marjorie said, but he shook his head and she put the liquor away.

"We need get him up the hill and into the wagon," she told Callum and Tinny.

"Where to?" Tinny asked. Anthony hadn't said where he lived.

"Columbus Circle is the closest."

"On three," Tinny said, and they hoisted the stretcher, beginning the awkward journey up through the stones. Marjorie trailed, her walking stick supporting her slow climb.

The air was cooling as the sun began its descent over the Hudson. White remembrance markers glowed in the amber light and on the sleeping Anthony's head. His scalp was scabbed and Callum looked closely at the oddly patterned skin. A thin wire wrapped around his head, attached to a sparkly bit behind his ear.

"He's got something there."

"Just a charm," Tinny said, struggling up the last steps to the Riverside Drive where they rested the stretcher in the car. Tinny raised the wagon's back panel.

"Callum," Marjorie said. "You have Frannie Stein's mark on your back. Did the Touched One visit?"

"Yeah."

"Are you sick?"

"Nah. She just checked me. My brother's sick," Callum said. "It's the fever."

Marjorie hugged him, and stroked his long hair. She removed the cape from Anthony, returning it to Callum who covered himself against the breeze off the Hudson.

"Thank you for your help," Marjorie said, giving him a second hug. Callum thought she had a sad look in her eyes. "Drink water if the fever comes. "Remember that."

Tinny lifted the handles with a grunt and Marjorie poured a dark liquid over Anthony's chest. More stinky stuff. The man roused for a moment, then fell back as Tinny pulled the wagon south, Marjorie trailing slowly behind, her cane making little taps on the hard road.

Sneezing the stinky smell from his nose, Callum retrieved his roller from the plaza and started home.

LAHARA

THE SUNSET'S SPECTACULAR oranges and reds spilled across the sky as Beatrice and Lahara began their crosstown hike along Seventy-ninth. Mosquitoes buzzed around their eyes and head in the heat, but thanks to a splashing of apple vinegar, the bugs refrained from biting.

Just east of the First Avenue Stones, Beatrice slowed and stopped to listen to a hammering in the sprawling rubble. Lahara watched her niece uneasily. The girl was withdrawn, and she worried for her mood. She followed Beatrice's gaze to the man swinging an axe, sweating in the dusk as he broke a concrete column into pieces small enough to cart off.

"If you make me an altar of stone, you shall not build it of hewn stones," Beatrice called out, her voice too deep. "For if you wield your tool on it you profane it."

The man looked up and Lahara recognized Jak from the field north, and knew he was come to gather hard pieces for the building of his son's house.

"Halloo," she called, hoping the sound of his axe had covered Beatrice's words.

He waved and leaned against the wall of a crumbling stone stairs leading into the ruins. Pulling his shirt off over his shoulders, he wrapped the gray cloth around his head to soak the sweat of his hair.

Beatrice drew back, grabbing Lahara's hand before calling out again, "And you shall not go up by steps to my altar, that your nakedness be not exposed on it."

"She speaks *whispers*," Lahara jumped in quickly, shrugging helplessly at Jak.

He climbed down from the rubble. "Can't say I envy you." He crouched to tease a sharp scrap from the rocks. "Was a time I wished each night to wake Touched. Now I thank each day my mind is right. *Whisper* hearers are crazier each season."

He held the piece of salvage up, a long dark blue shard of glass that caught the last of the setting sun, reflecting lavender and purple on the pale stone. He blushed at his own words. "Not to offend, Touched Ones."

"Not to offend," Lahara repeated, mesmerized by the lights and vibrations in her head. She squeezed her eyes shut and when she opened them again, it was an immense room and bright, unfocused colors surrounding her. Her *whispers* clicked, revealing windows of blue and red and gold and green, sun streaming through the deeply colored glass to light the vaulted space in rainbow washes.

A sweet, dry perfume tickled her nose, come from an old man in long white robes who waved a ball of smoke over and around the glistening center aisle.

She sensed rather than saw her niece beside her on the dark bench. "Sweet spices with pure frankincense." What was the girl saying? "Of each shall there be an equal part and make an incense blended as by the perfumer, seasoned with salt, pure and holy."

Burning candles in tall red glass filled rows of shelves, the jeweled light falling across the floor in overlapping pools. A chorus of voices was singing, her niece's clear notes among them. The music reached the highest ... *rafters* ... of the ... *church*. The ceilings were so lofty, so gilded, and the music so deep and all encompassing, Lahara felt pulled into something so huge she lost her breath in its enormity. And underneath the awesome spectacle coursed a hum—a current—calling Beatrice's name.

"No," Lahara said, or thought, and the hum retreated and her mind cleared. She was in the rubble, the reds and yellows of the church's stained glass simply the purple and blue of the shard Jak held to the sun.

Beatrice's face was flushed and she trembled with excitement. Lahara recognized the euphoria, dangerous even in this second wave of Touched. She reached for her niece's hand, but the girl's face darkened, and she turned, pointing to nothing at all, accusing, "You will not deal falsely with me or with my descendants or with my posterity, but as I have dealt kindly with you, so you will deal with me and with the land where you have sojourned."

Lahara nodded a quick good-bye to Jak. She didn't understand these *whispers* and the sharp edge frightened her.

"We'll drink a tea from Myra," she said, and the girl walked with her without protest down the ramp and through the cool tunnel beneath the Stone.

On the far side of First Avenue, Lahara pulled the metal sticks in correct sequence and slid the heavy gate, closing the district behind them before climbing out of the passage to the outside.

"Halloo Myra, teas for our travel," Lahara said, handing the vendor two vouchers. The tiny woman who bartered sweet and spicy drinks from a wheelbarrow on the corner was deaf, but she could read the words in Lahara's mouth, and she poured cool drinks into drinking cones fashioned from rolled husks.

"We're to Meet the new baby tonight," Lahara said, sipping the tea and chewing the leafy pulp at the bottom. She tasted peppermint and basil and dark honey.

In the cold months, Myra served her tea hot from a pot on a kettle fire. In the extreme winter she sought shelter in one of the small, sleek houses dotting the avenue. Glazed homes built from a compound of sand, stones and glass, the mixture sculpted on metal frames and left to dry in the sun. Beatrice had lived in such a house shaped by her mother's own hands before the onset of the *whispers*, the house given to a weaver in exchange for blankets toted when they went forth with the Group that Left.

"Myra?" Beatrice said, reaching over the wheelbarrow. "Who has made man's mouth? Who makes him mute, or deaf, or seeing, or blind?"

Myra wrinkled her eyebrows.

"Maybe now isn't the time," Lahara suggested.

"You shall not curse the deaf or put a stumbling block before the blind."

Lahara took Beatrice by the arm, with a "Many thanks," over her shoulder to Myra, but the girl wasn't finished, and shouted, "You shall fear your God: I am the Lord."

The sunset blinded as they crossed Second Avenue. The hard road was cooler here under a canopy of vine-covered trees, but steam rose from wet half-buildings on either side, and feral pigs rooted in the swampy frontage, grunting as they turned over damp soil and muck for acorns and grubs.

"I didn't mean to scare the tea woman," Beatrice said.

At the west side of Third, Lahara and Beatrice splashed themselves from the trickling water between the rocks, resting a moment in the spray. Lahara slipped her feet from her short boots and dug her toes into the mud, enjoying the coolness and breathing deep the scent of the wild gardens stretching north.

"Some flowers for the new mother, niece."

Underground rivers found outlet along this stretch in bubbling creeks that circled homes set on poles in the marshes. Beatrice filled her hands with tiny buds growing along one of these streams, and Lahara was thankful the girl's *whispers* had gone quiet.

They set out again. Lahara was tired—the day had been full—and their pace lagged. Her gift-laden pack chafed in the humidity and she was beginning to regret filling the bag with such bounty.

Beatrice, too, fell behind, stopping over and again to contemplate things visible only to her. Lahara, powerless to help the girl process what she didn't understand herself, kept close, trusting her nearness would be some comfort.

"How did this happen?" Beatrice asked, at one point, in tears.

"I'm not understanding what Touches you," Lahara said. "Everything changes and we can't know the whys. The transformations are difficult to witness."

"No," Beatrice said. "That's not what I'm talking about."

They waded across Lex and stepped up onto the cracked cement on the far side, dripping on the hot pavement. "Maybe we can find the flat ride," Lahara said, but Beatrice was back in her *whispers*, speaking too softly for Lahara to translate.

They just managed to meet the rolling platform. Lahara had to drag Beatrice down the last half block to Park Avenue where the brothers who pushed and pulled the flat ride were right then almost passed by.

Lahara shouted, waving her arms as they ran, hoping the men would hear. They did. Peter, the smaller of the brothers—the puller—raised his banner and the flat ride stopped.

Lahara rarely bartered a flat ride as walking was mostly

quicker. Also, finding the ride was not so simple. The brothers ran just a single platform up the Park Avenue from Sixty-third to Ninety-seventh and back again.

The ride often tipped, unbalanced from crowding, and Lahara was glad the platform wasn't full now. Only a few passengers waited for their boarding, a young man—Lahara knew him to be named Joshua—carrying a legless toddler across his shoulder, and two veiled women who hung on the back railing.

The men pushing and pulling worked hard. Park Avenue was clear north of Sixty-third, but even with the level path—wide footbridges crossed the streams where they intersected the Avenue—the men's skin shone and they grunted and panted in their labor.

Lahara and Beatrice faced forward, holding tight to the railing, Lahara in front of her niece. The wheels vibrated the wood and metal panels, and conversation wasn't easy for the noise. When Beatrice murmured behind her, Lahara turned. Beatrice said nothing further and Lahara left the girl to her *whispers*.

The second time she heard Beatrice talking to the back of her head they were passing a noisy salvage. Neighbors taking advantage of cooler twilight hours used squealing pulleys to remove containers of stone and brick from a pit between two buildings on Eighty-third.

"Niece?" Lahara said, turning back. "I missed that last."

"I said nothing."

Darkness descended as the flat ride bumped uptown. At Eighty-sixth Beatrice confronted the young man holding the little boy. "Choose for us men, and go out and fight with Amalek."

He shifted the toddler to his other shoulder. "Who's Amalek?"

"We're off here," Lahara called, and the puller raised a hand signaling the pusher.

Lahara led Beatrice to the ground. The befuddled Joshua shifted the toddler again—the little boy laughed—and, descended too. "Who is Amalek?" he repeated, but Beatrice didn't answer, so he shrugged and slipped into the marsh reeds to the east, heading home to one of the small rice farms that began at the widening waters at Ninety-third and Lex.

After a moment, the sway of the ride left Lahara's legs,

although her head still buzzed lightly, and she and Beatrice walked, climbed, and tunneled the last two blocks along a trail that led through the rocky salvage of the Avenues.

Lahara smelled the fire pit as soon as they entered the Central Park. Low flames in the oil trench lit the path on the east side of the reservoir, and campfires burned in the lots below, but the fires couldn't keep the night bugs away, and Lahara swatted flyers from her face.

In the field at the top of the path wagons were blanketed and parked for the evening, crests flying above each. Switch's cart was among them, a resined tarp covering materials traded from subway salvage. Lahara wondered where he'd tied Horsey.

A young girl with splotches of uneven freckles jumped down from the rocks ahead, startling Lahara. She recognized the redheaded girl Vella, whose father, Beetus, was a Great Lawn falconer. Vella was thin, her leanness accentuated by the thick brown glove on her arm, a resting pad for the sharp talons of the bird she carried.

"And when birds of prey came down on the carcasses, Abram drove them away," Beatrice said, dashing ahead, arms outstretched to reach for the gray bird with the pointed beak and black eyes

The falcon spread his wings and launched skyward, his squawking harsh in Lahara's ears. Tethered by narrow strips tied around Vella's wrist, he hovered above her like a cape shielding her from the moon.

The falconer's daughter shook her head. "Abram? Abram's gone south for a new start," she said. "Are you to Meet baby Moham?"

"We are," Lahara said, pushing her niece through the trees before she might say anything further.

They emerged from the woods circling the Moham settlement to a roaring center fire that threw orange light over the guests and drummers filling the plaza, and they were greeted by the smell of catfish grilling on the grate.

Bal Moham, a slight man with a wide smile and skin the color of the darkest summer plum, waved his grill stick with the music and gestured them closer, wiping his hands on the rough fabric of his skirt. In a hammock next to him, shielded from the smoke by a wooden panel, Bal's youngest wife Celina nursed the newborn.

"All best to your family," Lahara said, smiling at the parents and handing Keisha's soft cloth to Celina, fingers lingering on the baby blanket as she made the gift.

Celina's dark eyes lit to examine the weave and color of the bunting. "Many thanks to yours." She removed the baby from her breast and faced him forward, as custom dictated. "Nared vay Moham. Meet Lahara, friend of your uncle to the east, and Beatrice, daughter of her husband's brother."

The tiny baby was wrapped from head to toe in white crochet, his veil fastened back to reveal a wrinkled face, brown lips pursed, still sucking. He opened his eyes—they were gray—and closed them again right away. He hiccupped and began to cry.

"That's milk on his lips," Beatrice said as Celina returned the baby to suck. "Blessings of the breasts and of the womb."

"Help lay out the food we've brung," Lahara said quickly, turning Beatrice and her *whispers* from the hammock.

They emptied her backpack of the onions, summer squash, red cabbage sprouts and thick branches of rosemary, piling them on a flat stone table already laden with gifts of fruits, vegetables, breads, fresh and dried meats.

"Much appreciation," Bal said, admiring the rosemary. He rubbed a sprig between his fingers and sniffed deeply before tossing the branch on the fire. The herb infused smoke made Lahara's mouth water, and she felt suddenly weak.

In her lightheadedness, her head seemed to buzz, and she swatted the vibration. "Is there a cricket in my hair?"

"Who can know for all the baubles swung from your curls?" Beatrice said, with barely a look.

Cheers went up from the reservoir, and the children ran dripping across the plaza. A contorting fish on their rope sent the guests in the courtyard rearing back in laughter and squeals. "We caught it," Marly shouted. "For the new baby."

Lahara scooped up her stepson, his damp robe cool in her hot arms. "You've been swimming without me," she teased.

"I can swim the reservoir's length," Marly said, and at Beatrice's sneer, quickly amended, "Well, by next season I will. Even Reko says."

"Where's your father?"

"At the field west. The one *Touched with Animals* brung oats and Horsey gobbles them like a beast." Beatrice stiffened at the description.

"Lots of neighbors to see Horsey," he added. "A Horsey Meet."

"I want to swim," Beatrice said, and Lahara wondered if she wanted to enjoy the water or remove herself from the horse talk.

"Me, too. Again," Marly shouted, jumping up and down.

"Auntie, say yes."

Lahara knew she couldn't shield her niece from the things she was hearing and seeing, but needed to try regardless. She spoke into her ear. "Swim, but if *whispers* confuse you or any other, you need find your way back to me."

Neighbors arrived and the hellos were ongoing. Lahara filled her cup from the pitcher on the stone table, sipping the tea, glad to gather with friends she hadn't seen in many weeks. The last Meet had been early winter for the twins at Kips Bay. The journey itself had taken a whole day into night with the snow and quakes, but the trip had been worth the effort for seeing the newborns.

A familiar woman with long blue braids fanned herself at the plaza's edge, and Lahara worked her way through the neighbors toward her. "Cousin Grindle?" she ventured, and the granddaughter of her own great-grandfather turned in surprise.

"Lahara," she cried, crushing her to her bony chest in a hug.

Grindle lived way south on the tip of the island, married into a tiny clan that harvested snails for the dye. Lahara had visited as a child and remembered shelves of dyed cloth, and open, downtown waters that frightened her. She hadn't seen Grindle in many years, but easily recognized her father's cousin by the blue of her hair.

"I hope for good news of your husband," Lahara said, eyes scanning the crowded plaza. "Is he come?"

Grindle shook her head. "He's not made the trip. He's … he's changed," Grindle said. "Tark is changed."

"How so?" Lahara remembered the burly blue man she'd met

as a child. Older than Grindle, he'd be ancient now.

Grindle considered. "It's his mind." She tugged her braids. "Though some days he's right as rain."

"Is he *Newly Touched*?" Lahara asked. "It happens like that."

"I don't think so. We've been overlooked for *whispers* in the downtown."

A small woman with deeply lined chestnut skin and tight gray curls interrupted. "What a night," she giggled, raising her pitcher.

"Inez," Grindle greeted her. "Do you remember Lahara? She's come to celebrate your grandson's birth."

"Welcome," Bal's mother said, and poured the honey wine carefully, first into Grindle's pink plastic salvage tumbler, then into the hammered metal cup Lahara had carried from home. "We're gonna drink 'til we sing and sing 'til we dance."

Lahara and Grindle laughed, raising their cups to Inez's toast.

The sun had set leaving the humid night in its shadow, and Lahara twisted her heavy hair off her face. The children were returned from their swim, and to Lahara's relief, Beatrice was playing with them amid much laughter. Switch had also returned, the horse settled in an old thatched lean-to west of the plaza, one favored by the horses in days before the *whispers*.

While the women prepared the feast, the men danced and sang in the courtyard, arms high. Twirling, hopping, bending and swaying, the baby Nared was danced through the air by his father in small dips, passed to each of the men in their family.

Reynaud, the uncle, swayed with the baby to the music before handing Nared to his father. Husbands and brothers and fathers and sons of the people moved in a collaborative circle to drum and flute and the unison hum of a hundred closed mouths singing.

Shoulders and hips relaxed in the music, Lahara pulled sweet orange roots from the fire with bare hands, juggling the hot pieces and dropping them to split as they fell on the stone, steam rising from their centers. Her fingers burned and she blew on them to cool the singe. Bal's older wives scooped up the split potatoes, filling a huge bowl with the tender mash.

Inez slid long flat sticks on the grill to move fish to wide platters, and Grindle put cool fruit and torn bread alongside the plates. As they prepared the food, they gossiped, and laughed, and Lahara blushed at the hammock complaints and praises spilling from the neighbor women's mouths.

Lahara scanned the darkness for Beatrice. The girl had been setting mushrooms and garlic in vinegar, but she'd disappeared. The men were winding down, their sweated bodies collapsed in a heap, the song's hum tapering. Lahara heard a buzz behind her, and thinking her niece had come back to sing, turned to the sound.

Nobody was there.

"There's my wife," Switch said, coming alongside her. His braid had untied and his long hair fell wet with the dance on his shoulders. Lahara wrapped a damp tendril around her finger.

"Let me feed you, husband." She gestured to the brimming tables and guests who filled broad leaves with their feast. Her hair again buzzed, and Lahara shook her head, tossing her curls upside down and brushing through the knots and bangles with her hand.

"What's wrong?" Switch asked.

"My head vibrates. And yet it's not a *whisper*."

"It's you needs eat," Switch said, sitting her down on one of the wide logs around the fire pit.

He set a plate filled with supper on her knees. Ravenous, she pushed the mat to her mouth and ate every morsel of hot fish, burning her lips, but unable to help herself. She licked the last bits and pulled tiny bones from her mouth. "Better," she said.

The sound of distant neighbors singing drifted across the night. They sang an ancient funeral song, one of a handful survived, and a lump grew in Lahara's throat as she listened. Somewhere in the park a procession was leading a wrapped body west to the Remember.

Should old acquaintance be forgot,
and never brought to mind?
Should old acquaintance be forgot,
and auld lang syne?

"That'll be the eldest Spencer boy," Switch said. "He passed this afternoon, the reservoir keeper was telling."

"A boy born, a boy died," Lahara mused. She knew the Spencer boys. The older one had flown his falcon in the autumn games, the bird with the blue feathers winning top honors.

"He has a brother Beatrice's age," she said, and for one horrible moment she imagined her niece wrapped and carried west. She ran her fingers through Switch's hair, untangling the snarls. "I have news about your brother's daughter."

"Go on."

"She's hearing the *whispers*."

His mouth twitched. "*Newly Touched*?" he asked. "Is she to go crazy? Is she to not remember who she is?"

"She knows who she is."

Switch closed his eyes, but said nothing further, and Lahara smoothed his hair, wrapping long strands around each other. She picked through the ornaments in her own curls and found a piece of wire to fasten the neat braid hanging down her husband's back.

"What if she's taken like her mother?" Switch said. "What if she's carried away by whatever stole the Group that Left?"

Beatrice's voice rang out from the darkness. The children were laughing now and Lahara could hear her niece's giggles. She sounded happy.

"Your brother and his wife left without shackles," she reminded Switch. Marly was running around the trees, the chasing game mostly obscured by the dark. "We know about the euphoria now," she continued. "Beatrice comes *Newly Touched* surrounded by those who can help. None of the first had that."

A long shriek, and shouting—that was Beatrice, suddenly harsh over the laughter. Lahara stood, unable to see what was happening. Vella was screaming, and the cherry trees dropped a storm of pink petals as the redhead tore through, falcon high on his tether, the moon reflected on his wings.

The children shoved in chase, circling Vella—the girls from the Chelsea Wood, the Moham brothers and sisters of the baby Nared, and Marly, sweet, young Marly reaching for the falcon with a disturbing fervency on his face, shouting nonsense.

And then, from the darkness, Beatrice high on the horse's wide back, thin legs pale against the mare's dark skin. As she rode to the center of the plaza, the children ceased their chants and chase, and the falcon girl scrambled away, up onto the low concrete wall.

"What in the fux dangum?" Switch's face was stone. He turned to Lahara and she reddened under his glare.

"You've no business," he called, starting toward his niece.

A hush fell over the Meet and for one short, curious moment— there in the plaza surrounded by the sound of crickets in the humidity and her husband's anger—Lahara felt she must be caught in a *whisper*.

The horse reared, snorting. Beatrice leaned in for balance, one hand clutching the strap around its neck. She thrust her torch up—at the sky, at the falcon—and broke the strange silence. "Let us have sacrifices and burnt offerings," she proclaimed, and the children echoed, "Burnt offerings, burnt offerings."

Parents and elders dropped food and drink and ran to the children, unable to get close for the skittish horse so menacing in the torchlight. Lahara moved with the crowd, eyes back and forth from Marly to Beatrice.

Beatrice called out again. "He shall tear it open by its wings, but shall not sever it completely. And the priest shall burn it on the altar, on the wood that is on the fire. It is a burnt offering." The young ones cheered her strong voice.

"Burnt offerings. Burnt offerings." Marly scrambled up the wall toward Vella. "Burnt offering," he told her, as if in explanation.

"Don't," Vella said, backing away. She unpinned the leash from her sleeve and waved the falcon free. The bird flew to the treetops, tether trailing like a kite.

Were they all gone Touched? Lahara edged closer to Switch, but he was moved now behind the horse and motioning to Reko who had joined the clamoring at the wall.

At Switch's signal Reko snatched Marly from the ledge, the younger crying, "Let go' me," as Switch vaulted onto the horse, behind Beatrice, grabbing the leather and kicking in one motion.

Beatrice shouted as Switch brought her away. "Our livestock also must go with us. Not a hoof shall be left behind."

The children scattered, the odd event dismissed as rough play and over joy from the energy of the Meet. Vella accepted a drink of cider from one of Bal's wives, comforted with the attentions.

Marly ran to Lahara begging a sweet and ran off again just as quickly. The women whispered some, but Lahara ignored the words and pushed through the trees. Switch was holding Beatrice's hands while they spoke quietly, the girl seated on a stone ledge, he leaning against the same. The horse was tethered—all menace gone—to a bent tree just beyond.

Beatrice looked so much like her uncle in the darkness, the two with hair escaping their braids to fall into their faces. Switch raised his eyes to Lahara and she braced herself, words of defense at the ready. Her husband would hold her accountable for Beatrice's *whispers*. He would be annoyed, and she would be more so for his accusations.

But Switch only stared, and where on his face she expected anger, there was alarm instead. "Wife, a spark's in your hair."

Lahara flinched—the knots tugged her scalp as he reached into her curls and ripped a bead from the tangle. The jewel crackled red and white, lighting the darkness, and hissing like a snake.

"It blinks with a wild eye," Switch said, holding the strange piece up to the moon's light.

Lahara stared, puzzled. "It's the dangly from the mare's headpiece." She took the bit, trying to find the light within.

"Drop it else it burns," he said, swatting the gem from her fingers.

The bead bounced in the matted undergrowth to land at Beatrice's feet. She picked it from the moss, holding it to her ear. "The dangly speaks."

"I hear only hisses and pops." Lahara said. "Can you understand the words?"

Beatrice listened, then shrugged. "I was wrong. It's silent," she said, handing the jewel to Lahara as she skipped away to rejoin the children.

THE GIRL

DAISY LEIGH took the voucher from the sobbing old man and stuck the payment with the other wrinkled chits in her pocket. The tears made it hard, but fifteen-year-old Daisy was used to them. Sometimes, when a family member would come for their kin, instead of finding a loved one waiting in safety and ready to leave, they'd find one died, and unfortunately for the old woman on the mat, that was how this old man had come to find his wife.

"She was only to the blackberry slope," the man cried. "What happened?"

He and his son-in-law had left for the Columbus Circle soon as the Tweet arrived, but the trip to the Wait from his farm at the Trump had taken almost until the numbers in the black sky were to change, and he was inconsolable.

"I wasn't here when she was brung," Daisy told him, "But Ma said she was already gone when the cart got her. I seen it a lot. Sometimes they just go."

Daisy set the standing screen around the mat and left the man to be comforted by his own. She didn't mean to be abrupt, but another woman called in the corridor and others as well lay in the dark—two more come in this evening—each one needing something while they waited.

The woman on the next bedroll grabbed Daisy's leg as she passed. "I need void."

Her matted white hair stunk like hot carrion and her chin was shiny with spittle and food. "Where's my brother?" the woman called Starly whined. "Didn't you send a Tweet?"

"Shhh," Daisy said, helping her up without telling that her twin brother had come and gone. The drunk woman had a young son and when she was sick with the wine her brother would care for him while she slept away the liquor.

The brother also made himself sick with wine, but he and Starly managed to take turns in their incapacitation. Daisy was very familiar with this family who lived in the Theater district.

The pale woman's Da—also white-skinned like the full moon—was disappeared now half a season with drink and a confused mind.

The heavy floors swallowed their footsteps as they made their way to the back. Daisy held the swinging doors with her good hand. Her lantern cast a skewed light in the canopied outdoor stall, and Starly stumbled in, retching a dark cherry wine into the watery trough that carried her vomit away with the force of the diverted Broadwaterway.

"I don't wanna wait for my brother," she complained, rubbing her eyes and smudging the dark liner. "I'ma get my stuff and go."

Daisy put a hand out to keep her from falling, nudging her back to the bedroll she'd already wet and muddied in the few hours she'd been at the station. She mumbled something about her flask as she picked through her backpack, slowly closing her pale lavender eyes and tipping to rest her head on the guitar she was never without.

Daisy peeked behind the privacy screen. The man had wrapped his wife, and with his son-in-law's help, placed her on the wagon brought east for just this purpose.

"Stay until the sun rises?" Daisy suggested, but the man shook his head. "My daughter needs know what happened to her Ma."

She accompanied them through the huge doors—kicking the bent and damaged side, as the metal tended to stick—and onto the circular plaza cut through by the Broadwaterway, which, wide enough here for canoe passage, veered northwest.

Scraps of steel frame and sheets of broken glass in the surrounding hills reflected the light of the star fields above. The Wait, tucked into the Columbus Circle's western rise was just far enough from the southern rubble to avoid its scalding steam. Daisy placed a small log from a pile on the fire under the everstew. Although the stew was low in the pot this time of night, the savory aroma filled her nose just the same, making her hungry after so many hours without break.

The man took the light stick from the smoldering embers, touching the glowing tip to the resin-soaked rags on his staff. The flames caught easily and the torch threw dark orange shadows across his face.

"Smells like rain," Daisy said. The place where her crushed

hand had mended ached as it did when storms were not far. She rubbed the throb and shook her wrist to away the pain.

"Thank the cart man what brung my Romell from the street." He searched through his cape, and handed her an oversized mushroom collected on the journey east. "For the stew."

Daisy nodded. He grabbed the wagon for support as they eased its wheels over ancient cables snaking through the broken pavement. For a few moments, the girl watched the old man shuffle alongside his son-in-law and the remains of his wife. Then, breathing in the earthy aroma of the mushroom, she broke the gift into pieces and dropped it in the everstew, adding a ladle of water from the barrel and stirring the thick porridge up from the bottom.

A shout inside made her put her meal on hold, and Daisy raised her lamp in the doorway to determine who was making such ruckus. Pulling the dented metal doors behind her, she followed the sound of the hollers to the man at the end of the corridor.

She held the lantern close. He looked her father's age—well, the age when he Left—but except for the years he was nothing like her Da. Under the blisters, this man's face was smooth and pale as compared to her father's rough, sun-browned skin. Her Da had light blue eyes and a thick hair and beard. This man was bald—no eyebrows or lashes either—and his eyes were dark in the lamplight.

"Watcha on about, Anthony?" Daisy asked.

He tried to sit, but restraints held him against the pallet. His eyes darted about and he thrashed his body, oblivious to the wounds on his shoulders, and the lacerations made wet from his movements with new pus and blood.

"Be still," Daisy said. "Don't hurt yourself more than you've had done already."

He twisted free, and his hands flew to his hair and scalp, his neck, his ears. "My Connex-Link? Where's my earpiece."

Daisy examined both sides of his head, certain she misunderstood. Ear piece? "There's nah missing from either." She thought he might have the mind sickness.

"It's a small bead," he said.

Daisy shrugged. This wasn't the first time one come to the

Wait had words that made no sense. She lifted a box from the foot of his mat. "All you had would be here."

Anthony tore into the empty box, running his finger along the seams and shaking it upside down. Finding nothing, he threw the box down, the clatter echoing throughout the station. At once, voices yelled in complaint from the darkness.

"Simmer yourself. You're not the only one waiting."

He lay back down, closing his eyes. "Where am I?"

"You're at the Wait."

"Where is that?"

"Columbus Circle," she said, having been asked the same before by countless disoriented others.

"How'd I get here?"

Daisy sighed. "The wagoner Tinny brung you. The Touched One was along. She's the one told your name was Anthony."

"What are the charges?"

Sometimes people who found themselves at the Wait worried about the barter, or having a debt, and Daisy found the best approach was to answer truthfully. "Well, now, most give a voucher, or add to the stew..."

The man stared at her and Daisy blushed, thankful for the shadows that hid her embarrassed face. "But that's just as you see fit." She trailed off. "No matter."

"I'm free to go, then?" he asked.

Daisy shrugged. Nobody was forced to wait. "Go or stay, but it's long until dawn and you come to us without a torch."

"Why was I restrained?"

"So not to hurt yourself," she said, struggling to keep her voice low. "Enough yack yack. I still need sweep the floor and hang the mats. My Ma's to wake soon and I look forward to taking her hammock."

As she started away to retrieve her broom, the walls shuddered. The floor rumbled a response, tickling her feet and knocking Daisy to the ground. Her lantern skidded on the concrete where the flame flared briefly before going out.

"Are you all right?" Anthony called. "What was that?"

"Just the hillside settling." She regretted she hadn't already made her sweep. The day's dust tickled her nose—she sneezed from the irritation—and bits of dirt and grass poked her bare skin as she crawled toward the lamp. She grabbed the lantern from the darkness and her knee came down hard on something sharp.

"Dangum," she cursed, digging a pointed pebble from her skin with the tip of a cracked nail. She stuck the stone in her bandana so not to step on its sharp edge again, and went to light her lamp.

A blast of hot wet air blew in as she opened the doors. Great heavy drops of rain fell to the dry earth, little puffs of dust rising where they landed. She ducked her head to the downpour and rolled the waxed awning out over the everstew and fire. She touched the lightstick to the wick of her lamp, the flame catching right away.

"Can I borrow a canteen?" Anthony asked, and she turned to him. He held himself steady in the doorway, hand on the wall.

She shook her head. "You can drink from the barrel and eat from the everstew, but I've nothing to send with you," she said, curious about the bare-chested man who must certainly have the mind sickness to want head into a night like this.

"How can I find the wagoner?"

"You can send a Tweet, but what will you trade? You have no vouchers."

"I can work for trade. What kind of work is available?"

Daisy threw a hand up. "What question do you ask? Have you never earned a voucher? There's building and gathering, farming, repair, hauling. Salvage. You look like you'll heal to be a fit fellow. If you can run down a hog or trap a squirrel, you can barter the flesh or the skin. But surely there'll be none of that tonight. Yeah?"

"Can I work for you?"

Daisy laughed. "Here?"

"There's nothing you need done?"

"We need everything done but have nothing to trade and no vouchers to spare. All we have is a place to wait."

"I need a place to wait."

Rumbling thunder rolled through clouds blowing from the north. Lightning flashed, a long jagged streak that illuminated briefly the treetops in Central Park to the east and the churning Broadwaterway just steps from where Daisy stood.

There was definitely something odd about this man. "You'll be no use to anyone in your condition. Let's think it in the daylight."

Another flash. This one even closer. The night seemed blacker for the lightning, and the darkness hid the figure come upon the station. Only when the woman was right on her did Daisy hear her cries through the storm.

"Help me." She held out her arm, a deep gash spilling red beneath her elbow's crease, staining her robe anew as quickly as the rain washed the crimson away. She babbled, holding Daisy for support. "I should have stayed at my brother's the night but thought to make a swift journey. The rains came unexpected and my cart slipped. I only found the Wait for the kindness of two Disconnects come to lift me up..."

The woman slid to the ground, gesturing to the Disconnects who were nowhere but perhaps in her mind. Daisy looked on helplessly, watching the blood flow. Anthony lifted the arm from her body.

"A tourniquet," he yelled, over the thunder and pounding storm. "I need a tourniquet to wrap the arm. She'll bleed out without it."

"I don't know what that is," Daisy said, tears mixing with the rain on her face.

"Give me your hair band," Anthony said. "Quick."

She yanked the bandana from her head, dislodging the tiny sharp object stashed in its folds. The bead hovered a moment, sparkling red and white, and dropped.

And then, while Daisy followed Anthony's instructions in the rain, as they stopped the flow of blood that threatened the life of the journeywoman, a rivulet of the downpour caught the sharp stone, and carried the bit away into the Broadwaterway.

Daisy turned to its wild blink as the piece sank, shrugging at the disappeared flash that was likely, she thought, only a trick of the storm in her eye.

LAHARA

DAWN BROKE HOT, the saturated ground releasing its water in the morning sun, steam rising throughout the Moham settlement and infusing the summer air with a mist that reflected the reds and the turquoises of the painted bungalows.

Lahara rolled over, stiff from the hammock-less sleep on the porch a Moham cousin had so generously padded for their visit. The rains had come suddenly, and though the children were long asleep, piled on Inez's deck, the men had been roused from their games of chance and the women caught in the downpour while dancing the hours off midnight into the new day.

It had been a wondrous feeling, the water come upon the feast, but Lahara was anxious now to return home to examine the fields and cistern and tenement roofing that might require patching after such a soaking. Certainly the molds would need a scrape and the cellar a mop.

The sounds of guests preparing their own journeys home filtered throughout the campsite—creaking wagon wheels, tarps shaken and rolled, and a few unpleasant squeals as small animals were trapped, skinned, and tied. Some had been up before dawn in order to make first start, and as the sunrise spilled yellow across the plaza, there was much hugging and crying amid promises of return visits.

She pulled the thin blanket closer around her bare shoulders. The heavy rains had washed away the sweat of the dance, but not the worry of her niece's *whispers* or the puzzlement of the strange sparkling bead that had flashed and murmured before becoming dark again and silent. In the morning's clarity, Lahara wondered if the light they'd seen hadn't been simply a firefly caught behind the gem, and not of the bead at all.

She still clutched the faceted ornament in her hand. She'd held it all night and her palm was creased with its imprint. Cool to the touch, the transparent piece of silver seemed to disappear against the pale light.

She twirled the gem in her fingers. It caught the sun come over the rail, creating diamond flashes on the ceiling. Lahara closed her fingers around the sphere to extinguish the reflections, and after a moment's thought, twisted the strange jewel back into her hair.

"Auntie?" The top of Beatrice's veiled head appeared around the carved railing. "Are you awake?"

Lahara put her finger to her lips and gestured her niece come around quietly. She wasn't worried about disturbing the women on the far side of the covered deck—they'd been up in talk long after she and Switch closed their eyes, and were sleeping soundly now—but she didn't want to wake her husband, as he slept lightly and in fits.

She disentangled herself carefully from their shared wraps. Switch opened his eyes as she slipped from the bedroll.

"I'm sorry," she said, "The morning calls."

He sat up, braid hanging loose again down his back. His eyes were far away, and Lahara was saddened to remember his words.

"This girl is to be watched," he'd said. "Watched closely." Once the distraction of the blinking bead had faded, the spectacle of his niece in the darkness had gripped him with fear and anger. He'd taken the horse to stable and not returned until the rains came.

Lahara hoped the waters had washed away his fury along with the dust and heat, but Switch was no different than any of the neighbors suffered a loss to the *whispers*. The memory of his brother led away by a Touched would always linger, and he couldn't help it coloring his feelings—even toward his own Touched wife, and now his niece.

She picked her robe from the floor. The air between them was heavy, the night's conspiracies unresolved. Lahara waited for her husband to say something—anything—but he just rubbed the back of his hand across his eyes.

"It is what it is," she said, finally. "And a new day."

"I'll bring the horse 'round and prepare the wagon," was all he said, his voice raspy from the long night's smoking and singing. "Collect the children. See the girl's *whispers* are attended to."

"Her *whispers* are not an illness begging cure."

He had no further response, and she climbed down from the porch. Beatrice sat in the grass, back against the bungalow, knees pulled to her chest. The circles under her eyes were apparent even through her veil, and Lahara pulled the lace up for a closer look.

"Did you not sleep?" she asked, touching Beatrice's cheek.

"The girls from Chelsea Wood shared our mat. They squirmed and made sounds the whole night. Marly, too, was disturbed."

Lahara nodded. Onesies rarely journeyed beyond the Wood, but the girls' father, still a Moham cousin though many generations removed, had brought the Onesie north by river raft to the Meet. It was no wonder they squirmed and giggled at such an adventure.

"And my dreams," Beatrice continued. "All night I followed a pillar of smoke tall as the sky. The ground was so dry. My feet blister as if I actually did wander so far."

Beatrice's dream sounded to be a *whisper*, but Lahara would keep that to herself, fearing to upset the morning calm. "What is a pillar of smoke?" she laughed. "I myself dreamt of a boy I once knew at the Carl Schurz. Such green eyes he had."

Beatrice smiled, but still looked troubled. "I wore sandals. Somebody was shouting in my dream and I was to remember what he said, but I've already forgotten."

Lahara's stomach twisted. She held her hand over the tender spot to soothe the ache. Her skin pulsed beneath her touch. "Are you washed?" she asked, and Beatrice held up clean hands for inspection. "Bring Marly to breakfast, then," Lahara said, "and I'll make my own cleanse."

She waited until Beatrice ran off before hurrying around the back of the bungalow. Several neighbors, her cousin Grindle among them, were queued at the shed, and Lahara waved in dismay until Grindle pulled her to the head of the line.

"Are you faring well?" Grindle called from the other side of the wood. Lahara cracked open the door with her toe and grabbed her cousin's hand through the tight space.

"My insides feel to pour out with my void, cousin."

"It's the feast in your belly," Grindle reassured her. "I'll brew a mint tea."

Lahara stood shakily over the waste drain. "Thank you for your kindness, but I think the fires inside have eased," she said, relinquishing the shed and walking the few steps to make her wash.

The barrel was much fuller this morning than when they had arrived, and Lahara dipped her fingers, then hands, in the fresh rainwater. She stood a moment to allow the heat of the fast-rising sun to dry her robe and ease the chill inside.

She found the children around the flat stone table laid out with breads and jams and nut butters. Baskets overflowed with blueberries and sour plums, and dripping hunks of honeycomb were piled on a hammered metal platter. The older wives of the baby's father made room on the crowded table for bowls of fresh laid eggs and platters of dried fruits wet with vinegar and syrup.

"Look," Marly called to Lahara, holding up a thick piece of honeycomb, bees still swarming around the wax. "I choosed my own and didn't get stinged."

"Can I have some sweet?" Beatrice asked.

Lahara swatted the fat bugs away, breaking off a portion for her niece. Beatrice sucked the dark honey hungrily. Nibbling a cracker, Lahara was pleased to find her stomach stopped complaining.

"Might I offer a hot drink?"

Reko's uncle Crispin, a thick-skinned man with deep-set bright eyes, held out the chicory carafe. Lahara turned her head to avoid the sharp smell, but the queasiness returned, and she held perfectly still until the wave passed.

"Thank you, no," she said, smiling at the two blond heads peeking from behind Crispin's robes.

They smiled back, and came around shyly. Although Lahara had seen the man from the Chelsea Wood dancing during last night's feast, and had seen the Onesie with the other children, this was the first the girls had made a greeting. "Pleased to be halloo'd to you," they said in unison, identical faces pink from the sun and sticky with breakfast, curtsying the short, stout body they shared.

"My daughters are anxious to stroke the horse again," Crispin said. "I wouldn't mind another look, either. Seems we once had an animal that color, one disappeared in the black of a night. If this is that horse, it would only be right to bring her south again."

"Yours without hair, too?" Bal asked. He winked at Lahara. "The same story I've heard all day and night. More horses remembered than ever roamed this island, I'd say."

"Still and all," Crispin insisted, helping himself to a brown egg and slurping the wet yolk noisily.

A sudden cramp seized Lahara. She stumbled from the table, beyond the plaza to the reservoir path, away from the scents and sounds of breakfast. She breathed deeply and willed her stomach to settle, but everywhere she turned, the nausea had encouragement. A crow pulling a fat worm from the wet earth, an antlered buck nibbling new green shoots in the mulch, a compost heap, the cesspool. She covered her mouth.

"Auntie, what?" Beatrice cried, dragging Marly to catch up, startling the deer in the thicket that bounded away, white tail high.

"It's nothing," Lahara said, shaking her head.

A moment later, the tangled limbs of the girls from Chelsea Wood came tumbling down the path. Wispy yellow hair flew behind the Onesie as they scampered toward the reservoir. Switch's apprentice followed, red-faced and out of breath for the chase. "No swimming, you're to leave for below Crease, your Paw tells."

Beatrice's eyes widened at the mention of the Crease, but Lahara's hand on her shoulder bid her keep her thoughts to herself.

"Reko, na bad y'self," the Onesie shouted back, squealing at a joke Lahara didn't understand.

Reko blushed, shrugging an apology. "First time my cousins are to the uptown."

Lahara crouched, ill again, a wet warmth come on her thigh as she vomited.

"Did you drink old water?" Beatrice asked.

"I'm to be fine," Lahara said, pulling herself to stand and spitting bitter remnants from her mouth. "There's peppermint in the brush. Gather leaves I can chew."

She kicked dirt over the mess, and as she did so a clot slid from deep inside her to the ground. She looked down at the sleek, gelatinous clump shining purple and red in the morning sun.

"Oh," Lahara said.

Marly pointed at the blood trailing down her leg and backed away, fingers in his mouth to whistle a long, solid tone. After a moment, two wavering twills responded—Lahara thought that would be Switch—but the sound was too far away to be certain.

Afraid to move, she stood perfectly still, paralyzed by the blood that pooled beneath her, yet swooning and almost unable to remain standing from the same.

Inez was first to appear to answer the call, as she had been just at the edge of camp to spill her night waste and her container was still in her hand.

"She's dying," Beatrice cried as Inez helped Lahara to the ground, lifting her feet to rest on the wide trunk of a tulip tree still wet from the rain. Lahara pushed against the rough bark as another cramp seized her, arching her back to relieve the spasm.

"It's her Bleed come," Inez said, pulling Lahara's understrap to the side. The tulip tree's broad flat leaves cast shadows on Lahara's bare legs and she watched the shapes shift like a flock of birds crossing the river.

"Ya gots to stay alert," Inez said, pinching Lahara's ankle.

Her niece cried out to Switch, who had appeared in a thunder of footfalls, dropping next to Lahara to slide his wrap beneath her head. She squeezed her husband's hand.

"The Bleed is our friend," Lahara said, repeating what her mother and grandmother and grandmother's grandmother had told, each in their own times.

The burn ran the length of her body and she cried at its pain, but in her safe place, inside, away from the scorching cramp, Lahara was laughing at the force speeding through her, and she drifted in the joy, remembering how her mother danced and how in the dancing, she would reach for her and they'd dance as mothers and daughters had done in an unbroken circle since the beginning of forever.

"Look at me girl," Inez was saying, as she slapped her arm.

The muscles in her legs and back contracted, twisting Lahara off the ground and she seized a hand—it was hot and sticky—that hovered above. She was angry now, in a rage of blood that pooled beneath her and stained black like crushed cherries her clothes.

A cool cloth wiped the sweat from her face and it was Switch, she saw, who held her hair back while the sponge did its work. She wanted to run her fingers along her husband's shoulder, but straps she had no memory of being tied to held her arms. She tried to speak her deep love for this man but the words seemed small and she left them behind, done and already rushing away.

Did she shimmer? Lahara searched the faces of those kneeling before her, but found no answers, and she rose, as if on a wind, cool and vaporous, from her body. She recognized her own wet curls tossed on a quilt of many fabrics below, and the recognition pulled her back into her hungry body.

"Hot wine," Switch was saying, as he tipped a beaker toward her lips. The broth burned her mouth and Lahara coughed, choking on the alcohol vapor.

"Get her up," Inez instructed, her old arms moving Switch out of the way so her own daughters could scoop Lahara onto a soft pallet.

Lahara ran her tongue gratefully over drops of honey Beatrice spread on her lips. Encouraged, Beatrice wrung sweet tea from a cloth into her mouth, and Lahara's throat was soothed.

"I've covers in the wagon," Switch said. "We'll start home."

Inez shook her head. "Not yet. She needs to be tended. It's dry now, but the Bleed comes fast, and these hours and days want to steal her."

"She'll be safe with me," Switch argued.

"No," Inez said. "She needs be with women."

"Last Bleed her cousin come from the Carl Schurz. Lahara has women."

"The blood shall be a sign for you, on the houses where you are," Beatrice said, touching the dark smears on her aunt's legs.

"Control yourself," Switch said, pulling her hand away.

"And when I see the blood, I will pass over you, and no plague will befall you."

"Go east with your uncle," Inez told Beatrice. "We'll bring your aunt home when it's over."

Switch shook his head. "I won't leave Lahara without family.

Close as the Mohams are, her great-grandparents share no blood."

Lahara longed for a bite of bread or sip of soup. The scents of everstews bubbling beyond the path were unbearable in their callings. Exhausted now, Lahara thought of all to be neglected at home for her Bleed. The crops ready for gathering, the ferment, the gardens with new plantings. She understood her husband's fear—he had lost one wife already—but to stay would cost dearly.

A smooth hand brushed the hair from her eyes. "Not to worry, husband of my cousin," Grindle was saying as she stroked the tension from Lahara's face. "I have been through the Bleed and I am family. Don't forfeit all in the east. I'll care for Lahara with the kind help of the Moham women." She raised her eyes to the sky. "She'll be dried by the time the middle number spells 16."

"Ten sleeps," Reko calculated from Switch's side.

"What of your husband?" Switch asked, but Grindle waved away his concern, blue braids wrapped like a crown shining in the summer sun. "Tark is well attended. It's of no regard."

Switch knelt beside Lahara. "Tell me what to do."

She turned a weak head toward him. The new baby was crying in the distance, and Lahara smiled to remember his milky smell. "Bring the children home," she whispered. "I'll be soon through the worst, then dry until winter."

Switch brushed his lips to Lahara's cheek as she rose to meet his touch. "After a sleep we'll see you again," he promised.

She nodded, and fell back, and as the mattress below became wet again with the red and black, she closed her eyes and drifted, smiling, in the fertile places of her mind.

WINTER

ONE TOUCHED WITH SCIENCE,
ONE WITH MATH

ROLF JAY leaned out from under the canopy, lifting his face to the night and the biting saltwater wind. Fat snowflakes landed on his eyelashes and he wiped them away with a chapped hand.

Standing on the upper platform of the Watchtower at the river, arms braced against the crossbeam, he surveyed the waters from the southern sunk-city Battery to the west across the Hudson. All was quiet, and Rolf was glad he had nothing to report to the coming Watch, as his brother was waiting.

He could just locate the bobbing lantern a few blocks south at the End's landing—that would be Roman loading their gear. Heavy clouds made bright by eternal sky-lights concealed the stars, but the twins didn't need stars to guide them. They'd marked their course through the shoals, and the solar buoys would shine until sunrise.

Skin drums pounded for the opening gates, and Rolf turned to track the fur-bundled woman, Lady Pan, leaving the walled community at the edge of the Chelsea Wood. She cut a line through the drifts, following pale green lanterns almost obscured by snow.

Rolf lost her for a moment as she passed behind the smokehouse, but here she was again—a dark shape below—climbing the ladder now toward him.

"What goes?" she asked, pulling up onto the creaking platform.

"All still," Rolf said. "Too cold for the beasties tonight."

She held her hands over the fire lantern hanging from the crossbeam, rubbing her fingers in the warmth, then took a container of hot tea from her pack, twisting the top open to sip from the wide mouth. A spicy steam rose between them.

"It's a windy one," he warned.

"Yeah, gonna tie on, fa sure." She brushed snow from the

forged metal gong, belting herself to the tower against the buffeting winds.

"I'm out then," Rolf said. "Keep the bogey man away." He scrambled down the ladder, twine burning his hands as he lost his footing to slide the last few rungs. Roman was already hoisting the sail as Rolf sprinted toward the landing.

His twin—identical but for the black hair where Rolf's grew yellow—loosened the mooring. "Ya coming?" he challenged, and the wind pulled the boat from the jetty.

Rolf slipped wildly on the snow-blanketed planks. Grabbing the weighted tether at the edge of the pier, he swung out over the water, calculating—one, two three—and let go, soaring into the icy night to drop hard just before Roman navigated out of range.

He landed feet first and slid to his bottom and along the deck, coming to rest against the wide spool of cable they'd salvaged, over a mile of thin wire to be uncoiled through the sea and shoals before night's end.

"I'll trip ya numbers someday," Roman teased, securing the line as Rolf reviewed the angle and speed and distance he'd processed on the fly to reach him.

The small craft rose and fell on the choppy water, sail snapping in the wind. Rolf's stomach clenched. They'd spent months planning, and here they were, tonight, almost at the finish. Yet so many things could still go badly.

"Is the snow making danger? Ought we wait for clear skies?"

Roman kept his eyes to the water. "Done waiting," he said. "Think what coulda been accomplished by now if we had Pulse."

They'd been Touched more than five years, Rolf with the math *whispers*, Roman with the science, and they'd figured out the Pulse since almost the first. Ma hadn't wanted them to take their Adventure, afraid they'd be caught up in the Ones Leaving, but at a certain age the young people of Chelsea Wood always took their Adventure above Crease, and theirs had been arranged before the *whispers* began.

Rolf and Roman insisted they'd keep each other safe, and as soon as the gripping headaches subsided they'd set off up the Hudson, their Ma and siblings shouting their names as they left.

By the time they reached Inwood at the north, they'd

identified—aided by their combined *whispers*—two of the Pulse rods. Waters churned in telltale froth that burned skin, and fish kept their distance where the transparent rods rooted.

In a short time, again directed by *whispers*, the brothers traced those roots to where they joined underwater foundations of the stacked roads circling the island. The rods had once powered the highways and the twins got busy figuring how to harness that idle power for their own use.

"Hey, ya," Roman said sharply, and Rolf shook his head of the memories. "Pay attention. I don't find the markers. Give your eyes to locate them."

The moon shone a diffused light over the water through falling snow and fog. "There," Rolf said, pointing to the faint line of phosphor buoys at the southwest.

They'd answered many questions during their half-year Adventure. Camping at the Norte Inwood they'd explored the Hudson at the riverbed crack, a rift that caught and spun and released like a slingshot whatever flowed over it. For several weeks they studied how the rift and tides and currents interconnected, and except for the runner Janelle who every morning passed where they moored, none of the clan in that north forest showed themselves.

When they were ready to move on and continue their Adventure, the twins had overlanded west. The channel that connected to the Harlem River dead-ended in a sludge dam, but Rolf and Roman had prepared for this. Their canoe had runners along the bottom and only twice did they have to carry the heavy outrigger over sediment and rock.

A congregation of robed Disconnects—visible in the ruins across the dry waterbed—had watched them drag their boat east. Roman shouted to engage the hooded ones, but they simply melted into the bluff across the channel.

Although they'd been warned not to venture into the domains north of the city—remnants of burst and burn pockets in the sand and beasts in the wilderness were a danger—the twins pursued the Disconnects through the marsh, turning back only at the shrieks of long-limbed, hairy creatures beating their chests and showing their teeth in the trees.

As they retreated, Roman saw the footprints they'd left in the marsh were now glowing green. He stopped to shovel bunches of the shimmering mud, and that night, camped in a cove on the Harlem River, he began his work, assembling his first lamp. He'd built a hundred since—all the Chelsea Wood used them—lamps that stored sunlight and glowed green in the dark, and in a more recent variant, lamps that shined orange.

The wind shifted, and Rolf grabbed the railing. Roman navigated around oyster-encrusted islands and past the sprawling rubble ridge to open waters where the snow turned to ice, striking the brothers. He pulled the boat beside glowing floaties they'd chained to salvage underneath. The water here was rough in the wind and they bounced on the crests and murky swirls.

The moon continued to provide some light, as did the radiant numbers—01.02.2257—shining through the night despite the cloud cover, but Rolf's anxiety grew. He tried not to contemplate what lay below, underwater ruins home to coiled eels and enormous hard-shelled creatures, and razor-mouthed fishes.

"Secure us," Roman said.

He cranked the wheel and lowered the hook. After a few moments, arm growing numb from the repetitions, he reversed the motion, relieved to feel the anchor catch on a concrete scaffold.

"Got it," Roman said, unfolding a package stowed beneath the forward bench.

"Maybe overnight is a challenge unmanageable," Rolf said, the thoughts he'd been worrying come to surface again. "Wait 'til day rather, yeah?"

"Can't lock with the sun interference." Roman smoothed the wrinkles on the plastic sheet he'd set on the deck. "If it was nah submerged so deep, maybe."

"North at the channel mouth c'be easier?" Although they'd found twelve remaining Pulse rods in total, only two—one at the top of the city, and this at the bottom—were steadfast, the others intermittent and requiring complex repair to stabilize.

"Got the Disconnects there. Can't have watching. You know they watch," Roman said. "We already decided." He stood, dropping his cape and under wrappings. Teeth chattering, he stepped naked onto the plastic.

Rolf nodded. They would tap into the energy as planned.

He lifted one edge of the clear, blended plastic, supple even in the cold, and pulled the cover around Roman, straightening the frame as he raised it over his brother's head and snapping the edges to inflate the orb.

He examined the sewn chambers that would fill and empty with seawater and ran a finger along the seam to check the seal, smoothing the attached paddle sleeves and double-checking the knot that tethered the bubble to the boat.

"Issa perfect job," Roman said, his voice muffled from inside the clear ball. He rubbed a phosphor filament on the spiny frame and an easy orange glow filled the sphere.

Rolf bit his lip. He recognized he had done careful work, but the calculations worried him. What if he'd mistaken the integers or transposed figures? If the chambers collapsed, his twin would either drown, trapped with the bones of the ancestors, or be swept out to the unfathomable and further.

Rolf fell into the math *whispers*. Calculations flew back and again. Suddenly, nothing made sense, the sums meaningless as snail tracks in the sand. But even as doubt overtook him his *whispers* insisted the computations were correct.

"Stop," Roman said, pressing a hand against the plastic. "I trust your *whispers* as you trust mine."

The wind had died down. Rolf unwound a length of wire from the spool and connected the braided end to one of the paddle sleeves. The cable would follow his brother into the ocean.

Roman grinned. "G'wan. Do it."

Rolf took a deep breath—they both did—and rolled the bubble over the starboard side. It bounced on the surface—Roman went head over toe—and disappeared under the waves.

The slack of the nylon tether pulled through his hands, following the sphere, and Rolf counted ticks to keep pace with his brother's descent. Not too quickly. The bubble needed a moment to right itself and Roman needed time to fit legs and arms into the paddle sleeves. It would take time for the pressure to stabilize and for Roman to kick his way down to the submerged rod.

As he focused on the passage of time, Rolf's *whispers* overtook him, compelling him to count the beating of his heart and the space between contractions, the pull of his lungs and the quiet between breaths, the blink of his eyes and the echo between each closing of the lid—every increment a percussive tone around his own name.

He might have stayed in the song of time forever but for a splashing come over the deck. He sputtered, salt water in his mouth, and heard what he'd missed for the *whispers*. A rolling gong—the Watch alarm—echoing over the open sea.

Rolf turned to the shore, but couldn't see anything in the darkness. The gong repeated, faint for the distance, along towers to the east and north. Out on the water an unidentified pinpoint of light grew larger. What in dangum? He looked back at the spot where his brother had gone under. Fa sure there wouldn't be time now to uncoil cable and bring Pulse back. They needed return.

Rolf yanked the tether to signal Roman as a vibration like an earth tremor rocked the boat. The light on the water swelled upon him. "Halloo," he called.

A strange white and silver vessel like none he'd ever seen had pulled along his port side. A brilliant blue ball spun at the top, illuminating brighter than a midday sun, and causing the spellings painted across its hull—*ALPHA*—to gleam.

A ramp slid from the tall ship to the twins' boat and the rumble ceased. A woman called to him, her accent unfamiliar, peculiar. "You're the Touched?"

"Who is it?" Rolf shouted.

She climbed aboard with footfalls that rattled the metal of the walkway. "Hey, easy," Rolf cried as the stranger pulled his arms up hard behind him.

The woman—her face was scabbed and peeling—waved a flashing stick over Rolf's body, and when the rod clicked, she shouted, "Confirmed."

Rolf struggled but she covered his face with a cloth and he breathed in the sweet ferment. Gagging—his throat felt to close and at once he was ill—his knees buckled and he slid to the deck.

The woman was strong. She hoisted Rolf over her shoulder and carried him up the ramp, dropping him like dead weight at the feet of a tall, well built, bald man. Rolf took deep, clearing breaths, but the taste and smell of the ferment remained.

"Seth, there was only the one," the woman was saying, small dark eyes on the stick's flickering lights. "Discrete Mathematics."

The man Seth examined the stick as the woman bound Rolf's hands and feet. "The second is the same coordinates, Marilena," Seth said sharply. "You missed him."

The woman started back for the twins' boat and Seth followed. Searching the small space, they moved the cable, peered under the benches, and unfolded the sail. Seth picked something from the deck and shook it. Roman's cape.

Rolf was confused, not afraid. Of all the things he'd worried might happen, he could not have imagined this. It felt to be a dream. Anyone they'd explained about Pulse looked forward to joining the ring of current that once circled and lit the island. Why would these strangers interfere? It was incomprehensible. Unless Pulse wasn't the reason these two had come. They had barely glanced at the cable, after all.

"Seth," Marilena shouted. "In the water."

Roman's orange bubble had surfaced. Seth grabbed the tether, pulling the orb—and Roman—toward the boat, and she helped maneuver the deflating sphere.

"Hey what goes, yeah?" Roman shouted, flailing at the flashing stick across his naked body. The woman placed a cloth over his face, holding the weave against his mouth and nose until he crumpled, covering his cold skin with the cape.

"Confirmed," Seth said. "Biophysics."

"What is this?" Marilena asked, pointing to the wire in Roman's plastic suit.

Seth examined the glowing cable that snaked from the spool through the paddle and he peered over the railing where the wire disappeared into the rubbled ocean. "I was right to grab these two. They've connected to something live," he said. "Secure it."

Marilena unrolled the cable behind her and lifted the spool onto the deck—close enough to Rolf he could almost touch it—and she cut the wire and twisted the still glowing slack edge onto a line come through a panel on the floor.

After checking the tension of her new connection, she tossed the spool into the water, its weight pulling the plastic wrap and paddle over and under with it.

Seth hoisted Roman over his shoulder. Rolf feared his brother would end in the ocean as well, but the bald man carried his shivering twin up the ramp, dropping him next to Rolf.

The gangway retracted and the boat began to move.

Roman stirred. The brothers curled into each other for warmth, watching the clear line come up through the floor glowing with the Pulse and feeding the sea with its length, and as they sped away, the twins fixed their stare on the lamp hanging on their own small craft, the green light fading behind them in the distance.

ANTHONY

ANTHONY STEELE was in a deep sleep when something woke him, pulling him fast from the depths of unconsciousness. His mind lurched, clouded by the transition, and he opened his eyes, body ready in spite of the disorientation. As his eyes adjusted to the darkness, retrieving points of reference—the toppled refrigerator, the pipe leading nowhere, the rusted sink—Anthony recalled where it was he'd holed up for the night.

The long abandoned apartment was like ice, his breath white in the frigid air, but the metal door at street level had been unmarked with the red X warning of cholera and other diseases of disaster, and the stairs had seemed sound when he climbed them earlier in the evening seeking refuge from the storm whiting out the city.

Anthony flexed his fingers, and, still in his bedroll, unsheathed his knife, listening. All still save the scramblings of the mice drawn to the heat of his body.

He shoved off the wrap, and the rodents scattered. Crouching, he shifted his shoulders to relieve the pressure of the backpack he wouldn't remove even in sleep, the bag heavy now with the medicines—antivirals, antibiotics, vaccines and more—retrieved from the Safe cache. He'd left the generator, but would return when the weather cleared to collect that heavier piece of equipment. For now it was the antivirals he had to get to Marjorie and the sick ones. He'd paid a Tweet before the storm to bring news to the one *Touched with Medicine* that he was en route with the doses, and it was urgent he keep that promise.

He listened carefully to the sounds of the building, wary, for although he'd surveyed the floor below when he first arrived, he hadn't continued up the dark stairs to explore further, instead dropping, exhausted, to settle in the first room with enough space to accommodate him. He regretted that lapse in caution now.

He stood slowly, knees cracking, the pops like shots through the dark. With his back to the water-stained wall, Anthony moved across a floor wet with snow filtered through the broken window. He lifted the heavy, mildewed drape and looked down to West Twenty-ninth Street.

The snow had stopped while he slept, but scattered gusts blew the accumulation in sideways whirls. A wolf, mangy and thin—he'd heard this animal's howls the night before—pawed at an abandoned, overturned wagon, its pack circling behind him.

Snow piled undisturbed in window frames and doorways of surrounding buildings that were likely empty. Although travelers might stop here, none stayed, for barely a half mile out hissed no-man's land.

He could smell the sulfur in the air and even inside, at this distance, hear the cracklings where the landscape folded in on itself, a scorched canyon created by subterranean vents blown miles deep through bedrock to rip a hot gash—the Crease—straight through from Eleventh Avenue to the middle of the island.

Soft mounds of snow were falling to the street. His eyes followed the avalanche to the height of the building across. The remnants of an ancient cornice hung from its damaged frame, snow sliding off in melting clumps. The sight stirred a memory of some wintry childhood game. He shook the thought away, banished to a place he wouldn't visit.

He slid his knife back into its sheath and forced the broken window up. The wooden casing cracked and the wind whistled in along with the sound of distant shore alarms. The last time he'd heard gongs they'd preceded a beaching of creatures that swam in the Hudson and came ashore for meat. Meat, when no deer were found, meant humans.

He leaned both hands on the cold cement ledge and craned his head, stretching to see as far as possible east and west. When he'd first arrived on Manhattan, Anthony saw Vaulters in every movement. Real? Imagined? Who knew? He'd felt stalked and tracked and paralyzed by the chase. When Marjorie removed the tracer that Seth had implanted in his thigh—implanted in all their thighs—he'd begun to feel safer, but still he had to assume they were looking for him.

Vault was definitely visiting the island. Disappearing Record holders—the native's called them *Touched*—made that clear enough. At first, Vault teams had removed the Records with a knife and left the bodies where they fell. The families blamed the deaths on hungry beasts come over from the far shores. But now, the people rejoiced the leaving of the beasts—no bodies had been found in some time—and mourned instead the Touched gone missing. What was Vault up to?

He studied the clearing sky, locating the Big Dipper directly above the satellite corridor. Heaven lived in those servers, but although they were lit, the open receivers and transmitters on the ground were gone. Admin and the Interface between Heaven and the earth they supervised had disappeared as a result of the same events that ripped the city in 2078. The beginning of the end.

The night was silent except for the cracklings of the Crease and a soft whisper he couldn't at first identify. He listened to the sound—all but imperceptible—tracking the slow whoosh as it increased to a shriek that seemed headed directly for him.

He drew back instinctively, arms up in defense. At its crescendo, a searing flash lit the sky, reflecting green and yellow with shots of red on the white of the city, setting the wolves below to barking and growling.

His heart pounded at the sight of the flare. Vault cruisers exchanged information with each other through light and color, and although Anthony had never used the flares himself—his work had been inside—he'd trained with them. He'd seen them lighting the sky from time to time since his arrival—the people called them sky-paint—but he'd never before been well positioned enough to decode their messages.

He sprung into action—pulling a book from his pack to record the symbols—as the rainbow faded to reveal a series of lines and dots in the sky. A second flare—blue and white—responded in another section of sky, and when those patterns faded, he copied those lines and dots, a Morse based text, before they too disappeared.

He laid the book flat on the windowsill and scribbled beneath the markings, and as he translated, a slim hope rose that he might be able to intervene and save a Touched One this night.

The initial flare had launched in the southwest, and according to the skyward code, Alpha—Seth's team—had retrieved two designated targets and was returning to Vault.

The second, responding flare, had risen south of him—the dots and lines a communiqué informing that Bravo—Racine's crew—continued by water in-mission. The grid system used for Data Recovery fixed their destination to Sector 5-D, a four-block radius from Fourteenth to Eighteenth Street on the East River and west to First Avenue. Salt collectors, mostly, lived in this barren area, and a clan of blue-dyers and fishing families made their homes in a small colony set in the river ruins at Seventeenth Street.

Anthony flipped through the pages of notes that he and Daisy and Marjorie had compiled, a comprehensive record—names and locations—of Touched. The information hadn't come easy, but with conversation, barter and stealth, the list had grown.

He had recorded only a single Touched in Sector 5-D, the entry punctuated with a question mark. At the time of the breach, Vault determined southeast sectors were not affected. No pings were detected, and anecdotal evidence backed the lack of southern Record holders. But at the spot where Fourteenth—the people called it the End—and Avenue C intersected, Anthony had shared a meal with an old fisherman, and though he hadn't asked and the man hadn't said, Anthony had recognized a certain look in the old man's eyes. If he were indeed Touched, he'd be an easy mark. And if Bravo was in the southern waters, they'd be to him by dawn.

He pulled a map from his pack and unfolded the frayed, woven cloth, examining the tunnel system sketched in black grease. To enter the tunnels running under the island he'd need to get to Park Avenue—three city blocks from the building he was holed up in—a treacherous hike at night.

He'd met the Touched fisherman by following this same tunnel route, searching for a Safe cache deep in a cellar of the Bowery Mission near Houston Street. A woman he'd encountered at Murray Hill—she was above Crease for trade—warned there was nothing below the End, but Anthony hadn't understood.

"Bowery where now? Go on and crack ice water, yah, that's all ya find, to go down. Raft south to Union, or tunnel the way. The beasts are hungry if you walk it. Wah, you'll find it the true," the woman had said when he asked how to reach the Mission.

Certain he misunderstood—the slang was, after all, confusing to translate—Anthony had hiked from the bazaar on Second Avenue to Park, and after a small trade in the tunnel—seeded bread for access—he'd walked the subway to where it ended. When he finally emerged Topside via the pulley system that screamed as its gears turned, the truth of the journeywoman's words had hit him.

He'd stood dizzy on a bluff at the southern and easternmost edge of the island, blinded by the sun after so many hours underground. East Fourteenth Street was a jagged cliff overlooking black water. Anthony could see part of the old Con Edison power plant, a configuration of silver transformers below in the waves, and way out to the south the feet and foundation of the Brooklyn Bridge, its roadway missing along with the entire of the Manhattan and Williamsburg Bridges. Brooklyn was far and east across the open waters, her coast broken, her shape distorted.

He'd scanned the waves and spinning ice for any sign of the downtown he'd known until his mind and body became numb with the effort and grief. Greenwich Village, Wall Street, the Lower East Side—it was all gone.

As he teetered at the end of the world, the sky turned orange in the west. Two, then three whales breeched, leaping in the wide, endless southern waters. For a moment his heart leapt with the silver beasts and he thought God had given him a sign, but then he remembered God was nowhere in this city, his higher power now just wits and luck.

After a time, Anthony had turned from the water. Signs of habitation, an old fire pit and a canoe overturned on wooden planks in the rubbled clearing, were losing definition in a light snowfall.

Almost invisible, the old man with the long, braided beard sat at the water's edge, leaning back in what looked to be a section of a vinyl sofa on the curb, holding a broken fishing pole and taking occasional sips from a bottle balanced on his knees. Had he been there the whole time or just arrived, Anthony didn't know. Beside the man, a fire burned in a metal drum. The old timer raised a hand stained many shades of blue when Anthony caught his eye.

"Put away your work and eat, Theo," the fisherman had called, gesturing to a sack beside him. "Before the storm hits and the beast smells what's to sup."

Anthony hadn't eaten in so long, he'd hurried over without correcting the senile man who'd confused him for someone else.

The man laughed to see him, mumbling a bit about a baby named Willem, but never spoke again as they ate cold salt fish together. Anthony, however, for some unclear reason—maybe it was the weight of the changed world pulling on him—shared with the old man some of his own story, a story of loss he wasn't able, in this new existence, to tell. That the fisherman was busy drinking his fermented maple, and likely not listening, didn't even matter.

That was two months ago, and for all he knew, the old man with the blue hands had moved on. But if not the fisherman, someone else was the target, and Anthony needed to try—he had the information—to intercept the Recovery.

He stuck his head into the dark hallway and took a tentative step out. A thick sludge covered the linoleum—he'd slogged through the muck on his way in—and the stale territorial spray of cat burned his sinuses.

He covered his mouth as he negotiated a path through the slime. He eyed the stairway down, but headed up instead to avoid the wolves just outside. He climbed carefully, holding the smooth banister for support as the stairs groaned beneath his weight.

Long strips of peeling paint hung from the ceiling, brushing his head as he made his way to the roof, and he swatted at the rustling pieces as if they were alive, not knowing, in the dark, if they were.

Anthony stepped onto the last landing and stumbled over a haphazard pile of furniture stashed against the door to the roof, cursing at the sound of metal and wood crashing down the stairwell. He stood still, and when the last echo died, he listened intently, hearing only the wheeze of the old building.

He wondered against who or what the roof had been barricaded. A sliver of frosty neon snaked its way in through the warped doorframe, partially illuminating the landing. Anthony guessed it was the SolSat, orbiting, reflecting, and calculating the date even after all this time, that lit this cluttered space.

He made a swift search of the area. The fire extinguisher was too heavy to carry, so he put the centuries-expired tank back on a stack of moldy, empty boxes that slid sideways when he jostled them.   He prodded a crumpled tarp in the corner with his foot and, curious, peeled the cover back.   The remains of a woman— mostly bones, but also soft black boots, and a pocketbook and a gray skirt—lay beneath.   And hair.   Wisps of dark hair still attached to the skull.

"Hail Mary full of grace," he whispered, only a little horrified as he rifled through the woman's cracked vinyl handbag.   A pair of mirrored sunglasses went into his pack.   He found a rock hard lump of gum, recognizable only by its pink and orange wrapper. He stuck the flavorless gob in his mouth, and sucked it, tongue and teeth working double duty to finish the prayer while teasing the colorful waxed paper off the fossilized treat.   Using the vinyl bag as a broom, he swept the skeleton to the side, uncovering, and pocketing, a gold wedding band.

A jagged, wooden table leg was jammed one end through the door's handle, the other through a ring hammered into the wall. Time had swollen the wood, and Anthony couldn't pull the wedge out.   He yanked the handle and splintered the warped frame. Kicking the door, he dislodged a panel, breaking pieces from the old wood until he opened a gap large enough to squeeze through.

With one last look around he decided to take the boots from the woman, shaking small bones from the suede and folding the footwear into his pack for barter.   He crawled out to the roof.

The sky was darker now, the moon set and new clouds moved in.   The thick blanket of snow, however, reflected the SolSat, and Anthony slithered on his stomach across the radiant snow cover to the roof's easternmost edge.

The connecting building was in greater decay.   The water tower had fallen there, leaving great gaping holes filled with snow and ice through which gnarled trees, leafless now in the winter, rose.

He crept along the abutment to look down onto Twenty-ninth Street.   The wolves were frenzied.   They'd uncovered a body beneath the wagon, a frozen traveler caught in the storm, and they jockeyed for position, growling and snapping, strong jaws pulling at human carrion that reddened the snow.

He backed off the ledge and crawled to the opposite side. West Thirtieth was a long, gently sloping rubble mound almost as high as the rooftop here, diminishing in height to the east, and without another option, he sat to push off, landing hard on the uneven surface below.

His foot caught on a slab of composite camouflaged by night, and he stumbled, falling to his knees. He brushed the snow from the board and considered, standing to brace one foot on a cement gargoyle. The grotesque face leered as he pulled the board out.

The thin panel was light enough for his purposes and he laid it on the snow, holding the scrap in place with his foot, allowing himself a moment to remember flying down a snowy driveway with his sister. Anthony almost smiled but the memory would soon enough morph and he shut it away with the rest of what he could never change.

Stomach down on the board, he shoved off, gripping the sides of the sled as he bounced and slid down the long, long hill. In just a few short minutes the friction had shredded the tops of his canvas boots and scraped his arms raw where his wrap pulled away. As he neared Park Avenue, he dragged his hands to slow his descent, and spun himself to a stop into a snow bank.

He climbed out of the drift and oriented himself by the landmarks sketched on his map—a bubbling geyser and an old restaurant's strangely intact glass façade reflecting the night sky. Partial tracks in the snow led into a narrow alley of trees—to the tunnels—and Anthony slid the last few feet down to follow.

A hundred yards south, Anthony rubbed his frozen hands. He lifted the heavy sidewalk grating by the knotted twin handles—the rough rope pricked his fingers—and moved the cover to the side. A ladder leaned against the wall below, disappearing in the dark.

With his back to the entrance, Anthony got to his knees, feet resting over the edge. Somewhat awkwardly, he lowered himself, stomach sliding over the lip of the grate, hands and arms hanging over the broken pavement, nails digging into the cement. His feet kicked gently, searching for the ladder.

Earlier this winter, looking for a Safe cache in one of the old Port Authority buildings, Anthony had fallen through a rotted floor, landing in the covered living space of a woman below. With lightning reflexes the startled woman had struck out at him with a weighted whip—a series of scrap metal pieces tied to a cord—slicing the right side of his face and scalp in the few seconds before he'd been able to scramble back out.

Mindful of this as his foot caught a rung and he began his slow descent, Anthony called out to the people down in the alcoves and platforms of the underground labyrinth.

"Coming down," he shouted. "Coming down, coming down."

Little light filtered into the tunnel, and Anthony continued down the long ladder slowly—forty rungs below the street now—in darkness, one step at a time, keeping his heavy pack balanced between his shoulders. At sixty rungs he called out again, and at seventy he found the ladder submerged, stepping off into icy water high as his knees, an unexpected surprise as his previous foray in the tunnels was low tide, the water just puddles and shallow pools.

Gentle lappings against the curved walls and a soft rustling above—bats, maybe—were the only sounds. Anthony smelled the smoke of a wood fire and the sharp, salty tang of the sea that fed these tunnels from somewhere along the coast. Unable to see ahead or behind, he held his arms out and sloshed along until he felt the slimy wall of the tunnel with his fingertips.

He drew back. Soon after arriving in Manhattan he'd begun his search for Safe caches. Although tunnels along Broadway were flooded and collapsed, a wet but intact maintenance room near Ninety-sixth Street still remained. A church hosting a cache had once stood above that transportation storage area.

Anthony had climbed into that bleak space without caution and breathed the spores of a rippling, black mold so bitter he'd vomited all night and the whole next day, and Daisy nursed him for a week or more—the fever blurred the days—at the Wait.

Concerned the walls here might be covered with the same, Anthony plunged his hands in the salt water and rubbed his fingers clean. His legs burned with the cold rising tide—his feet were numb—and he splashed blindly looking for dry sanctuary.

A yellow wash lit the tunnel, casting long shadows across the walls. He turned to see, across the water, a flickering torch behind an overhang, its bearer hidden by the wall.

Anthony called out, self conscious as he tried to approximate the oddly stilted language of the island people, "Here, friend. Barter for passage through the high waters this night?"

No response, but the torch moved down, across the water, illuminating what Anthony had missed in the darkness—a pontoon bridge spanning the width of the tunnel.

"Whatcha got?" a thin voice asked as Anthony grabbed the hand reaching for him and climbed onto the floating walkway.

The fuzz-headed girl—at least he thought she was a girl—couldn't have been more than nine-years-old. Bare, scabbed legs and feet stuck out from the knee length plastic quilt wrapping her.

"Is there a boat?" Anthony asked.

"Depends," the girl answered, repeating, "Whatcha got?"

"Boots."

"Ya maked 'em or dug 'em?"

He held out the soft suede boots he'd taken from the corpse. She raised the torch to examine them. A series of short whistles from the shadows seemed to convince her, and she nodded. "Ya can't keep the boat," she bargained. "Where ya to?"

"The end, south and east."

"My brother'll collect the boat where ya leave it," the girl said, taking the boots.

She slipped her feet in and Anthony followed as she shuffled across the pontoon. She untied a dingy from its mooring and pulled the boat hard from the crawl space beneath. Rough cut wooden paddles balanced in the oarlocks and a short torch—the girl lit it with her own—was shoved in a cleat at the bow.

Anthony climbed in, setting the boat to rocking, and sat carefully on the bench, his feet framing the NYC DEP stenciled across the bottom. The girl pushed him off, and by the time he got the paddles in his hands and turned to thank her, she'd already disappeared, leaving the tunnel behind him in dark silence.

THE ARTIST

THE SUN HADN'T yet risen, but the sky was lightening and night would soon be extinguished. The old man waited patiently by the open shutters, anticipating the colors that sunrise would bring and sipping the last of his absinthe before sleep.

He preferred working in the quiet of the night and had been occupied since dusk, plotting colors, sketching with charcoal, and writing long, rambling letters to his brother by the light of almost supernatural stars reflected in the river through the open window.

Nighttime was easier. Sequestered in the darkness, reality didn't clash with the one in his head. Tonight the church bells at Arles had been ringing and under their calming tones he'd made satisfying progress on his current study, the sunflowers.

A ruckus in the street disrupted his drink, but before he could investigate, the door to his yellow bedroom opened wide, his candle flickering wildly in the gusting, incoming breeze, and he jumped, startled by the visitor's rude entrance.

"Come, Tark," a soft voice commanded. "Tark, pay attention."

He stared uncomprehending at the tall woman gesturing urgently from the shadows. "Sien?" he asked. "Is it you?" Where were the children? Many years had gone since she returned to the street. Did she even still breathe?

"It's Grindle," the woman said, holding her lantern to her face. "The shore alarms are ringing. Don't you hear the Watchtowers at the west?"

He shook his head, trying to sort the battling worlds in his mind. Leaving his sketchpad on the night table, he looked out the front window into the public gardens of Place Lamartine, ignoring the woman who threatened his peace. But she persisted, and when he turned back to her everything had changed, the window, the pine bed, the chair, the table, the towel on the hook, the door leading to the guest room—gone—his space now a bare area with an unlit fire, peeling floor, and sleeping pad separated from the rest of an extended room by a tattered curtain.

Voices blended, untranslatable, behind the drapes, and the rustlings of a people waking and moving in the night disturbed him. He closed his eyes, trying to summon the church bells, but they were departed, replaced by the ominous peals of the gongs.

"You're half frozen," Grindle said, wrapping a blanket around him. "Let's go."

He grabbed his bottle and allowed himself to be directed along a corridor, joining a slow moving line of people. He expected Theo in the candlelit queue, but his brother didn't pass, and he was desolate to think he might be left behind.

His chest ached and he slowed to catch his breath, leaning against the exposed brick. He began to cough, throat and lungs raw, and the woman—Grindle—handed him a cloth. He spit into the towel, and spit again as the red mucus kept coming.

"Don'a stop," a crone in a dark cape said. "You'll find plenny time for the pains when we're to Salt."

"Why are we to Salt?" he asked, befuddled again.

"Tark, the alarm sounds," Grindle explained. "We need to protect ourselves."

"How do we know the alarm doesn't sound for rising waters?" a woman asked, stooping to avoid a crumbling overhang as she passed. "We ought head for high ground."

His heart stuttered at those words and he tried to sidestep the column of people, pushing back in the narrow space. "Lemme pass, yah. I won't leave my paintings again to suffer the torrent. I've no made copies. I'm begging you."

Grindle put an arm around his shoulder and moved him artfully into the flow down a concrete ramp. "It won't be the flooding, Tark. Waters be rising in the spring. Fa sure it's the beasts, so we're going to the Salt."

The beasts—oh, the beasts—were repelled by sea salt, and the people had been hiding from them in a dugout shelter beneath the piles for as long as anyone could remember. He shuddered. "Why no wait for the Runner? She'll explain about the alarm."

"The weather delays her arrival," Grindle said. "We need conceal ourselves now."

The incline was slippery from water seeped in and froze, and the old man inched carefully down so not to lose his balance.

Black waterbugs skittered around their feet, and negotiating the dimly lit corridor with poor eyesight he thought he must have stepped on one of the fat beetles. He tugged his braided beard nervously and began to cry, soundlessly at first, then with big gulping sobs that echoed in the passages leading from building to building to building.

Someone shushed him. "You'll wake the babe." But the warning came too late and an infant's wailing filled the corridor.

He clapped a hand across his mouth. Had he woken Willem? He had sketched Sien nursing Willem over and again. He missed the little one and wanted to ease his discomfort now, as he had then, with honey pudding. Why was he bawling so?

Embarrassed for having been so noisy, the old man began to whimper anew. Grindle offered a piece of dried apple from her blue treat bag, and he sucked the scrap in his toothless mouth, extracting every bit of taste, then gummed the remnants, softening the leathery sweet with a slug from his near empty bottle.

The line moved calmly now, practiced, as if they had marched this journey a hundred times, and some of the old timers had. The old man whistled random notes from the back of the line, glad now for the steady hand guiding him. He glanced sideways at the woman called herself Grindle. With her long blue braids and unblemished skin, she was prettier than Sien.

He thought about Sien's pockmarked face, her beauty already stolen by the time they'd become lovers. He had drawn her a thousand times in a thousand poses. Even now, he could feel the hard cut of her chin, the soft round of her stomach. "Vincent, bread is on the table," she'd say.

The line came to a sudden stop and, lost in his memories, he stumbled, grabbing the woman in front to keep from falling. "Watch yer step," she rasped. "I got troubles enough keeping my own steady balance."

He blushed for the reprimand and tugged his beard, ashamed.

"Count off. One," a woman at the head called, and in response, the people returned their positions. *Two, Three, Four* and onward—a census of the traveling group.

"Tark, I can speak your number if you need," Grindle said.

The enumeration continued. *Fourteen, Fifteen, Sixteen.* A

man with a deep voice stuttered at *Seventeen*—perhaps he didn't know what followed—but with a small correction the count proceeded.

"Twenty-three," Grindle said. She nudged the old man.

"Twenty-four," he cackled, and beamed for remembering.

"All counted and accounted," the woman at the head declared, and she opened the door to the outside.

The twenty-four moved quickly through the exit onto the snow-covered path that looped maze-like through trees and around the remains of dozens of buildings. Sunrise approached and the numbers above shone silver against the lavender sky— 01.03.2257.

The old man shivered, looking back at the shelter they'd abandoned, a squat brick building, one of many facing the river and salt flats. "Why are we here?" he whispered, suspicious. Tangled brown vines snaked over the park's center oval. He'd painted this scene—*The Courtyard in the Hospital in Arles*— during a summer, but did not recognize the plaza now. When would his attendant arrive to escort him to breakfast? Morning bells were ringing and he craved the porridge served each daybreak in the hospital.

"We must continue," Grindle said, guiding him down a terraced ramp past one of the many signs—*STUYVESANT TOWN*—rising from the snowy ruins.

He didn't recognize the spellings. Was he in France? The Netherlands? He searched the landscape for any clue as they crossed under a section of scorched, layered roads curling out of sight above.

"A little further. We're almost arrived," Grindle said, pointing to piles of salt beyond the chain link fences on the shore.

His eyes lit on the sparkling waters. He'd painted that river— *Starry Night above the Rhone*—and loved the swirling turbulence, but those stars were disappeared now. Pink, salmon, slashes of orange, yellow—his favorite—and the palest blue of dawn stretched the length of the sky. He needed return to his brushes before the colors receded.

"You've finished your maple?" Grindle asked, propelling him forward. "I've more sap below. And biscuits waiting. Come."

He followed the people onto the uneven salt path. Crystals crunched beneath his feet and he pulled the blanket tighter around his shoulders, slowing against the strengthening wind. The line moved ahead and he listened to their feet make cracklings as they did. He liked the sound.

He stopped, coughing, and kicked salt over the chipped and rusted sign—*East River Drive Historical District*—frozen beneath his feet. Grindle paused to wait and he called to her, clearing his phlegm. "Go on, yah, help another. I'll be right along."

He'd been hearing the gongs for the whole of the excursion, but something blended with the alarms now—a hum disguised by the wind. Was it the train from Paris? Had Gauguin returned?

"Tark," Grindle called from across the way. She held open the wide planked cellar doors that led to the chamber beneath the piles of salt. People were disappearing into the hatch, heads down against the fierce shore wind.

"Tark," she called again. "I need that you focus. Come now."

The group had vanished into the hatch, and Grindle fought to keep the door up, her body braced against it to resist the wind.

He was just starting for the hideaway when the sound of the hummings and rumbles surged, and a boat—so oddly shaped—appeared from behind a dip in the coastline, floating slowly, deliberately, toward them.

He pointed and Grindle turned to his gesture. A clear blue orb spun at the bow. Oh, if he could create a pigment in such a shade. Three men on the approaching boat faced the shore, and one raised a yellow cone to his mouth.

"We seek the Touched One," the man called to Grindle, his voice amplified above the river and wind. "We have food and warm blankets to exchange for the Touched. Tell us where he is."

The old man got a funny feeling in his stomach at these words. Grindle stood motionless, briefly, and then waved to the men. "No Touched, here," she shouted, her voice tight.

She turned from the boat and crouched behind the cellar door, gesturing frantically. The old man took a step closer, but now she was waving him away.

"Go," she shouted.

Go where? What about the boat? Did the men have news from

the gallery? Had he sold a painting? Received a commission?

"Tark, run," she screamed again.

He searched his pockets for a calling card. These patrons had certainly come to see him, and he wouldn't miss the opportunity. He would invite them to the café and show them the yellow house. They would discuss his plans.

Grindle allowed the cellar door to slam shut and ran back across the salt to him. He looked with confusion from her to the men who manipulated the boat through the rocky shallows. The woman slid on the ice and her blue bag fell from her cape in the tumble. It seemed fun to go so fast, but she wasn't smiling.

"We need hurry." Her braids flew up and around her face—he loved the blue—and her lips were chapped. "Tark, husband, please, don't delay."

"My guests have arrived from Paris," he said of the men attempting to disembark.

Grindle put her face close to his. "Listen to me, Monsieur Van Gogh." She held his shoulders in her hands. "You are in danger."

The old man gasped, tears filling his eyes. The ever-simmering dread he only just managed to suppress rose and slammed his gut. He couldn't breathe for the fear.

"Come with me now," she comforted, leading him away from the river and the men shouting after them. Quickly and surely, the old man and the braided woman slipped back into the Stuyvesant ruins through a camouflaged entrance, to disappear in the unmapped maze of buildings on the river.

ANTHONY

HE HAD BEEN smelling the meat cooking for a while now, though Anthony couldn't tell, in the torch lit glow of the labyrinths, just where the smell was coming from. The night had been exhaustive and cold, and the scent was almost painful. He seemed to be getting closer to the grill. His eyes smarted, and his throat, already dry from the frosty air of the tunnel, burned.

The tide was pulling out, and the current took his boat, relieving the arms that had rowed against the flow to make it south to Union Square. The relative quiet of the pre-dawn journey through the Park and Lexington Avenue tunnel system had transformed abruptly at the cavernous Fourteenth Street hub.

A nocturnal community spread along multi-level platforms. Leather and plastic-wrapped men with metal breastplates and silver hats huddled around a fire pit and shouted down to him, the dialects impossible to translate. Lights from dozens of torches lit open stairways leading up and down throughout the sprawling Union Square station.

On a platform below the men, a woman stood over a simmering vat. What was going on inside, Anthony couldn't tell, but the steaming tub warmed the air and eased the dryness in his throat. Anthony loosened his wrap and breathed deep the salty, humid air.

A rhythmic clanging echoed through the subway repeating the signals from the shoreline Watchtowers. Men and women moved like shadows on catwalks suspended over and across the tracks and Anthony saw long, heavy bundles transported in the dark. Torch-lit faces peered from graffiti-covered vestibules as he descended deeper into the system through tunnels both manmade and earthquake forged.

A section of sidewalk must have collapsed and opened high above because his small boat was pulled into a pale gray light—sunrise could not be far off—shining from the surface. Snow piled in drifts on the subterranean platforms and stuck to the walls.

Anthony put an oar down to slow the boat and was surprised to hit bottom with the edge of the paddle. The water level had decreased substantially. Barnacle studded rails were visible below him in the morning light. Low tide. A few moments later, the dinghy ran aground on the tracks.

The old Third Avenue Station was just ahead, yellow paint corroded by salt water still apparent on columns rising from the platform. Two girls, long sharpened poles in their hands, were jabbing at the exposed tracks on the opposite side. Torches in the wall cast shadows on the inlaid tiles and graffiti—jagged letters and numbers—painted over the station's mosaics.

"There he is. Go, go," one girl pointed, and the other jumped down several feet to the tracks to chase her prey through water just barely covering her silver-wrapped feet.

"Yaha, I gots him, fat one, eh?" she shrieked, her metal shoes clanging on the tracks as she hopped up and down in excitement. She raised her spear and through the indistinct light Anthony could just see the impaled shuddering rat. "Come away," the girl up top said, holding a hand down. "Ma said quick back to soothe the baby. Sun time. Sleep soon."

The girl climbed up, prize held aloft, and grabbing the torches, the two scrambled away, heavy shoes muted in the scattered, soft piles of bat guano that covered the platform.

Anthony stood, his cold, stiff leggings cracking as he did so, and stepped out of the rowboat. He splashed lightly across the passage, banging the boat's bottom along the rails as he dragged it to the side and secured the rope to an iron ring set in the concrete.

Snails and other shelled creatures large and small clung to the smooth tiled walls of the subway tunnel and in shallow puddles along the tracks, exposed by receding tidal waters. He scraped a few of the spiral shells, crushing them in his hands and slipping the briny bits into his mouth hungrily.

He unfolded the hand-drawn map. A passage led to the surface to the east but he'd have to scale exposed rock three flights where the stairway no longer existed. The other option was expensive. If he continued by foot through the tunnel he'd reach the pulley near First Avenue. He'd ridden the shrieking cables and basket powered by muscle when he'd come this way before, and the lift had cost him a sack of cornmeal from Murray Hill. This time he was broke. He had the meds and supplies—some dehydrated foods and water purifiers—from the Safe cache, but not much to spare.

Anthony yanked the torch from the boat. He hadn't arranged this additional trade but he needed the light. He rifled through his pack and found a bottle of chewable vitamins for payment, thinking he should add a note explaining the fruit flavored tablets weren't to be eaten all at once.

He realized he had no idea if the girl or her brother who'd collect the boat could read, so he took the vitamins back and dug from his pocket instead the wedding ring he'd removed from the stairwell corpse, placing it on the rowboat's center bench where the gold caught the torchlight, winking in the gloom.

The pitch-soaked rags had burned almost all the way down by now and the torch was smoky as it sputtered. Anthony blew on it gently to feed the flame. He hoped the fire would get him to the pulley before completely dying.

Keeping close to the tunnel wall to avoid the wind that whistled through and to protect his remaining light, he stumbled east and back into darkness. As he walked, he went over his rough plan. Find the fisherman and get him to a secure place, and divert or disable the Vaulters and their boat.

He still hadn't worked out how to find the man or convince him to go with him or how much information he could share without exposing his own origins. And he had no idea how to deal with the Vaulters. He'd been examining different scenarios since he got to the city five months ago and not one of them seemed right. Regardless, he had to get Topside.

Rubble narrowed the passage here to the width of a single track. Bats darted above and around and Anthony tripped as he ducked to avoid them, their destination the columns separating the once eastbound and westbound tracks. The thick pillars rippled with thousands of the colony returned for their daylight sleep.

Lights flickered above. A group moved along a wobbly pathway that swung over the rails. Anthony watched them cross overhead, carrying something that knocked against the sides of the narrow walkway. They stopped a short distance away, and after some jostling began to descend.

A thick-bearded man wrapped in what looked to be lawn bags was the first to appear on the ladder that hung from the scaffold. He dropped to the tracks and his glass lantern cast a small circle of light where he stood. Setting the lamp aside, he reached up to help manipulate an unwieldy board tied with twine—gravity helped—placing the pallet on the ground.

Two women followed. They lifted the long board, one on each end, and moving slowly behind the bearded man, inched steadily closer, kicking up the shallow water.

"Hello, I'm here," Anthony called, raising his failing torch.

The bearded man held his lantern up. "What's your turn, stranger? There's an alarm. Go to your people."

"I'm a journeyman, looking for barter."

The women put the board down, careful to place it away from the damp. One of them, light-haired with bad skin and a vest of a plastic that looked, from the bits of metal poking from the seams, to be stuffed with silver shreds, grabbed Anthony's arm.

"Why tonight, of all nights, with your unfamiliar face?" she demanded.

Anthony raised his free arm in peace, and spoke softly. "Easy, now. I came down at Twenty-ninth to escape the overland and make a speedier travel."

The woman's nose was running. Her eyes shone yellow and her skin had a mustard cast. "He hears the alarms yet continues towards them?" she pondered out loud.

The second woman, older, maybe forty, with loose dark hair threaded with gray, wore a short spear—its top sharpened like a pencil—strapped to her leg. She coughed, a hacking that began deep in her chest.

Anthony drew back to avoid the phlegm spraying towards him. She spit onto the wet tracks and convulsed again. The jaundiced woman pounded her back.

"The alarms mean nothing to me," Anthony said in a calm voice. Manhattan was a peaceful island, but a bloody history was not far behind and this all-night alarm would be making the people anxious, suspicious, and potentially dangerous. "I'm not afraid of the beasts when barter's expected."

"It's no the beasts," the yellow woman said. "We'd throw salt in their eyes and be done. It's something else. Something strange heading through the waters this night."

"What then?" he asked, though he knew the answer.

"One of ours went Topside before dawn to check a trap at Fifth," she said. "The Watch told of a boat heading east. A boat vibrating like a thousand beating wings." She paced, eyes narrowing, and pointed at him. "Have you seen this boat of dreams, or passed others who describe the same? Nothing good can come in a strange night boat."

Anthony shook his head. If the lookout at Fifth Avenue had seen Bravo, the cruiser had likely by now, daylight, rounded the tip of the island. "I've seen none," he said, falling into the natives' speech pattern. "Perhaps you've seen none as well. The waters hypnotize. If you contemplate the crests, you can see what's surely not there."

"That's the true, cousin," the bearded man agreed. "It's said the Europes surface in the waves when the moon is fullest."

"The Europes is fantasy, Joe Soho," the jaundiced woman said. "Something genuine comes direct toward us." She crouched next to the wrapped board. "Such an awful night for the alarms."

"I've need move on, then," Anthony said to the bearded man, hoping not to upset the women. "I'm headed for the pulley."

The man didn't respond, and the Tunnelers, blocking his passage, did not step aside. Anthony shifted. His feet were wet and uncomfortably, painfully, cold. The bearded man and jaundiced woman exchanged words, the dialect too hurried and clipped for Anthony to understand, but the woman's expression hardened. He froze, and slid his hand, hidden under his wrapping, until his fingertips touched the handle of his knife.

A long moment passed.

"You've come to barter," the woman said, finally. "Who do you trade with?"

"There's a Touched I want to visit."

"We've no Touched," she said, pinching a drip from her nose.

"This man has a braided beard and hands stained blue. Do you know him?"

The woman considered. "That's Tark, by your description. Topside," she said. "He's nothing to barter, unless delusions fetch vouchers. What would you want with such a man?"

"I've been told he has salvage I might find useful. Where I can find him?"

"He has no salvage, and I wouldn't tell to a stranger any words about him. I don't know your history."

Anthony'd been expecting this. Lineage kept the populations connected and introductions would include a genealogy. He hesitated. Referring back to university studies, he sometimes feigned *Touched with Literature*, or *Touched with Poetry*. It was easy to do, as the people here knew less about those things than he did. But he'd already introduced himself as a journeyman trader so he went to a persona he'd been using since his arrival last summer, one that served him well.

"I'm called Anthony," he said, introducing the cover story. "My history I can't recite, I apologize. I remember nothing from before the fall into the salvage pits."

A small, slick-furred animal scurried past. The coughing woman slid the spear from her leg, suddenly motionless, but sheathed the weapon again as the animal slipped into a wall. Water dripped methodically from a rust-stained beam above, settling in a small puddle at Anthony's feet.

The yellow woman was first to speak. *"Ikh nite getroyen im."*

Anthony turned, startled. He'd only heard English and related dialects spoken in this new world. He'd wondered what had happened to Spanish and Chinese, both spoken extensively on the street in New York before he joined the Project. Had the woman just spoken German?

"Zayn opgehit, vayb," the older woman interrupted and the yellow woman nodded, taking a wary glance at Anthony and mumbling, "It's *mishegas*."

Not German. Yiddish.

The older woman gave the other a small shove. "Your turn," she said, and the younger frowned, disinclined to speak although convention demanded she reciprocate. "My name is Rowena," the jaundiced woman began, all trace of the Yiddish gone. "Born Topside at the Union Square under the number 10." Her eyes went distant. "Mother said the trees were gold and red."

October.

Rowena pointed to the older woman. "My wife, Nadia. She comes to me from the estate of my uncle, born also at the Union Square." With a nod to the bearded man, she finished. "And there, Joe Soho, the son of my grandfather's sister."

"You will come with us," Joe Soho said to Anthony.

"No. I've traded passage, a fair barter, to get here. You'll not dictate where I can travel."

"Go, fool, if you insist," Rowena said. "The pulleys are disengaged for the alarm. A stranger wouldn't be safe wandering alone. We've creatures, and there are chasms without bottom."

"You'll come with us," Joe Soho repeated. "To the Fires."

Anthony didn't know where that was but nodded as if he did and considered his options. His body was stiffening from the cold, tense from the standoff. He wouldn't make trouble. If Bravo had already arrived at Sector 5-D, there'd be little he could do on his own. Perhaps these Tunnelers could help intercede. "I'll go along," he said. "I need food, though. I can trade."

"Take one end of our burden," the coughing woman Nadia said. "Give Rowena relief."

"No," Rowena said. "I'll not relinquish my hold. It's my place."

Joe Soho took Anthony's arm—his hands were inked in a dark crisscross pattern—and the men fell back so Rowena and Nadia could advance with the board between them, lanterns balanced at each end.

They followed the women up a rutted incline to the north, a narrow slope that encouraged Anthony's hope he'd locate an exit as they climbed. The air was warmer here and soon the chill left his body.

Joe Soho opened wide a sewn pocket under his plastic. "Eat."

Anthony reached in carefully—its contents weren't visible in the dark—and grabbed a handful of something soft. Tiny mushrooms.

He crushed the chewy pieces into his mouth, surprised at their deep, salty flavor. "Thank you," he said, grateful, and Joe Soho opened his pocket again without concern for the barter.

They stopped at a tilted ladder and climbed onto a mesh bridge swinging above the end of the trail. There was sulfur in the air, and a dank smell of deep earth fumes. Anthony's head ached behind his eyes.

"Sharp teeth below," Joe Soho said.

Anthony peered over the bridge's handrail but saw only a mangle of parallel east-west tracks buckled beneath them. His torch, reduced to smoldering red fibers and throwing no light, was useless now. He dropped the stub from the catwalk, and heard, after a lengthy fall, a faint splash where it landed.

Single file, sandwiched between Joe Soho and Rowena, Anthony treaded carefully along the swaying walkway—they all did—as the sides were open save for the slim rope handrail and occasional splintered wooden posts, and even the smallest of movements set the whole construction to trembling.

A crack rang out.

"Heads," Joe Soho shouted as a shower of debris rained down.

Anthony ducked, arms up. A heavy chunk of something hit him in the shoulder and glanced off, shattering Rowena's lantern and knocking the pallet from her hands.

The unexpected weight of its release pulled the board from Nadia's hands as well and it dropped to the slatted walkway of the rickety bridge, setting a swaying that compelled Anthony to grab the woven handrails for support.

"No," Nadia screamed, as the wrapped board slid toward the open edge, headed for a fall to the chasm below.

Anthony moved quickly, pushing past Rowena to grasp the canvas handles and keep the pallet from sliding away. Nadia fell to her knees and threw her body across while the catwalk swayed.

"One at a time," Joe Soho said to the women.

"Take hold of my cloak," Anthony said to Rowena but she waved off his offer of help, and after a moment, straightened slowly, arms out for balance while the bridge steadied.

As soon as Rowena was stable, Nadia stood carefully, too, and lifted the board. Rowena took the other end from Anthony and the group moved on, passing above the blackened remains of a subway car, its back end rising from the chasm, its nose in the depths.

Anthony smelled boar or pig roasting again. He was so

hungry. The suffocating heat rose as they climbed the steep approach, and he felt dizzy from the lack of oxygen.

"How much longer?" he asked, to no response.

The trail ended in a northern blockade of pipes and stone and tile and crushed, unidentifiable metals. Rowena pushed through a heavy gate in the wall to the west with her shoulder. A wave of blistering dry air roared onto the trail and Anthony followed the women into a stifling, strange chamber.

The whole of the back wall was ablaze—a thirty-foot wide fire that sent flaming tendrils skyward toward screened gates opening Topside. A small, grim man, muscles bulging and sweat pouring off his bare back, shoveled hunks of combustible salvage into deep trenches that fed the flames. Thrusting a flat iron paddle, he tipped, then righted, one by one, the five metal grated platforms above the trenches, emptying piles of ash and debris from each. His face was scorched crimson, and he coughed often, the sound drowned out by the thunder of the fire.

Behind the man, a table overflowed with packages, baskets, duffels, bottles, a covered hamper and even a cluster of lustrous winter berries, the items placed in utter contrast to the smoke and pitch of this hellish furnace.

Nadia and Rowena maneuvered their pallet into a storage alcove alongside the fires, stacking the thick board with a dozen others similarly wrapped and bound. An elderly man sat against the wall, legs out and his head bowed to rest in his hands.

Anthony thought the man slept, but he raised bleary eyes to the women as they passed. "She's gone."

Nadia crouched beside him. "I know. It's bad." She hugged his thin body. "The fever emptied O'Far as well," she said, gesturing to the pallet she'd just surrendered. She stood again, holding Rowena for support. "He was not yet five years, my son."

"Every night more taken," Rowena said. "So many, so fast."

Anthony listened with heavyhearted realization. This was a crematorium. The illness had spread throughout the tunnels. He counted twelve wrapped stretchers in the alcove. How many more had already been disposed of?

The muscular fire-man slid a board onto one of the metal grates above the fire. The flames licked the offering, catching the rough shroud and quickly overtaking the entire bundle.

Anthony gagged at the stench that had deceived him at a distance. Hair and flesh and bone burned, much of the thick smoke pulled up out of the station through open screens above, but enough trapped in the enclosed chamber that the walls were black and the air horrible to breathe.

The door opened, scraping the cement floor. Two more were coming into the chamber, a man and a woman carrying a wrapped body between them. They passed, the woman singing softly, and they positioned the stretcher into the alcove with the others.

"I know this illness taking the young," Anthony said. "The people are fighting it all over the city."

He looked at each in the chamber—Nadia, Rowena, Joe Soho, the fire-man, the old man, the newcomers. To the one, they turned away or returned fatigued, empty stares.

"The sick need to be quarantined," he tried again. "Kept separate from those uninfected."

Rowena spoke. "Quarnteen? Then who would care for them?"

"They would be taken care of," Anthony said. "Hasn't a Runner come with instructions from the Touched?"

"No one runs this far south in the snows," Rowena said. "And do you think any have been able to reach the Middle Road since the dying started?"

"Listen to me," Anthony said. "I have medicines to give to the young who are not yet sick."

"No lies," Nadia said, coughing into her arm. "You can't help."

"I speak truth. I can't help your son, but for the healthy there's still time."

"We have none healthy," Rowena said.

"I saw children on the way in. There must be more."

The heavy door banged open once again and a man entered carrying a wrapped bundle across his chest in a sling.

"We need to get the children to a safe place," Anthony said. "Topside would be preferable. Fresh air. Gather them together."

"Who are you to relay such things?" the old man asked.

Anthony untied his satchel. He'd start by distributing the anti-virals. Marjorie's kids would have fewer doses as a consequence, but he had no choice. He'd have to find more. "I've seen the illness myself. The city is infected."

The fires roared as the muscular man added new bodies to the platforms and the room became thick again with ash and smoke. The old man got up slowly. Rowena took Nadia in her arms, the two unsteady in the foul air. Joe Soho placed a slender bottle with the other offerings on the fire man's table and turned to Anthony.

"We're returning now," he said, eyes veiled. "You can linger with us until the alarms end and the pulleys begin again."

"You're not listening to me. I have remedies."

Joe Soho pointed to steps cut into the stone, camouflaged by soot and grime, leading to the surface grates and out of the crematorium. "Or you can remove yourself Topside here if you prefer. You'll exit the north of the Union Square Park."

"Why won't you gather the children and let me help?"

"We'll take our chances with our own," Rowena said, pulling on the heavy door leading away from the smoldering fires.

"*Nisht vider*," Nadia whispered. "*Keinmal mehr.*"

"I don't understand," Anthony said.

"It would be best if you surface here," Joe Soho said, holding the door for Rowena and Nadia. "Last time we were asked to gather our children sick with the headaches and mania, they were brung Topside and forever away with the Group that Left."

BRAVO

THE THICK WATCHBAND irritated the patchy skin on his arm, but Racine liked the round face and old school analog hands marking the time. He pushed the cuff of his wool sweater up and took a quick look—just after 8 a.m.

Failure had come quickly for Bravo this morning. Although they'd disembarked and attempted pursuit, the Meta-Record holder had eluded them, disappearing into the ruins with his advocate before the team could negotiate the multiple barriers on the perimeter. The natives cowering in their crude bunker had given up nothing on the escapees, either genuinely uncomprehending or uncannily sly.

The sun was up and the cruiser's cells recharging, a sluggish charge but enough that Racine could take his time navigating under solar power without running the battery down.

The way out had been a different story. The worn cells held less and less charge, and when the remaining percentage fell below minimum level, he needed to choose between using Sonar to negotiate subaqueous debris or Cover protocol to remain unseen by the damn Watchtowers. Concrete below the Hudson's waterline had abraded the hull—operational damage as of yet unassessed—and he'd been forced disable Cover and set Sonar instead—leaving Bravo exposed and vulnerable.

The tower at Chelsea Wood had spotted them immediately and banged its never-ending gongs. Racine didn't understand why the Watch believed them threatening. No cruiser had ever before been visible in the offshore waters and Vault had projected that if and when it happened, the simple people would consider it a curiosity rather than a danger.

Having underestimated the people's response, and with Alpha still out in the western waters working a double Recovery tagged as highest urgency, Racine had tried to navigate Bravo farther south to avoid additional scrutiny. But Sonar malfunctioned, underpowered even with Cover disabled, and it had been necessary to hug the coast instead   , still visible, continuing their own mission east.

How the natives managed to maneuver around the detritus without technology he couldn't fathom. They were a peculiar, dim people, these children of Manhattan, and Racine was both intrigued and repelled by them. Although primitive, today this gangly, braided woman showed a troubling streak of cunning and sophistication, spiriting away the Record holder with unexpected defensive and evasive behavior, disappearing into the labyrinthine ruins like rats in a wall. Racine could kick himself, and them, for allowing that to happen.

The Sonar pinged, adjusting their course and sending a spray of seawater across his faceplate. He removed the mask—they wore them whenever possible to avoid the sulfur—and without its cumbersome filters he sucked down cold marine air. The craft veered suddenly and he lost his footing on the slick deck. The mask flew from his hands, and he smacked his shoulder against the wheel trying to catch the hard plastic and rubber shield before it clattered across the deck.

The pain was a welcome distraction, but the endless loop of blame continued to play. Although the Meta-personality wasn't technically Van Gogh, it might as well been. The whole of the body of the artist's life and art encapsulated was in one grimy islander who without the Records wouldn't know a masterpiece if it hit him in the skull. How much civilization—art, science, music, literature, history—mislaid in these people, and how bleak the thought of future societies stunted by these forfeitures.

For certain anatomical reasons, these enhanced personality Records couldn't be sliced from Metas like regular Records were excised from the Holders—their connection wasn't understood— and Seth's protocol required grabbing the whole person for storage at Vault. He shook his head. It was less bloody but having to interact established multiple opportunities for mistake.

Racine realized he was grinding his teeth and he unclenched his jaw, rubbing his face. He would not take blame for Van Gogh's getaway. These freaking Meta-Record holders—*Newly Touched*— had been on the loose for too long.   If not for faint radio signals finally identified—somebody was asleep on that job and thank god it wasn't him—Vault wouldn't even have discovered the second breach and the release of the Meta-nanos. They hadn't produced enough energy to remotely monitor those servers for two years and the last visual inspection had been over a year ago.

The heavy transports with caterpillar-tracked road wheels were designed to negotiate the dense, overgrown route to the aboveground data center west of the Hudson, but on their first trip overland one of their vehicles had become lodged in a deep earth crack, and subsequently abandoned to the quakes. Unwilling to risk additional losses with a second transport, they'd ridden Aja, their only remaining horse, to the next scheduled survey.

That had been the final examination of those servers before Anthony stole the horse. And what did his treason accomplish? His tracer had stopped transmitting within days of his betrayal. Certainly he was dead. That's what his treason accomplished.

The cruiser was edging closer to the shore and Racine scanned the barren snow-covered southern edge of Manhattan. Yesterday's storm softened the torn landscape but left still visible a row of abandoned army tanks, pivoting turrets long dismantled, set back on the bluff that used to be Thirteenth or Fourteenth Street.

Engrossed in trying to discern the artillery's age—circa 2080 he approximated—he didn't notice two girls lobbing snowballs down at the cruiser until one of the soft mounds splattered on his shoulder.

"Punks," he shouted, confused initially by the engagement, and then, as realization set in, furious at Lear for not re-enabling Cover even though he himself had forgotten to issue the order in the chaos of the morning.

A Watchtower ahead, partially obscured by pine trees grown tall in jutting rubble, would observe them as soon as they cleared the outcrop, so Racine stepped quickly to the console to override Lear's input from below and set Cover—a trick of light and waveforms—rendering the cruiser invisible.

Lear would chafe at being overridden, but the hell with him. He was a weak link. Five years together on Bravo hadn't yet made them friends. If it weren't for having to replace Elizabeth, Lear would still be inside. Why Seth chose him Racine couldn't guess. Melly had been transparent in his leadership. Seth, paranoid Seth, kept his reasoning close to the vest.

Racine sighed. Even without hair, Elizabeth had been hot, and the few short months together working on Bravo had provided, if not relief, grist for his fantasy mill.

He found his teeth clenched again and made a conscious effort to relax his jaw, punching the code to set Cover. The expected confirmation did not display and Racine realized he'd been mistaken. Cover was already set. Bravo was already invisible. The girls had simply been throwing snowballs into the sea. Whatever. They were still punks and Lear still a weak link.

He turned from the console and headed below. The winter sun would provide enough continuous charge to keep both systems running, he calculated, but there would be little to store. If need be, he'd disengage sonar and navigate manually from the main.

He ducked to descend the spiral stairway and pushed on the metal door at the bottom. Something obstructed his entrance and he shoved harder, knowing Lear's feet blocked the door.

With a groan, his subordinate bent his knees and retracted his feet onto the too-small couch, and Racine entered. The broad back of his communications guy, Driscoll, blocked Racine's view of the Connex display on the desk, only a white glow visible from his workstation.

Racine poured a cup of a tepid dark drink from a machine bolted to the sidebar and threw a look of disgust at the man on the hard plastic sofa who picked a bleeding scab on his bald head.

He pulled off his wool hat. His scalp itched, too, and the blast of cool air soothed. At times, the itch—a consequence of the Cocooning—was unbearable. Some aspect of the process stripped them of their hair and caused a chronic irritation on their unprotected skins. The wool exacerbated the discomfort, but helped keep the accompanying fungus at bay.

Driscoll stood to stretch and Racine took the opportunity to eye the Connex that hadn't refreshed since the morning. Although intermittent connectivity was a chronic issue, today it was a gift. "Vault doesn't have our position?"

Driscoll shrugged. "As soon as the system has enough charge the transmission will send. We're running on empty."

C Team—Charlie—was on a scheduled day patrol checking

interior assets and needed to be updated on their status. "I'm not flaring C," Racine said. "Is Alpha out or back?"

"Seth's last flare put them heading to Vault. They should have been inside as of 0-100."

Racine rubbed his neck and stirred a protein syrup into the faux coffee. Seth expected Bravo back to Vault, but without Van Gogh in hand, a confrontation would be impossible to avoid.

The success of their next mission, a high-profile Grab slated for less than twenty-four hours from now—and assisted by Racine's own informant—would do much to make up for the loss of Van Gogh. But that didn't help him now.

"We didn't fail, you know," Lear said from the couch. "We just haven't succeeded yet." He sat up, his misshapen head creased from the lumpy pillow, his eyelash-less eyes red and runny. "We'll stay out," he yawned. "After tomorrow's Grab we'll hit Sector D again on our way back."

Racine considered. If they returned to Vault with a failed mission, they'd not only suffer the embarrassment of such— Charlie would love that—but it would take a lot of tap dancing to keep Seth from assigning Van Gogh to his own A team or even worse, to Charlie.

The bitter synthetic coffee irritated his stomach and he set his cup, just a few sips taken, in the tiny sink, his mind already on the One-hundred-eleventh Street pier. They'd stay out and he'd refresh his spirit there. After the respite, they'd Grab the target Seth had ordered them to find—a target Racine would get credit for—and on their return, he'd make a second, successful pass for the one-eared artist.

He laughed. Would the islander actually cut his ear off? From what he'd heard, these Metas really lived the life of their Records, but Seth kept those they'd retrieved buried deep in the Vault, so who really knew?

"Configure a flare," he said to Driscoll. "'Retrieval in progress.'" Driscoll nodded and Racine turned to Lear, his mind on the tall, native asset who accepted his visits without question or complaint. "Set course for Sector 23."

"Too far north," Lear said, pulling his sweatshirt over his head as he stood. "I propose anchor down in the cove at East 48th.

Setting course for Sector 18."

Racine stuck a finger in Lear's face. "I'll set you ashore for insubordination."

"Just trying to stay on-mission."

Racine paced the length of the cabin. The East River girl with her dark hair and pouty lips had an old Hollywood look that in another life would have placed her out of his league, but in this world, living in a junkyard with an extended family of scavengers who spent their days digging in river garbage, she was lucky to have him. Even if he only visited once a month. Or less.

"You've come back," she'd whisper, accepting his wine and stack of vouchers without a blush. Vouchers he tore into squares from rags. Racine rolled his eyes. These people were ridiculous. For the life of him he couldn't understand how the trading of homemade chits worked as a system of barter. Elizabeth, know-it-all, had tried to explain it to him but he'd tuned out at the ethics portion of her lecture. Whatever. Unlimited funds as long as he had rags.

The native girl would serve him, too—smoked fish and duck, hunks of roast yam, dried fruit puddings—and she'd him give dark, thick beer to drink. He could only hope the one brother would be away doing whatever he did with his peasant boat. The dreadlocked man with a penchant for gambling made him uneasy. The other brother, the Digger, was a wild card, but Racine made sure to bring him liquor, too, and the payoffs kept him mostly distracted and quiet, except for when he got angry. That the whiskeys and vodka were synthetics didn't matter at all.

Racine glared at Lear. "Intel acquisition is the mission. We drop anchor at our Randall's Island post. We'll set cover and charge all systems to 100%. I'll take the inflatable to meet my asset."

He smirked. Seth had turned the Project into some sort of freaking CIA, and all team members managed assets. Men and women—even children—that they'd developed relationships with, and who supplied information, often unknowingly.

Lear worked that albino pimp who lived somewhere on the west side with his drunk sister and her mute son. Driscoll had been developing a young girl whose mother absorbed Chinese language Records, but they'd disappeared from their Hudson River hovel in what the locals called a new start and he'd lost contact. The loss of his asset made the little man Lear bitter for all Racine's own successes. Too freaking bad.

He looked at his watch. Tuesday. He loved seeing the names of the days of the week. Nobody used them anymore but he held on, perversely. His mother enrolled him in Tuesday piano classes when he was a kid. He hated the lessons but liked the lemon soda that his teacher, an old lady whose name he'd forgotten, served after each session. He missed those lemon sodas.

One night would hardly be enough to satisfy, he thought. It was difficult to accomplish anything when the spirit was distracted. He smiled at Lear and Driscoll, feeling generous as he thought warmly of the girl he'd be seeing shortly.

"Let's hit it, fellas," he said. "Tomorrow's a big day."

ANTHONY

ANTHONY SLOSHED EAST on Seventeenth Street, his ripped canvas boots covered in plastic sheeting pulled from the top of a salvage pile. The smell of the crematorium clung to him, unmoved by the wind that blew across the island.

Temperatures had risen slightly. Yesterday's snow was soft, the sun blinding where it pierced the cloud cover, reflecting off the wet landscape. The sunglasses he'd found were pinching his nose, but despite being scratched across the lenses, they worked well to shield his sensitive eyes from the glare of the day.

Sector 5-D was still some long blocks away, but so far he'd seen no sign of the fisherman Tark, no sign of anyone at all. The hours in tunnel lockdown had cost Anthony the chance to intercede in Vault's plans, the idea a stupid one to begin with. Delivering the meds should have been top priority. The virus was spreading, children were dying, and he was miles away from helping anyone. He'd fucked up, wasted the night in his scattered attempts, and not many options remained.

He rubbed his face where the skin was peeling. Travel uptown was dangerous on the eastern trails. He'd be days working his way north through the woodlands. If he retraced his steps across Union Square he could attempt hiking the Middle Road uptown and if the weather held he might find a Runner to deliver news of his delay to Marjorie.

If only he'd followed his original plan he'd be halfway up the lower Broadwaterway by now on bartered canoe or kayak. Well, this wouldn't be his first time flying by the seat of his pants.

He continued on autopilot, reviewing the night's events, and before long, turning back became less of an option. He was making good time, walking through difficult terrain in a wide rut left by the drag of a passing sled, until Third Avenue, where the trail ended at a fence, the abandoned sled frozen in a snowdrift.

He examined the weathered barricade that ran up the avenue into the distance and south to an embankment of collapsed buildings. Cinder blocks shoring the base were stained orange with rust from knotted chains hanging between each panel, and the boards themselves were mildewed black.

He shoved the fence with his shoulder. Although the wood was warped with age, it was sturdy. With a quick look around—the streets were empty—he climbed up and pulled himself over the graffitied blockade.

The other side of the fence was as bleak as the avenue to the west. A blue plastic drum stood derelict and overflowing under a thin yellow waterfall running over rocks between Sixteenth and Seventeenth. Yellow and black tarps covered digs, held in place with hunks of brick and concrete. The sidewalk and paved road were buckled, and he tripped more than once on twisted metal cables sticking up from the ground.

Holding the bars of a rippled cast iron fence, he stopped just once to look briefly southwest where Friends Seminary should have been, but there was no sign of the elite school his niece had attended. No sign of St. George's, either. Anthony missed the meetings in that basement, a penance of sorts, being so close to his sister's daughter's school. He hadn't expected the church to be standing, but felt a certain anxiety to confirm its disappearance.

He could use a meeting. What would he have now? Two centuries? "One hell of a chip," he congratulated himself, the sound of his voice surprising in the emptiness.

A flock of geese rose in unison, honking as they lifted to the sky. Oversized birds with striped heads and white wings he'd never seen in the old world. Did any Touched hold Records of migratory birds or avian mutations? For a moment Anthony remembered the reason Vault was charged with Data management, and the recovery of lost Records. So much information at stake. But, no. Recovery came at too high a price.

A man in snowshoes crossed an elevated field where the woods had burned out just southeast, and to the north, a bundled figure rode a limping, gray horse toward the avenue.

Anthony let his eyes linger. He and Aja had been separated five months. With Daisy's help—the Wait was a useful conduit for news—he'd traced his horse to a salvage man on the East River. He had every intention of reclaiming her, but for now they were still safer apart.

A loud banging echoed between buildings and ruins. Anthony peered into an alley. A man was pounding the runner of an overturned sleigh, each strike causing the wooden chassis beneath to shudder. He looked up at Anthony, hammer raised mid-strike.

"I used to have a spare," the man said, his words slurred in an odd lisp. He swung his hammer down on the metal runner. "Gave the sled to my son's daughter when she went to marriage." He hit the steel again. "What was the sense in that? Shoulda given a rack of rabbits instead." He snickered. "Where do you go, stranger?"

"I'm looking for passage uptown."

"Ahh," the man said. He wiped his nose with the back of his hand. "You'll be wanting Mack. Most afternoons he's ferrying north from Twenty-third."

Anthony whistled his thanks. "Much appreciated." The hike would be manageable, but he'd still need to figure out a barter.

The man swung the hammer again, somewhat unsteadily. "I could use your help, journeyman, if you've the time."

Information had its price—a swap was expected—so Anthony entered the area between the brick of a slender, intact brownstone and the rubble of a collapsed apartment building. A semi-ceiling of planks offered shelter but left the alley in shadow.

He pushed his sunglasses to the top of his head. The man at work was older than he sounded. Wrinkled skin sagged and his body was thin, hunched over an upside down sled. A dark bottle—Anthony smelled the alcohol—rested on a crate next to him.

"What happened?"

"Came down hard on the ridge." The man pointed to a slight bend in the runner. "Can you hold her steady? She's slipping."

Anthony crouched in the narrow space. The runners were set atop a wooden box frame fitted with a high handle. Anthony reached around and grabbed the polished wood, bracing himself against the wall.

"And go," the man said as he thwacked his hammer. "And go."

Anthony held on despite the burn that shot from his hand to his arm, and in a few minutes, the runner was straightened and the old man reached for his bottle.

"Some bread?" the man offered. "My wife has the fire going."

He took a swig and grinned. "Or would you rather a drink."

"Just information, if you will, and then I'm to the ferry."

The man's eyes narrowed. "What did you say your name is?"

Here we go. "Anthony," he said, prepared to defend his bare genealogy, but to his relief, the man just nodded.

"I'm called Harlin. Harlin of Rutherford Place."

He drank again and Anthony frowned. Was there unending wine in that flask? "Do you know a man called Tark? Bearded braid? Blue hands?"

"I know Tark," Harlin said. "And his wife Grindle. We're all the downtown." He set the bottle down and hoisted the sled from its bay with strong arms, the muscles in his neck straining as he righted it on the ground. "See, the fabric is dyed blue from the snails she gathers," he said. "It's the same on his hands."

Anthony ran his fingers along the deep cobalt padding sewn around the wooden bench. "Can you tell me how to find him?"

Harlin grabbed his bottle. Anthony smelled the must of his coat and the damp alcohol sweat of his body as he squeezed past. He followed him into the street.

"They're might to still be at their Hide a cause of the alarms," the old man said, shielding his eyes from the bright sun. He drank again and confided, "All the way east beneath the salt piles."

Anthony noted the location and kept still as Harlin continued. "Some need hear all clear from the Runner before they emerge. But where's the Runner in the snow, I say. Not gonna stay in my hidey-hole all day. There's other ways news travels. News comes to those who listen. Can't always wait for the Runner."

He took a thick piece of sticky tobacco out of a pouch and stuck the wad in his cheek. "They said a ship raised the alarm. Well, I'm not afraid of strange ships in the sea," he said, spitting a dark liquid into the snow. "There's a whole world gone below the waves and from time to time things rise on the currents." He nodded at his own words. "They fall below again soon enough."

"Did you see it?" Anthony asked, knowing this particular ship would not be falling back below the waves. Harlin shook his head.

Anthony's feet were cold. He stomped them in the wet snow and asked casually, "Is Tark a Touched One?"

Harlin paused to move the tobacco in his mouth. "No Touched

130

in the downtown." He shrugged. "There were the Tunnel kids, five of 'em Touched all the same. *With the ABC's.* Don't know what those are. But they Left. You tell me, where's the sense in that?"

Anthony had heard this twice now, and he didn't understand. He'd seen the entirety of the Group that Left, Record holders frightened, strangely docile and submissive in their incomprehension as they were brought through the chambers for processing. There were no children in the Group.

The old man took a long draw from his bottle. "Tark's not Touched. Just crazy. All mixed up. Has some strange name for himself. But what's the harm? He's content until he's confused." He laughed. "Last time he passed this way my tongue forgot the name he answers to. Got him all riled. What a yelling. Can't blame me is what I say. It's not a name easy to remember." He wiped his mouth where liquor mixed with tobacco spit.

"Name?" Anthony asked, encouraging him to continue.

"Yeah," he said, thinking. "Old Tark insists to be called Old Joe. No, Van Joe or such. And don't mention the downtown around him. He calls this place *Arles*. What's the sense in that?"

Arles? Anthony stared at Harlin. "Van Gogh?"

"Maybe," he said, tilting his head in thought. "That could be the one." He shook his bottle. "Empty, dangum."

It seemed Harlin might say something else, but he just slipped back into the alley with his bottle, no doubt looking for a refill.

Anthony barely noticed the steel girders above as he hiked toward First Avenue, mind spinning. The man with blue hands called himself Van Gogh. Was it happening again?

Five years earlier, a subterranean explosion had released billions upon billions of nanobits—each a complex code encompassing any of a trillion disciplines—into the city's air and water, and each person who'd absorbed one of those bits, by mouth or nose, became a repository for the data within.

The data had been culled from everywhere—histories, books, poems, maps, archives, databases, journals, textbooks, hyper-combined resources, images, video, audio, news, art, language, science, magic, religion, medical, historical, genealogical and government records, every piece of information ever recorded from children's scribblings to scholarly works of the most abstract and specialized fields, from holographic renderings of architecture and space to 3D realizations of chalk art painted on sidewalks that existed for only hours until washed away by rain—and the *Global Data Management Project* had captured everything, including live camera feeds and calls and texts and social and community media and virtual worlds and images from satellites recording in real-time—tagging, cross-referencing, processing and storing the tremendous *Global Collect.*

It was the backup of the total of the human race's experience and knowledge saved in a gazillion little bits, designed to be restored in any number of worst-case global scenarios.

A second undertaking—the *Humanity Restoration Collect*—had been safeguarded in separate server containers off the main grid, and when the initial breach occurred, the *Humanity* cores had remained secure.

Those Meta-Records were created to reestablish, also in a failsafe, pivotal and determinant figures from the history of humankind. Artists, philosophers, inventors, prophets, teachers—individuals deemed critical to a re-evolution of mankind.

Vincent Van Gogh was one of them.

Was the *Humanity Restoration* breached and the Meta-Records tagged Vincent Van Gogh restored to a living person? Bio-bits fused to an unknowing host? To Tark?

Anthony didn't know if it was worse to consider that Meta-nanobiotics had been released and were being restored, or that those unabsorbed would fall after a period, inert and lost. Is this why Vault had targeted the fisherman?

By the time he reached First Avenue the clouds had thickened, and a bitter wind whipped through his cloak. The remnants of a landing strip covered most of the western side of the avenue to the north. Anthony identified a helicopter, rotor blades like a bent pinwheel on the landscape, and the sleek frame of a small jet, stark against the gray sky.

To the desolate south, exposed building skeletons disguised by drifting snow, dangling wires, charred streetscapes, low forestation, a cliff and then nothing—a reminder that the edge of the world loomed just a few blocks away.

He forced himself to move on.

Stuyvesant Town spread for acres east of First Avenue. The sprawling complex of red brick buildings had once housed more than twenty thousand people in thousands of apartments stretching north to Twenty-third and east to the river. There were only half as many inhabiting now the entire city, not enough bodies to fill Yankee Stadium to even one-quarter capacity.

Did the Bronx still exist?

Anthony had studied some of the final satellite images with Melly. Ground stability didn't occur in that direction again until Westchester at Yonkers. Swamps and marshes covered most of the territory north of Manhattan with pockets of habitable land to the east.

It had been unclear from satellite data what population remained in the remotest areas. After Melly died, Seth had classified those feeds and Anthony hadn't seen them since.

He kept east, following a network of paths, low railings along the walkways his only guideposts. Thick snow muffled every sound but the rasp of his breath. He veered slightly north through a row of trees to cross a flat expanse that looked to be a shortcut. His sliding feet exposed the faded green tennis court.

He could smell the tide, and as he came around one of the easternmost buildings he saw the parkland highway covered with waving yellow wild grasses and iced bare trees, and beyond the stacked transit expressways, the river.

The late morning sun was too feeble to disperse the steel shadows of the overpasses, the silvers of the sky, the platinum of the snow covered riverbank, the white of the piled salt mounds and the charcoal black water carrying swirling pieces of ice and debris upriver—the whole vista a strikingly beautiful and depressing monochrome.

The wind had knocked a gate open just past a bend in the river. It smacked back against the fence, rattling the chain link. Anthony climbed through drifts and over bramble to reach the gate, passing through the cold metal into the wild shore flats.

Rounded salt mounds on wooden platforms, some covered

with protective mesh, lined the river. The coastline straightened to the north, undisturbed, but here in this bend footsteps marred the snow. Someone, many people, had trampled it recently.

He crossed the frozen expanse. Where the salt had scattered, the ice melted, revealing black earth beneath. Anthony spotted something blue exposed in the swirling drifts, but lost sight of it when the wind covered it again. He kicked through to where he thought he had seen the color flash, finding nothing.

The riverbank met the water in a muddy strip of ice at the bottom of a short incline. Anthony slid down to inspect deep grooves sliced through the wet earth. Something had moored here. Rocks visible in the shallow water's edge were scraped and algae displaced by long scratches on the top surfaces.

He adjusted his sunglasses and scanned the dark water. If the Vaulters had been here they'd moved on by now. He turned back to face the scattered salt.

"Tark," he called to the emptiness, feeling foolish. A sea bird at the edge of the water screamed back.

The old man Harlin said Tark would have hidden under the salt. Anthony examined the white and gray clumps piled on the low platform. Kneeling, he brushed away the snow. Where he expected dirt, there was wood. Two hinged sections interlaced with a length of chain and a heavy lock.

He pulled on the wood but the chains held fast, secured with a thick padlock. He had a small collection of tools. A safety pin bent straight and a thin tipped flathead screwdriver would work. It took just a few minutes to maneuver the pins and turn the cylinder. The lock clicked open and he pulled it from the chains knotted around the door's metal handles.

"Hello," he called into the interior, lifting the wood. "Anyone?"

The low-ceilinged cellar was empty, blankets and cushions scattered on the floor. In a plastic stacking crate, a child's doll and some dried flowers. A bucket of water.

He resealed the chamber and sent a prayer up for Tark, though if Bravo had gotten him no prayer would help.

In the gusting snow he saw again the glimmer of blue. He dove into the drift, catching the crocheted blue fabric of a small bag. He untwisted the knot, digging his fingers into the sticky interior, certain he must be dreaming. The bag was filled with dried fruit. He put a piece of apple in his mouth, chewing slowly to savor the flavor and letting the calories refuel him. He ate another—a strip of pear dusted with maple sugar—and his hunger eased.

The sun was higher in the sky now. Anthony tucked the bag away—he'd ration the sweets—and started uptown the five blocks through the shore park toward the afternoon ferry.

A busy trade crowded the pier where boats and rafts moored at Twenty-third Street. Anthony stopped briefly to eye a table of books in varying states of decay, spines stamped *NYPL*.

"All new today," the woman behind the display told him. "We pulled em from the second shaft before the snows. If you got the spellings, I'm gonna be the only one trading these kinds of words."

She opened a crate labeled *Epiphany Library, East 23rd Street, NYC*. "I'll trade the whole lot of shinies, if you want," she offered, exposing a silver DVD, but Anthony didn't know why anyone would swap for a disc already obsolete in his own time.

He found the uptown ferry, a longboat with a mast and ivory sail, tethered to the dock with yellow cables. Although crew attended other boats on the pier, the ferryman was nowhere to be seen. Anthony reached into his pack for the rectangle of cloth he carried—his flag—and tied the banner to the cord, reserving his passage. That done, he scanned the port for the ferryman.

"Try the Game," a girl selling hot drinks suggested, gesturing to the covered bazaar beneath the stacked roads to the west. "Mack's gonna be at the Game."

Anthony thanked her and walked down the pier to the bazaar. A man worked a firebox at the entrance. Long brown razor clams and blue-black mussels spit steam as they opened over the flames. A pack of dogs lurked hungrily, pawing discarded shells and bits of trimmed clam as they jostled for position.

He ducked into the hot, crowded plastic tent. A barker stood on a ladder calling numbers, and the players, betting and tossing chits onto a table, hollered and catcalled at two men—one with a wide teased out beard and close cropped hair, the other with a head full of twisted dreadlocks—throwing dice on a slab.

The noisy competition seemed to end with the eruption of cheers and groans, but the bearded man stood to full height and shouted, "Count six, ya cheater, I'll not give ya a second chance to do. G'wan, ya drink sees ya double, give the right number."

The barker shook his head and the dreadlocked man, dressed in layers of faded salvage—Anthony recognized the upscale logos on his clothes—spit on the ground and raised a fist full of vouchers above his head, crooked teeth grinning at the whistling crowd.

The winners grabbed their markers and the losers shouted for rematch, but the bearded man threw down the dice and pushed his way from the throng.

"Vouchers, gone. Dangum, I'll be carting 'til I'm under stone to make my losses," he groused. "Gonna hafta hike uptown now."

Anthony's sunglasses had fogged in the warmth of the tent, and he pulled them from his face. The bearded man caught his eye and did a double take.

"Your look is familiar," he said, furrowing his thick eyebrows in concentration. "Do you owe me on a Game?"

"Aww, Tinny, sore loser," the dreadlocked man interrupted, wrapping an arm around his shoulder. "Ha. I take you on my ferry. No voucher."

Tinny turned, relief on his face. "Yeah?"

The man grinned and pushed Tinny toward the exit. "You load my crates. I find John Ellen. Then we sail."

"Wait," Anthony called, catching up. "You're the ferryman?"

"I am," the man said. "Mack McKay."

"I tied my flag to your line. Swap passage?"

Mack headed out, stopping at the firebox to exchange a voucher for a cone of shellfish. Steam rose from the container as he fished out an open clam. With a long blade pulled from his belt he sliced the meat, shoving the chewy clam steak in his mouth and tossing the shell to the dogs.

"The oars are already promised," he said, spitting an inedible bit into the snow. "Six paddles. Three men."

"Wasn't John Ellen to meet at the Game?" Tinny said.

Mack laughed. "But for the snow I would have his vouchers, too. Ha, there may be time yet for another Game while we wait for our passenger."

Tinny shook his head. "I'm out."

"Take me," Anthony said. "I won't hold up your schedule."

"Blast," Tinny said. "I remember you. You're the stranger carted to the Wait. Anthony, yeah? I brung you to the Columbus Circle. I'm Tinny."

"Tinny the Wagoner?" This man had saved his life. "I was told your name when I woke, but you were gone. I owe you." Wishing he'd had a chance to eat just one more piece, Anthony passed the crocheted bag to him. "Fruit," he said. "Many thanks."

"Not necessary. The Touched Marjorie settled the barter the same day you collapsed in the Remember, but I'm glad to have your thanks." He tore the pouch open and poured the dried slices—every one—into his mouth. Anthony licked his lips.

"Lucky for you Tinny wasn't winning that day," Mack said, plucking the last shell from the cone. "The man only carts when his losses need fixing." He slurped the mussel. Anthony tried to think of anything but food.

"You had no hair," Tinny said, still chewing, spittle dribbling into his beard. "Smooth as a mushroom. Not even eyelashes."

"No lie?" Mack asked. He pulled Anthony's hood down, exposing his bald scalp and the patches of psoriasis around his ears. "Dangum. I'd wager there's no hair on your manny, either."

Tinny made a lewd gesture. "How would you know?"

Mack looked at Anthony thoughtfully. "This mariner, same type, comes around. My sister Fee tends him. No eyelashes, no eyebrows, no manny hair."

Anthony raised his hood but the ferryman kept on. "This hairless man visits, but doesn't stay. Fee can carry babies. She's bleeding each season. Why wouldn't he give her babies?"

"Hairless babies," Tinny laughed.

Mack whispered to Anthony. "You're his clan. You will direct him stay with Fee? Yes? We need babies."

Anthony sighed. There was no way to explain he didn't know this hairless mariner, that his own alopecia was a consequence of Cocooning. Each time he'd woken to wider patches of bare scalp. At the fourth Awake, he'd been bald. There'd been no hair left on any of them. He remembered the handfuls of curly blonde hair falling from Elizabeth's fingers, and how sad she'd seemed.

He shook his head to turn that loop off in his brain. Mack—looking so hopeful—waited for his response.

"I'm a journeyman," Anthony tried. "Estranged from my clan."

The ferryman persisted. "In our settlement there's only Fee to have the babies. We're all the rest male. We care for the elders. But who will have the babies?"

"You need barter wives," Tinny said. "That's what you need."

"I will find this mariner kin," Anthony said. It seemed the easiest answer. "I will tell him to give your sister babies."

Mack smiled. A huge grin full of teeth and shellfish. "Our clans will join," he said, hugging Anthony. "You'll be my brother."

Tinny hugged Anthony, too, and pulled a flask from his tunic. "To the joining," he toasted, drinking from the container before passing it to Anthony, who passed it to Mack without sipping.

"What kind of brother would I be," Mack said, gulping the spirit, "to leave my own kin south when he needs passage north?"

Tinny grabbed the drink from Mack and slipped it back into his pocket—Anthony was not sorry to see it put away—with a toast, "To passage north."

"Passage north?" Anthony repeated.

"John Ellen is late, brother. I can't hold sail forever. Six paddles, three men. I take you uptown. You meet Fee at One-hundred-eleventh and tell her the news. Good trade." Mack took off, long legs carrying him easily over the snow and slush.

"Wait for me," Tinny shouted, scrambling to catch up.

Anthony did the math. He was sixty blocks from his destination through near impossible terrain. Taking advantage of the ferry passage to One-hundred-eleventh Street, he'd be thirty beyond. Good trade.

Putting his sunglasses back on, he sprinted after them, trying not to fall on the slippery path.

VELLA

THE IMMENSE ROOM with the high, high ceilings was cold, even with the fire crackling behind the tall gates at the far end, and Vella was mad to be there, mostly because of her birds. They'd be winter mating, and here she was stuck in this stupid Quarnteen. It was Vella who would keep their nest boxes filled with gravel and water. It was Vella who would track them and make sure they returned home. It was Vella who kept their wing tips painted gold and pink like the sunset. Who would do all these things if not her? Da? She didn't think so.

She missed her friends, too. Well, she didn't have so many, anymore, and the few who survived the summer outbreak were at Quarnteen with her, but they didn't much want to play, and Vella, so awfully tired and stomach aching, didn't want to play either.

She had thrown up during the night. Someone in a cloth mask had come in to clean her sheets and give her a fresh robe, dousing the shiny cold floor beneath with a sour wash. The smell of the rinse had almost made her vomit again.

Vella tried to ask about her falcons but the person had whispered, "Close your eyes," and slipped quietly away. She'd fallen back to her hot sleep, and in the morning had thrown up again, a yellow puke that burned her throat. This time she'd managed to reach the bucket, pushing the sloshing pail across the floor when she finished so as not to inhale the awful mess, and there was no person come in to comfort her.

When she woke again, a long time later, the clear winter light that had been streaming in through windows at the ceiling was gone and smoky lanterns were lit for dusk. She listened for her falcons. They'd be singing for each other now from twisted bare branches in the aviary and waiting to fly in the set sun, but the birds' songs didn't carry through the solid walls.

She unwrapped herself from the sheet and sat up. Her red hair had been tied back with a string. She rubbed her eyes—they were sticky with dried tears—and she tried to wet her chapped lips with a dry and bitter tongue.

She called out for her father and remembered Da had abandoned her in the Museem where she felt like the last ember in a dying fire. She fumbled for her water bottle. It was empty, but she put the soft straw to her mouth and pulled anyway, moistening her lips with the remaining drops. She swallowed carefully, her throat sore from vomit and bile.

Da had brought her to this place in the middle of a night. Maybe two days she'd been arrived. She couldn't remember. He had been crying, but Vella, squinting in the bright moon, had pretended not to see the streaks on his face, tears fallen from his dark eyes and disappeared into his thick beard.

She'd fallen asleep on the sled that sliced the icy snow, and woken when Da carried her through a room filled with stone tables and sideways statues and up the open stairway. He hadn't said when he'd return, just hugged her until she couldn't breathe, and stood without moving while someone poured that horrible liquid over his hands and arms.

They were left alone, she and the others who slept on and off in this cool room, though she dreamed a kind hand had wiped her face with a wet towel. She knew someone must be coming in. Food she wouldn't eat covered banquet benches, and somebody had been emptying the metal void boxes set against the stone figures, and wouldn't there be someone to replenish the fire? But she hadn't seen anyone do those things, and the large room and the ones beyond the arches were empty but for the sick.

Quiet voices echoed from somewhere, and Vella got up to investigate the strange words. "Forty counted as of today," a man said. "And more coming now the snow's done and the Runners have spread the news. There's another Quarnteen started across the park at the History Museem."

A second voice, a woman. "Anthony sent word he has enough medicine for whoever many comes. We can only hope he's here before long."

"If he's not arrived soon we won't need medicines. Just carts to the Remember."

"Thirteen already wait in the snow for that trip."

The words meant nothing to Vella, but the adult voices

comforted her. Thirsty, she dragged her sheet past listless children come from everywhere, laid out in rows—some asleep, some awake and staring—in the semi-darkness. She stopped at the water bucket, her slurps loud in the brittle, marble room.

"Vella?" a small voice whispered, and she turned to a boy sitting in the shadows against the wall that connected the arched doorways.

"Yah?"

"Vella of the falcons?" he asked, looking up at her, the light from the burning logs behind the gate illuminating his raised face.

Vella wiped the water from her mouth. "Key?"

He nodded quickly and gave her a thin smile.

"Key, why are you here?" The dark-skinned boy with swirling white tattoos was the son of a salvage man who lived in the settlement called Tudor, on the East River at Forty-first. The boy's father had claim to a large plot and her own Da swapped fresh killed birds and hard eggs for the wrapped cans and tubes of the soft salty and sweet foods she'd loved before she got sick.

"The Runner told to bring the sick to the Museem," the nine-year-old said, teeth chattering. "To keep the fevers from jumping. He said medicines would make us better." Key pointed to the supper laid out in one of the arched doorways—cake slices and a tureen of broth cooling on the ledge. "I'm hungry."

"That's good to be hungry," Vella said, handing him a piece of dense yellow potato cake. She crinkled her face in thought. "I don't think there's been medicine," she said, trying to remember through the fog of her sickness.

Key shrugged. "Well, ma didn't want the fever to jump on my little sister, so she brung me away to the Quarnteen."

"Long trip," Vella said.

"As soon as the Runner said, we left. It took all the day and some of the night," he said, looking at the cake in his hand. "Did you hear about the twins gone missing at Chelsea Wood?"

"We haven't had news since the snow," Vella said. "What happened?"

The boy took a small bite and grimaced. "Oh," he said softly as he stood. "I've voided."

Vella turned from the smell as Key twisted to clean himself

with his robe. He started to say something else, but gurgled instead. Bloody vomit came up and out his mouth and nose with a force that sent the bile spewing across the room.

If Vella had been concerned about being left alone, the next eased her mind. The person who had come to her during the night was at the boy in a flash, scooping him into her arms—it was the one *Touched with medicine*, Marjorie Jane—and now she was carrying Key away.

"Where are you going?" Vella called.

"Shhh," Marjorie said, stopping by a stone figure of a bird-man that blocked one of the arched doorways. "I'm just to clean him and put him to cool the fever in a tub."

"When is my Da coming back?" Vella yelled. But the Touched One had moved on with the young boy, Key.

Vella wrapped the sheet around herself. A wind coming from the hallway chilled her, though the fresh air cleared her mind. She wanted answers. If Marjorie couldn't provide them she'd find somebody who could. The Runner should be passing. He'd give a relay on the Museem steps if he saw the flag, so Vella would raise the banner and wait.

An endless series of hallways and staircases spread throughout the Museem, but Vella had been roaming in and rummaging around in the vast rooms her whole life—for play, for salvage, and for shelter during the worst of lightning storms and flooding—and she knew this big, drafty gallery with the floor to ceiling gate was just a short distance from the terraced steps on Fifth Avenue.

She waited, hand against the wall, for a dizziness to pass. She may have dozed there, standing, but when the room came into focus again she set out.

Quietly, she went through the doors at the end of the sick room and into the Museem's torchlit entryway. The height and width of the hall dwarfed her, and she faltered for a moment in the empty space stretching forever in either direction. The air was so cold. The doorways facing the Fifth Avenue stairs were open to the wind, and although long canvas sheets hung over gaping breaks in the thick frontage, snow and water had come in and slick patches of treacherous, almost invisible ice covered the floor.

Vella took small steps across the frigid hall, stumbling as her foot stuck to the ice and barely noticing for the cold the skin ripped as she dislodged it. She pulled the heavy panels of cloth up with both hands and raised her face to the outdoors.

The wide steps to the street were covered with snow, but a narrow, partially cleared path wound from the top plaza down to the first landing, where what looked like mounds of dirt were piled along the white ice.

Vella took a tentative step out, letting the canvas fall behind her. She stood between two columns, the sky darkening indigo as the last of the sun faded behind to the west. Crisscrossing deer tracks and sled trails marked the snowy Fifth Avenue but there was nobody on the road.

She wrapped the sheet tight around her almost naked body, and holding onto the burning cold handrail, limped barefoot down the icy stairs. She heard an owl in the distance and smelled pine. She ripped a length of her sheet and tied it on the railing to flag the Runner, but wasn't sure if he'd notice the banner there.

The dusk had deepened, Fifth avenue obscured in shadow, so she sat carefully, her bottom burned from the frost, on one of the black dirt mounds, setting her sights on the street directly below.

"Vella," a worried voice shouted from the top of the steps, and she turned to look at Marjorie. "Oh for dangum, what are you doing out there?" the Touched One cried, sliding down through the slush and ice.

Marjorie lifted the girl over her shoulder, wrapping her own warm cloak around her cold skin. Vella watched the black dirt mound recede below as they climbed back to the Museem.

She was frozen, toes discolored with creamy white patches, her bare legs red and itching, and too exhausted to even say the words aloud when she realized the black mound was not dirt at all, but rather young Key of Tudor, died and left wrapped with the others, his small spiral inked hand still clutching the yellow potato cake.

ANTHONY

ANTHONY'S SHOULDERS WERE stiff from rowing against the wind, his face chapped from the spray that had hammered him all afternoon. The ice had made travel nearly impossible, even with the north running tidal current, and at times it had seemed they weren't moving at all. He estimated they'd been on the river almost five hours.

He was thankful when the ferryman relieved him of the oars and directed him to sit on the covered crates instead and stoke the fires in the small stove for warmth, and now, as the sky darkened, for food and light. With the sounds of gulls in his ears he'd dozed a bit, but the uneasy sleep left him seasick on the choppy water.

Hiding behind his open cloak, Anthony unzipped a tube of Safe cache protein and poured the dehydrated flakes into the everstew, mixing the mash into the fish bones and broth before sliding the casserole back into the fire.

"G'wan, lady, we're starving," Tinny shouted, laughing. "Serve it up, yeah?"

Anthony rolled his eyes at the big man and ladled stew into metal cups, passing the supper to the men. He sipped from his own cup, closing his eyes to the salty, hot soup thickened by the protein.

The wind was stronger, now, and Mack raised the sail. At Eightieth Street, the setting sun threw long, weak shadows over the low ridges of the East River and the fields just beyond its banks. Anthony had seen these fields—images—when he'd come out of the Cocoon the first time. Farms had been created over the obsolete FDR Drive, and glass needle towers overlooked acres of wheat and soy that stretched to the river. Few of those towers' frames—home to nesting birds—remained now, but the fields were still cultivated along the river.

Tendrils of mist brushed his face, blowing across from the rocky, fog-shrouded Roosevelt Island to the east. The island shimmered on the water like a ghost, half the length Anthony remembered, and twice as misshapen.

The ferry moved quickly past the Carl Schurz Marina where tethered boats banged against pilings and a column of antlered elk made their way along the shore. A few moments later they entered the widest part of the river. Anthony braced himself, expecting converging currents to challenge the ferry and her paddles, but instead, perhaps due to the shifted lands in the Long Island Sound and waters dammed with pieces of the RFK bridge, the currents were smooth and passage was swift.

The river narrowed to the north and the city's shore was hidden behind high walls and gates designed to keep the beasts from climbing to land. What used to be Randall's Island rose in a sloping forest at the east. The people called this mid-river island Blowburn, a name referring to the explosive charges buried in the perimeter, and Mack gave that shore a wide berth.

The aggressive wind pushed the ferry towards the high dock looming over the stone and metal seawall. "Oars," Mack called, yanking the sail. "You, too, hairless brother. All hands," and Anthony abandoned the fire to pick up his paddles. Working in unison to a chorus of barking dogs, the three manipulated the boat to the foot of One-hundred-eleventh Street.

The jetty was wider than long, and Mack's ferry was one of several moored to pilings that reached from the river bottom to the platform five feet above the surface. Great honking geese gathered beneath, biting and rustling against each other in the current, and the wood smelled of bird and fish and salt.

Tinny went first up a creaking ladder that swayed with his weight, lifting the crates Mack hoisted. By the time Anthony pulled himself up, wringing the river from his cloak, a young man wrapped in fur was stacking the last of the crates on a sled. Dark, muscular dogs paced in the shadows. Anthony hoped they were tethered.

"You've rocks mixed with the cargo, cousin," the young man said, struggling to balance the tied cartons as he started across the buckling frozen field.

"The library dig is birthing, Carlo," Mack called after him. "Tell the aunts and uncles I've brung a hairless friend to Meal."

Tinny shuffled his bulky shape. "I'm south to catch a Game before morning. There's a player owing me vouchers." He turned to Anthony. "Wager some of what you carry, hairless one?"

Anthony tightened his wrap around his pack. "I've nothing to wager or barter," he said, worried Tinny would press the issue—he had a gambler's tension—but the moment passed.

"Go," Mack told the big man. "And may the dice be like family."

A coyote—or some hybrid—howled in the distance, and the dogs set up barking again. Mack flashed a hand signal and the pack settled with low growls. Anthony took the torch he offered and followed the ferryman across the field, sliding on the ice in his shredded foot wraps and grabbing a fence to stop in front of an ancient automobile propped against the chain link.

"Dragged from the river," Mack boasted. And then, confided, "Had a couple Disconnects jump in when the metal beast almost pulled me under." He laughed. "It's good to be watched, yeah?"

Anthony nodded. He'd heard stories of Disconnects showing up in the nick of time. Maybe the tales he'd dismissed as legend contained some truth. The river car had been here a while, he guessed, from the looks of the seagull droppings covering what was left of the paint and pitted shell. He raised his torch to the stripped interior. The rearview mirror hung unbroken, and by torchlight, his reflection—red-rimmed sunken eyes, hood over his head—stared back like a ghoul.

Time had beaten him down. He was chasing his tail with no resources and no idea how to accomplish what he'd come to do. The tracking numbers had shown 483 natives absorbed Records. Anthony's scribbled notes named slightly more than 200. How would he find the rest? Why couldn't he figure a way to retrieve the data without harming the hosts? He wasn't a nanobiologist. The solutions were too complex.

And now the dying children. He had to locate more Safe

caches. He didn't have enough doses to stop the spread. Anthony felt would travel up and down Manhattan forever, incompetent and unable to do a damn thing for any of them.

Mack put a hand on Anthony's shoulder as they tramped across the park. Stacks of salvage were visible under the melting snow. Cinder blocks, bricks, sheet metal, rolls of plastic, rubber pads, tires. Anthony passed a football, chairs, a baby carriage, all organized in rows. Along the fence, tarps protected even more reclaimed riches.

The ferryman stopped under an orange basketball hoop. He lifted one of the plastic sheets and held his torch over the contents beneath. "Barter now?" he asked slyly, and threw his head back, laughing as the flickering light revealed a mound of reclaimed shoes and boots—hundreds of them—salvaged from a warehouse or basement or container somewhere in the ruined city.

Anthony's eyes lit. He needed boots. He pulled his pack around, looking for anything to offer in exchange. Hopeful, he handed the vitamins to Mack. The ferryman examined the label, unscrewing the top to sniff. He scrunched his nose.

"What is this?"

"You swallow one each day," Anthony said. "To keep healthy."

Mack nodded. "I've heard of such remedy. Good for the elders." He grinned his crooked smile. "Here's more shoes than we'll trade in many seasons. Choose."

Anthony found a pair of water-stained boots, and when he pulled them over the plastic covered canvas, they fit well. He stomped on the thin layer of snow covering the basketball court, and settled his feet in the leather.

"What else do you carry?" Mack asked. "You added to the everstew and it tasted like no other. Where'd you pull that? You dig in a good salvage?"

Anthony bent to straighten the stiff tongues of his new boots. He'd been careless with the food from the cache, underestimating this street-smart ferryman. But he'd been so hungry and the gruel so thin. He didn't know how to answer.

"You've found the right brother, hairless one," Mack said. "If you've specials, I can make trades. I've got ins and outs mad crazy, dontcha know."

Specials. What they called the rare finds. Eyeglasses, vacuum-sealed food, clothing, canned goods, toothpaste rock hard in the tubes. Anthony had seen bras bartered as specials. Cracked, faded lipsticks. Peeling bars of soap.

"It's true," Anthony said, too tired to lie. "I carry specials, but not to trade."

"What specials?"

Once the information was offered there'd be no turning back. Anthony had gone down this path with only two others, the Touched Marjorie and Daisy from the Wait. He'd gambled then—luck was with him when he trusted the women with his truth —and he'd be gambling now. Well, here goes, he thought. "I have medicines."

"Medicines?" Mack punched Anthony in the arm. "Medicines? You crazy, bald duck. I'll barter the whole lot."

"No," Anthony said, trying to explain. "They're spoken for." But Mack was talking over his words. "You'll need attend David first, " he said, dragging him by the arm along a narrow shoveled walkway. "He's the oldest."

Anthony tried again. "They're for the children."

Mack wasn't listening. He let go to run ahead, his long legs taking him faster than Anthony could follow. "David's sleeping, but I can wake him," he called back. "It won't take but a small time. You'll see."

Anthony lost Mack at a twist in the path and found himself outside a courtyard lit by a center fire. The incredible aroma hit him first and he stopped, stunned at the sight of huge crispy-skinned birds on a spit dripping fat onto the flames. The geese gleamed a deep brown that brought to mind, unbidden then rejected, roast ducks hanging in Chinatown windows.

He licked his lips and watched the skin sizzle. Fueled by the crackling grease, the flames jumped and threw light on a path cleared of snow, and the old woman on a folding chair at the edge of the bonfire.

He took a tentative step in and she beckoned him closer. "You

Anthony?" she asked, pushing herself up with a wheeze. She was a big lady in a fur-quilted vest, thick legs covered to the knees by layered socks, feet in hot pink sneakers. "I'm Auntie Lou," she said. "Born by the River, gonna die by the River."

Anthony nodded at her brief genealogy, hoping she'd overlook his lack of a reciprocating history. "Sorry to bother," he said. "I'm with Mack. Did he pass?"

"Yah. Mackie run by like his feet was burning." She hiked one end of the wobbling rotisserie off the flames and Anthony jumped to take the other end from the fire. "He said you'd help cart meal. Right there," she directed, gesturing to a cart in the shadows.

He slid the birds with his hands onto the cart, and licking the grease and charred bits from his fingers, followed Auntie Lou west, past a debris-filled dugout—a city pool—and a row of small, lopsided houses set back in the field. Fires in front of each cottage lit the exteriors—red, pink, green, yellow, now a blue, a purple, orange—and dark alleys ran between them. Someone must have scored a mother lode of paint, Anthony thought.

The woman was sure-footed in her light, neon running shoes, leaning on the cart for support, but when she began to wheeze in the winter air, Anthony offered his arm. A noxious wind whipped through the park and Anthony coughed, covering his mouth and nose. "The black banks," Auntie Lou said.

He nodded. More than a century's time hadn't soothed the stench of the melted uptown financial center, but the smell was gone as quickly as arrived and he spit the last of the foul taste into the snow drifted against the building at the end of their path.

Auntie Lou banged on the wall. A tall, red-eyed man flung open the metal door. Dreadlocked and wide-mouthed like Mack, he lacked the posture of the ferryman, and stank of the ferment.

"Ah Digger, rude boy," Auntie Lou smiled. "Give some love."

He tweaked her ear and grabbed a bit of bird. "I'm starving," he slurred, pulling the cart inside. "All day raising the shovel. Mouth's ready to feast."

They followed him into a warm, lamp-lit room. A dozen elderly men and women barely acknowledged the food Digger rolled past them, so busy were they at their tables, sorting through the crates Mack had ferried uptown.

"Is he here?" Anthony asked, looking for Mack in the dim interior, but Auntie Lou just shrugged and hung her vest on a wall jammed with coats, joining the others examining stacks of books.

"You," an old man called, eyes buried beneath shaggy white brows. "Are you the hairless one?" He poked an old lady with skin as thin as cellophane and a faded green turban. "Didn't Carlo say another hairless come up with Mack?"

"All I heard from Carlo is arguing with Digger." She eyed Anthony suspiciously. "So, you also with no manny hair?"

"Sister Bob," Auntie Lou cut in. "It's not polite asking such things of a stranger."

"I'm not Digger," the turbaned woman complained. "Don't make rules at me."

Anthony coughed softly. "Has Mack been this way?"

The thick-browed man regarded him with intelligent eyes. "Ya got the spellings?"

Anthony hesitated, and the man held up the book he'd been reading. "Cause if you don't have the spellings you're gonna miss out. Look what Mackie brung."

Anthony blinked and blinked again to see the blue book. He'd carried the digital version on his Com, of course, but once upon a time he'd actually found a Big Book at auction and won. When he joined the Project, a lifetime ago, he'd had to leave the dog-eared hard AA bible behind, along with everything else.

Could he barter now for the volume in the man's hands? What trade would suffice, he wondered, turning sideways to read the lettering on the broken spine.

"It's a good one, yeah?" the old man asked.

Anthony nodded, disappointment physical in his gut. It wasn't the Big Book at all. It was *The Hitchhiker's Guide to the Galaxy*. "A good one," he agreed, laughing—what else could he do? The elders laughed with him until a clattering in the hall distracted them and the giggles stopped.

"Make space," Carlo called, bringing trays into the room with Digger, setting bowls of bird and soft bread on the tables.

The elders shuffled their belongings away from the grease. Digger high-fived his uncles and tweaked his aunts' ears. Showboating now, dancing backwards with the trays, he tripped over a crate and lurched awkwardly, the food flying from his hands. Bird and bread bounced to the floor. He kicked the mess and he kicked the crate.

"Fux all Mack's stuff." He looked around. "Where is he?"

"At David's," Carlo said. "He won't be long."

"And Fee misses Meal, too? Who allows that?"

Auntie Lou stood. "That's a tone you're not to take, nephew."

Digger grabbed a fur from a hook, bowing deeply with mock formality. "May my tone be pleasing to your ears, old ones," he said, and gave the crate one last kick before heading out the door.

Digger had the long legs of his brother and Anthony struggled to keep up. He'd followed the distressed man out, hoping he'd lead him to Mack, and Digger accepted the distraction, steering Anthony toward the row of painted houses.

The cold air—or the flask he drew from—had brightened Digger's mood. He pointed to the red house, the only without an everstew. "My Mother lived there," he said, and then sped off, leaving Anthony again to catch up.

The ferryman's brother ran his hand over the glass and metal chimes hanging over the green door and slid the panel open. Soft music spilled across the threshold. He put a finger to his lips as they entered. Mack was sitting between a narrow bed and the source of the music, a spinning plate connected to a horn fashioned from a plastic milk jug. A drumbeat and voice filtered through the contraption. The words were too soft to understand, but the style of music was one Anthony had been familiar with a long time ago.

"Did you build it?" Anthony asked, trying to get a closer look at the gramophone.

"Uncle Stava designed the music maker from an idea in a book. Old David likes the songs." He touched the sleeping man's cheek. "I tried to rouse him, but his slumber is too deep. I'm sorry. I spent good time when you should already be away."

"Why do you bother the uncle of our mother?" Digger asked.

"I wanted him to agree to a trade." Mack bowed his head. "Even though I know my hairless friend's medicine is promised to another."

The old, old man opened his eyes. Dark irises stared out of deep sockets in the sunken face. Thin speckled brown skin hung from his bony neck. He licked his lips.

"Try this," Anthony said, pulling a box from his pack. He snapped the top off a pale pink nutrient tube and put the end in his mouth. Old David sucked hungrily and closed his eyes. "You can squeeze if he's too weak to pull."

As Mack twirled one of the tubes in his hand, considering the value, the music stuttered and slowed. The ferryman turned a crank and when the song came back up to speed and volume he took his uncle's hand, humming.

Anthony listened, remembering the dance this song made popular decades before his own time. Before he knew it, he found himself slapping his knees and jumping with a knock of his hips.

"You're Touched," Digger spat, eyes cold.

"I'm not." Why had he let himself recognize the music? "I'm only a journeyman to visit your sister."

"What does he say?" Digger asked his brother, disgust—or fear—on his face. "This Touched will not see Fee. I won't let him give us the Touched."

"You know it's not spread like fever," Mack said. "Let him be."

But Digger was already shoving Anthony toward the door. "It was somebody gave it to my Mother," Digger said. "And to her sisters. And their spouses."

"Stop," Mack yelled. "He's going to have the hairless mariner make babies with Fee. It's his clan." And then, more softly, "She was my Mother, too."

One final shove from Digger and Anthony was outside, the door slid shut behind him. He was torchless, but everstew fires created staggered pools of bronze along the walkway.

At the sound of metal on wood he drew into the shadows. A purple door, some houses ahead, was sliding open and a tall woman came out, waste bowl in her hands, and disappeared around the side of the house.

"Fee," a rough voice called. A shadow fell across the doorway, and a man stepped out—Fee's mariner—silhouetted against the firelight. "More beer," he shouted, rubbing the back of his neck and hairless head. "And put it in a clean jar, for chrissakes. Don't skimp on the foam."

For a long moment, Anthony watched his worlds catapult toward each other. The man's familiar accent. An old school manner of speech. Something in the syntax, the syllables stressed and words chosen.

Anthony turned away instinctively but forced himself to look again. The woman had returned and her arms were reaching. The two shifted and the man raised his face to the light.

A surge of adrenaline coursed through Anthony and his worlds collided. It was Racine of the Vault running his hands under her robe in this East Harlem park.

Anthony tensed, prepared for flight, afraid to move, afraid of being discovered in the flickers of gold firelight nipping at his shadow cover. He willed himself invisible and held his breath. Why was Racine here?

To the east, another door opened, rattling chimes, and he dove into the alley between two of the houses. "Hairless Anthony, I see you making your away," Mack called. He cringed to hear his name shouted, and stumbled through a trench half frozen with sewage.

He hesitated at the end of the alley, flat against the windowless wall. "A word with our sister is what you promised," the ferryman yelled, his voice carrying easily through the suddenly still night.

Racine joined Mack's shouts for Anthony, and Fee raised her voice in complaint. The voices were back and forth now—Mack's bursts of explanation, Fee's questions and Racine's, above all others, demanding, "Get him back here."

Anthony slipped from the passage to find escape north blocked by a barbed fence. Trying to place the location of the voices in the dark he continued west along the rear walkway, stopping to peer into an alley before moving quickly across to the back of the adjacent house and a row of furnaces.

At the sound of Mack's calls, now somewhere behind, and of Racine's rants somewhere ahead, Anthony dashed between two houses hoping to lose his pursuers again along the front path. It was barely a moment his head stretched out of the alley. A single moment exposed and Racine was on him from behind, pulling Anthony's hood down with one hand and grasping his chin with the other to thrust his head back.

"Blast from the past," Racine whispered and Anthony felt and smelled his onion and whiskey breath on his throat.

His hand went swiftly to the blade at his waist, and he wrenched himself free. Racine shoved his knee into Anthony's groin. Anthony doubled over, still clenching the hilt of his knife, and the Vaulter clamped his hand on the back of Anthony's neck.

"How are you even alive?"

"Racine?" a soft lisped voice said, and the man's grip tightened. The Vaulter narrowed his eyes, shaking his head slightly before releasing him, and Anthony understood. He would keep quiet.

"Away," Racine said sharply to the tall, dark-haired woman. "My brother's come to discuss private matters." Fee backed into the purple house without argument. The Vaulter and former Vaulter regarded each other.

"Brother," Anthony began.

"I'm not your brother," Racine shot back, momentary truce dissolved. "Give me one reason I shouldn't crush your head right here," he said, spit flying.

Racine's tunic was unzipped, his bare chest mottled from the cold. He was unarmed—a weapon would be visible beneath the thin linen pants—but his hands were strong and Anthony had seen them break concrete. In fact, it was Racine's hands that had pulled Anthony from the rubble when the deep quakes unseated the Cocoons. He owed his life to this man who would surely kill him just as Anthony would slice him with his own blade.

"This isn't about the Project. It's a flu," Anthony said. "The children are dying. The virus is spreading. They'll be wiped out."

"We're not the Red Cross."

"Admin would've interceded. At the very least, you need a healthy population to restore to."

"These inbreds aren't candidates," Racine snorted. "Most of 'em can't even read for fuck's sake. Seth's protocol requires we self-restore."

"There aren't enough of you," Anthony said. "Even if you restored to Civ-staff. How many are left?"

"We'll have plenty of hosts," Racine said. "Vancouver. Ha'il. Mexico City."

"Those Vaults have been dark since our first Awake. Are you even still capable of a restore? So much data's now irretrievable."

"We're raising Heaven."

"Not possible. You don't have access," Anthony said. "No Vault had access."

"Seth says a full restore from the backup is going to happen."

Anthony's blood went cold. "But Records are already propagated. Think what would happen to them. To the holders."

"Not my worry." Racine pried a salvage board from the snow and tested its weight. "City life doesn't agree with you, old friend. You look like shit."

Anthony heard footsteps and spoke quickly. "Don't do this." He drew his knife. The Vaulter grabbed his arm, twisting his elbow sharply and shoving him against the house. The blade fell. Racine swung the board.

Turning to deflect the blow, Anthony saw out of the corner of his eye Digger and Mack burst from between the houses. The board went flying and Racine collapsed with a shout, yanked away by the thick net Digger had thrown over him. Anthony retrieved his blade and stood back, breathing heavily.

"Get this the fuck off me," Racine grunted, struggling against the knotted twine.

The purple door scraped open and Fee flew out. "What's happening?"

"Man dropped like a bird over the Crease," Digger said, tightening the net. "I kicked the back of his knees."

"But why?" Fee cried.

"Would you have Cain slay his brother on our mother's land?"

"You illiterate shit," Racine snarled. He'd managed to twist himself into a low crouch, restrained by the twine. "What would you possibly know of Cain?"

"I've read that book," Digger said. "And I saw what you did." He turned to Mack. "He meant to kill his brother. You saw it."

Meal must have ended because torchlights were visible through the trees. The indistinct murmurings of the elders grew louder as Carlo, Auntie Lou at his side, led them onto the path into the light of the everstew fires.

"What's this about?" Mack asked, eye on the approaching aunts and uncles.

"Tell them, Anthony," Racine said. "How you abandoned your post to protect a race of simpletons. A race of simpletons holding Records we are mandated to Recover."

"You would destroy the people for the Records," Anthony said, and Mack wrinkled his brow at the words.

"These hairless share dementia," Digger said to Mack.

"You're an idiot," Racine said. "You know nothing about it."

Digger leaned in and pointed a finger in Racine's face. "I know you come in secret and leave the same way. I know my sister vouches for you so we don't request your lineage." He shook his head. "But you're finished and I will row you across the water."

"No," Fee cried. "I won't let you leave him with the beasts."

"Cut him free," Mack said. "We have no call to hold this man. Business between brothers is none of ours."

"Dangum, Mack, he's mad crazy," Digger said.

"All the more reason he be on his way. Release him."

Digger tensed his jaw but did as his brother asked. It took just a few cuts of the cable before the Vaulter shoved him off and pulled the net up and over his head.

"Get my things," he ordered Fee, and she ran to his command. Racine's black eyes held Anthony's and if there was a message in them, Anthony couldn't decipher it.

The door to the purple house slid open, and Fee, wrapped in fur, approached, Racine's bag in her arms. The Vaulter strapped the satchel over his shoulders and took a step backwards. Then another. He smiled, a smug twisting of the mouth.

"I'm to go with you," Fee said, reaching for him.

"No."

"I can help. Didn't I already help?"

"Shut up—"

"But I told you where the Touched was," she said. "I'll find more for you."

"What are you saying, sister?" the ferryman asked.

Racine grabbed her arm. "Not another word, stupid girl."

"Fux no, rude hairless," Digger shouted, and he flew at the Vaulter, head butting Racine and slamming him to the ground.

"Stop," Fee cried, clawing at her brother. "He's to help us."

The men tumbled, cursing and kicking up snow and dirt. "You don't understand," Fee shouted. "It's what we wanted."

Mack jumped in, pulling his brother from Racine. The Vaulter twisted and grabbed for the ferryman's long braids. Racine was strong but Mack was quick and he dove at Racine's legs. An everstew kettle went flying, soup spilled and embers scattered.

They somersaulted, interlocked, onto the dark field. Digger ran alongside, unable to help for the speed in which the two switched positions. Over and under they fought—one moment Racine on top, the next Mack.

"Who did you locate for this man?" Anthony shouted, grabbing Fee as she tried to follow Racine.

"I'm not to say," she said, struggling against him.

"Listen to me. You know of Touched gone missing or left for dead?" Fee shook her head, but there was hesitation in her denial.

"The Touched he seeks is in danger."

"I win," Mack shouted. He had Racine pinned, his knee in the small of his back.

Carlo was doing his best to restrain the elders but Auntie Lou pushed past onto the field. "Keep him down 'til we sort this out," she yelled to her nephew. "Don't you let him up."

"Stay back," Mack shouted, but his aunt came closer.

"Fee," Anthony said. "Look at me." He took her face in his hands and turned it toward his own, distracted a moment by her long black hair. He'd known many of her type in his time. Women blind to the men they stuck by. Such a woman had once loved him. "Please tell me who Racine asked you to locate."

"I speak only to defend him," she said, finally, looking out from under long lashes. "He asked how to find Lahara the Touched. She checks her nets at midday and I told him so."

Anthony knew who Lahara was. Her husband Switch was the metal man caring for his horse.

"Why Lahara?"

"Her *whispers* will help rid us of the Touched infection."

Anthony tried to process. Lahara held Records of the city's infrastructure, of architecture, geography. What information did Racine seek? The Vaulter would grab her, hurt her if necessary, to retrieve it, whatever it was. Anthony wouldn't let that happen.

Fee had wrenched free and was running onto the field. Anthony followed, eye on the Vaulter still pinned by Mack. He had a bad feeling, and as he approached the group he saw Racine's hand snake out in the darkness into the satchel lying beside him.

A flash of silver.

"Watch out," Anthony shouted, but as Mack and Digger turned to his voice, Racine grunted, and Anthony watched the Vaulter flip over and sweep his Prod across Digger and Mack and Carlo and Auntie Lou, discharging the current. They dropped, each one, soundless and twitching, to the ground.

Fee stopped, hands raised in defense, but Racine passed her, ignoring the screams of the elders, to train his Prod on Anthony. The charge pulsed and Anthony fell, paralyzed but for the shuddering.

A slow sear radiated across his chest, and through a half conscious haze he watched Racine grab Fee and disappear into the trees. The elders, still shouting, scattered, and before Anthony could think a single other thought, his world dissolved to black.

SWITCH

SWITCH CLIMBED THE ladder leaning against the house and tied the wooden shutters down with a strip of leather. The banging had woken him from a troubled sleep, and he'd slipped from hammock to make the fix before the panels shattered the glass behind them.

He examined the rope he'd replaced in the moonlight—chewed through by animals come down from the roof and gutters—and he made a mental note to return in daylight and set metal around the shutters instead. The winter had been long, and frequent snows sent rats and squirrels into their stores and along their walls to gnaw whatever they were to find. Hemp was flavorful. Leather would be as well.

The sky numbers were the same as before he'd gone to hammock—1.03.2257. So little time elapsed? It felt he'd lain through a dozen darknesses but the moon told a different story. He'd been asleep no time at all. He breathed the cold air, sleep banished and the worries returned.

His apprentice was on Watch until the sun lit the river, his rotation from dusk until dawn. Switch would have caught him up in the morning, but with sleep finished he'd go now. Other sleepless would be at the Watch as well—dice games ongoing—and Switch might find news of his niece.

The wind followed him inside, and he stomped his feet to loose the snow gathered in his treads. He stirred the hearth fire, adding wood to the red embers. The heat would rise through the cut ceilings and he hoped the warmth would keep Lahara and Marly in their hammocks until morning. Although they'd all fallen to bed following supper, it was a restless sleep taken. Marly had cried in nightmares, and Switch's hammock rocked from Lahara's anxious turnings.

He wrapped a flannel skirt around his leggings, hungry now. When he'd returned home for supper after hiking north and south, failed in finding Beatrice, and exhausted, his appetite had been worried away and he'd sipped only broth. His hunger was stronger now, so he helped himself to a piece of twisted salt bread covered with seeds, washing a bite down with ferment before putting the crust and flask in his pocket.

Where the dangum was that girl? His eyes burned from too little sleep and too many miles. Had two days passed or three? New snow covered the ground on the morning Beatrice disappeared. He'd gone out before dawn to lead the blanketed horse to winter grasses. There was nothing to see or hear as he set out, but when Lahara woke at sunrise, Beatrice was already left, along with her clothes and cup and the rolls of dark red and purple cloth she'd been dyeing and sewing since summer.

Marly coughed in his hammock and Switch stopped to listen until the boy quieted. The boy had been distraught at his cousin's leave taking and Switch was thankful his wife knew how to comfort him, but surely he wouldn't have been as upset if he'd spoken out before Beatrice departed.

Marly had observed his cousin preparing her away during the night, but the girl, in her peculiar manner, made him promise to be silent. Just before sunrise she'd dragged her belongings through the snow up to the York and Marly'd watched until she was no longer visible for the weather and distance.

Lahara had found Marly curled in Beatrice's hammock and he was easily convinced to tell what he knew. Beatrice had confided she was to "Rise up and go forth," but none knew what that meant.

Vendors laying wares on the York had seen the girl pass north, and mute Myra selling tea gestured she'd continued west, but even as Switch and Reko picked up Beatrice's trail on Seventy-ninth, the flurries began again and by Third Avenue her tracks were covered in soft white and it was as if she had never been at all.

Switch set his hood over his long tangled braid and lit an oil stick in the hearth. He stepped quickly outside with the smoky torch, staying the chimes with his hand and closing the door tight behind him. The fire beneath the empty everstew hook was days dead and he stared at the reminder of yet one more thing beyond his comprehension.

Beatrice had taken the pot. Why? She could have shared any stew along whatever journey she made. To steal an everstew was

... Switch struggled to find the right word. It was wrong. Just wrong. He frowned. They'd need replace the silver kettle, but that was another day's worry.

He should have seen this end in the beginning. In fact, he had seen this end, but Lahara had convinced him of Beatrice's safety. False safety. Hadn't his wife spoken of Beatrice's odd words? Words that increased in fervor in the days before her leave-taking.

The girl had directed her aunt to paint the top and sides of their doorframe with the wet of a cut beet. Why should they mark their home? But Beatrice insisted so Lahara had made the blood red marks to appease her only niece.

Switch rubbed at one of the stains with his thumb but the color was deep in the bare wood. It would take salt and strong wheat wine to remove the marks. He'd let Lahara see to that, as it was she who'd indulged the girl.

He crossed the dark street and climbed the rise to the snow-covered path running along the side of his gated workshop and behind Reko's hut. He followed the path through the low rubble hills between the York and the river, holding his flame ahead to watch for tiny beasts whose teeth were sharp.

The night was quiet enough that he could hear river splashings as he traveled south. The only structure remaining on this path, a building similar to his tenement, had been abandoned when the family's oldest died and the youngest moved west to make a new start. Switch had scaled the back scaffold recently to reclaim the last of the building's glass for his own window frames. The wind whistled through the broken walls and the sharp smell of fungus burned his throat. He hurried past to avoid the razor mouth creatures that inhabited the open and crumbling rooms.

The Watch at Seventy-second overlooked the river from the plaza above the fields. It had been many years since the East River had kept a day Watch, and many years since all four lookouts along the river were filled at night, but this platform was active in the dark, and every person of age and fortitude rotated time.

The message birds roosting below had homed there for many generations and journeying neighbors were encouraged to carry a bird. Switch often traveled with one of the larger sleek gray pigeons, transporting the messenger to salvage or trade in a woven grass basket and letting it fly back with spellings from afar, but his favorite had been found died recently in the roost, and he hadn't yet chosen another.

He stepped from between the steel skeletons lining the north side of Seventy-second and onto the torch-ringed plaza. Gamers huddled around a fire calling wagers, and at the far end of the overlook the tented Watch platform had a clear view of the river and shores below. Switch recognized journeyman Tinny in the local group of sleepless—no surprise seeing him gaming here.

"Horse man," Tinny called. "Throw your vouchers at me." The gambler laughed, but his expression changed as Switch approached. "Wha?" he said. "Bad news?"

"My niece's gone two days now," Switch told him. "Any word?"

"Ari's daughter?" he asked, and when Switch nodded, his eyes became sad. "I've been at the downtown," he said. "Haven't heard anything, my friend."

"It's likely she went north," Switch said, remembering that Tinny lost a sister to the Group that Left—they also had gone north. From all over the city Touched had gone north. Like fish pulled in a current. Some, like Ari and Beatrice, followed a loved one pulled. Tinny's sister had snuck away before he knew to follow and had never returned.

"Sometimes people make new starts," Tinny offered. "Made one myself. Much time passed before I saw my Ma again."

But Switch knew Beatrice hadn't left for a new start. The fux Touched stole her, like what made her mother leave.

The stacked roads above threw moon shadows across the brick and stone clearing. When he was young there had been a ramp— since collapsed—and he could climb the lowest level of the construction that circled the city. Hard clear tubes edged each level of the road, smooth as stone, transparent as water, and the children found sport in slinging rocks at them for the tone they released when struck.

The gambler threw his dice, grinding his teeth as they fell. Switch waited until chits were exchanged before speaking again. "What news from the downtown?"

Tinny pulled a flask from his wrap and removed the stopper, scrunching his face in concentration. "More curse of the

Touched," he said. "Two brothers missing. Twins. Their uncle found their boat anchored in the southern water."

"Drowned?" Switch asked, thinking of the dangerous sea below the city.

"Who's to know?" Tinny said. He clicked his dice. The other players, ignoring their conversation for worry of the game, clicked their own dice in response. "There was a shore alarm, too," he added. "I was lucky to be gaming for surely there'd be no sleeping through it." He shrugged and took a long sip. "The true be told, I think they're jumpy raising the gongs in the south, but Mack McKay brung me uptown before the Runner come to tell what the alarm was on about."

Switch leaned in and spoke softly, a bad thought crossing his mind. "About those twins gone missing," he said. "Where from?"

Tinny considered a moment before answering. "Chelsea Wood. One *Touched with Science*, one with *Math*," he said, and Switch's heart sank at his words.

Reko had his back to the Game, facing the river under the oiled canopy. Switch whistled, feet crunching in the snow, and Reko turned, eyebrows furrowing at the sight of his mentor out during sleep times.

Switch stuck his light stick in the drift. He broke the crust he carried, dropping half into the Watch everstew, and poured the rest of his ferment into the kettle with the bread. The liquid hissed against the side of the pot and he lowered his face to the steam.

"Brung news?" Reko asked, his concentration split between the man and the river.

Switch regarded his apprentice. His cheeks were ruddy in the cold and his uncovered head, dark with ink, was shiny with applied oil. Lahara thought his attentions vain but Switch knew it was clan pride compelled Reko display his crest and brands.

"You see Tinny?" he asked. "Sleepless with the dice tonight?" Reko nodded. "He just come up from the downtown."

"Is Beatrice gone south?"

"I don't think so," Switch said, dipping his cup into the

everstew and tasting the yeasty soup. "It's likely she went north from Seventy-ninth."

"We found no trace on that road," Reko said.

"No trace at all," Switch agreed. He opened the roost below the platform, tossing the rest of his seeded bread inside for the pigeons. "But a ricer come to trade told a covered raft had been on the Lex stream in days past. So I went north across Third."

"Beatrice got on a raft?"

"Maybe. I followed the water uptown. Slippery going. After many hours I get more news. A man on the ridge at Ninety-eighth says a raft sailed north on the same morning Beatrice left."

"If she was on water," Reko said thoughtfully, "she'd be ashore by One-hundred-seventh. The stream ends at the rocks there."

"I run out of daylight to keep searching, but both men said this. They heard a singing from the raft and thought it was a Disconnect. That strange sound they make. I say it may have been the girl. In her Touched she also has made odd sounds."

At first she'd hummed, words obscured with a hand, but more recently she'd been singing a loud, strange melody. Switch had no idea what those rippling notes and unfamiliar words come from her meant. He had begged Lahara to make the girl desist.

Shouts of recognition went up from the sleepless as the silver numbers in the sky changed from 1.03.2257 to 1.04.2257. Switch whistled and Reko clapped along. For a brief moment Switch felt the renewal brought with the changed number, but the feeling was fleeting and in the next he was once again thinking of the lost.

"We'll follow the Middle Road tomorrow," Reko said. "Vouchers will find someone who knows where Beatrice is."

Switch held up a hand. "No plans until you've heard my words."

"What words?"

"The Runner's not been for some days, but distressing relay arrives with Tinny. From below Crease."

Reko's eyes grew large and he looked quickly to where the bearded man wrestled arms with another, their wagers echoing across the plaza. "What's happened?"

"It's your brothers. They're missing on the water."

When Switch returned from the plaza he found Lahara standing in the dark, cold kitchen, the fire gone out and the lamp unlit. He wrapped his arms around her growing belly, a belly so large even at this early date he predicted triplets slept inside.

She started at his touch. "I woke and you were gone. I meant to make tea for your return." She yawned. "But *whispers* held me and the tea is unboiled."

"No matter," Switch said. "You're back to hammock now. It's not many more sleep hours before sunrise."

"Reko will hike with you tomorrow?" Lahara asked, as he guided her up the creaking stairs, hand on her elbow.

The thin quilt of her robe threw sparks in the darkness. Lahara would miss the boy—Marly would be dejected—and Switch chose his words carefully. "I'll take the horse," he said. "Reko will be returning below Crease when Watch ends this night."

She stopped on the landing. "What? Why is Reko to leave?"

Switch shook his head. He wouldn't upset her with discussion of Reko's brothers. Beatrice gone was worry enough. "This talk will wait," he said. "We'll need help Reko prepare his away tomorrow, then I'm again to search for the girl. We'll sleep a while. First light will come sooner than we're ready."

ANTHONY

THE TEMPERATURE HAD dropped and the sky was lighter to the east, the path and parkland slipped from charcoal to pale gray. Sunrise was not far off.

Digger was shouting. Anthony's head was pounding. He grabbed his pack and started towards the ferryman. Mack was on his knees, heaving into the snow, a blanket over his shoulders. Auntie Lou was still down, covered with a weaving, and just beyond, Carlo was helping Digger up, neither solid on his feet.

"I will paint that hairless mariner with honey and invite ants to feast," Digger screamed, falling backwards, and Carlo coughed, wrapping his arms around his chest.

With shouts and a ruckus, the elders were spilling out of the little blue house. Sister Bob—Anthony recognized the aunt with the light green turban—yelled, "They're waked," and an uncle shouted, "Fill the flasks."

"Easy breaths," Anthony said to Mack. Legs tingling, Anthony tripped in his boots and they lurched together to the ground, the landing softened by a quilt he hadn't realized he was wrapped in.

"Auntie Lou," Mack croaked. Her eyes, clouded but visible through partially open lids, fluttered at his voice. Mack slid his arms around her, lifting himself and his aunt in one motion. He swayed beneath her weight and took off toward the blue house. One of her pink sneakers had fallen off and lay in the snow.

"Dangum fux I can't feel my feet," Digger howled.

"I know there is much to explain," Anthony called, scooping up the sneaker and limping to catch up. "Hear me, Mack," he said. "Fee has left with Racine."

The ferryman staggered at his words but didn't slow. Digger, coming up fast behind with Carlo, roared, "Left for where?"

"To find Touched Lahara."

"You are no friend," Mack said, walking backwards as he accused. "Why didn't you warn what he would do to my family?"

"I will track them like supper," Digger shouted. "I will drag my sister back and feed that man to the river."

Anthony pressed his hands over his temples. "I didn't realize who he was until it was too late," he explained, hurrying alongside the ferryman. "Your sister is helping him. She admitted as much to me. And there are others of his kind just as dangerous."

"What kind is that?" Mack shouted. "He's your brother."

"He isn't. I promise this is true."

Mack missed a step and fell forward to one knee, just managing to keep Auntie Lou from tumbling out of his arms. Anthony crouched beside the ferryman, knowing his explanations sounded deranged, but needing to speak the truth. "He, and others like him, have come from across the Hudson, from below the ground, to claim what's theirs. To take their *whispers* back."

Mack climbed to his feet. "I am not Touched but I know of *whispers*. You can't take back dreams. Or thoughts. Or words."

Anthony closed his eyes. He'd walked down that corridor. Seen the naked bodies. The splattered walls and sticky floors. He opened his eyes and looked directly into Mack's and again, told the truth. "Yes, you can," he said sadly. "With much blood."

In the five minutes since the ferryman had carried Auntie Lou into the house, the pale sun had lit the eastern sky and the forest had come alive. Digger followed his brother inside, but Anthony, unsure if he was invited, had stopped at the door. Although Mack had sent the elders back to their own houses to sleep, Sister Bob remained outside, and the bushy-eyed uncle kept vigil, too.

Anthony paced. Every hour without antivirals meant more sick, more infected, but how could he leave for the Museum before securing Lahara's safety. Sister Bob approached with a cup of everstew. "It's Brother Stava dragged you all closer to the path," she said. "A long night's work."

Her brother dismissed her praise. "The sisters brung hot blankets and rang bells until morning to keep the wolves away."

Anthony realized he still held the pink sneaker and he handed it to Sister Bob in exchange for the stew. The bitter broth was thin, but the seeds and dried vegetables were chewy and helped fill his stomach. "Thank you. I will find payment," he said, and Sister Bob put her hand to his cheek. "Your face is sad, hairless man."

The door to the blue house slid open and Mack stepped out with his brother and cousin. "She's sleeping," Mack said, "but will need seeing after. You'll make a rotation. Like with old David." Sister Bob nodded, and hurried inside.

Brother Stava, face grim, waited until the door closed, then grabbed Mack's arm. "It all happened so suddenly and our niece was making her away. I tried to intervene, but they were off the path and the darkness stopped my feet."

"Don't worry, uncle. We'll fetch her home."

"They'll have gone to his cruiser," Anthony said. "Hidden somewhere on the water."

"We need more eyes." Mack said. "I can pay big prizes for assistance. We have much to compensate a search team."

"No need to search," Anthony said. "Fee told me Racine will be at Lahara's nets by midday. Just get there first."

"Carlo will attend the elders while we're gone," Mack said.

Uncle Stava spit in the snow. "We can stoke our own fires and care for David and Lou. Carlo goes with you."

The ferryman nodded and wrinkled his brow. "Hairless Anthony as well," he said, looking for confirmation. "Yah?"

Anthony shook his head. "I can't delay this medicine delivery any longer."

Mack held his hand up. "You will help find Fee and remove Racine from our river. The medicines are not to make worry. Carlo will deliver your goods." Anthony hesitated, and Mack continued. "I will trust you and you will trust Carlo. Good trade."

Anthony regarded the ferryman's cousin. He'd spent the night unconscious in the field, felled in an act of violence he'd not experienced before. His face was scratched and his eyes were pained, but he was uncomplaining, unquestioning and attentive to Mack's request. Having Carlo transport the medicine was a good idea. This was his territory and he knew the shortcuts to reach the Museum quickly. Anthony nodded. "Good trade."

❖❖❖

"What about weapons?" Anthony asked as they escorted Uncle Stava into his small orange house. "I have a knife."

Mack lit a lamp, revealing windowless walls lined with books that smelled of mold and spice. "We're not to need weapons," he said, helping his uncle onto the bed. "I will trade for my sister."

"Racine won't barter. Do you have knives?"

"Why these questions when we need catch the current?"

"Because Racine threatens everyone and won't stop until each *whisper* is recovered. The people have to defend themselves. This isn't going away."

Mack shook his head. "This conflict ends today. My sister will return home and we will not again allow Racine near us or Lahara or her family."

Uncle Stava smacked his hand on the bedroll. "You are not hearing his words."

"Uncle," Mack said. "Sleep now. We'll secure Fee and fix everything to good."

"Do not condescend," Uncle Stava shouted. His face was flushed and his mouth trembled. "If a beast were galloping on the avenue you would bang a drum. If the waters were rising to overflow the riverbanks you would move your neighbors to higher ground. You are a child of peace and don't know the signs, but I recognize what is happening. Never again the Bad times. You need send warning. You need help send all Touched to Hide. Your father and his grandfather would agree. It's the Bad times come again and it's the *whispers* brung them to us."

Mack flinched at his uncle's words. The Bad times were not so many generations removed that the threat of their return didn't haunt the people.

There was much Anthony couldn't know about what had happened during the years of Cocooning, but the second time he'd been stirred to consciousness, wakened by the steady chirps and hums of a system come alive, the Vaulters had found themselves right in the middle of those Bad times.

It was an unrecognizable, isolated city in 2123. Treacherous sulfur waters circled the island and feral animals ruled ruins and charred rubble. New York had been divided into enclosed districts, the passages home and highway to violent journeyman and outsiders. Fresh water was a currency and the island's natural springs and wells were battlegrounds. A fungus had destroyed much of the food and the resulting shortages created desperate people. The population was half it had been fifty years prior. Melly sent two men into the city one night during that short Awake to try and restore network updates. They'd crossed the Hudson near One-hundred-fourteenth and were never seen again.

"Your ignorance will not change the circumstance, nephew. It wouldn't take many men or many days to seed the Bad times."

Mack bowed his head. "Understood."

"I have something," Uncle Stava said. He climbed down and dragged a wooden crate from beneath the bed. "You brung me spellings, a long time ago." He rustled in the straw, holding a book to the lamp. Although the cover was peeling, the title was still legible—*Classical Weaponry of Japan.*

Anthony took the book as Uncle Stava lifted a heavy staff with pointed knobs along the length. "Kanabo," he said, handing the weapon to Mack. He dug again, pulling out a carved wooden stick with a studded weight chained to the end. "Chigiriki," he explained, waving it over his head, letting the chain and weight fly.

Anthony and Mack ducked. "Uncle," Mack asked. "Where do these come from?"

"I copied from the pages," he said. "Poured the metal myself." He tore through the dried grass and lifted from the bottom a shallow tray filled with black stars and iron spikes and thin discs.

"Shuriken," Uncle Stava said proudly, touching the sharp point of a star and watching the blood bubble from the puncture on his fingertip. "Throwing weapons."

Anthony would have preferred to travel camouflaged by trees and steel on land, but water was the fastest route to Lahara's fields. The idea of sharing the river, being visible in the morning sun yet unable to see the Cover-enabled cruiser, made Anthony uncomfortable.

He looked over his shoulder but saw only a flat raft receding in the distance and shadows of the steel skeletons on Randall's—

Blowburn—Island across the choppy water. He reached for Uncle Stava's ninja stars and felt for his knife. It helped to know the sharp weapons were just a pocket away.

Mack wanted to paddle south through the tall weeds at the shoreline, but Anthony, afraid they'd run into the cloaked and moored Vaulter cruiser, insisted they sail mid-river. Neither Mack nor Digger could fathom an invisible boat, and no explanation convinced them. Anthony likened the cover protocol to a magician's smoke and mirrors but the brothers had no reference for that either and after a quick discussion—argument—Mack threw his hands up and paddled out to where the current propelled them downtown.

Digger, the chigiriki's weighted chain sticking from the cuff of his boot, used a battered long glass, some type of telescope, to scan the coves along the riverbanks, looking for what Anthony had described as a clear outline around the Vaulter boat, the only indication of its location they might see in the sunlight.

With the wind behind them, the light canoe reached the wide section of the river in just a short time. "We'll put to shore inside the stone," Mack said, pointing to the white wall that ran to the coast at Seventy-ninth—the East River district's northern border.

A ramshackle lean-to on top of the wall, the remnant of a Watch platform, threw shade on the dense cattails growing along the riverbank and on the fur-draped man crouched outside digging the tall, starchy plants from the frozen mud.

"Halloo, Charles," Mack called as they came ashore.

"Mack McKay, what brings you off the water?"

"We've come for Fee. She left last night, joined with a nasty one called Racine."

The man broke the cattail stalks in his hand. "Hard to lose a sister that way," he said, stuffing the roots in his bag.

"I won't lose her. She'll be brung home, the man dealt with."

"He's a stranger dressed as a lover," Digger said. "He spit a fire at my aunt and she's almost half dead."

"There's Bad times in his eyes," Mack said. "He comes with his clan. Hairless, the all. My friend is recently left them for a new start and speaks the true of his people."

Charles's expression didn't change. "My grandfather's father had fires put on his family during the Bad times," he said. "It was a clan come from the Queensland." He slung his root bag over his shoulder. "I'll raise a flag for the Runner and send relay."

"There's more to tell," Mack added. "I say this to you now, Charles, to protect your son and the others hearing *whispers*.

"You, with no love for the Touched, are to protect them?"

"Who loves a disease?" Digger said, anger in his voice. "Your Reynaud resisted. Our mother was away with The Group that Left and our arms couldn't hold her back."

"That's no matter now," the ferryman said. "Listen what I speak. The hairless plan is to harm all Touched. We go now to warn Lahara. Send your son to Hide."

"We surely won't leave," Reynaud's father said. "Never again the Bad times."

Lahara's fields began at Seventy-seventh Street behind overgrown hedges. Tangled roots wrapped over and through the splintered boardwalk and the river splashed against the crumbled sea wall, spraying the men as they walked toward the jetty at the foot of Seventy-fifth.

"There's peoples on the shore," Digger said, looking through his glass, and Anthony froze. Had Racine already arrived?

Mack took the scope and studied the scene. "That's Switch. And Lahara. And Switch's boy from below Crease." He lowered the glass. "Looks like they're pulling the cloth from the outrigger."

The husband of Lahara didn't understand what Mack and Anthony were telling him, but Lahara listened and watched with intent eyes. She and a young boy were trying to keep a fire lit in a circle of bricks, placing hay knots and braided grass on the smoky wood. Clay pots balanced on the brick, and Lahara was checking each with a finger as she eyed Anthony and the McKay brothers.

"This is about the Touched, you're saying?" Switch asked, neck muscles tight as he and his apprentice whacked the canoe with their fists, trying to break the ice around the lateral support.

"It's about Lahara. Because of her *whispers*, yes," Anthony said, stealing a glance at the woman who'd lifted a pot from the fire and was splashing hot water onto the ice. The morning sun reflected on beads and glass tied into her dark, shiny curls, and she turned to catch his eye. Embarrassed, Anthony looked away.

"Friend," Mack said, helping rock the frozen outrigger. "I wouldn't leave my ferry a day to share nonsense with you. There's a danger approaches."

"Why would a man bother a woman with a belly full of baby?" Switch asked.

"He wants her *whispers*," Anthony said.

"Have 'em," he snorted. "No good come of *whispers* in my house."

"Switch, be true," Mack said. "Remember Lahara told where to dig for cans? You traded a long season with what you pulled from that salvage."

Lahara spoke now. "And when the sliding muds filled the Trump it was *whispers* revealed a stairway between rubble and water," she said. "Saved a man that day."

Switch shrugged and Lahara turned back to the fire. It was an old argument she didn't seem inclined to continue.

A gust of wind off the water fanned the small flame and the hay balls caught with little puffs of smoke. Lahara warmed her hands over the blaze without speaking again.

"You're asking me to send my wife inland when my house is already broken," Switch argued, shoving the canoe with the heel of his boot. "My niece is *Newly Touched* and absent three days. Reko heads below Crease as soon as we get this fux boat on the water, his own brothers missing and a mother needing comfort. What next?" He pointed to the boy who picked barnacles at the end of the jetty. "Should I send Marly to dance with Disconnects?" he asked, underscoring each frustrated word with another kick, and as his tirade finished the canoe broke free of the ice.

"What harm sending Lahara away for a day?" Anthony asked.

"You have Mack believing your words, but I'm not so quick to agree," Switch said. "Any stranger can tell a bedtime story."

"I'm no stranger," Mack said. "It was a bad one left us lying for dead. Me, my brother, my cousin, my aunt."

"Then you should be home with yours, not here with mine."

Anthony scanned the river. The shone so brightly and the air was so fresh and this family so busy in their morning. Lahara and the apprentice were loading Reko's possessions into the canoe. Switch put his hand on his wife's shoulder and she smiled at him. Marly stood at the very end of the jetty, half a city block's length into the river, arms above his head singing into the wind, joyous, and spinning, his cape blowing around him. Why would any of them believe this crazy story of danger and *whispers*?

Sunshine. And then, a shadow fell and a flock of the strange river birds rose en masse with a rush of wings from the fields. The ice creaked along the jetty and pulled apart in dark, lacy cracks that widened and filled with water splashing on the concrete.

"Quakes," Switch shouted over the deep vibrations, but Anthony knew better, and just a few seconds later the air shimmered and Anthony felt he was looking through tiny, scattered bubbles of a hand blown glass.

Lahara dropped the bag in her arms. Its contents, cloth and leather, spilled in the wet reeds. She shouted to Marly, but the boy was transfixed, watching dark and light coalesce on the water. The sleek white ship—*BRAVO* shining silver on its hull—shuddered into view just a few feet from Marly, and the rumbling ceased and the river went quiet.

"Fux, what?" Switch whispered, letting go of the outrigger. Reko grabbed the canoe, and Switch ran to the jetty, leaving his apprentice knee deep in the frigid shallows to hold the boat steady.

Anthony crouched in tall winter grasses as Racine came down a gangway, silver Prod in hand, tailed by two Anthony recognized as Driscoll and Lear. Racine spoke a few words to Marly and wrapped an arm—the one clutching the Prod—around the boy's thin neck.

"Don't you touch him," Switch hollered, as he and Lahara, with Mack and Digger not far behind, ran out onto the river.

Marly squirmed from Racine's grasp, but the Vaulter grabbed his cape, jerking the boy back and discharging his Prod in the process. A stream of sparks and flame lit the river's surface, churning water and ice into steam where it connected.

"Stop there now," Racine shouted, waving his weapon, and Switch paused, gathering Lahara to him and holding out his arm to keep Mack and Digger from passing.

"Lahara, come alone," the Vaulter called. "Do it and the boy will not be harmed."

Lahara pulled from Switch's arms and backed away, turning to call, "I come to you now."

Anthony eyed the span from the shore to Marly, and then crawled through the weeds to the riverbank. "I'm going out there in your canoe," he whispered to the shivering Reko. "Distract the stranger. Run and make noise on the other side."

Reko didn't understand what was happening but understood the directions, and he raced along the shore to a spot beyond the jetty, shouting in his downtown dialect, "Stranger yah, g'way, yah, ya mad man skink."

Racine turned to him—Driscoll and Lear did, too—and Reko waved his arms for the audience. Mack, following his cue, began to shout as well, and his brother cursed and hollered with him.

Anthony climbed into the canoe and pulled out by hand, head down, concealed under a lip of steel extending the length of the jetty. The current had turned, flowing north now, pushing the canoe against the concrete with soft scrapes and splashes, but he reached the far end undetected, and looped a tether around a bit of protruding metal.

He peeked over the edge. Marly and Racine were just inches from him—so close he could smell the rubber of the boy's boots—and Driscoll and Lear held their thin, silver Prods at the ready. Lahara was almost upon them. She stopped an arms length away and reached for her stepson, her voice strained and her face pale. "Marly, make your good byes and come away to me."

"That's not how it's gonna happen," Racine said, his tone conversational.

"What do you want?"

Racine eyed her. "We need your help finding something. It won't take long, but you'll have to come with us."

Anthony whistled softly to attract Marly's attention but the boy was fixed on Lahara. Switch and the McKays, still some distance away, inched closer, and on the cruiser's upper deck, a shadow passed across a porthole. Was it Fee?

"I don't understand," Lahara was saying. "What boat is this?"

"Like it?" Racine asked. "We've got heat and food and wine."

Anthony struggled to remain concealed as the current lifted the canoe above the edge of the jetty, slamming it against the concrete, but at the dull clangs of metal on cement Racine turned and locked narrowing eyes with him.

"Set Cover," Racine shouted, and Driscoll thundered up the gangplank at his command.

Anthony slipped one of Uncle Stava's weapons from his pocket. The Vaulter must have seen the slight movement, for he raised his Prod, discharging a stream that scorched the cement as he shoved Lahara and Marly up the ramp.

Anthony tried to find a clear shot as Switch and Reko and the McKays rushed the gangway. "Incoming," Anthony warned as Lear discharged his Prod from halfway up the ramp.

The current glanced off Reko's arm and the boy tumbled to the ground. Switch dropped to him, shouting, "What did you do?"

"Heads down," Anthony cried, lobbing the razor star. The shuriken caught Lear in the neck and the Vaulter fell and slid head first to the bottom of the gangplank, blood from the embedded points smeared in a trail behind him.

"Stop it," Fee screamed from the upper deck as Anthony flung a second shuriken at the cruiser, then a third, and a fourth onto the deck. One struck Racine's raised Prod, knocking the weapon from his hand to slide under the inflatables tied to the railing.

"This is finished, swamp gas," Digger called, swinging his chigiriki as he climbed the ramp.

Racine grabbed Marly by the scruff of his cape and lifted him to dangle over the fast moving current. "I'll drop him," he threatened, and Digger stopped, uncertain.

"Mack," Anthony called softly from the canoe. "The Prod."

The ferryman nodded, taking the silver laser from the fallen Lear. "There's still breath in your friend," he called to Racine, fingers on Lear's neck. "Your man for ours. Good trade. Yes?"

Anthony let the current pull him around the deep end of the jetty, under the cruiser's raised bow. He tethered the outrigger loosely to a set of hooks on the hull. Marly's legs dangled above, kicking gently.

"No trade," Racine yelled down to Mack.

Anthony stood carefully, taking advantage of the parallel support that kept the canoe balanced. Marly was out of reach. He stepped onto the bench, one hand braced flat against the cruiser, but still the boy was too far above him.

"Raising and retracting," Driscoll called, and a rumble of the ship's engine made overhearing further conversation impossible. At almost the same moment, the cruiser jerked in both a forward motion and starboard turn, and in the surge, Anthony was knocked into the icy water.

Marly shouted to see Anthony flounder and Racine looked down as the cruiser plowed ahead. "Don't worry, old friend," he called to Anthony. "I wouldn't leave you alone in such a state." He smiled broadly and tossed Marly out into the river.

The boy grasped at the air, fingers curling around nothing, cape and tunic up around his neck exposing bare skin as he fell. The ship flashed in the sun and disappeared—along with its passengers—under its cloak of light and waveforms.

Anthony grabbed the canoe, and holding it in front of him, he kicked, letting the tide and his own legs propel him toward Marly. The boy's head was barely visible, the flow carrying them both north and into the mid-river.

Anthony shouted as he navigated closer, and the boy grabbed on, coughing with lips blue from the cold. "Climb in," Anthony directed. "Take the oar." Marly pulled himself up, shivering in what remained of his wet clothes.

· Anthony's frozen hands, unable to grasp any longer, slid from the outrigger. Brackish water rushed into his nose and mouth. He tumbled in the current, and in just seconds the canoe was out of reach. Although Marly flailed with the paddles, he didn't have the strength to turn the boat. Anthony watched him drift north toward the marina at Eighty-fourth, hopeful the boy would find assistance there.

Anthony's teeth were chattering, his exposed skin blue and gray. He'd been in the river nine or ten minutes and knew at these temps he didn't have much time left. The tide was pulling him toward a long stretch of high seawall he'd be unable to climb onto, and although Roosevelt Island to the east was more dangerous, the shore was wide, and Anthony fought the current, swimming a sideways crawl toward the shallow water of the island's beach.

His strokes shortened as his exhaustion grew and soon he stopped, clutching the remains of an old boathouse just off the mid-river island. He felt warm—sweaty, even—and struggled to remove his tunic.

He floated, eyes closed to the sun, watching red and black lights behind his eyelids. Trapped between the splintered, ancient pilings, he could no longer feel his arms or his legs. Someone was speaking to him. Pulling him. He protested, twisting from strong, insistent hands. "Not now," he complained, disturbed.

"Open your eyes," this someone was saying with a voice that smacked his ears.

He peered through squinted eyes. A pole raft. Voices now. Many of them. His bare back scraping over sharp debris. A face was close, breathing onto his skin and into his ears and nose. Hands all over him. Wet clothing pulled off, peeled away, cut away. Blankets covering him. Warm tea poured into his mouth.

"Anthony," a voice insisted. "Anthony." A hooded figure with pale, freckled skin. A Disconnect. He squeezed his eyes shut and opened them again. Deep blue eyes stared out at him from under the light hood. Deep blue eyelash-less eyes. A heart shaped face with no eyebrows.

A long-fingered hand reached up and lowered the hood. "Anthony," she whispered, and he stared, confused. For the Disconnect who had pulled him from the river was not a Disconnect at all.

It was Elizabeth.

SPRING

NADIA

NADIA PULLED HER knees close and held her hands over her ears to away the sound of the screeching pulleys. The ride Topside took only a count of ten five times, but the noise would likely bring on the *whispers*—it had happened before—and she needed not to wander in her mind but to get quickly to the Watch. A Tweet had called from a grating high above the Tunnel, relaying that finally, and thankfully—for Nadia had begun to have worried nerves—Joe Soho's message bird was flyed home and roosting beneath the white-blossomed trees surrounding the tower at Second Avenue.

The sun had risen warm, and as the basket bumped to a stop, Nadia shoved her dull, graying hair under her headpiece and adjusted the flat metal visor to keep the light from her weak eyes. She stretched, extending her arms first to the newly lit sky and then to her feet. Her bones popped in complaint from what had been a short, but cramped journey.

The pulley puller, muscles shiny with sweat from this first exercise of the day, took her payment of a soft skin and wiped his face with it before stashing the leather in a box behind him.

"You're metaled?" he asked, and Nadia raised her tunic to reveal the fine mesh between the cloth and her body. "Don't look thick enough," he said, revealing his own layer of chain and tin.

She shrugged. Her *whispers*, and those of others in the downtown, had remained secret for nearly six years now, shielded from detection, unintentionally in the beginning by deep Tunnels and basements, and later, by design, covered in metals to hide what they had inside. By now the metal was a habit, but on a warm spring day Nadia was inclined to wear less protection for the sake of speed.

It was her husband—*Touched with a Science difficult to explain*—who had discovered that Touched emitted what he called radio waves. Before he died he'd shown how to block the *whispers* from signaling. He reasoned if *whispers* sent messages, it was somebody or something meant to receive them, and that didn't sit well with the cautious communities downtown and in the Tunnels.

They'd been metaling for over three years now, wearing steel and aluminum even before they'd learned of the suspicious men and women come from another place. They'd begun concealment on just the tellings and *whispers* of her husband. There was a word for that. Nadia closed her eyes and let her own *whispers* speak. The word was *emune*, in Yiddish. *Faith.*

The uphill path west—the End—was overgrown with flowers and tangled, knotted vines. White, purple, and orange bursts waved on tall stems, and a clean sea breeze made its way over the low mounds and fences separating the path from the high cliffs that dropped to the southern water.

She whistled hello to a rock climber examining rope knotted in iron rings at the top of the bluffs, and waved a hand to Tunnelers come out to check traps. The woods along the north side of the path were quiet—deceptively so—for she knew eyes followed her.

Neighbors had taken heed the warnings of the hairless man Anthony and the uptown resistance that had grown this winter. Well-hidden militia watched from trees, from rubble, from the roofs of half buildings and scaffolded towers. Her own Rowena would be later with the group patrolling at the Union Square.

She stepped over a narrow chasm stretching from curb to cliff. Sea water churned below, a tiny inlet joining the wide ocean that covered the south forever and completely but for the ribbon of broken towers—the Battery—that jutted from the endless waters almost too far away to see even with the best eyes, and beyond the skyscraper reef, the X Island. The people steered clear of the wide, skull-shaped land, its shores marked with X's taller than three men and wider than two.

That the X Island faced the rancid Brooklyn coast was yet another reason the people kept a distance. Although Nadia had never been so far out in the sea, others had paddled against the waves and come back to repeat the warning of the X's.

Would Joe Soho have gone if not for the medicines? The Vaulters had paid Runners to bring their offers to the people. They would trade medicines and wines and foods for labor—salvage, transport, and strength. They sent gifts of unknown fruits and foods—chocolate, pineapples, bananas—to prove their benevolent intentions. In the Tunnels, the people ate the strange food but ignored their words, for Runners also shared news of violence, theft, and threats.

But then the Vaulter Marilena arrived, come on a ship silver and white like the moon, and when Joe Soho went Topside, the brown-eyed hairless woman made him the same offer circulated before. They would give the sturdy man work on Governor's Island, what they called the X Island. Joe Soho said yes.

The sun felt good on Nadia's skin and she breathed deep, thankful for the eased cough. Rowena said Marilena was a *bracha*—a blessing—for the Vaulter had given Joe Soho the capsules that saved her wife's—Nadia's—life. But Nadia disagreed.

A volf farlirt zayne hor, ober nit zayn nature, she thought. *A wolf loses its hair, but not its nature*. Although the bald woman seemed come with a fair trade, there'd been too many tales of bad deeds and secrets—this was not in dispute—and when Joe Soho left with Marilena to pay his debt doing the Vaulter's work on the X Island, he carried two message birds wrapped in cloth and hidden at the bottom of his travel box.

Nadia looked to the sky, eyes blurry for the tears the glare brought. It had been many days since she'd been Topside, and the silver gray numbers visible though high wisps of clouds crossing overhead today spelled 06.05.2257.

Joe Soho's first message bird had flyed home on the day the numbers shone 5.21.2257. The strips wrapped around the bird's pink leg were covered front and back with many, many of his own careful marks, long spellings that told of digging and carrying stone, of untwisting lengths of cable and porting metal tubes across the tiny island. He wrote of Vaulters onsite connecting small wires with hot tools according to diagrams in hard books, using lenses to make clear the miniature pieces, and of frustrations over failures and lashings out for the same.

Two women come to the X Island for their own barter were

found to be Touched. Although they had no *whispers* heard, the shiny Vaulter stick had made the sound of discovery and the women were disappeared and Joe Soho heard them blamed for the errors and delays. A Vaulter told they'd been removed for treatment and would be sent home. Nobody spoke of them again.

Nadia flinched to remember. Joe Soho's message had raised her own *whispers* of the horrible-place. Men, women and children sent in trains to disappear. Crying. Screams. Smoke.

The Yiddish *whispers* both comforted and terrified, and five years of living Touched had not made it any less so. Even as she remembered the starvation and despair of the horrible-place, the *whispers* lurked with the savory, warm scent of crisp *latkes* and cooked apples.

Nadia smiled. She'd prepared these *latkes* herself, cutting thin slices of dark potato and onion, and mixing the roots with wet egg and grain and salt before dropping spoonfuls in hot oil. She'd boiled apples made sweet with honey and spooned the mash over the potato. *Latkes* with applesauce.

And that wasn't the only recipe the *whispers* had provided. There was the *yoykh*. *The chicken soup*. Nadia had taught the Tunnelers how to make this *zup*. They had no chickens but pigeons and sparrows and plenty of gulls come, and roots and herbs were easy to harvest and barter for Topside. The vats of *yoykh*—like their everstews—simmered day in and day out on the Tunnel platforms.

She was hungry remembering these foods, and felt in her front pocket for the chewy sea plants she carried. The Watch was just a half block further along the path. She'd drop the vegetables into the pot and help herself to a cup of the oyster stew.

Vines rustled at her feet, and instinctively Nadia's hand went to the short spear strapped to her leg. She held still. Although her eyes were weak in the sun she sensed the shadowed movement along the ground behind the brush, and she dove with sure motion, thrusting into the green and black leaves. Ignoring the thorns, she pulled apart the branches and removed the dead rabbit, its pale brown fur just barely damaged by her sharp blade and skilled attack.

She tied her kill to the sash around her waist. Rowena would skin the animal and they'd grill the meat tonight before sundown and light the candles her *whispers* insisted upon every seven sleeps. *Gut shabbos*, she'd say, and those who partook of her Yiddish—more and more in the Tunnels had come to participate in the *whispers* she shared—would respond in kind. *Shabbat shalom*. These were quiet greetings. And if a Vaulter or journeyman stranger were in the Tunnel, the words would not be spoken, the candles not lit, and the *whispers* suppressed. A necessity to remain safe. And most Touched, in their own way, understood this now, and acted accordingly.

The trade tables at the Second Avenue Watch were covered with goods, and a small crowd browsed the wares. Spring vegetables, cooked pies wrapped in cloth, and potted meat were peddled along with medicinal mosses and plants collected from marine cliffs by dangling rock climbers, and chunks of the same cliff ground into powder and offered as poultice.

Rolls of fabric and coils of twisted rope dyed shades of blue were piled over a wooden bench, Grindle's work, a sure sign she had returned and was at market to trade, though Nadia didn't see her friend from the east buildings in among the neighbors. The tall wife of Tark had been away from the downtown seeing to her husband, and Nadia hoped for news of the man who called himself Van Gogh.

Passing over the food tables for the everstew pot beside the platform, Nadia piled her ruffled brown seaweed into the kettle and stirred from the bottom up with the ladle. Harlin of Rutherford sat on the platform overlooking the cliffs this morning. The old man reeked of the ferment, but the day Watch was a short rotation and the path was busy with many eyes to cover his failings. Nadia filled her cup and sipped the stew carefully— someone had contributed a pepper and Nadia's mouth stung with the spice.

"I sent the Tweet at you, ya know," Harlin called down from the wooden tower, glancing away from the southern waters to look at her. "Saw your bird fly in when I came on at dawn. Coulda waited for you to come out whenever ya did, but what's the sense in that? Thought you might want to have your spellings." His eyes narrowed craftily. "It's Joe Soho carried the bird away?"

"Here's your pigeon," a familiar voice called—interrupting—and Nadia turned to the blue-braided Grindle crouched at the bird coop beneath the trees. She had an odd look on her face—one of warning perhaps—so Nadia nodded to Harlin, handing up a voucher in thanks, and came around toward the lanky woman holding the fat gray bird.

"Friend," Grindle said, pulling her close with long arms and whispering in her ear, "Careful the Watch man. *Moserim.*"

Nadia's lip trembled slightly at the Yiddish. *Moserim. Informers.* Neighbors bartering locations of Touched and private information of all types for bread and spirits and vouchers and in some cases, Nadia had heard, an awful trade—the barter of intelligence or errand for the promise no harm would come to a child or sibling stolen and held hidden.

Nadia had seen the long black wagon on thick crushing treads. A Vaulter wagon that rolled through the districts with gifts. Menacing gifts. It was Bad times come, and *Never Again* the rallying cry, a rustle murmured in the night, passed from Touched to neighbor to Touched again. A promise of resistance not easy to keep. *Moserim.* Their own were betraying them.

Nadia smiled and waved back at the old man on the platform. He raised a silver bottle at her and she recognized the shape as one filled with whiskey and gifted by the Vaulters. Aside from the drink he clutched, he seemed most interested in her and the bird. More so than in keeping his eyes on the waters and cliffs.

A flutter of white petals fell on the women—message birds flown up into the trees loosened the flowers—and they laughed a false happiness, whispering behind their smiles, arm in arm. "Come," Grindle said, handing the pigeon to Nadia and pulling her out of the old man's sight to a clearing behind the coop.

Nadia fingered the message fastened around the bird's leg. "Tell me," she said to Grindle. "What of Tark?"

Many Touched had gone to Hide. In the downtown, the Tunnelers had removed ladders and closed entrances. The pulley was disengaged but for certain times. Of course other ways in and out of and through the Tunnels existed, and these secret routes were used to transport supplies, deliver relays, and ferry Touched to safety. Grindle had been hiding below with her husband since winter and the old man with the blue stained hands had recently been taken away through the covert passages.

Grindle twisted her braid in her hand. "The Tark I knew is gone. Any memory he held of his life and family is lost. Van Gogh ... we must call him so ... is well and safe to the north. I won't see him again. He does not know me. He will not miss me."

Nadia saw the sadness in her eyes. "*Es tut mir bahng*," she offered, thinking of her own losses. Her husband. Her young son.

Grindle shook her head and continued. "I'm joining the Vault Companion initiative," she said. "I go tonight to meet the group crossing the Hudson. So many neighbors leaving to make a new start with these strangers. I suppose it's for the vouchers they give to the clans we leave behind." At the confused look on Nadia's face, she added quickly, "No, no, you misunderstand. I mean to search for Lahara. The Vaulters don't know we share ancestors." She smiled a sorrowful smile. "I visited Switch on my return. He's been unable to learn anything of his wife. I made promise to find if Lahara still breathes. And the babies in her belly."

The pigeon in Nadia's hands cooed and she stroked the top of his pearl gray head. "It's what you need do," she said. "I don't have to tell you the danger. You'll be alone."

"In the Vault, yes, but support grows all over the city. As we are doing in the downtown, the people are doing even more in the uptown," Grindle said. "They fill the woods at Fort Tryon and the Norte Inwood and the corridors below the old highways. New Watches are set along the Broadwaterway and across One-hundred-sixteenth. Not just Touched and their families but neighbors who have only memories of the Bad times as told by their great and greater grandparents. The Vaulters may pretend they have no evil in mind, but they queue on our beaches and send their hairless into our communities. We are ready."

The pigeon turned in Nadia's hands—the flutter of his feathers tickled—and he pecked at her finger lightly. She stared at the bird blankly for a moment, so wrapped up had she been in Grindle's updates she'd forgotten about the message.

She untied the thread holding the spellings. The bird flew from her hands as she straightened the thin cloth against her palm. She needed squint for the blur and when the words sharpened she read them slowly, trying to find meaning in the Yiddish that Joe Soho had written.

He'd released the message bird shortly before dawn. Work on the X Island was terminated. The Vaulters had left with a ... *technology*—Nadia didn't understand this word—recovered from ruins. The laborers were to be brung to new assignments.

"No metal will shield the Touched," he had spelled in Yiddish to avoid his words being understood if intercepted. "No Tunnel will hide the *whispers*. I can only guess that distance might help. Leave the city with as many will go," his message instructed. "Send a safe Tweet to find the hairless Anthony. Tell him Vault authorizes a *FIELD WIPE* and *FULL RESTORE*. Few days remain while they finish their work."

Nadia didn't understand these phrases and stopped a moment to contemplate the words and message made more awful for her incomprehension. Only one untranslated line remained at the bottom of the cloth. She squinted to read it, and when the spellings again blurred, it was this time by her tears.

"What?" Grindle cried. "What has happened?"

She was once more in the horrible-place. Men and women and children naked, crying. Screams in the lost languages of lost people. The awful smell. Smoke. She shook her head of the *whispers* and read Joe Soho's closing words aloud, translating as she did.

"It's a *Holocaust* they create. No Touched will survive."

LAHARA

SWEAT CAME IN waves, damping Lahara's drawstring pants and long wide tunic. She pressed her fists into her eyes to shield against the light reflected off the black walls and floor. The glare, inescapable but for the pressure of her hands, was everywhere, and it magnified the pain.

She'd been birthing half a day and a whole night, now in the second day. This is what the blinking symbols told, marking time, but there was no sky to check for the true, and no sun or moon to tell in this Level Twelve room the Vaulters called *Infirmary*. At Level One she might see stars or the sun through the viewing ceiling, but she'd never been to the top of the Vault.

She let her breath out slowly—*one, two, three*—and the pain released her. "I know nothing of this," Fee said, fingers hesitant over Lahara's swollen belly. "Racine tells that Marilena will be returned by nightfall. Her hands will be more help than mine."

Lahara closed her eyes. "The women are birthing and bleeding in the fields," she said, speaking a nonsense she hoped sounded like *whispers*. "They are dying and I will be dead by nightfall, and the babies in my belly, too."

Fee looked troubled. She feared *whispers*, and this was good, for Lahara wanted her uncomfortable and gone away. True be told, the icy-hot birthing was clearing Lahara of the endless *whispers* that had become her constant state of mind. Each seizing cramp made her stronger and pulled her from the fogged world so difficult to escape. She would keep these thoughts to herself, though. Better Fee believed her mind clouded and weak from suffering.

The alerts had been crackling all morning, the lights flickering on the walls. The bursts of sound and symbol that Fee ignored with disinterest relayed a variety of things if you paid attention, and Lahara had been paying furtive, careful attention, learning, most importantly, that the cruiser carrying Seth and Marilena from the X Island—the place Lahara's own *whispers* had sent them—would be returned to Vault much sooner than nightfall.

The onset of the birthing had changed Lahara's options but wouldn't stop her. In fact, Level Twelve put her nearer where she meant to go. No matter Seth was returning. She still had time.

She'd pinched bruises on her leg marking the sleeps between power downs, the purple welts reminding her, when the *whispers* kept her captive, of the schedule she was monitoring. She had counted the marks and knew a power down was slated for this day. Fee would surely leave her as soon as the warning sounded. Fee always spent the brownout with Racine, and Lahara depended on that today. Racine and Fee would be distracted in each other, and she would be free to explore as planned.

Curled on her side, she closed her eyes, hoping for a rest before the tightening began again, but the babies kicked and pushed, pressing against her belly and back. Sabat with the strange voice and peeling skin had come in earlier. He'd pulled her legs apart to feel inside, said it was an *unproductive labor*, and left again without discussion.

"Is he a *doctor*?" Lahara asked Fee, using the Vaulter word, for Sabat had been more than once to check her since Marilena left and she wanted his eyes away. Fee had only shrugged. The dark-haired woman of One-hundred-eleventh, this woman of Racine's, asked no questions, and the not-knowing suited her.

The birthing alone was not easy. At home she'd have hot wine and massages with light oils, and the women would rock her hammock and sing the genealogies. Here there was only Fee, grown with brothers and male cousins, and Marilena, whose own experiences were so foreign that Lahara found little comfort in her attentions. She missed her husband. She missed Marly.

Seth had said she'd be to her home soon, but she didn't trust his words. There was deceit in his eyes. Hadn't he also said there were no other Touched in the Vault even as Lahara knew their *whispers* lurked?

She'd demanded exercise and Marilena obliged her, giving her unaccompanied access to the corridor where she'd walked the loop of Level Eight many, many times, testing doors and finding them always locked. But she kept trying, because she knew there were Touched behind some door, somewhere.

To release the locks she needed the charm the Vaulters wore on their bracelets. She'd watched Marilena hold it up to doorways they passed through. She'd seen the piece that looked like glass under the cuff of Sabat's sleeve. Each Civ bringing meals or attending her private wore the bracelet with the flat, clear square laid over the inside pulse of her wrist.

· The pain wrapped around Lahara's back and hips and she clenched her fists, digging her toes into the mattress. The room darkened, but she wasn't afraid.

"Breathe," a rough voice commanded. Sabat. She hadn't heard him return but here he was, lifting her shoulders and placing a plastic mask over her nose and mouth. "Again," he said hoarsely, and she did and the room lightened as breath filled her lungs. He handed her a robe. "Get up," he said. "You need to walk." And then more gently, "It will help."

The length of the corridor was deceiving, turning in a wide circuit around the exterior of Level Twelve. Lahara had been walking its curve now with enough steps to bring her through two periods of tightening—she crouched to the slick floor for each— and three periods of release, and she hadn't yet circled all the way back. The Infirmary's glass door was still ahead and out of sight.

The hall was quiet but for her own grunts and Sabat's soft footsteps behind her as he followed without comment. Lahara would have tested the handles of the corridor doors but under Sabat's gaze she kept her hands clasped below her belly. That the doors were closed was no surprise. They were always closed, her contact with others minimal.

When she was down to Level Fifteen for the sessions there was only hairless Seth with the deep voice, and the bald woman Patrice who worked the strange panels that joined with her *whispers*. And when she was locked in her small room on Level Eight—her private—any one of several detached Civ-staff serving her meals spoke only to ask what she'd prefer if the food disagreed.

She had no invitation to share the communal meals up on Level Three. She ate alone, as did Fee, though Lahara had visits from nobody and Fee had visits from Racine.

Lahara heard the Vaulter at all hours come to Fee. The sullen woman lit only to his attentions, though his attentions were sporadic, he gone with his cruiser—the boat that brought them— often for days at a time. Lahara overheard arguments between them as to his leaving, but the overhearing had no advantage for her and when they quarreled she'd sink back into her *whispers*, a relief from the shouting.

A siren sounded the power down warning, and Lahara crouched with a pretend tightening, her eyes on the patterns of light scrolling across the wall. There were just a few moments to respond to the siren and Lahara would feign at the birthing until those moments were passed and the hor-verts disabled.

When they were first arrived, Security Civs escorted Lahara and Fee to their privates at power down, but eventually they were given hor-vert codes and directed to return on their own. If they were unable to reach a hor-vert between first and second warning, and if the lifts had gone dark, they were instructed to use one of the stairwells found along each quadrant of the corridor instead.

Lahara had deliberately been late to use her codes last power down in order to explore the nearest stairwell. She'd peeked at Level Ten as she climbed from Fifteen to Eight but had seen nothing and nobody, and the stairs themselves had been deserted.

The siren sounded again and Lahara hugged her belly. She heard Fee ahead, out of sight en route to the hor-vert that would bring her to her private. That left only Sabat to deal with. Lahara wouldn't return to Level Eight. She needed stay on Twelve.

The stairwell clicked open. All doors opened during power down. For safety, Marilena had said. Lights were lowered and air blowers stopped. Lahara would often listen, through the temporarily unlocked stairway, to footfalls and conversations echoing up and down. Sometimes she heard Sabat—no mistaking his odd voice—as he descended to a level far below. He'd be needing head that way now.

"The birthing consumes me," she lied through gritted teeth. "There's not time to get to the moving chamber and push the buttons with the codes."

Sabat was also watching lights on the curved walls. "I have my own wait-duties," he rasped, "but I'll climb first with you. Fee can watch your progress until power up."

"Fee? Her attentions are well on Racine." Sabat's face darkened at the reminder. Fee had told that many resented her keeping company with Racine. In response, vouchers had been paid to men and women to join as companions for other Vaulters. Lahara shook her head. "No matter Fee's business. My swelled feet won't make the steps. I will return to my Infirmary pallet."

"All Touched have to return to their privates at power down."

All Touched? Lahara kept her eyes averted, thankful the false creases of pain she'd created hid the expression of recognition. There was no mystery why Vaulters were not to exchange words with her. How easily a mis-speak carried news. *All Touched*, he'd said. There were others. Sabat gave confirmation.

"No," she insisted, taking a deep breath. "I can't make it."

"I'll carry you."

"There is no sense in that," Lahara snapped. "Nothing happens so quickly in my belly. You yourself said so. My water hasn't even fallen." She sighed. "Isn't my mattress here the same as the one in my private on Level Eight? I spent the last sleep on Level Twelve and my meals have been brung. True, yes?"

Sabat furrowed his face at her argument. "All right," he said. "Power down is just sixty minutes and you will stay in the Infirmary. I don't expect your labor to change in one hour." He held his hand out. "I'll return for you."

Lahara grabbed his cracked palm and pulled herself to standing. "Thank you," she said, moving swiftly around the loop toward the Infirmary as Sabat slipped into the stairwell for his own climb down.

Every morning after first meal, Seth or the woman Patrice arrived to accompany Lahara to Level Fifteen. Every morning she reclined in a chair with a wide belt around her chest and the strange panels glowing on the table beside her. Every morning questions were asked. Pointed questions that raised her *whispers* like she hadn't known possible.

At home her *whispers* came random, scattered and undirected. In the Vault, wrapped in the belt, access to the *whispers* was guided and specific and on demand.

They'd brought her here to answer a particular question, and she had done so for them. She'd found the building called *Admin*, a secret place unmapped, unmarked, its location unknown even to the men and women who took their directions from those inside it. A building broken now and tumbled in pieces on Governor's Island—the X Island—buried deep under a refuse carried by floodwaters.

But after Lahara located Admin, and described the damage and depth of the materials once held in a series of bays in the *Global Data Management Project* headquarters, they informed her she was not yet finished. Seth was exuberant with the success of her *whispers*, and as he left to survey the X Island ruin and begin salvage of the mysterious dense cube that her *whispers* called the *Heaven Interface*, he'd promised her work in the Vault would soon be over. Soon.

And so the routine was established, each success creating another need for answers and more time in the chair connected to belt and panels. Winter turned to spring and as the Vaulters' access to her *whispers* grew, so did Lahara's belly, and her time spent in the *whisper* world grew longer and deeper. She grew more frightened as well. She'd been promised punishments—locks never opening, light turned to shadow, sound removed—for non-compliance, and she expected such to materialize at any time.

Lahara grasped the cool metal railing and took a long look down through the power-downed stairway, twisting her neck to make certain Sabat was away and not to return. Satisfied at the silence, she stepped off the landing. Although the stairs were dark, red glow spots and arrows along the edges gave some guidance.

Barefoot, leaning backwards to balance her belly, Lahara descended carefully, reaching with her toes for the rubber treads on each step. At the sound of voices below she stopped, but both the voices and her alarm faded as the Vaulters speaking quietly exited at Level Fourteen. After another moment—waiting to suffer a tightening that left her weak and sweaty and clear headed—she continued down. At Level Seventeen she opened the door.

The corridor looked the same as those on the other levels. Symbols on the walls told forty-six minutes remained until power up. Not wanting to waste any of them—she didn't know exactly how fast the numbers changed—Lahara set off to find the double silver doors singular to this level. Doors leading to the Rails.

Lahara had spent many *whisper* sessions exploring Admin. Although Seth cared only about the Heaven Interface and a reconstruction of its movements within the rubble, in order for Lahara to locate it she needed to understand the layout of the Governors Island building. Floor by floor, she'd inspected the rooms, studying each at length, and cataloguing the contents.

Joined with the glowing panels that Patrice manipulated, Lahara could expand the details of her *whispers*, framing and holding them stationary, and while they hung frozen, she could turn and refocus, moving through the space and through time to uncover layers of information and the true within them.

It was during one of these studies that she had first seen it. The *model*—instinctively she kept the *whispered* word unshared with Seth and Patrice—was the height of two men, and round as a tree trunk too wide to wrap her arms around. She'd held the *whisper*, manipulating the background clicks as Patrice had shown how to do, examining the shaft.

Several extensions—branches—radiated out at different heights. One stretched from the tower at the height of her knee, another at an arms length above her head and a third at the very top, twice her own tall away. She didn't know what the model was meant to do and she inspected it more closely.

At the prodding of Seth—the Vaulters grew anxious when *whispers* caused her go silent—Lahara turned her attention from the curious column and instead described bookshelves and the shape of the white tiles on the floor. In her first act of non-compliance, she omitted from her description the room's focal point, the pillar rising from that tiled floor.

The strange construction remained in her thoughts even after the session ended, and back in her private her *whispers* rose free to bring her to the same place. In the familiar crushing hum, she was pulled into a group of men and women observing the model. She watched a man open the column along a seam, like two sides of a walnut, she thought, but before she could see inside, a pressure pulled her from the *whisper*.

The next morning she was anxious to begin exploring again. Patrice connected the belt and panels and in a few clicks Lahara entered Admin, opening the model the way she'd seen done, kneeling to examine the interior, beginning at the bottom. There was much to see, and by the time she stood to continue her inspection, Lahara knew what she was viewing. The Vault.

She recognized specifically the gardens filled with rows upon rows of miniature plants. She stepped back to see the very top and counted down the divisions, one number for each section. The countings confirmed her guess. The plastic garden corresponded to the Vault's Level Eleven. The hothouse gardens.

It was just a few seconds in real time—a whole afternoon in the *whisper*—before Lahara was pulled back by the admonishing words of Patrice who grew impatient when answers to her questions were slow in coming. Undiscouraged by her attentions diverted from the model, Lahara made time the next day and for many days after, in moments stolen from the sessions with Seth and Patrice, to examine the column, learning much about the Vault and its branches.

She discovered communications on Level One. Cocoons and stasis on Levels Two and Three. Living quarters on Eight through Ten. Infirmary and laboratories and mortuary on Twelve. Kitchen and water services on Fourteen. Power on Eighteen and Nineteen and a core of incomprehensible machinery and catwalks running through the center of the model from Sixteen through Twenty-four. Security on Twenty-six.

She found stables and leisure rooms, libraries, dining halls and vast, unlabeled spaces. That she didn't understand the functions of many levels or even the reason this place existed at all didn't matter. What she did grasp was enough for her purposes.

The branches radiating from the model indicated passages out—to the Bridge on Level One, to the River on Level Six, and on Level Seventeen to the Rails.

Forty-two minutes until power up.

The silver doors seemed further from the stairwell than indicated on the model, and Lahara grew anxious as she followed glow dots along the circuit. To her left, a long glass inner wall reflected some of the light flickering on the outer, and although the interior was shadowed, she could see into the rotunda and the convoluted machinery reaching the height of the level and descending below, surrounded by catwalks and ladders and cables.

Bracing the small of her back with her hand, she hurried down the corridor toward a huge black gate, stopping briefly to examine the steam pipes surrounding it. She'd seen similar. On her first day in the Vault, Lahara had been led through a wet cave and tunnel to the same type of enormous entrance. Racine had directed her and Fee into the moving room he called Freight. The journey to Level Fifteen—to Seth—in the Freight had been terrifying, the descent wrenching her ears and drawing vomit to her throat.

Continuing past the Freight as a cramp caused her cry out, she stumbled ahead. After one minute, according to the symbols on the wall, the tightening eased, and thirty-six minutes remained.

The heavy doors to the Rails opened with a pop sounding like the stopper loosened on a ferment bottle. It was a stale, earthy air come in from the darkness, a scent of iron and ash and rock, and Lahara wrinkled her nose and sneezed at the dusty whiff.

If she were home she'd be carrying a fire stick. In the Vault there were no fire sticks, for dark turned light the moment a door opened or a corner turned. But this entry raised no lights, not even the dims of power down, and the meager glow spilled from Level Seventeen was just enough to make visible a ramp, the width of the doors, bordered by stone walls on each side, disappearing into the darkness.

Lahara hesitated, waiting for her eyes to adjust, but the black ahead offered no glimmer, no symbols on the walls, no glow spots on the floor. Immobile between the open doors, she stared into the dark without a plan, and the minutes passed.

She'd not known what she would find. The different branches on the model were labeled only *Bridge* and *River* and *Rails*, and her *whispers* had proved to be of no use in illuminating the actual Vault or its passages.

In the single accounting given as to her *whispers*, the Vaulter Patrice had described their scope. She told that Lahara's encompassed a physical area covering the old New York City and waters, including islands and other nearby lands they called boroughs. Bounded by time, Lahara's *Records*—the Vaulter word for *whispers*—stretched from pre-history to the termination of the transmissions, a length of time and concept too large to comprehend. But, like much happened in her world, she could ignore without consequence all that confused.

The relevant portion of Patrice's disclosure was that New Jersey and the Vault were not included in her *whispers*. Briefly, Lahara had wondered if anyone had those Records, or had those little bits been lost on a wind carried them away?

In the end she'd put away her curiosity and instead set out to determine, by investigation rather than *whispers*, which passage would bring her home.

Forcing herself to surface from the daze created by the sessions, Lahara had, with great concentration, discounted first the passage leading to the Bridge at Level One. Many Vaulters climbed to levels above her own during power downs and it would be risky to head the same direction even though exiting at the Bridge would be ideal.

She turned her thoughts to the second passage at Level Six, the one through which she'd come into the Vault. The problem discovered in the model was that stairwells did not open on Six— the only access through either the hor-vert or the Freight.

She had no code for Level Six. The code she'd been given transported her by hor-vert only to Level Eight, either up or down, depending on where she was coming from, and then around the circular Level to open at her private. The Freight was not an option either. Apart from the day she'd arrived, Lahara had not been inside it, and she had no knowledge of what made it work.

And so she focused on the passage labeled Rails, though she didn't know how far the passage extended or where it would emerge. She required more information to proceed. This power down and the *whisper* relief brought by the tightenings might be her only and last chance to find what she needed.

Thirty-one minutes.

Lahara crouched in the doorway, pain gripping her once more. The babies kicked through the cramp and she rubbed her belly, reminded that if she slipped back into *whispers* or inaction without passing through the door, and if the minutes ended while she did so, many days would pass before she could again attempt this. Breathe, she said to herself as she inhaled and exhaled clarity through the tightening.

Thirty minutes. The numbers changed so quickly and she was anxious with the hurry. She needed move now. She stepped through the doors held open by their own weight. The ramp was cool under her feet and she took another step on the ridged metal, her purpose stronger than her fear.

Moving from slim light into the black, she kept her arms out front, feeling her way as she continued up the incline. After just a few moments in the darkness, the tips of her fingers hit a wall, bending to the knuckle and scraping against what smelled like the old steel her husband salvaged.

Hands on the wall for guidance, she shuffled slowly to the right where it continued unbroken to the far stone. She moved back the other way, more quickly now, and before reaching the left stone her fingers found a long handle in the metal. She grasped the rod with both hands, forcing the lever down with her weight.

The wall moved, and Lahara gasped, startled, as it slid open. Slivers of penetrating green light—searing after the deep blackness—jumped out from the other side.

She blinked, trying to away the spots made in her eyes. Sparkling jeweled bits hung suspended like drops in a mist, and she moved toward them, stopping abruptly when she realized the slivers were not suspended at all—it was an illusion in the dark—rather they crawled on the black walls and low ceilings, glowing green worms, as many as stars in a night sky.

The worms lit the passage and as Lahara's eyes grew

accustomed to their dizzying glow the details of the space became clear—a long platform and what she recognized from *whispers* as a train, doors closed and dark, and on the other side of the platform, wheeled transports stacked and abandoned. The air smelled like stone burnt in fire and she shivered, rubbing her hands for warmth.

Before she could explore further, the power up warning sounded. Lahara paled, arms protective over her belly. Civs and Vaulters would be flooding the hor-verts, each chamber going up or down or around the perimeter to return the staffers to active duties. She needed get to the stairs while she still had time.

"Damn, fux," she remembered. "The locks."

She ran, fearful to be trapped in the passage, turning to pull closed the gate at the top of the ramp then flying down through the silver doors. As she entered the corridor the second alert sounded and the wide doors closed behind her, clicking shut along with all other temporarily unlocked doors.

She'd not be able to enter the stairway now, but she ran toward it anyway, heart in her throat, babies twisting, her insides crushed against her lungs.

Voices came from around the corridor. She looked wildly for a place to hide but found no alcove or niche save for the machine shadows in the rotunda, a maze of scaffolded metal she feared to enter. There was the hor-vert, though, and without thinking, survival instinct kicking in, she entered the only codes she had—for Level Eight—and waited, breathless as the Vaulters neared.

She shifted her weight and her water fell and her thin pants were drenched with the fluid. She threw herself in the first lift to open just as Civs in white jackets came around the curve.

The door closed and the hor-vert vibrated lightly. No reason would explain her arrival back on Level Eight. She'd been forbidden to leave the Infirmary and was non-compliant. It would be punishments come. She would never again see her family.

She slid to the ground, punishments gone from her thoughts as a new and fiercer tightening crippled her. And when the door opened on Level Eight, she was too busy birthing to notice.

ELIZABETH

WHEN ELIZABETH WAS a little girl, a trip to the Bronx Zoo in springtime was a family tradition, for so many of the babies were born then.   Every year, on a Sunday in early June, her father would turn off his Com and leave his research to spend the day with the family in the sprawling public park visiting cubs and chicks, and ending always with a walk along the Bronx River so her brothers could see the snapping turtles.

After her father left, the yearly excursions stopped. When she was a teen, and the layered roadways circling Manhattan and the outer boroughs were completed, she'd returned for an excuse to ride the express rail on the highest tier—a seven-minute trip from Bleecker Street to the Bronx—but once she finished school she'd visited the zoo for the last time. The last time, that is, until two hundred years later.

The morning mist had burnt off in the afternoon sun, but the path was still damp under the forest canopy. Woodbine and poison ivy climbed together throughout the red maple swamp, and Elizabeth skirted the vines as best she could, stopping a moment to listen for the beasts—especially the big cat—lurking nearby.

The trail she followed now had little in common with the zoo of her youth beside latitude and longitude, although the tigers and great gorillas and bison did still give birth in the spring, just no longer in the ancient enclosures. The animals, free for many, many generations, bred and lived and hunted in the open forests and wild miles, inhabiting—ruling, even—the stable lands in every direction.

The Lens had an ages-old connection with the beasts and they moved through them without fear. Elizabeth had no such personal bond. She'd seen a bear at dawn along the slope, an aggressive brown hybrid, but the female had been concerned only with her cubs in the berry bushes and Elizabeth had been able to back away from the animal without confrontation.

Trekking again now outside the barbed fencing, Elizabeth

attempted to avoid the tiger stalking her. She'd seen flashes of his orange coat through the trees, and had only been able to discourage his approach by discharging her silver Prod into the air every few moments, the warning sparks catching the dense foliage and returning bits of charred confetti-like leaf to the ground.

A rustling directly behind startled her, and Elizabeth spun, Prod leveled at the tall girl who stared back, unafraid, hood down.

"I might have struck you," Elizabeth said. "You shouldn't be outside the fence."

"You're a hunter mighty as Nimrod before the Lord."

"I'm not hunting," Elizabeth sighed, lowering her Prod. She chose her words carefully. It wouldn't do to condescend. "Please, Moses, keep in mind that the others follow your lead. It's for their safety as well as yours that you stay inside."

The girl didn't respond, rubbing her hands through short, shaggy hair blonde in shadow and red in the sun. She'd cut it with a dull knife recently, leaving long tresses for the wind to carry off.

"All right," Elizabeth said. She wouldn't send the girl back along the path to Zoo House by herself, especially with the cat nearby. "The raft is returning. If we have newcomers you can help make them welcome."

"Of course," Moses told her. "As the Lord said to me, 'The stranger that dwelleth with you shall be unto you as one born among you, and thou shalt love him as thyself; for ye were strangers in the land of Egypt: I am the Lord your God.'"

Elizabeth smiled. When Moses spoke, especially when she quoted the books attributed to her, the words rang clear and contemporary and conversational. She brought a vitality to the biblical Moses that made believing in this Meta personality easy. It was easy to believe in all of them, and because the Vault's Meta-Records were programmed in English—other Vaults had stored different versions—it was fascinating to speak with these figures from all over the world and all periods of time.

She held out her hand and surprisingly, the girl took it, the gesture likely just a memory of the girl's native self. Beatrice had become deeply dormant over the past months, and although Moses would ultimately occupy her without any input from the originating personality at all, there were still, now, occasional appearances of the girl who'd arrived at the Zoo in the middle of a winter snow with offerings of silver—the everstew kettle—and dyed cloth.

Elizabeth and Moses climbed down the trail to the abundant, green shoreline reflecting in the river before them, the waters home to a rich and varied wildlife. A pair of muskrats watched from the rocks beneath the falls, and the far bank showed signs of beaver activity—young willows newly felled with branches dragged off, and larger trees stripped of bark and chewed almost completely through.

Elizabeth was anxious for the raft's return. A Resistance of Touched and their defenders assembled in Manhattan's northernmost forest, and Anthony had gone to the Norte Inwood with the big man Tinny to enlist their help.

The spread of the winter flu had not slowed. Although the virus hadn't yet reached Zoo House, Elizabeth anticipated a refugee or returning Lens or bird would carry the illness to them, and come the fall, the virus would mutate and circulate again through the city, attacking the same families already affected. The population was decimated—close to twenty percent lost—and Elizabeth didn't think it could survive another hit.

Many, many thousands of doses of universal anti-flu and anti-pathogen lay in Vault storage and she knew exactly where they were shelved in the Level Twenty-five warehouse. Her father had assigned her to Inventory, deep in the bunker, to allow her some relief from those who would never consider her a colleague.

Alone in her work, she'd catalogued Vault's extensive resources and now, with no move on the Project's part to distribute the meds, Elizabeth meant to steal them. She would meet Anthony at the Norte. From there they'd cross the Hudson with the Resistance and enter the Vault.

So they had planned. But the Bronx River overflowed its banks in the torrential spring rains—the Manhattan waterways had done the same—and the Lens were delayed, waiting for the swollen waters to recede. The tunnels across the Harlem River, the ones Elizabeth, and Moses, too, came through, were also flooded, and no one had returned to Zoo House in many days. The arriving raft should bring news as to the status of their plan and Elizabeth hoped to leave for Inwood as soon as possible.

Moses was distracted, hands pulling long grasses from the water to braid. The tiger must have moved on, but Elizabeth kept her Prod ready regardless, and before long she heard a deep male voice singing, and Moses pointed downriver, shouting, "God leads the people out."

The canopied raft drifted slowly upriver, poles in the water. The Lens traveled this route with ease and had been doing so, according to their own records, for one hundred sixty-eight cycles. Elizabeth assumed these to be years, but that was only a guess. Vault hadn't even known the Lens existed. None of the satellite images showed settlement in the Bronx and they had never been recorded.

Zoo House was isolated, its gates locked to visitors, but travelers did not happen this way often. Safaris might come through for the big game, but they often fell prey to the same animals they chased. Even more rare, the journeyman crossing the Harlem River to salvage in the Bronx's burnt streets. The prevalence of beasts made digging highly dangerous and unprofitable, and years could pass between attempts.

The song grew louder as the raft neared. Elizabeth stood on tiptoe to see better, but the awning was zipped. That the raft was covered meant passengers were inside, and Elizabeth was glad for this, for though she broadcast daily via the Connex Panel she'd brought with her when she fled, she couldn't know who heard the messages, and Record holders always arrived unannounced.

It was this same technology that had compelled the Group that Left to head north, but Elizabeth's transmissions didn't betray as Seth's manipulative directives had, and she tempered her broadcasts with suggestions of calm to quiet the mania often accompanying nano activity.

The robed and hooded Lens waved as they approached, and Elizabeth returned the greeting. Even after six years she did not know any of their names. Perhaps they had none. She'd named each in her own mind, though, and it was the dark-skinned older man she called Crinkle—for the lines around his eyes—who climbed ashore first, tossing a rope over a pole.

Still humming, he held her shoulders and kissed the top of her head. "The man and his wait," he said softly with a minimum of words. "Depart sundown."

Crinkle's wife, Halo—she looked like a painted, golden icon, her hood stuffed with teased yellow hair—unzipped the canopy along the base of the raft, and rolled back the canvas panels.

Elizabeth smiled at the refugees—a woman, a child, and a man. The man seemed uncomfortable to see her hairless head, recognizing her as a Vaulter, but Elizabeth ignored his discomfort and helped gather their things.

"*Ni kan, lao gong,*" the robed, newcomer woman—they all received robes and hoods to travel in—whispered to the man. "*Yi qie dou hui hao de.*"

Chinese. According to the list Anthony compiled, this would be Nina from the East River at Eighty-fifth Street. She held the linguistic history of the Mandarin dialects, and appeared to not only use her *whispers* but to be teaching them, too.

That was good. They'd be joining the Farsi and Portuguese and Old English language Touched already here. Elizabeth was familiar with Mandarin. Nina had just told him everything would be alright, though the tone of her words seemed more an attempt to soothe her own worries than her husband's.

"What a huge dangum clan of Disconnects," Nina's husband Leo said as the gate opened to a hundred Lens singing a welcome. Nina backed up at the sight and shifted her daughter in her arms.

"What do the Disconnects want with us?" she asked, frightened.

"They call themselves Lens," Elizabeth corrected her gently. "Disconnect is your word. And they don't want anything. They offer you a place to live safely with your *whispers.*"

Behind the Lens, dozens of Touched and their families, including many Meta-personalities, spilled from the central building. There was the old man Van Gogh and the younger Plato, and the women Hildegard and Jimi Hendrix and Mr. Tesla.

Nina's daughter Rieni squirmed out of her mother's arms and pointed to the children waving in the crowd. *"Kankan, mama, zheme duo xin pengyou."* *Look, mama, so many new friends.*

The children ranged from toddler to young teen. The ones longest here were the Touched from Union Square—part of the Group that Left, the five boys and girls Elizabeth had refused to process on the Hudson. She'd fled with them six years ago, led by Lens to this sanctuary. Martina Belle had been at Zoo House for several months—she held a European folk music archive—and the little girl Meta Hannibal had arrived fairly recently as well. Then there were the siblings and children of a variety of ages and tenure who held no Records of their own but who learned from the others' shared *whispers*. Rieni would indeed have plenty of new friends. Smart, diverse, special friends.

Elizabeth put her hand on Nina's arm. "They look forward to meeting her."

"Zhuyi limao," Nina whispered to her daughter as she wiped her face. *Mind your manners.* Rieni giggled and skipped away, already singing Lens songs as she did.

Nina turned to her husband. "Two new starts I've made before my daughter is tall enough to pick her own apples. I uproot her as carelessly as a weed."

"This wasn't careless. Here we have no need keep one eye always open for the hairless man talking to her," Leo said. "It's done." He surveyed his surroundings. "Although I would feel better to know where we are in this place."

Elizabeth left the newcomers to their discussion. Sometimes this happened. They'd abandoned family and friends, and doubts set in. The raft's closed awning kept the route secret, and when they arrived, without reference, refugees often felt displaced and confused. A recent arrival insisted on returning to her old life, and although the Lens acquiesced, they'd brought her back to the city across a convoluted, days-long, beast-filled overland route impossible to remember or share.

Elizabeth moved through the gathering. A young man—Jared Hopes—touched her robe shyly. "I made something for you," he stammered, pale blue eyes blinking rapidly, and he handed her a richly gleaming yin yang amulet, warm from his palm. "When I spoke your name the gold transmuted from the lead. You made it pure." He blushed and melted back into the crowd before she could respond.

Dangerous business, Elizabeth thought. Schoolboy crushes and transmutation. She didn't know how much Jared Hopes— *Touched with Alchemy*—understood the actual processes he worked with, but if he had been able to change base metals into gold, he was manipulating protons and had built a technology involving tremendous amounts of an energy difficult to control.

So many Records in the hands of so many innocents. The Lens opened their gates to all refugees seeking asylum. Elizabeth and the Union Square children had been the first, and a catalyst for all the others. The combined knowledge at Zoo House was staggering and the Lens provided a stream of resources for the Touched to pursue their *whispers*, whatever they were.

Jared Hopes had come seeking perfection in the form of gold. Van Gogh, tortured by a catalogue of work he was compelled to recreate, had been brought by his wife. Mothers came to protect their children and sisters to protect their brothers. Moses had come by herself with a fire ready to ignite a religion.

Elizabeth had been a little concerned when Moses arrived— maybe concerned was too strong a word, for the Lens had been only ever accepting—but even so, the Lens were a spiritual group existing unchallenged for almost two centuries in a religion-less world. Did the idea of a Moses distress them? It seemed not. The Lens had just kissed her on the head, as they did all the arrivals, secure and unblinking at this new reality.

The welcome songs had long died down, the newcomers feted and brought to their apartments, and the sun sat low in the sky below the evening SolSat blinking 06.05.2257. Elizabeth regarded the numbers curiously, reminded her birthday was in June. The Lens didn't celebrate birthdays. She'd had not a single well wish in the six years here with them. How old would she be?

She'd just celebrated her thirty-second when her father returned like a ghost after twenty-five years in the Project—it was

2073—to bring his family into the Vault. Though her brothers wouldn't leave their lives, and her mother wouldn't leave her sons, Elizabeth put her affairs in order and went with Melly into the classified bunker.

Thirty-two when she went in, and now, one hundred eighty four years later as close as she could figure, if she didn't count the time Cocooned, she'd be turning forty. Forty years old, living in a wilderness, fighting for the survival of this damaged underdog of a city. She'd never been happier.

She laughed and Crinkle smiled in response. Mosquitoes and other twilight bugs were beginning to swarm as they walked past the long, open work building toward the outer field, but the tiny insects ignored her peeling skin as they usually did.

Fingering Jared Hopes' amulet, Elizabeth looked for the young man in the exposed workspace, but he wasn't at his bench. His fire was snuffed, his chalks neatly stored in the pail beside a notation covered board, and his carry-box gone. She'd have to thank him when she returned. If she returned. No, that wouldn't do. She sent the Lens words out before her. *Already done.* They would be successful in retrieving the vaccines. They had to be.

"She prepared meal," Crinkle said, referring, Elizabeth knew, to his wife, and he handed her a wrapped package and canteen.

"Thank you." Although the overland journey would be long— they'd follow the river past the waterfalls, then move across the remains of the charred Bronx through the night—and they likely wouldn't stop to eat or drink, Elizabeth appreciated the food and water and would enjoy the provisions when they did take rest.

Elizabeth had put on tall boots for the journey and changed into a lightweight and waterproof—the threads were waxed before weaving—robe and hood. She clipped the canteen to her sash and stashed the meal in a deep interior pocket, adjusting the pouch holding her fire sticks and the cubes, some as big as her fist, of dried and seasoned hunt-meats they'd toss to distract the beasts.

The queue was already in place. She could see the Lens through the second fence, assembled in the pasture around the fountain, and beyond their formation the verdigris bronze double zoo gates she remembered from her childhood.

They climbed down the long wide steps together, and when

they reached the fence, Crinkle kissed her head and veered away without a word. Elizabeth clamped the door shut behind her and joined the queue, wetting her hands and face in the fountain's pooled water as she did.

Five Lens in front, five behind. With her eyes fixed on the pale robe ahead, Elizabeth held her position in the formation—*already done*—and the eleven filed silently through the sculpted bronze gates, under the setting sun toward Manhattan.

ANTHONY

THE CIRCLE OF torches ringing the center fire at Norte Inwood had been burning all night, and although Anthony would have preferred to be in his bedroll, the boisterous Never Agains, Tinny the loudest, were up drinking whiskey, throwing dice, and smoking the cured, blended leaves brought from the south.

One of the women, a curvy albino with dark paint lining pale, lavender eyes, plucked a stringed instrument and circled Anthony, eyes narrowed as she sang. He blushed, awkward in her musical talons, and ducked back with an uncomfortable smile.

Anthony had been following the activities of this group, almost thirty strong, since the end of winter. Although he'd funneled information to varied militia, this Resistance was the one that acted most aggressively on his anonymous intelligence. Not a week after he sent the location of cloaked Vaulter cruisers docked under the Palisades, these Never Agains had boarded and destroyed the light converters on all three ships.

Lying flat on rafts and paddling with their arms, they'd crossed the Hudson in stealth, and after identifying each by their silver outlines in the moonlight, they'd climbed onto the docked cruisers, pulled the blue orbs from their poles and tossed them overboard to sink in the murky water. Mission completed, cloaking protocol destroyed, the Resistance had paddled back undetected.

Much of what Anthony knew of them came from Touched Marjorie, via her cousin Drake from the Mount. This group had a mix of skills, purpose and daring, and Anthony's plan to steal the vaccines was devised with help from this very Resistance in mind.

But reaching them, like reaching him, was not simple—they moved quietly and in small cells, out of range of all but the most underground of Tweets. When Marjorie informed him they'd built camp at the Norte, he grabbed the opportunity to approach and enlist their help.

It would be safer, and legitimize him, to make his introductions with a native in tow, so Anthony had set out first for

Mack's, where Tinny was helping build walls around the ferryman's compound during the day and at night betting the spring games, high stake contests that saw gamblers from every district wagering all manner of strange and unique items.

Tinny had enjoyed a winning streak at the games and feeling flush, agreed to join Anthony. As they rafted miles up the Harlem River through hills of sand and steel and rubble he offered a trade. "Won it off a journeyman come east. He told it was stole from a hairless laying cold out, new arrived and drunk with sex at what they call Civ camp. Near the Trump."

Anthony was still trying to follow this provenance when the gamer unwrapped a thin package. "Fire stick," he boasted, raising the silver Prod in his hand.

Anthony ducked but Tinny shook his head. "Shiny as a new egg but I can't make the sparks fly." He grinned. "For you," he said. "Maybe you have something for me?"

Anthony took the weapon—there was a safety catch—and smiled at his friend. "I will definitely find something for you."

Surrounded by centuries-old trees on the rocky hills above the Hudson, Anthony addressed the militia. They knew of him as the Vaulter who'd exposed the rest, but even so, there was much distrust, and tensions were high. A pony-tailed man grabbed his arm with strong, bony fingers. Tinny lunged but Anthony cautioned him to stop. He recognized the *whispers* rising in the man's eyes, as did the group encouraging him.

A dark man tattooed with white spirals called to the man with his hair tied back. "Whose blood runs through this Vaulter? Is he one of the hairless entered the Mount this season to displace your own? Or is he related to the hairless who put fire in our digs at the Tudor? Tell us his line, Drake."

Drake. Marjorie's cousin was *Touched with Genealogy*, data created not only through historical records, but composed as well in real time using DNA and other micro markers found in molecules of sweat on skin. Drake's nanobits connected each person he touched to the Global Tree, transforming the man himself into a server of these histories.

"Like drops of water without an ocean these hairless arrive," another shouted.

Anthony held his breath, unsure what Drake would find in his lineage and how it would impact this standoff. After a long moment the Touched One released his arm. "This drop of water has an ocean," he said. "He connects to a descendant in our city."

The man with the white tattoos called to those in the back, "He's connected," and the others relaxed, concerns eased, ready now to hear what Anthony had to say.

But Anthony was distracted, processing the genealogist's words. Did Drake speak the truth about a descendant, or did he lie to protect him, respecting Anthony's friendship with Marjorie? After two centuries, what would such a person be to him?

The Never Agains shuffled uneasily waiting for Anthony to speak, so he held his own questions and began again. "You've all lost someone to the fever. Each of you has family or friends to care for. To defend. I ask you to follow me into the Vault and carry out medicines to heal and protect your families."

The albino woman leaned in to him, her breath raising goose bumps on his skin. "How do we know what you say is true?" she challenged, and he turned his face from the scent of cherry wine.

"What way inside?" a lean girl named Bo asked, twirling the ends of a rope she carried. "Men've tracked Vaulters to where they hide like foxes. There's a Watch. Bodies been drowned for getting too close. My brother one of them."

Anthony nodded at the girl with the blue hemp rope, a climber from the southern bluffs at the End. Vault's river entrance and cruisers were well guarded now, and Vault had set Watch at the Bridge wall as well. "Correct," he said. "There's no catching them unawares here. But a half day's sail north is another access."

The Rails were to have been sealed a hundred seventy-five years earlier. Although Vault believed the entrance sealed—the office administering the transportation center had been reassigned and the trains slated for removal—Elizabeth's father had in fact returned to unseal the entry for his wife and sons, hoping they would join him. But they hadn't come, and as he had confessed to his daughter, the entrance to the Rails had remained open, though abandoned, since that time. Elizabeth would lead them to it.

"Are you with me?" Anthony asked, and the Never Agains shouted a unanimous yes, rallying around the challenge.

Over the next few days, Anthony refined the plan. Half the group would head upriver, one boat at a time to avoid suspicion, Anthony and his team leaving first to anchor just south of the rift and wait for the others.

The Hudson widened at Yonkers and the combination of a deep crack running through the riverbed and the outlet of a wide channel from the west created a current that made travel a perilous undertaking.

Only one among them had ever been beyond the rift, the young man, Pep, who'd sailed out with a brother looking for their mother gone with the Group that Left. He'd returned alone from the journey. His advice to the group, relayed with much of the story untold—"Hold tight and don't ever put to shore in the marsh."

In preparation for a travel over steep slopes and cliffs, some of the group practiced maneuvering on the Norte rocks, and then later, they hammered iron points onto walking sticks for each.

This afternoon they'd tattooed themselves with the letters NA—and although not everyone had the spellings, they understood the symbols meant Never Again. Anthony's ink itched, the purple letters raising welts, but he didn't complain—it was important he be accepted as one of their own.

They shaved their heads—the women, too—and the men their beards, to blend in with Vaulters above and below ground. This last was Tinny's idea. "Some Vaulter puts eyes on me while I'm inside, I won't have my beard saying my name," he'd declared, sliding the blade over his face. Anthony wondered if Tinny had ever in his adult life been beardless, the white skin beneath was as telltale as the hair he removed, but he kept that thought unspoken.

So here they were, bald and inked, pumping hormones and sweat, and blowing off steam with the bottles. Anthony left the group and climbed down the rocks to a wide path, eyes scanning the canal that had gone from dry to teeming in the spring rains and now swirled with a mud glowing green and orange in the dark.

The night was quiet except for the faint music filtering downhill and a persistent owl in the trees. He shielded his torch. Paranoid their plan could be betrayed—Vault offered a high price for information on the militia—Anthony imagined Vaulters right now journeyed toward them under cover of night.

He'd heard of groups assembled in the hills below the Bridge, and in the Remember all along the river. As men and women joined the Never Agains, so there were as many joining the Vaulter causes. But no lights and no sounds disturbed the blackness tonight, and he was relieved, thankful that although Vault cruisers still traveled the waterways—sometimes cheered, sometimes spat upon—at least they were no longer invisible.

He hiked a short distance west, rocky heights on one side, mud channel on the other, and crossed beneath the remains of layered highways spanning the canal. The ages-old Hudson dam to the immediate south created a still, deep water, and their own boats were moored, unflagged, below. Across the river, just beyond the Palisades, smoldering, toxic caverns lit the sky a soft red.

As long as they could navigate the Yonkers rift they'd avoid the overland beasts on the east. Westchester was overrun with natural and migrated and mutated wild life, and Prods would not be enough against the creatures.

The western riverbank, below the cliffs in New Jersey, was passable only in short sections. Fast moving channels of white water moved through split and fallen cliff into the Hudson, and the burning caverns made travel though even the shortest lengths of unbroken shore a trial, not only for the fumes, but for rocks and steam raining down without warning.

It was a lateral eruption of such steam and debris from those subterranean fires that had breached Vault's nanobiotic facility, forcing the Records into New York's air and water. The same blast had cut support to Vault, rupturing the chemical and power flow that maintained the Cocoons, its vibrations rocking the foundations of the pods and sending the Vaulters into their unscheduled, final Awake. Three men died in their Cocoons that morning and of the horses, only Aja remained when the rubble was cleared.

Anthony turned back, climbing to where the night's final Runner would hand the news to Janelle Duyvil who would begin the sequence again at dawn. Anthony had watched Janelle set out every morning this week, even through the downpour dropping in sheets for three days flooding the roads and forcing mud into the valley, a rain that drowned rabbits in their nest under the brush where Anthony made camp and, except for the incessant pounding, had stilled the highland forest as birds and animals and hunters sought shelter to protect their own.

The Runner Janelle would be sleeping now, but her Grandfather, the blind man, had wandered from their settlement beyond the outcrop to drink sharp ferment with the Never Agains, telling tales of his sighted days in this spot where the Harlem River ship canal met the Hudson. The group had been raising hollers and encouraging his chronicles, toasting each adventure and coughing the harsh tobacco as he narrated.

Voices cheered suddenly in the dark and a drum pounded deep in the woods. The SolSat changed numbers at midnight, and as happened every time, those who witnessed the change called out in recognition. Anthony checked the sky—a new day—06.06.2257.

The drink would keep the group awake until the jugs were empty, but Anthony needed to sleep. Dawn would come soon enough, and Elizabeth with it. He climbed the second slope back to camp where Drake and another, a Touched woman called Mahindy, swayed together, Drake dancing steps made complicated by inebriation, and Mahindy reciting—singing—her *whispers.*

Anthony recognized the words of one of the few poems he'd actually read and enjoyed in high school. Hoping to capture *Beowulf* before the poem was gone again, he quickly scribbled some of the lines, managing only to scrawl a single verse before the performance dissolved into debate.

"I hear the mistakes in your stomps," Grandfather called to Drake. "You'll trip on your own feet keeping up that way."

"Old man," the genealogist teased, chugging from a leather wrapped bottle. "We've danced like this for generations on the Mount. You g'wan then and show the spring steps to us."

"When I was young," Grandfather said, "I danced the moon to her bed." He dragged on the cigarette burning between his fingers. "Now I only wait the buzzards." He coughed, and his blind eyes grew teary. "I once brought the fattest deer and highest flying birds to the fires. I fished the whole span of the river. Even the hot side where the ones hugged the rocks weren't fish at all. Seals they were called, but the last has long swum to other waters."

"Seals?" The dark-eyed man from Central Park, the falconer Beetus who'd lost his daughter to the fever, snorted. "Nah."

"I would believe it, yah," the leathery man Crispin said. "We've had them below Crease. They lay out on the offshore rocks when the weather's mild."

"I remember rafting across and following a fat one into a cave," Grandfather said. "And what did the bugger lead me to?"

"More seals?" the dark man with the white spiral tattoos asked.

"No. Crates. Crates marked with old world spellings."

"What was in 'em?" Tinny asked, eager. "Cans? Specials?"

"Don't know. The ground was full of slicers. Cut my foot bad to bleed and the sun was coming down. I had no fire so I paddled home. Never went back. We had enough salvage on the cold side without risking the burn."

"That's no end to a story," Tinny complained. "You coulda made a better end."

"It's the true." Grandfather ground his cigarette into damp leaves. "Not a story."

"Do you think you could find that cave again?" Anthony asked, guiding the old man back to his camp, all thought of sleep gone. Grandfather's discovery didn't sound like salvage. Crated weapons came to mind. If military supplies had been uncovered in the hot slopes of the Palisades sixty years earlier, would they still be there?

"I know where it is," Grandfather said, leading him into a dense wood. "I can't make the rafting any more but I can tell ya exactly and you'll find it like you got a map. It's a strange thing, waiting for the buzzards. I can't remember yesterday, but I can remember the color flower my wife wore the night we first made the dance."

Anthony nodded. Getting old hadn't changed much in two

hundred years.

"Start across at the triple rocks," the old man said. "Used to be a face like a lady across on the cliff, and she was my guide. That rock's collapsed a long time but if you paddle straight you'll end where she was. I walked north a few minutes in the fumes when I seen the seal jump into a water. Follow the water back. If the stream is dry, climb between the boulders—it's one big rock split in two, and going between the pieces will find ya the cave."

The old man pulled a curtain of vines and Anthony thought he saw fading yellow flash in the sky as the night was revealed. Flares? His stomach clenched. No, most likely summer lightning.

"I go alone from here," the old man said, dropping the vines between them to cover the sky again and leaving Anthony no opportunity to say thank you.

The sun had just barely come up and the Never Agains were out cold, sprawled around the dying campfire, embers glowing under thin streams of smoke visible only for the stillness of the dawn. The torches had died, some knocked over, and raccoons were pulling apart the pile of discarded corncobs and oyster shells.

Tinny lay with his head on the guitar, and the woman who had been strumming had her head across his feet, arms wrapped around her pack. Crispin from the Chelsea Wood had strung a hammock but lay underneath, and in every direction, crumbled, smudged and newly bald Never Agains were passed out.

As the sky lightened to the palest clearest blue, Anthony heard the call. A song, a warble that could be bird or beast but wasn't, and he scrambled up and hurried to the ridge, raising a scope.

On the far side of the canal the Lens appeared from the ruins, moving down the hill in a precision line, breaking formation at the bottom to drag a raft from the rushes and into the muddy channel.

Anthony half climbed, half slid down a double rock slope to the canal's bank, careful to stay within the marked boundaries as blow pits lined the shore to defend against animal crossings. He counted eleven on the raft, Elizabeth indistinguishable from the rest. She blended as well as if she had been born to them, and she deserved the family, he thought. She'd never had that in the Vault.

The first time Anthony ever saw Elizabeth was less than a week into the first Awake. They'd been Cocooned for over two decades and she was with her father Melly, the head of Nanobiotics. He was herding her into a hor-vert lift against the advances of a small group of agitated and accusing Vaulters, Racine one of them. Elizabeth had looked upset, and though Anthony caught her eye, the elevator had shut and spun around the corridor out of sight and he'd not seen her again before the next Cocooning.

Anthony knew all the Specialists in the Vault—they'd trained and lived and worked together since the beginning—but of the hundreds of Civ-staff embedded with them, Anthony knew only a handful. He'd assumed at first that Elizabeth was Civ-staff, but that wasn't the case. Elizabeth was neither Specialist nor staff. She was family. After twenty-five years inside, Melly had left Vault to find his now adult daughter and bring her into the Project.

He'd told Elizabeth that Admin had approved her admission, and she had no reason to question her father, but at the next Awake she discovered, as did everyone else, that no authorization had been granted her to board the Rails fifty years earlier. Not only had there been no authorization given, but the Rails had been decommissioned, and her father's use of that passage illegal.

That she replaced a Vaulter who'd died during the first Cocooning did little to mitigate the resentment toward her, and at the second Awake, a group snuck out in search of their own descendants, returning empty-handed. It was then the sanctions for unlawful furlough were put into place. It hadn't made the Vaulters like Elizabeth any better.

The Lens climbed off the raft and one by one took Anthony by the shoulders and kissed the top of his head. He should have felt honored by such a greeting reserved for their own, but in fact it made him self-conscious, reminding him he'd never liked the hand holding or peace-be-with-you bit in church. He startled himself with the thought. He could use a hand to hold.

There she was, eyes unmistakable under the hood before him.

She kissed him lightly on the head then watched the others return to the raft and shove off into the muddy water. A Lens waved from the middle of the channel and Elizabeth looked at him curiously before waving back. When they reached the other side the Lens covered the raft and climbed single file into the ruins on the bluff.

"You okay?" he asked.

Although she'd walked miles through hazardous land throughout the night, Elizabeth looked rested and energized. She nodded, and they began the climb up back up to camp.

It didn't surprise him. The day Elizabeth dragged him half-frozen from the East River, Anthony had been able to walk in formation with the Lens across Roosevelt Island almost immediately.

Was it hypnosis or some sort of walking meditation? He didn't know. All he knew was that Lens could travel long distances without rest. And although he'd seen them eat and drink as they journeyed, he suspected it wasn't necessary. When in formation, they needed very little.

At the top of the first set of rocks Elizabeth stopped a moment to catch her breath and look north across the canal to where the Hudson dipped out of view behind the bluff. "I can't see it," she said, and Anthony nodded. She'd see the massacre landing soon enough. They'd be sailing past it.

"I don't suppose they survived very long out there. The ones that got away, I mean." she said. "They would have come back by now if they did."

"A few did come back," Anthony reminded her. "Beatrice, for one." And then he added, knowing his words wouldn't help, "You saved as many as you could."

They'd decided to begin the staggered trips up the Hudson just before midday, when the tide, for a couple of hours at least, would be pushing north. Anthony, with Elizabeth and Tinny, would lead, crossing the river first to investigate Grandfather's cave.

Tinny had grabbed Anthony in a bear hug at the news of this detour, excited for the specials he planned to find, but Elizabeth was more cautious.

"Is it worth the time to chase his memories?" she'd asked, and Anthony considered it again.

Military provisions had been cached—contingency arsenals—throughout New York and New Jersey and it was possible Grandfather's crates were part of those armaments. "Firepower would help our chances," he'd said, and Elizabeth nodded.

After the cave, the plan was to paddle north. The Never Agains would be watching from Inwood, and when Anthony's boat was no longer visible upriver, the next would set out, and when it sailed out of sight, the next, until all seven boats were en route to assemble just below the rift at Yonkers. Although unlikely anyone would question their travel north, each boat carried fishing nets as explanation.

Three men would stay behind in the Norte, moving deeper into the forest, clearing the remnants of their camp and hiding their provisions in primeval rock hollows. The remaining group had split up to travel south and east, back to their own districts, spreading disinformation as they journeyed.

One had woken early enough to pass a false news to the runner Janelle, telling her Anthony had become ill and was to quarantine on the East River. The Runner would add his name and prognosis to the updates relayed at each of her stops, unknowingly disseminating the misinformation.

Thin, high clouds were moving in from the west, but the sun was strong and Anthony's neck peeled in the humidity and his pack irritated the skin under his shirt. Although Elizabeth kept her hood up Anthony could see the peeling around her eyes, too. He bent to fill a cup from the stream splashing down the pebble slope, and handed her the cool water. She dabbed it on her face, soothing the sore patches, and he did the same.

"On my way," Tinny called, sliding to where their borrowed boat was tied on the shore. Six other boats of various sizes were moored along this stretch called the Tracks, and the Never Agains made their way toward them to ready their departure.

Starly, the pale guitarist, waved a long, sinewy greeting to Anthony from the hill. He blushed and hurried to untie the canoe, dragging it to the three rocks that Grandfather had described.

Tinny stashed a box stuffed with dried cobs and a smoldering coal under the forward seat. Each boat would transport its own fire. A few carried birds. Tinny had Mack's in a small, mesh basket on his waist. The ferryman would do what had to be done if Tinny sent the pigeon to fly home.

Elizabeth stepped into the canoe, holding her robe up to keep dry. Anthony followed, and with a quick look back at the others assembling and preparing their boats, he pushed off into water made still by the half-dam to the south and the slack tide.

"Until the upriver," Tinny called back to the Never Agains, and the boat cut west across the Hudson toward the spot where the cliff used to look like a lady.

They pulled onto the narrow strip of shore, a dry and struggling forest slope just steps away, deteriorating cliffs above. The air smelled of sulfur and the tall grass between the rocks on the shoreline was yellow and brown. Anthony wrapped a bandana around his face, as did Elizabeth and Tinny.

They set out north, in some areas picking their way over landslides that had sheared entire columns from the Palisades. They passed the remains of an ancient marina, pilings visible in the river, and watched geese pecking at the algae covered debris. A short distance beyond, a metal tower was fallen over boulders the size of small hills, many split as Grandfather had recalled.

Anthony shaded his eyes and examined the cliff—dark vines and leaves twisting through the cracks, and faded illegible graffiti along the face. The forested slope extended as far into the distance as he could see, at its foot the shore, mostly cobbled with debris but occasional patches of pebble and tough grass beach remained.

A blue heron flew overhead and circled back to a flat area just beyond them. Tinny pulled the bandana from his mouth to rub his razor-irritated face. "That's water that way," he said, pointing to where the bird moved out of sight into the rocks. "Those long-neckers like to walk in it. A stream comes out of the hill."

Tinny was right. Water flowed from the slope into the river, but they weren't able to follow the stream back too far before it disappeared under boulders leaving little room for passage.

Anthony climbed onto the large rocks and looked across into the talus, but saw nothing. Nothing cave-like, at any rate.

"What do you think," he asked, sliding back down. Tinny shrugged, leaning against a rock twice his height and wiping his face with the bandana now brown with dust. Anthony turned to Elizabeth, but she'd disappeared, and he shouted her name.

"I found it," she called from the other side. Anthony and Tinny scrambled around to where she crouched in a dry streambed between sections of the immense rock.

"The water's been diverted," she said. "The entrance is partially sealed, but you can feel a breeze coming through."

Anthony ducked his head and moved sideways along the narrow gap in the rocks, the smell of dirt and stone in his nose. Elizabeth followed, but Tinny shook his head. "Small spots and big shoulders aren't friends. I'll keep watch out here."

Pebbles slid from above and Anthony flinched at the sting on his scalp. "Go back," he said to Elizabeth. "If there's anything—if I can get through—I'll holler."

She nodded. "Be careful. It's not stable."

He squirmed along for a short distance, then climbed, hunched, on stone that shifted under his feet, loosening a torrent of gravel, raising dust and dirt.

"Are you all right?" Elizabeth called into the gap.

"It's okay," he yelled down, waiting for the motion to subside, feeling just the tiniest bit claustrophobic in the pressing rocks. He continued up with careful steps, hands grasping sharp edges as he climbed. The passage opened into a small, surprisingly cool chamber created by the layout of the fallen rocks.

Some fortuity of the cave's design had produced a ventilation that swept warmer air through and kept inside temperatures much lower than those outside. He felt chilled in the flow. Thin shafts of light illuminated ledges and stacked, slatted wood boxes.

He stepped inside to examine the crates, feet crunching on broken glass. He picked up a long, brown shard and turned it over, catching and reflecting the light in little points against the dark gray walls. An upturned crate was wedged in the corner, broken bottles partially covered with dirt and rock and what looked like ice trapped under and between the stones.

With a strange feeling in his stomach and the trace of a familiar scent on his fingers, he stood to examine the crates more closely. They weren't military. The boxes on the ledge were handmade. If the fragments on the ground were any indication, he'd be smart to leave now. But he couldn't. He had to be certain.

He nudged one of the heavy crates, the wood stained and splintered and rotting along the side and bottom. As he took the box into his arms the slats gave way and cloth wrapped bottles fell, some breaking even with the protective sleeve, filling the cave with alcohol fumes that burned his eyes and throat.

He slid a bottle from its flannel. It was unlabeled except for a small square marked with handwritten initials, but Anthony knew his booze. In another life he'd collected and owned a similar antique, one he'd paid too much for. His had been empty. A ray of light streamed through the liquid inside, and he gently swirled the Prohibition whiskey brewed a hundred years before he was born.

It wasn't hard to guess how this moonshine ended up in this cave. Whiskey runners had used the Hudson to convey their goods and one such runner had probably stashed his cargo here and never returned. How ironic he would be the one to find the hooch more than three hundred years later. How fucking ironic.

Anthony held the bottle for too long, then slipped the whiskey into his pack. "I'm coming out now," he called down, grabbing two more of the slim brown bottles.

He descended the wobbly stones, loosing more gravel as he did, and squeezed through the narrow passage into the sunlight.

Elizabeth and Tinny looked at him, questioning. "Nothing there," Anthony said, shaking his head. "Nothing at all." And then, "Let's get back on the river."

MARLY

MARLY NEEDED DROP water but wouldn't complain because his Da brought him on this journey and something big was to happen—something, according to his listening, about Lahara and the Vaulters who stole her.

The Tweet had run all the way to the Upper East Side from the downtown yesterday but Marly and his father had been at salvage below the Stones at the south and not returned until this morning. She'd waited for them—the message was too important not to— and it was Marly first saw her sitting in the road smoking leaves as they turned off the York toward their house by the river.

He'd been sent up the stairs when the Tweet started to tell, and although he couldn't hear all the words for being up there, he heard some of them—they needed find Anthony—and not long after the Tweet left, his father called him down. They were going on Horsey and Marly needed fill the canteens.

Marly leaned back against his father, enjoying the wind, hands gripping the leather straps. Horsey ran fast, taking advantage of the long stretch of the flat Central Park road, and sweat damped her dusty skin. Some falcon kids from the lawn waved and called for a ride but Marly was galloped past before he could wave back.

Bouncing was usually fun, but he was uncomfortable having to drop water, and with the blanket beneath slipping, every bump wanted to fly him into the road.

He hadn't ridden in a long time. Ever since the hairless Anthony told that Horsey belonged to the bad ones, his father had kept her hidden away. Some mornings, before the sun shined, she was let out to graze or exercise but mostly she stayed in the airy, locked shed built for her across the road and it was Marly's job to wipe her down and shovel her mess.

His father kept dogs in and around the stable and if anyone came too close they would bark, but one time, another hairless man come into the East Side—nobody would say how he got through the Stones—and he used his shine stick on the dogs and one died. The hairless wanted to steal Horsey but couldn't figure the lock and while he worked on the gate someone banged the drum and the bad man run away.

Marly had been sad about the dog. Vaulters didn't care who they died or hurt. Marly's chest still ached sometimes from the river water he'd breathed after the Vaulter tried to drown him. He didn't remember all what happened that day, but he didn't need remember for his chest to hurt when he ran or sang at Tent.

"Can we pick yellows for my cousin?" he asked, turning to his father behind him. The dark stone walls on either side of the park road were covered with flowering vines and Beatrice loved the yellows. His father had told him Beatrice went to live with friends for safety. He'd promised they'd visit, but hadn't said when.

Marly thought his father must not have heard him. He took so long to answer they'd already passed the thickest vines, turning out of the park headed downtown. His father's face was tight and his eyes hard, but when he saw Marly looking back at him again, his expression changed and he just said, "No flowers."

The road south was clear of rubble but neighbors clogged the street and Horsey slowed to pass around their wagons. His father didn't say anything when some pointed and called to them, but Marly waved and smiled at the attentions, worried only about the History on the right, a whole long way full of hulking, ruined buildings mostly empty but for the giant Tarium at the back where the Westers gathered like his own meeting Tent on the York.

Marly hadn't ever been inside the History but Reko told the buildings were filled with shifting shadows and razor animals that hid in the broke walls and jumped out to bite your face. Lahara always said Reko's words were stories and not the true, but she wasn't here and Marly felt relieved when the History was passed and he could see the lake on the other side of the road and the big feather birds grooming themselves on the wet banks.

"Da, swim?" Marly begged.

"Not today and not here," his father said, kicking the horse to gallop again away and fast from the crowds. "We need find the where of Anthony before the day is gone."

Marly's stomach clenched at those words. He would never say, but Anthony scared him. Not so much the sight of his skin peeling where his eyebrows should have been, but more that Anthony reminded him of the one who had whispered those awful things to him. The thought of Racine made his insides shake. "I need drop water now, Da."

"Ahh, boy. Quick, then," his father snapped, pulling the reins, and Marly slid off to spray the slabs of black marble stuck out from the low hills. He peeked west as he did. The narrow path at Sixty-second showed the Broadwaterway at the end and he watched a raft pass on the stream made fat by spring rains.

"What's the time wasting?" his father called "We need move," and Marly jumped at his voice and climbed back onto Horsey.

Great piles of tumbled stone and risen rock just to the south spat steam and his father warned against going near the hot fountain or the market tables beyond, and cautioned him to give not a word away. "Stay sat right here with lips together," he said, jumping down and tying Horsey to a pole half hidden behind a scaffold in the middle of the glass and metal of the Columbus Circle. "I'll be only a short time and we're safer without catching more eyes or ears."

"Yeah, Da," Marly said, twisting on top of Horsey to look around, wishing he could dip from the Wait's everstew and wondering if his father had noticed all the neighbors already seen them here—the boy fishing at the foot of the Broadwaterway, the man just come out of the Wait with a limping old woman, and that hairless one—Marly's stomach twisted to see him—speaking to others at the benches across the way.

His father hurried to the metal door and opened the creaking gate set back in the stone. "Daisy," he called softly into the Wait's dark inside and Marly felt worried, and hoped Daisy would come out with Anthony who the Wait woman called *brother* even though he was the hairless. Marly wanted all this would happen soon so he could go swimming and pick the yellows, and leave Anthony to take care of whatever made his father fearful.

But Daisy came out without Anthony, speaking quiet words with Marly's father. Daisy reminded Marly of Lahara, but with light flyaway hair instead of dark curled, and one bent hand where Lahara had two straight. She filled a cup from the water barrel and shaded her eyes against the sun.

Still in hushed conversation, she walked with his father away from the Wait door where the man, having dropped two handfuls of leaf greens into the everstew, was settling the limping woman into his wagon.

Marly listened to his father and Daisy's words carried in pieces across the Circle—something about blue Grindle, and the X Island and a message for Anthony—but their talk got quiet and the wind picked up just enough to blur the words, and Marly squirmed, and Horsey, too, was squirming, pulling the tether and nickering.

The Broadwaterway began its course here, and the Wester kid with a fishing pole hanging over the stream not many steps away giggled as Horsey stretched her neck at him. Marly didn't ruin his happy to say she was just trying to drink, but it was the true. His Da had jumped down so fast he hadn't filled a water bucket.

Marly turned to see if his father watched, but he was huddled with Daisy over a long cloth, eyes squinted like when he concentrated to figure an answer, so Marly slipped from Horsey's smooth back and unwrapped a length of tether. With enough lead now, Horsey maneuvered around the scaffold and drank from the water splashed over the cement.

The cool wet on Marly's toes smelled of grass and metal, and he knelt and reached his hand under the raised, pebbled concrete to touch the rush flowing from the south, where the Broadwaterway ran beneath the rubble mounds.

"Is that the beast stolen from the men who give us chocolate?" the little fisherboy asked Marly, his eyes accusing.

Marly sized the boy up. He wasn't supposed to talk about Horsey or the hairless, but it wouldn't do to have a Wester call him a thief. Certainly not one with falling out braids who hadn't caught any fish even though the Broadwaterway was full of them.

"Who give you chocolate?" Marly had tasted chocolate once. A journeyman come to trade at Bazaar had offered a bite for answers. Although the man had a head covered in hair, Marly—always alert for the hairless—thought the questions sounded to do with Vaulters and such, so he'd nibbled his bit and run off without responding. A bad trade. He felt ashamed but he'd not known what else to do. He wished he had some of that chocolate now.

The boy jammed his pole in the cracked pavement and stroked Horsey's leg. "Bald." he said, nodding. "Your horse looks like them. A whole clan raised a long tent near the Remember. Hairless, every one of them. They told about a horse stolen."

"They got the shine sticks?" Marly asked, worried and checking if his father noticed that others now come to use the Broadwaterway were whispering and pointing at Horsey. "The shine sticks can make you dead, ya know."

The Wester boy nodded and pulled a slim package from his knapsack. "Yah and I seen em myself," he said, lifting the paper.

"I seen em, too. And I been on their boat."

The little boy tore the dark wrapping carefully. "Lots been on their boat," he said with a shrug. "They come up the river every so and again. Boat full of fish and cakes and funny fruits." He pulled the paper back, revealing the flat of chocolate beneath. It was softening in the sun and Marly could almost taste it. "The trade is for answering," the Wester boy said. "Good answers get what they got. Seen a neighbor bring home a *pineapple*."

Marly frowned, hardly able to think for the chocolate in front of him. He didn't understand *pineapple* and there hadn't been cakes and fruit on the boat he'd been dragged onto. But maybe he was thrown in the winter river before seeing the goods for barter.

"You trade with them and you're doing rotten," Marly said to the little boy who licked chocolate from his fingers. "Everyone knows not to barter with the Vaulters. Never again the Bad times."

"Some think the Vault is bringing the Good times," the boy said. "And all this making bad talk about it is a lot about nothing."

"It's not a lot about nothing," Marly yelled, unable to stop himself. "My step-ma got stolen to the Vault and we don't even know if the babies in her belly still wriggle." He slumped with the weight of his words. "That's something," he said. "Not nothing."

A caravan of carts skidded across the Columbus Circle with much hurrying, and the pushers looked right at him and right at Horsey and their voices were loud and the hairless one across at the benches was looking, too and coming at him. His father—who had folded the long cloth into a square and was just putting it in his pack—turned from Daisy to the commotion, for the first time noticing Marly was moved from where he'd left him.

Marly cast about for a way out of the cart pushers' path. Their fervor frightened him and he wished he was still behind the mesh scaffold and Horsey in her stable safe on the East side. He tried to yank her from the water's edge, but she held her ground.

· "Son," his father shouted, sprinting with Daisy towards him, and all of a sudden Marly understood he'd done very wrong, and his face fell to realize he'd given words away, even though he knew to keep quiet and even after his father had reminded him. If only Reko hadn't returned below Crease it would be him here now with his lips set together and Marly home where giving words had no matter. Reko should have been journeying today instead of him.

The Wester boy looked at him curiously. "Don't be sad." He broke off a hunk of chocolate, wrapped it in a paper scrap and pressed the gift into Marly's hand. "I can barter more with what you told, so there's plenty enough chocolate to share."

Marly stuttered, blushing for the mistake, trying to return the treat. But the boy had grabbed his pole and was running away, and Marly hid the chocolate in his pack as his father lifted him to Horsey's back and climbed up after.

"The safe route is marked," Daisy said. "But danger spots change daily and it's a long time riding to Norte Inwood."

Marly yelped at the sting on his bare arm, and his father roared and turned to the barrage of stones and pebbles flung at them. Daisy held her hands up and faced the pushers. "Stop it," she called. "It's not right bothering those who Wait."

"Daisy Leigh, move aside," one shouted without slowing. "That horse has a price on it and we're to collect."

"There's nobody good puts a price on another man's horse," she called back.

"New times, Daisy. New times."

His father squeezed Daisy's hand and kicked Horsey to gallop north along the Broadwaterway. Without looking back, Marly held tight the leather, his hands still sticky with Vaulter chocolate.

LAHARA

THE DOORS ALONG the Level Eight corridor stood open and there didn't seem to be anyone to care if Lahara stepped in or out of the exposed rooms. She waited a moment in front of her own private to be certain she was alone, then made her way quietly toward the doors that had only ever before been closed and locked.

She carried her babies, tiny, wrinkled things, the both of them, barely a day old. Sabat had hovered like a grandmother, feeling responsible for the tightenings that had sent her alone into the lift for help, blaming himself for abandoning her during her labor. Lahara said nothing to relieve his guilt, as it suited her story. He had no cause to suspect she'd come from or been anywhere but the Infirmary on Level Twelve and he'd stayed with her and the babies all night, bringing straws of food they could suck to supplement her milk, and leaving her, finally, come morning, to her rest.

Seth had arrived then, with Marilena. Lahara feigned sleep and they removed themselves again without touching the babies beside her, and later Patrice had peered through her doorway. "After your third meal—Sabat insists on your rest—the sessions begin again. You neglected to provide a means for connecting the Heaven Interface to our network, a suspect omission. To avoid punishments, you will locate those instructions in your *whispers*."

Lahara had turned away at the threat, and when she looked again, Patrice was gone.

The babies—one boy and one girl—were strapped across Lahara's chest, cradled in a sheet knotted around her waist and shoulder, and they slept, puckered lips sucking even as they dozed. They were healthy, but nameless, and would remain so until their father greeted them. Those names were Switch's to give, and Lahara promised the twins they would soon have his gifts.

The walls flashed but Lahara barely noticed. Everything was different now with her belly emptied and the familiar current flowing again beneath her *whispers*. She might be far from home and under threat of punishments, but she was no longer alone, and felt wakened from the bad dream blurring the whole of her time here. She was returned to her own self, the afterbirth sliding from her womb taking with it the nightmare known as Vault.

Unattended by women during the birthing—only Sabat had assisted—and without the songs of the birth circle to support her, the pain, by some instinct, had forced her inward, pulling deep and fast and hard.

As the babies fought their way through her body, Lahara struggled through her own journey, down to where Touched connected, and with a cry masked by the birthing, Lahara had breeched the thick silence to penetrate that point below her *whispers*—a place lost since her arrival, eclipsed and obscured by the panels and clicks and sessions, made invisible or buried perhaps by some trick of the Vaulters.

Lahara wondered if they, in their endless scrutiny of her *whispers*, did even understand the undercurrent. Although at times here she'd been able to sense it and others—Touched—in its stream, this *whisper* flow accessed at home with just a stilling of her mind had been in the Vault simply unreachable.

Until the birthing.

Strong voices were waiting, and at the moment her babies left her tunnel and breathed and filled the room with their cries, Lahara understood the words clear in her mind—*Level Nine, We'll come from Level Nine*—and then the twins were in her arms and with them, hope.

The Civ woman bringing her second meal agreed to allow Lahara's door to unlock for a wall count of thirty so she could walk and soothe the fussing babies, and some short period after the Civ left Lahara entered the corridor without a plan but with her swaddled twins, and with food straws stuck in the folds of her sling, and it was then she'd seen the doors.

She stepped carefully. The slit where her legs met was sore, and she was musty with a sharp odor, some combination of blood and birth fluids. She ran her hand along the curved wall to the first door, and when she reached the opening, she peered in.

It was a private like her own, the mattress covered in a smooth gray sheet and soft black blanket, the floor pads clean. On the shelf was a woven travel box, and beside that, curiously, a walking stick. Neither were Vaulter items.

She hurried to the next glass door and stepped inside. "Hallo, halloo," she called, but nobody answered.

A quilted knapsack hung on the wall. She dug into the bag, empty but for a thin strip of silver, one she recognized from her own arrival. A shiny tag pressed on her arm but easily peeled away, later, that proclaimed she'd passed through the shower—what they called the purple light with no water—and was now rid of the bugs, the sweat, the dirt. Rid of the outside.

One of her babies shifted and burped, a gasp of air that began a soft wail, and Lahara stuck her thumb into the boy's mouth to soothe him even as her breasts loosed the milk and her tunic became wet. "Shhh, soon," she whispered, backing out of the empty room and into the corridor.

A banging thudded from further down the hall and she traced the sounds to Fee's private—the only one, except Lahara's own, with a closed door. After listening a moment, she knocked softly.

Fee pulled the door open and glared at her, throwing a hard book across the room, cursing as she did. "You with your babies attached like birds to sugar flowers," she spat. "Away."

Lahara ignored her venom. "Is Racine gone again?"

Fee pressed a hand to her eyes. "While you were birthing and yelling louder than a beast fall in a crevice, he left. He wouldn't tell where and he hasn't yet returned."

The twins were sniffling and making sounds that would turn to cries, and in their warmth they smelled both sweet and sour. "The doors are open," Lahara said, hoping to distract Fee.

"News like stale bread. I done them myself," Fee shrugged.

Lahara loosened the sling and pulled her tunic open, trying to figure how Fee could have unlocked the privates. She manipulated the babies with both arms and stood in the doorway, uninvited inside, setting them to sucking, and wincing at the sting as the hard, hungry mouths latched on. She shifted her hip to hold them steady but the girl detached from her breast almost immediately. Lahara jiggled her arm to keep the newborn from crying.

"A group of companions arrived last night," Fee said, offering no help. "The females are to private on this level. I opened the doors to show myself Racine wasn't with any of them." She shrugged again. "I'm still to look at the Level Nine privates. Perhaps Racine finds comfort in a male companion come."

Level Nine. What the voice in the undercurrent had spoken.

"I can add my eyes to your search," Lahara offered quickly. "We'll make fast work of Level Nine and find Racine if he's there."

The tall woman disappeared into her water room, but didn't close the door to the corridor, and Lahara took the gesture as an invitation. She stepped inside and sat carefully on the bed next to scattered clothes and books, adjusting the babies to sucking again, watching the back of their heads in the mirror on the far wall. The boy's scant hair was dark, the girl's closer to red, favoring Switch.

"Where are the companions now?" she called into the bath, trying to imagine which neighbors would come to such a place for such a reason.

Fee would know, as she knew much of the goings on here, her aloof, seductive insistence rewarded often with tellings that required for her part no more than a glance or half smile. Vaulters and Civ-staff both were free with words and favors around her, though Fee seemed to care little for either unless they were to do with Racine.

"The women are taken to meet who they're matched with," Fee said over her splashings. "The men will match with their Vaulters and Civs this evening. More companions arrive later."

Lahara wondered if Patrice was to be matched, or any of the Civs who carried the foods or gathered fruit from the gardens or mopped the rooms and left clean clothing.

The babies were squirming uncomfortably and Lahara moved Fee's things aside, laying the two on the wrinkled blankets. Their coverings were wet and she peeled them away, shocked at the red skin beneath. She pulled the yellowed cloth out from under each and folded the soaked squares into a pile, unsure what else to do with the wraps and without replacements.

She lifted her babies, one at a time, and held each against her, careful not to trouble their taped belly stubs, stroking their downy backs gently to release the bubbles. They were quiet then, falling asleep, and Lahara lay them back on the bed, hoping their silence spoke of contentment and not weakness. Their skin was so thin. Their bodies so tiny. As tiny as her sister's stillborn.

Lahara listened to the sounds of Fee's cleanse and wondered about the young woman behind the closed door. How would she visit Level Nine when stairs were locked and codes ungiven?

She picked up one of Fee's books. Lahara could read and write enough to encourage Marly and Beatrice, but the spellings confused her and she wouldn't understand a whole book full. Fee, however, had good spellings and spent long days with the Vaulter books. Had she found answers there?

Fee emerged, naked and wet from the bath, and unsealed a bundle of fresh tunics and leggings. "Racine can't give babies," she said abruptly, eyes down as she rifled through the laundry. "They are all, each Vaulter and Civ, made barren for this place. It was done at the beginning and cannot be changed."

Lahara put the book down, not understanding how one was made barren but believing Fee's words. "There are good men all across our city who can give you babies. We'll get home and you will have yours and continue your line."

Fee slid a white shift over her head and Lahara watched the thin fabric absorb the drops of water on her skin. "I've made my choice," Fee said quietly. "And it will never be the same at home."

The newborn girl hiccupped and let off with a wail that shattered the quiet and woke her twin, setting him to crying also. Fee frowned. "Would you like to hold one?" Lahara asked.

Fee's eyes softened and she leaned in, but as she did, a thick void spread beneath them. "That mess is where Racine beds me," she said, and although Lahara expected anger from Fee, there was instead—something else.

She carried her scowling babies to the sink to clean their skin. By the time Lahara dried them with Fee's bath towel and covered each with a folded square from the pile beside the basin, Fee had stripped the sheets and turned the blowing on to dry the mattress.

Lahara tied the babies back into the sling. Fee watched with that strange expression, twisting the ropes and half braids of her hair into a knot. She slid a glass bangle onto her arm. A Vaulter charm—one that opened locked doors—dangled from her wrist.

"Took it from a Civ musta thought she lost it in her work," was all Fee said as she walked into the corridor, and Lahara followed.

Fee sprinted down the hallway, shutting doors she had previously opened, and Lahara waited, leaning against the wall, weighted by the sleeping babies across her chest. She caught a glimpse of her reflection in the curved glass and recognized what she had seen in Fee's face.

Discomfort. Discomfort and a misguided notion that relief would be found in the other woman's circumstance. Lahara shook her head. Odd to have envy for the girl she'd believed—mistakenly, perhaps—to be useless for her devotion to Racine.

Fee disappeared around the curve of the hall and Lahara worried she had gone on without her, but in just a few moments she reappeared from behind, her long legs having carried her the full circuit of the Level Eight corridor.

Lahara's face must have told her surprise for Fee nodded and said, "I've much time to occupy when the man leaves. I have no *whisper* sessions and nobody applauds my secrets. So I've made the circle. Over and again. Every day my legs are quicker and stronger." She grinned, and Lahara couldn't remember if she'd ever seen her smile before. "I'm fit to be a Runner."

Lahara looked at her own legs, weak and skinny after the endless time strapped to the sessions chair without sun and without her daily work in the fields. She felt again the discomfort—no, jealousy. Sabat had warned of the hormones, but she hadn't understood. Her tears might have spilled then if not for a buzz come from inside her, and a deep rolling voice telling, *We are two! Can you hear us?*

Yes, yes, she sent back into the current. *Yes, I hear you.*

Fee had the charm to open doors but they still made cautious journey down the stairs, for Civs and Vaulters were up and down to their own tasks and there'd be no warning in their descent if any other entered with their glass. Lahara and Fee would be caught like mice in an oiled bucket.

"Are there Touched on Level Nine?" she whispered as they

slipped out into a hallway identical to theirs on Eight—dark doors on the inner wall, multi hor-vert lifts on the outer wall at the corridor's curve, and scrolling lights and muted alerts displayed and reflected on the slick floor and high ceiling.

Fee put her ear to the first door. "Touched? I wouldn't know." She listened where she crouched. "Someone breathes inside. A companion, I'm certain. I can smell the outside as sure as I can smell a Vaulter's scabs."

She tapped the charm at the handle and the glass opened wide. They looked in—a tall man lay snoring on the thin mattress. Lahara would have woken him, but Fee shut the door and they moved on.

The next room was empty with no sign anyone had been inside. Fee hurried to one further, and the door after that, and Lahara kept up, careful not to jar the babies in her haste. Fee was opening doors faster now—moving on without closing each again—but Lahara took a moment to latch them, covering the signs of their search.

She slowed to oblige the throb of her back and the twins shifted, sensing the change in motion. The girl opened her eyes, tiny hands flailing, fingernails scratching at the fabric wrapped around her. "Shh, shh," Lahara soothed, and the infant settled, hands relaxed.

Fee gestured to Lahara there was somebody inside the private ahead, making motions for her to hurry. A green light flashed to signal a hor-vert beyond would open in the wall at a count of ten, and just a brief moment later the bell sounded and Lahara knew only seven beats remained.

She quickened her pace as Fee tapped her charm. The private opened and Fee grabbed Lahara, pulling her inside and closing the door behind them without wasting a motion.

Lahara stumbled. Strong hands caught her, and in the surprising moment before a sticky plastic was pressed against her mouth and a dark hood pulled over her head, Lahara saw the tattoo on the wrist holding her—the Chelsea crest—arms and legs entwined with trees and roots in black and soft green ink.

It all happened so quickly. Wrists tied behind her, blinded and gagged, she tried to force her shoulders forward to shield the babies on her chest. She heard sounds of scrambling, and voices through the thick cloth covering her face.

"Fux, what? S'not the bald ones," a voice was saying, and another, "Dinna know more would come."

Other words she couldn't make out and then the bag was pulled from her head and Lahara saw a yellow-haired young man, cringing in horror, the hood hanging in his hands. The dark, soft headpiece was sewn with long stitches, shaped from what looked like the blanket removed from his own mattress, and he turned it over and again in distress.

"Shit sorry, dangum, it's the babies. Ahh no, did you hurt? Fux. Dangum fux."

Lahara peeled the plastic from her mouth. The young man was staring at the top of the tiny heads peeking from their wraps, and when he looked up, Lahara met the *whispers* in his eyes. She drew back in surprise, not only for the jolt of the Touched, but for the shape of his face, the slant of the eyebrows, the dark cream of his skin, the inked crest. He looked like Reko.

"I..." She stopped, unsure what to say, and turned to Fee who was backed against the far wall.

A second young man, looked like this first, but with black hair tied on top of his head, held a hood in his hands as he removed tape from Fee's mouth. "We thought you were the others."

Lahara heard voices from the corridor—they all did—and footsteps of the hard-shoed Vaulters. When the man with the inked crest moved toward the other to listen, Lahara realized they were twins. "You're Reko's brothers. Rolf and Roman." She looked at the two, remembering. "The Touched drowned at sea."

"Dinna drown," the dark one, Roman, said, finger to his lips.

"Hafta stop," Rolf whispered to his brother. "It's too risky."

"What is?" Lahara said.

Roman shook his head. "We do like we planned."

A knocking on the door. The sound of charm tapping handle. Rolf grabbed the black hood from his brother's hands and shoved both into the waist of his leggings, covering them with his tunic and diving onto the bare bed, curling on his side.

Roman motioned Lahara and Fee into the water room, and they hid quickly, sliding the door shut just as the dark glass to the corridor opened.

"Roman?" a woman's voice—Marilena's—was saying. "You're non-compliant to Farm task. Did the Civ not come to escort you?"

"Civ come and be gone. She left me to tend my brother who can't raise from his mat except to void. He pours sickness from both ends."

"Why wasn't I notified? Civ should have brought word to me."

"D'know why not," Roman said. "She told she would."

There was some mumbling between Marilena and a second voice—Patrice—who said sharply, "Seth needs you now, Rolf. Get up. You know how important this is."

"Rolf requires medicine," Roman said. "I can retrieve it as you be occupied with work. Le' me tend my brother. The nanos grow and are ready to receive data without my watching."

Lahara listened through the door. The babies squirmed as she shifted, turning red for the disturbance and arching their backs. "Do something," Fee said. "They look to cry."

She bounced the infants lightly, humming, and they closed their eyes again, but she knew their silence could change in a single breath. The alcove along the back of the water room was enclosed in thick plastic and Lahara raised her chin to it. Fee nodded and they crowded into the space, pulling the rubber curtain around to muffle sound and seal themselves in.

There was little room to stand. The damp compartment smelling of mildew and sweet soap was made smaller by a large pile of towels, and Lahara shoved them with her foot, jumping back at the resistance met, grabbing Fee who covered her mouth with her hand.

There was someone sat beneath the towels, knees up, pressed into the corner, black hood over the head, white-jacketed arms and white-skirted legs bound with strips of gray sheet. Lahara's stomach twisted. "It's a Civ."

"Does she breathe?" Fee whispered.

Lahara carefully pulled the hood off, holding it by the tips of her fingers. The Civ was alive—her chest moved up and down with breath—but her mouth was covered with the sticky tape and her eyes were closed in narrow unseeing slits.

Fee felt along the neck of the Civ's jacket, pulling a silver glass bead from the woven piping. "Don't touch her," Lahara cringed, but Fee was not stopped, and next reached under the Civ's sleeve to unclasp the glass charm from her wrist.

Sounds from the private carried in as the door slid open—words, coughs, pacing footsteps—and Lahara and Fee froze in their hidden alcove. "Be done with your business then I'm bringing you to your session," they heard Patrice say, and the water door slid shut again.

The air came on, blowing a loud wind, and the rubber curtain opened abruptly. It was Rolf faced them. He rubbed his spiky yellow hair. "Dinna plan you would see her," he said under his breath. "Roman figured a sleeping spray." He took the hood from Lahara and placed it gently over the Civ's head again, explaining, apologetic. "It's how we catch the spiny ones at home. It calms them. Don't worry. Civ'll be found when we're gone."

"Gone where?" Lahara asked, in a voice louder than she'd intended.

He started the water, splashing his hands under the stream. "We've not much time while I'm to be throwing my vomit." He gagged, speaking as he made his pretense. "We're to leave Vault. All of us. We were to find you but luck had you find us."

"How're we to leave?" Lahara asked, thinking of her own plan.

Rolf closed the latrine, the rushing void wash covering his words. "Roman's *whispers* figured how to work the Freight. We'll ascend to Level Six," he said, removing the hoods and strips of cloth from his waist. "And hike to the river."

Heavy knuckles rapped on the handle and Lahara jumped at the sound. Patrice's voice was sharp through the door. "Rolf?"

"Just finished," he said, moving to exit, but Patrice pushed in instead, forehead furrowed first in annoyance, then confusion, and finally in realization and shock and anger as her lashless eyes swept past Rolf to Lahara and Fee.

"Don't," Lahara shouted as Patrice reached for her Prod.

Marilena rushed in at Lahara's cry, Roman right behind her. He shoved the Vaulter and she fell on Patrice, tumbling across the basin with him. Fee grabbed the Prod as Marilena twisted up with her own, wielded. The two swung wildly around the small space, Marilena discharging the Prod onto the wall, shattering the glass doors and mirrors. Fee blasted Patrice's, catching Marilena who crashed to the ground atop broken glass and splintered wall.

The babies howled and Lahara wished to scream also. Rolf was removing little silver glass beads from the Vaulters' heads before covering them, while Roman bound them and sprayed the struggling Patrice from a small vial. Lahara averted her eyes at the woman's sudden stillness.

She squeezed past and out and sat on the bare bed, pulling the crying babies into position—first the girl, who relaxed at the milk, then the boy who whimpered even as he sucked. The sounds of dragging bumps in the water room caused Lahara guess the two Vaulters joined the Civ behind the rubber curtain.

Fee pushed out first, Roman behind her, then Rolf, twisting the silver beads taken from the Vaulters. "Give me the Civ's Link," he said to Fee. "A channel for us is just numbers I can manipulate."

"I won't," she said, rolling the transparent bit of silver between her fingers. "I'm to listen and find Racine where he hides."

"He doesn't hide," Roman said. "He's gone permanent outside as they make ready to rip our *whispers* from us."

"Let the *whispers* be gone. I'll join him outside."

"You're not understanding. Touched will die."

Lahara gathered her babies close. "Is it the punishments?"

Roman shook his head. "Copies of every *whisper* are stored in Heaven and they're to retrieve them through the Interface you found. But when they download, a Field Wipe will first erase the *whispers* already in us." He leaned in. "We wouldn't survive such, but I've a plan made, yah."

As Lahara tried to make sense of Roman's warnings, the sparkling pieces in Rolf's hand caught her eye. "The Connex are two," the yellow-haired twin said. "But without counting Fee, who carries her own, we are three in need."

"Wait," she said, untwisting from her curls the many-faceted charm that sometimes blinked with a wild eye. "I've worn this horse gem since summer last. Now the Connex are three."

❖❖❖

The wailing was like none Lahara had ever heard, a high-pitched shriek flying up and down in both tone and volume. The dim lighting of the arched passage had flared to a white pulse that lit every scratch in the dirty stone walls. She was running, mud-damped slippers fallen from her feet, babies crying on her chest. Footsteps pounded behind her, but she feared wasting time to turn and judge their distance.

They'd entered the Freight on Level Nine and when the enormous room lurched and opened again, they were on Six. Lahara smelled earth and water and fragrant mud, and knew that a walking distance through the winding, damp tunnel would find the river, but as they journeyed around a bend in the passage, the four came head on with an arriving group of outside men and women, one Vaulter at the front and one at the rear. Companions.

Lahara gasped to see, as the two groups collided mid-passage, a tall, blue-braided woman. Lahara was certain of her cousin Grindle even in the faint light. They recognized each other at the same moment, and before Lahara knew what was happening, there was pushing and scrambling, and Fee screamed at the lead Vaulter, "Tell me where is Racine? I'm his asset. He needs me," and Roman raised a Prod to surge the hairless, shouting to the rest, "Go back."

Lahara grabbed Grindle and Fee and they, with the Touched twins, ran back to the Freight, one downed Vaulter in their wake, the companions screaming, lights blinding and alarm disorienting.

Scalding steam from the Freight's pipes filled the passage ahead and Lahara was grateful for Rolf slowing and grabbing her hand, as she held Grindle's, to pull them through the vapor.

"She's my cousin," Lahara shouted over the siren as they entered the Freight.

"I come as a companion," Grindle said. "To bring you out."

"We're nobody out now," Fee yelled, tears washing her face.

"Level One?" Roman asked, maneuvering the metal to close. "Out the top and across the Bridge?"

"Nah," Rolf said. "All will be looking for us that way."

"Out again?" Roman asked. "Fight to the river? Suggestions?"

The Freight loosed sparks into the interior, tiny bits burning Lahara's arms, and Grindle pushed her back, blocking her and shielding the babies. The others, too, were hit with energy needles and molten drops, and quick blisters rose on Roman's face where the sparks touched his skin.

"Canna stay here," he said. "Their prods blast. Up or down?"

"Down," Lahara said. "I know another way."

By the time the Freight reached Level Seventeen, Lahara's ears felt to cramp from the descent. Roman opened the far gate onto the corridor where lights blazed as brightly as in the river tunnel and the sirens wailed as loudly.

"This way," Lahara said, running arm in arm with Grindle to the silver doors she'd been though just a day earlier. Had it really been only yesterday?

"I don't know where the Rails lead," Lahara said, catching her breath. "But it's a passage out and away."

Roman pulled Rolf close, speaking into his ear. His twin shook his head and Lahara turned her eyes from his anxious face. "Unlock it," Roman told Fee and she tapped a glass charm to open the doors.

Roman shoved Rolf toward the ramp revealed by the corridor's glare and his twin cried out, "Whya go changed your mind?"

"Dinna change it," Roman said firmly over the alarms. "Was always my intention to get you out to tell Ma our story. I've a plan to destroy the nanos and find the others I know are here."

"Please, brother," Rolf said. "We're stronger together, yah?"

Roman hesitated a long moment, then nodded. "Yah."

Grindle took Lahara's arm. "We need go now, cousin."

Lahara took only a brief moment to decide, as voices shouted from down the corridor. She lowered her face to her babies' sweet skin. "Take them," she said, handing the newborns to Grindle.

"What are you saying?"

"Three *whispers* are stronger than two. I need stay to destroy what threatens us all. Bring my babies to Switch. There's liquid in the pouch they can suck until you find a mother's milk."

Fee pressed down on the lever and the gate opened. "When the door is closed again," Roman told her, "Point your Prod at the metal. Melt the handles so none can go following."

"But how will you get out?" Grindle cried, clutching the babies to her body and stepping onto the ramp.

"We'll get out," Lahara said, and she pulled the heavy door closed, shutting her newborns and Grindle and Fee away in the dark passage.

They waited to see the sparks—Fee fired the silver Prod as instructed—and as Vaulters materialized around the curved hall, Lahara and the Chelsea Wood twins slipped into the rotunda to disappear in the Vault's vast machinery.

JARED HOPES

ALTHOUGH HE LIKED traveling in formation and the great distances he could cover while in the queue, Jared was glad the Lens had stopped on this outcrop overlooking the rift far north of the city, and glad to sit above the water with the others and eat the meal carried overnight under his journey robes—hard fired eggs, tart apples picked from Zoo trees, and a flask of juiced mint.

He had little to say. The few words he might speak, mostly musings about Elizabeth, seemed of no consequence in the beautiful silence of nine Lens sitting on this remote bluff with him, eating their own meals, flicking hands and eyes at each other and the world in tiny motions that had the ability to move mountains.

They'd traveled far, this day, their journey marked by faded signs covered in graffiti—*Spuyten Duyvil, Riverdale, Ludlow*—signs sprung from crumbling riverside platforms and tracks hidden beneath ages of dirt and sand and grass. And here, just above them now, the sign spelling *Yonkers*, the bleached letters still visible through moss and paint and black mold and decay.

Jared looked to the numbers—06.06.2257—watching the light play over the spellings, surprised at the sun's position, already late afternoon. The larger day animals would be resting in long shadows, night beasts still some time from waking for their hunt. Except for a pair of dolphins come to welcome the Lens, the river was calm and the sky, also.

How different from the night. Jared had slipped into the queue at Zoo House and dark-walked, safe in formation with the Lens—*already done*—to the Norte, where Elizabeth was to remove herself for other purposes. It concerned him she would be near that awful spot on the Hudson, and he'd quietly sworn to protect the woman pure as the gold he drew from dull metal.

They traveled a dangerous overland route, but their low, whistled tones kept hungry and predatory creatures in a wide orbit around the formation, and when they crossed the waterways west of the Zoo, crocodiles snapped only after they'd passed, and when wide-winged owls the height of half a man dove from overhead, it was away from the queue that moved toward Manhattan.

The Bronx woods and roads and burnt half-buildings were thick with cat beasts and long-limbed creatures and slithering hard-shelled animals crawled from the underground streams, and the Lens could see and smell and hear each in the night. Any other traveling through the wild places would be grabbed and gone, but the Lens dropped hunt meat as gifts and the beasts withdrew.

By sunrise they'd reached the spot where the choked Harlem River met the Hudson, and after seeing Elizabeth across the muddy flow, Jared had turned to look back at the forest once his home. He was connected to the Inwood clan he'd left for a life at Zoo House, and in the same way his *whispers* allowed him to sense gold in lead, and force in the atom, he'd sensed his aunt deep in the forest and waved, knowing she was well.

The Lens continued on without Elizabeth beyond the city, and when they reached the river cove just north of the canal, Jared glanced quickly at the spot he'd first ever seen her through a long glass from the Norte Inwood. The marshy inlet showed no scorch or stain, but his own eyes burned—even now—for the seeing, eased only slightly to remember hooded, robed Lens pulling Elizabeth and the children up the rocks and away from the awful spot.

He'd been still a boy then, held back by his aunt from joining the Group that Left. The call to follow pulled him, though, and he'd slipped from her custody in hopes of connecting with those already passed. He'd raised the long glass to mark their route, finding instead the Group's journey ended unexpectedly a short hike across the dead end canal.

Those not felled with sparks or chased into the water to drown were roped together and herded onto a long silver ship. It was Elizabeth come from that same ship to grab the children and run, and although he couldn't hear for the distance, the screams he imagined haunted his sleep to this day.

It seemed the Lens formation lingered above that awful place, but in fact the queue continued forward. Jared took refuge in his *whispers* as they journeyed, and in the moments between *whispers*, pulled back to position—seven robes in front and two behind—he sought further distraction by entering—anyone in queue could—the Lens mind, the group perception of all happening around them.

The midday sun sparkled on the river and the Lens mind knew many boats sailed north. Elizabeth was on the first, carrying the charm Jared had crafted from the negative and positive, and he kept his focus on her as she sailed beyond the queue.

Some time later Jared was pulled from his *whispers* where he'd been contemplating the radiating sphere—another design of balanced force—that he'd hidden in his robe. He found himself, in formation, passing between a sulfurous waterway parallel to the Hudson and a far-reaching line of tumbled brick. He could no longer see Manhattan to the south, and the land here was empty of journeymen, for the beasts were many and the insects hungry.

And yet, though no person would navigate this landscape, the Lens mind was turned to a horse carrying two travelers—a man and his child—not long behind them.

From within the queue, soft whistles—air through teeth—swirled around and out. The Lens directly ahead moved her fingers and tapped her thumb on her palm, lifting her robed elbow over and again in a rhythm Jared couldn't duplicate, and although sharp-clawed creatures thundered along a path at the top of the brick, they remained a distance from the horse they shadowed.

The Lens lifted their chins and smiled at those beasts and at the sting beetles clinging motionless to shifting leaves, and at the snakes in the fibrous trees that hung without twisting around those passing uninvited. And with the taps and whistles and smiles of the Lens—*already done*—the horse and its riders received protection in the wild place.

Six of the boats traveling together had passed by now. One final sailed behind, and the Lens mind detected another following further downriver, this last dinghy filled with air and crept out from the larger Vault cruiser anchored below the barren Wave Hill, a morning's hike south.

Sssssss. Sssssss. The Lens whistles pulled Jared back from a deep whisper trance and he tried to focus. The river was bright with sunlit ripples and seven small boats—Elizabeth in one of them—anchored mid-river, just south of the rift. He held his egg—uneaten—in his hand, and two green apples lay in his lap.

He offered one to the Lens beside him, but she smiled and shook her head, busy making the whistle sounds, so he bit into the fruit, eyes and mouth watering at the sour on his lips.

The man and boy—his son—had jumped from the horse, a sleek, bald animal, and, splashing in the shallows, the father was calling across the water to the boats, but his shouts failed to reach them for the distance and the boaters' own calls to each other. The Lens snapped fingers softly and the travelers' bare legs remained untouched by hungry creatures clinging to submerged river rock.

Jared peeled his egg and pulled apart the quivering white casing to reveal the soft, dark orange center. The tall silver birds on the Zoo shores had a short nesting season and he wouldn't have hard egg again until the next, so he savored the creamy heart melting in his mouth—it tasted of fish and sweet grass—then chewed the cool, rubbery white, and saving his favorite for last, crunched the shell, washing the hard bits down with mint.

The Lens rose in unison and Jared stood with them to watch the boats. "Is Elizabeth safe to cross the rift?" he asked, but the Lens beside him only touched his hand.

The first boat entered the whirlpool and spun, spit out after long moments. The next put into the vortex and the waters twisted over, clutching the boat even longer before releasing it into the calm of the north. Neither of the first boats crossing carried Elizabeth. Jared was certain he would know when the river had taken her in its spirals.

The third boat passed easily through the whirlpool during a fleeting lull in the gyrations to emerge quickly and safely across, but the fourth, hurrying to benefit from the same lull, became trapped in renewed turbulence, and in one blink of an eye was lifted—it hung in the air a moment—then was tossed back into the twisting water, pieces and passengers pulled irretrievably under.

The Lens remained motionless in the immediate aftermath, but while the man and the boy ran back and forth along the rocky banks unable to help the boats on either side of the rift, the Lens mind cleared and fingers began to tap again on skin, eyes flicking back and forth. They nodded to one another, blinking, and in response, dolphins and other large water animals gathered—some surfacing—along the shore and around the remaining boats.

At the sight of the beasts, the man gathered his son onto the horse and they backed away from the river's edge, and Jared, too, retreated—hiding a moment in the folds of his hood—so big were the animals kicking up foam and water as they circled.

The boats already crossed had anchored on the far side of the vortex and the three waiting held their position amid the water animals. Jared tried to detect Elizabeth, but the Lens mind overshadowed his probe, turning to the air canoe trailing the boats. The inflatable drew near, moving quietly at the shoreline, its hairless passenger mal-intentioned and dark in energy.

And now there was movement on the water. The boats were maneuvering around the dolphins, and the first approached the whirlpool. The Lens raised their chins and as the boat sailed into the vortex the animals buffered and protected it, keeping the small sailboat upright through to the other side. The second followed, and again, the animals swam close, the pressure of their bodies stabilizing as the boat spun out into the clear northern water.

Five had gone through, one was lost, and the last boat now was nosing into the rift. Jared felt Elizabeth on the spiraling waters, and although the dolphins and whales kept her upright, the rift force blasted her boat out and up to land hard at the east with a splash raining onto the river like a sudden storm.

When the water cleared Jared saw the boat was drifting within earshot of the father and son shouting, "Message for Anthony," and Elizabeth's boat moved closer still for the calling.

The hairless was moving too, scraping his air canoe along rocks overland, too far south to hear the words yelled, but close enough to see the horse and boat near the shore. The Lens had given the hairless a name—*Driscoll*—and knew the man carried a stick harnessing a deadly force.

What the horseman called from shore made no sense to Jared. *Heaven. Nadia. Field Wipe.* Elizabeth's hood had fallen—she was so beautiful—and she and her companions on the boat called back in acknowledgment of the man's message. After a few moments, the father and son climbed back onto the horse.

Driscoll watched from below the path, shouting, "Aja," and the man kicked to a gallop at the sound. The Lens tapped protecting rhythms over and again, even after the travelers were long out of sight south.

Jared fingered the radiating sphere in his pocket, knowing two things. One, he must never wake its power, and two, he would do so in an instant to keep Elizabeth safe.

Short jabs. Hard angled movements of the Lens. Jared let go of the sphere, aware now the Lens were shielding Elizabeth and the others. They clicked tongues and pointed fingers up and down in unison and the beasts in the highlands gathered and moved into the river valley. Jared heard teeth and claws and strong muscles snapping in their passage, and the earth shuddered as they lumbered and leapt to the rhythm of the snaps and pokes and rustling hoods.

Driscoll must have heard the creatures first, for he turned to the low hills rising at the east and began to run. A cat beast at the head of the pack caught him, leaping at his neck to bring him down to the grass. Huge birds circled, waiting for their due, and the long-limbed big-teethed creatures with flaring nostrils bounced up and down, beating matted chests with hairy fists and screaming a garbled language the Lens understood and smiled at.

And in an instant, to the beat of the fingers tapping, the dark energy Driscoll was removed from the Lens mind—*already done*—and the animals fed.

ANTHONY

THEY WERE A somber group, bandanas tied on their faces to protect against the fumes, eyes red rimmed from the same and skin hot for the dry, scorched air funneling from cracked stone. They gathered around the sputtering fire on a thin strip of beachhead between the cliffs and the river, the sun setting as they pulled the last of the fish from their sharp bones and threw what little bramble could be found on the flames.

They'd lost two in the boat that failed to cross the rift—a young man named Lon and the Touched woman Mahindy who'd sung her *whispers* at Norte Inwood.

Anthony regarded the fourteen who remained. Elizabeth, Tinny, Starly the guitarist, the rock climber Bo, Touched Drake from the midtown Mount, the young man Pep also from the Mount, the spiral-tattooed Brenny, arm around his similarly inked wife Nia, Crispin from below Crease, Beetus the falconer, old Martin from Carl Schurz come to put a stop, he said, to things unseen, and Touched Reynaud with his father, Charles.

Except for Starly, who'd arrived at the Norte just days before Anthony to replace a cousin called home, and Nia and Brenny, two newcomers also joined just days earlier following the loss of their newborn daughter a single season after the death of their son, most of this expanding group had been together several months, some since the beginning of the Resistance.

They'd fought successfully against a common enemy, and although they'd suffered together as well, their losses had come early this trip. Those losses, combined with the news brought by Switch on Anthony's horse, left them rocked and stunned.

"Field Wipe?" the falconer asked. "I have Touched in the Central Park. What of them? Are they to die from such a thing?"

"We'll stop it," Anthony said. "Vault doesn't know we've been warned. But we still have to get inside. The plan stands."

"We need be home, preparing our own to leave the city," Drake said. "We all have Touched in danger's path."

"My nephews are missing now a full season. Drowned? I dunna believe that for even one breath. That's why I'm here." Crispin rolled dry leaves and held the slim cigarette to an ember. "But my Onesie's below Crease still. Are they safe? Who can know for certain it's only Touched in harm's way?"

"There's nowheres to go, not for any," Tinny said. "Beasts to the north and east, fire to the west, water to the south."

"Some say Touched have gone to the Disconnects," Pep offered. "I've looked for their hidey hole. My mother may be with them. We can go there, too."

"They call themselves Lens," Elizabeth said, a deep sadness in her eyes. "Your mother is not with them." She turned to the group. "But even those Touched living with the Lens are not safe. We have to destroy the Heaven Interface."

"We can go further still," Brenny said. "If we follow this river for many days we'll come to the mountains. From there we can travel west or east. The grandparents of our grandparents knew of these places."

Old Martin ripped the bandana from his nose with gnarled fingers. His face and scalp were sunburned from the day's journey and his bright blue eyes burned hotter still. "I won't run," he shouted. "You're fools to think you can. Where will you hide? These Bad times will only follow you."

"Martin's right," Elizabeth said. "Vault's mission is to protect the *whispers*, but our Touched hold just a small portion of what exists. They would easily destroy ours to restore the entire treasure. We have to be as aggressive in our defense."

"I won't run," Reynaud's father promised.

Starly nodded, long white fingers clutching her flask. "Some of us can't run, you see," she slurred. "I won't run."

Pep echoed those words, as did another, and on around the circle the Never Agains repeated, "I won't run," until almost all had agreed.

Nia shook her head. "When our son fell to the fever our people brung us comfort, and when my hard birth cost us our newborn, our people brung us strength." Her husband put his arm around her shoulder. "Lon was only a boy. Mahindy leaves a daughter. We need return and tell their stories. It's what we do for our people," she said, and Charles glanced at his son, perhaps imagining the same fate for Reynaud.

Anthony held his hand up. It was true. He wasn't their people and he was reminded of this at every turn. But he was somebody's people, even if he'd left the one who needed him most.

"I'm very sorry for your losses," he said, angry for his isolation, his voice rising. He shook his head, not knowing why he was so enraged, why he was sharing. Self-conscious and uncomfortable, he was unable to stop. "You're not the only one, though. I had a family. A sister I lost. A niece I abandoned."

Elizabeth added thin branches to the fire. The Never Agains were patient, waiting for him to continue. Anthony shrugged. There'd be language they wouldn't understand, but he didn't care.

"Cut to the chase. One night my sister asks me for a lift into the city. Her car wouldn't charge. For a long time I blamed her battery. Blamed the weather. Blamed the never-ending construction on those damn stacked express roads. But I was drunk, and driving, and it was raining and I missed the detour off the FDR and went over the concrete into oncoming traffic."

He looked up at the sky. "My niece lost her mother that day. God only knows why they didn't pin vehicular manslaughter on me. It took another year to get sober, and by then I'd heard about the Project and came in. For a new start, I guess you could say," and he saw the men and women around the fire nodding. New starts they understood.

"But I'm clear-headed now. I see people. I hear them. And maybe I didn't know Lon and Mahindy like you did, maybe I'm not exactly one of their people, one of your people, but I listened to Mahindy sing and I copied her *whispers*." Feeling self-conscious again, he unrolled a rough mash paper from his pack. "Did any of you listen to her song?" Without waiting for a response, he read her words.

A high rising shore-cliff on heath that was grayish:
a path 'neath it lay, unknown to mortals
some one of the earthmen entered the mountain,
the heathenish hoard laid hold of with ardor.

He lifted his head. "Mahindy sang about us. It's an ancient story but ours as well." The Never Agains were silent—confused—and Anthony hesitated. "Don't you see?" he said. *"A high rising shore-cliff."* He pointed to the Palisades. "These are our shore-cliffs. *A path 'neath it lay, unknown to mortals.* The path to the Vault lies beneath. We enter the mountain to claim their hoard—medicines, supplies, provisions." He held out his hands. "Mahindy and Lon gave their lives for this mission. Why would we go back? How would that serve their memory?"

The Never Agains shifted. Anthony's face reddened. This is all beyond them, he thought, embarrassed at his outburst. They can't understand. He looked away. Maybe he was the one not understanding. Maybe he had totally lost touch with his confession. Maybe he was stupid to think this old, dead verse meant anything.

Tinny stood and Anthony waited for him to speak, for any reaction. "My sister also is gone," the big man said. "Such pain never feels better."

Another brief moment and Reynaud stood also, raising his arms. "For your sister, and for Mahindy and Lon."

The others followed him to their feet, repeating the words he'd given them, "A high rising shore cliff on heath that was grayish," and Anthony joined in, all fifteen reciting the Beowulf verse in soft unison for those they'd lost.

Anthony wasn't too surprised to hear rustling during the night when the tide shifted south, and murmurings at the shore where they camped, but he was surprised to wake and find it wasn't the white-inked couple who'd departed by the lights of the satellite corridor, but rather Crispin from below Crease, returned, according to the message scratched in the dry earth, to attend to his own in Chelsea Wood.

He scanned the water for any sign of the painted canoe on the current. The man was either gone beyond the whirlpool or pulled below. Nothing to see.

A stone and wood pavilion along the shore had survived the

ages beneath the cliffs, and further inspection showed while some of the timber posts were rotted, and a portion had been taken by fire, the foundation and roof—braced by steel—were sound. Old Martin, Reynaud's father Charles, and Beetus the falconer would remain at the river and shelter at the pavilion. *Watch One.* If a boat neared or a problem arose, Beetus would climb the slope and find *Watch Two* who'd relay to the next.

"Look to the numbers," Anthony said to the men. "06.07.2257. If we're not back by the time the center number spells 10, you're to leave to your families. Take the outrigger. It will be most stable."

"I'm to leave my son who climbs away?" Charles asked. He shook his head. "You best return."

"But, if we need go," Beetus asked, "What are we to do when we arrive home?"

Anthony kept his answer unspoken, as he didn't suppose, after all, that the men knew the word *Pray*.

Spike-tipped walking sticks in hand, the ten started up a steep northerly trail in search of the wider road Elizabeth knew to be cut into the cliff. Felled timber, stones, and a knotted underbrush made slow travel, and little black lizards hissed and darted in the scrub, disturbed by their climb.

The river splashed below and for the longest time, the voices of the men left on shore carried up through the brittle forest and still, suffocating air. Winding south, the trail became steeper.

Sweat ran down Anthony's face—partial cloud cover did little to cool the day—and as soon as the group stopped to rest under parched trees, he peeled his shirt off to tie around his head. Elizabeth removed her robe, folding the cloth into a narrow band to twist around her waist, and the others as well lightened their clothing to fight the heat and humidity and exertion and fumes.

Elizabeth set small red flags along their route as they climbed. Numerous times they were forced off the trail for boulders or brush too entangled to pass, and at these detours they pierced soft top layers of leaf and earth with their sticks to avoid precariously balanced rocks and narrow clefts concealed by overgrowth.

By midday, the group had gone as far as they could up the slopes butting against the cliffs, and still had not found the road. Dead-ended where the trail gave way, they looked over the huge drop to a jagged outcrop below. Hot gusts of air through the cliff face hit them again and again, and when storm clouds that had worked throughout the morning to cover the sky let loose their rain, they stood under the deluge to cool their baked skin.

"I'm certain we began our climb at the right spot," Elizabeth said. "The Alpine lookout is at the cliff top," she recalled. "This trail originates at the boat basin. I remember it all, but the road is gone."

"I can climb this face," Bo said, studying the towering cliff. "I'll lower a rope from the top to bring each up in a harness."

"Are you certain?" Anthony asked. "This isn't our only option."

"I've climbed the bluffs at the End over and again and brung neighbors up and down in harnesses. The rock is wet but yes, I'm certain."

Anthony nodded. "Tinny and Reynaud will keep *Watch Two* here. Bo, once we're up you'll descend again to join them."

"Understood." She pulled a length of blue cable from her back, demonstrating how to wrap and knot the ends to create each harness.

Elizabeth fingered her own rope and whispered to Anthony, "This handmade rope won't have the stretch of gear in our time, but as long as it doesn't snap, it's safe."

"Two yanks will tell you're ready to lift," Bo reminded the group as she reached and stuck her slender fingers into a deep crack in the column. Slowly, testing the rock for traction, she pulled herself up, toes of her rubber shoes grabbing the cliff face, one foot at a time. Knee bent, she removed one hand from the fissure, dipped it into a powder she carried on her hip, and stretched to a new hold.

Bo seemed to crawl like a long insect, arms and legs straight then bent, sideways then up and down, sometimes creeping diagonally or horizontally across the rocks. She stopped several times to wrap wire or bang rods into the face, or to crook a leg behind to wipe a slipper on the back of the opposite leg. During several rains she rested her weight on jutting ledges and waited.

Anthony gagged at the metallic taste of the rain running off his scalp into his mouth. Much to his discomfort, Starly wrapped her bare arms around him from behind, breathing fumes of cherry wine into his neck and face. He extricated himself, stumbling, and put a hand to the slippery cliff made blacker by the torrent. The ground turned to mud as the rain continued and the group held as still as possible so not to disturb the softening talus.

They were just beginning to get restless—and Anthony worried, as he could no longer see Bo—when a series of short, sharp whistles sounded from far above and a weighted rope crashed over the cliff and dangled near the ground.

He grabbed the homemade cable and pulled himself up a length to hang a moment before dropping to his feet. Satisfied the rope didn't snap at his weight, he turned to Elizabeth. "Okay."

She attached her harness and Anthony pulled twice. Elizabeth began to rise, hands held in front to keep from banging against the sharp rocks, and Anthony watched her become smaller and smaller until, finally, she disappeared.

The others rose in turn quickly without fuss, but when the rope dropped for the sixth time, Starly took her time wiping sweat from her white scalp and swallowing the last of her wine with a curse for the empty container.

She grabbed Anthony and whispered, "Don't think bad of me. I do what I have to." She attached her harness, and the pale woman with the smudged lavender eyes spun up and out of view.

After a time, the rope dropped for the final trip. A few moments later Anthony was yanked off his feet, the rope cutting into his groin as he rose, more quickly than he would have liked, up the rock face.

The vertigo was awful. To take his mind off the fact he was suspended a hundred feet above ground on a handmade rope surely weakened by the six gone before him, he turned in his harness from the cliff to the view across the Hudson.

Westchester spread from the far eastern shore in shades of green, the only reminder of another time the smokestacks rising from an orange brick building on the bank. Beyond, sprawling, pristine lands reclaimed by nature seemed ready for discovery. Rediscovery. If not for the beasts, Anthony thought.

The rope swung him close to the rock as he spun around, and he put his hand out, fingers swiping—crunching—not the cliff, but on and through an enormous, papery hive set back over a ledge.

"Shit," he said, jerking his hand back as angry wasps spilled from the tear, and although he was being pulled past the hive now, the roaring cloud followed.

He drew his legs up to protect against the onslaught and tipped forward from the motion, the horizon rising to meet him. He thrust back again to catch himself as wasps landed on his arms, his chest, his neck and his scalp, and he swatted at his face with wasp-covered hands.

The first sting felt like a lit match on his shoulder, the second and third like hot brands on his back. The wasps teemed over his peeling, exposed skin, and though the damaged hairless skin forged by the Cocooning might repel a thousand wasps, the stings Anthony had already suffered were taking their toll.

Dizzy, he reached for his Prod. The laser hummed in his fingers and discharged into the cloud of wasps. The energy arc jumped from one to the next with an awful sound, the bodies sizzling and dropping, the swarm decimated from the charge.

Anthony vomited over an arm still matted with crawling wasps. Unable to aim for the tremors, he dropped the hand holding the Prod, discharging the current in the same motion. The pulse hit his foot, blistering his toes, and as the energy coursed through him, wasps crackled and fell off. The weapon fell.

He was still rising, yes, but a darkness overwhelmed him and the last thing Anthony felt was the rain striking his skin, drops that hurt even as they refreshed.

The ground was hard under his back. A light cloth tickled his legs and chest, but below the sheet he was naked. Anthony cracked an eye to the starry sky, so bright under the SolSat's 06.08.2257 that the clearing glowed as if beneath stadium lights.

"He wakes," a voice called and Anthony focused on the small dark woman who appeared beside him, her white tattoos luminous under the blaze of the satellite corridor.

He pulled himself to sitting and the covering slipped from his arms, loosing dry clay from where it caked thick on his skin. "The numbers changed?" he coughed.

Nia offered a sip of water. His shoulder throbbed and his limbs itched. "Elizabeth" he said, turning to rustlings, but it was Starly rising from her bedroll.

"She's to the Rails," the guitarist slurred. "With Drake and Brenny and Pep. We thought you to die. We were waiting to—"

"Elizabeth found the entrance," Nia cut her off. "Near to this Watch. She returned to observe you during the night but she's gone again. It will take many arms to clear the way, she tells."

Anthony stood shakily, and the sheet dropped from his body. He looked down at his nakedness. "I'm gonna need my pants."

He went alone, leaving Nia and Starly at the *Watch Three* cliff top. The sun rose as he followed Elizabeth's red flags across a field of rough grass toward a low forest spreading west. The air tasted only faintly of charred fumes and Anthony sucked the oxygen in and drank frequently to flush the venom still in his system.

A herd of deer pounded alongside for many moments before pulling ahead, white tails high, toward parts unseen. A rusted sign—*Department of Global Data Management*—peeked through wildflowers taller than Anthony's shoulders, and Elizabeth's red flags directed him past these tangled weeds to a barbed fence and a gate forced open against the overgrowth and dragged across split paving beneath.

A stone building half hidden behind a metal annex rose over the vegetation at the end of the access road. Anthony pushed through the waist-high ferns—the plants bounced back behind him—and in a few minutes found himself at an open hangar filled with mud covered debris.

Elizabeth was holding a torch over unidentifiable wreckage and stacks of synthetic wrappings. He called to her and she shimmied to him through an obstacle course of equipment and stacked barrels.

"Thank God," she said, examining the welts on his arms.

"I'm okay," he said. "What do we have?"

She held his arm a moment longer before continuing. "The tunnel descends beyond this shed, but I don't know how much more of the blockage we can remove."

"Is there another way in?"

"When my father brought me into the Vault we boarded here on the loading platform. Like cargo," Elizabeth said. "This whole office was shuttered by then, the trains soon to be removed. We walked with a flashlight through many empty cars, down a long incline. At the very front of the train, doors opened onto a deserted, indoor platform. I believe that passenger platform should be somewhere below the main building ahead."

Anthony limped beside Elizabeth, joints feeling the effects of the wasps. Brenny and Drake carried picks and shovels dug out from the loading dock, and Pep was removing flags Elizabeth had placed at the cargo hangar, setting them instead along the path to the stone building. "Bread crumbs," she'd called them.

Signs forbidding access ringed what was once a paved driveway in front of the old stone structure partially fallen toward the rear, and black cameras hanging from metal frames pointed blind eyes in all directions. Almost invisible for the tall grass, a chrome van listed against a powerless charging station. Anthony kicked the huge off-road tires. A slim, white snake slithered away, disturbed by the vibration.

"Survey the grounds but be careful. The cliffs are just east," Anthony said to Brenny and Drake, gesturing to the property surrounding the main building.

He led the others inside. The floor was slick and overrun with rodents. Sunlight through a collapsed wall washed the room covered with moss. "If the passenger entrance was through here," he said, "there has to be some way down to the platform."

They crossed splintered floorboards to the rear of the building abandoned by the *Global Data Management Project*. A framed poster hung crooked on a cubicle wall—*Forever Saved, A Gazillion Little Bits* written in the clouds above an earth pixilated into all those pieces. A desk was upended in the muck.

Finding nothing on the first floor, they crept up a narrow stairway to a storage loft, also empty except for generations of squirrel nests. As they climbed back down, Anthony heard Brenny calling from outside, "There's something here. Under the dirt."

Anthony crouched to pull handfuls of loose earth from the rectangular shaft Brenny had uncovered, and Elizabeth's torchlight played over wide metal and enamel steps inside. "It's an escalator," he said, examining the brick foundation visible around the shaft. "The whole enclosure fell in."

The sun rose higher in the sky as they worked to empty the shaft, and after a couple of hours with shovels and hands, creating mounds of dirt and refuse, Anthony was able to lower himself in, squeezing through the path they'd cleared.

Under the light of his torch, the station at the bottom was revealed. Granite columns fallen across the escalator would need to be climbed over, but the platform was reachable.

He'd just turned back when the shouting began, and as he pulled himself out, the cries grew louder and it was Starly and Nia running toward them, Nia's face streaked with dirt, Starly's albino skin mottled red with the exercise.

"It's them," Starly was babbling. "We seen the hairless wagon. The long black one with them covered wheels."

"Where?" Anthony asked.

"It's a strong glass I viewed him through," Nia said, "stopped a morning's hike south."

Elizabeth paced. "This transport may have seen our travel from the heights, but he can't know where we are now or why."

"He knows," Starly sobbed.

"Listen to Elizabeth," Nia said. "She makes good sense."

Starly shook her head. "You don't understand. I told him. I sent his bird," she sobbed. "The hairless man took my son and I barter my betrayal for his safety."

"When did you send the bird?" Anthony asked.

"At the Norte. I made the spellings and told our route."

"Then even if he did follow, he has no way to know where the Rails are, since you yourself didn't know until we arrived cliff top."

Starly hung her head. "I sent a flare while Nia drowsed and you lay cold with the stings. I'm to light one at each location and add words as he showed me, and he will find us, and I must do so or he will hurt my boy. I have no choice."

"Which hairless is it?"

"I don't know. But he has no interest in the Rails or Never Agains, Anthony. Only you."

He frowned and took Starly's pack, over her sobs, and removed the flares. "Drake and Starly will remain here. Brenny, Pep and Nia, follow our exit plan and withdraw everyone onto the two heaviest boats—the weight will keep you safer across the rift—and return to the city."

Starly pulled a thin wire from under her cuff. A dangling bead—a Connex-Link—caught the light. "Take it," she said to Nia. "I was feared to be caught with it so I kept it hidden and unused. See and hear him before he sees and hears you."

Nia looked at the bead with confusion, and Elizabeth took the Connex from Starly and demonstrated. "Twist one way to enable the connection and twist back to stop transmitting. When it's open you may find a clue where the hairless is, but he may also find a clue about you. He gave it to Starly to keep tabs on her. Turn it on and off quickly when you use it."

Anthony nodded. "When you get on the river, release the message birds to each district with instructions to raise defenses. Assemble your people to wait on the Bridge's far, hot wall."

Nia, Brenny and Pep set off for the cliff, and as Anthony watched them cross the field, Drake grabbed his arm. "When we are home," the one *Touched with Genealogy* said, "I will introduce you to the daughter of Romell, descendant of your lost sister and your niece. Then you will understand what I already know. You, my friend, are also our people."

Anthony set to work slicing rubber from the tires of the van dead in the weeds while Drake rolled barrels stuffed with tarps and scrap from the hangar to the escalator. "Lemme help," Starly said, leaning in, but Anthony dismissed her. "Just stay where I can see you."

Elizabeth hiked back to remove the red marker flags, and by the time she returned, Anthony had finished stuffing the rubber shred into the barrels along with the other material, and he positioned the containers, one at a time, on boards just inside the shaft's entrance.

"Fire?" he asked Drake, and the Touched One handed him the box of smoldering coal he'd been charged with carrying.

"Get in. All the way to the bottom and away from the stairs," Anthony told them.

"What of my son?" Starly whispered. "I have to set the flare."

"I'll take care of it. Get below."

Starly and Elizabeth and Drake squeezed past the barrels and onto the steps. In a few minutes Elizabeth called, "We're down," and with one last check that everything was in place, Anthony squeezed himself into the shaft.

From the top steps of the escalator he wedged the flare he'd configured between the barrels, pushing the bases together above him until no room remained for a body to pass through.

He removed from his pack one of the bottles taken out of the smuggler's cave, unwrapping the flannel cover. His unexpected craving startled him. Working in the sun all afternoon had taken its toll. He was running on adrenaline.

The stopper in the centuries old booze was swollen in the bottle. He tried to jam it down inside but the head of the cork crumbled in his fingers. He tapped the brown bottle gently on stone, and then again harder, until the top of the glass cracked off. He sniffed the jagged opening. Harsh alcohol, and his eyes watered. He rolled the flannel and shoved the wick carefully into the whiskey. The other two bottles were also swelled with cork, and he repeated the same preparation, setting all three on the planks above.

Last chance. He imagined the taste. The warmth. He thought about how fearless he'd feel. How deeply he'd sleep. And he thought about his sister. And his niece. And what he'd taken from them. And how their descendant lived in the same world he now called home.

He shook his head and lifted Drake's firebox to the flannel wicks. When the cloth in each bottle caught and burned, he reached through the narrowest of spaces between barrels, tossing one flaming bottle of alcohol into each of the containers.

The booze exploded in the barrels, the rubber and scrap smoldering and set ablaze. Anthony pulled the switch on the flare, sending skyward colorful patterns the Vaulter would read, and then without looking back through the smoke, he descended after the others into the Rails.

RACINE

"WATCH THE POTHOLES, you morons," Racine screamed as he covered his Connex Panel against the puddles that splashed up from the pitted East Seventy-ninth Street pavement.

The commission to deploy to Manhattan had come, unexpected, and he'd left immediately to spearhead the island's transition from a free dominion of districts to a territory subject to the laws and command of the *Global Data Management Project.*

Runners had been circulating the martial orders and paid armies were moving into place. Racine was to oversee the construction of Civ stations in each district and had begun a tally of all assets held by the native population. Not a bad commission, and one he expected would yield personal gain. Who, after all, would notice the skim off a salvage society?

He rested his head on the hard seatback and smiled. Racine's report detailing poor old Lear's desertion during the acquisition of Lahara had placed him at the top of a short queue for promotion. There was work ahead but Racine hadn't invested centuries in the Project to land in a Neanderthal backwater. He'd make sure there was leisure as well, and amenities befitting a man of his position.

The wagon creaked over a rough wooden bridge spanning the stream on Lexington. The roads sucked. Infrastructure would be one of the first undertakings that Seth's mandatory volunteer workforce tackled.

The natives made their best travel by boat, but unregulated water access had seen its last season. The submerged energy recovered by the southern twins was proving a wonderful—and eventual profitable—means to control the rivers. Racine was anxious to see the Water Constriction System—developed using that ancient energy—put to use.

This was Racine's first trip across the island, as he'd been securing ID's and recording native capital along the west shore since his arrival. He felt exposed to the sulfur without his mask, but wouldn't appear weak wearing one.

He noted the unbreachable white stone walls along First Avenue—those would have to come down—and directed the men to turn north on Second, where expressionless natives watched them roll past.

The Runner had relayed that Anthony was taken to the Ninety-sixth Street Quarantine and Racine put his census taking on hold to bring the traitor into custody. It wouldn't be long now. He ran his fingers over his Connex, scanning for nearby embedded tracers, but picked up only his own and those of the three Civs pulling his wagon with the grungy native asset.

They turned east onto a narrow, deeply grooved road that passed under the remains of the transit highway. Ninety-sixth. "Stop here," he said, climbing down to approach the covered raft docked on the river.

He wouldn't board the Quarantine—no sense exposing himself, vaccinations notwithstanding—so he raised his Prod, as did the Civs behind him, calling in his most officious voice, "By order of the GDMP, raise your door and provide your identifications."

A slight breeze ruffled the tented raft. He stepped aside, allowing the Civs and native to board and unzip the canvas shelter. "Wha ho," the native said. "Gone."

Racine peered under the bleached tarp. No sick. No dying. No Anthony. "Jesus fuck," he said. "Where is he?"

The native shrugged, picking a scabbed tattoo on his wrist. Racine glared at the man's razor burned scalp and when he whistled a sharp tone Racine slapped his fingers from his mouth. "Where's Anthony?" he threatened. "Who had you guide us here?"

"Incoming," a Civ shouted, as glass, followed by stones and cement and more glass, crashed down from the tiered highway above. Racine threw his arms over his head and the Civs discharged their silver Prods into the air and at the native who was now fleeing north through the weeds and rubble.

Racine scrambled back into the wagon, and as the Civs maneuvered the vehicle away from the over-roads, the Vaulter looked back, catching a glimpse of, on the lowest tier, the nasty, matted braids of the scavenger Digger and his brother Mack.

FEE

THE BRILLIANT SUN felt to stab her, and Fee turned her face against the glare. With eyes calibrated over the past day and a half to the Rails' green glow, she was blinded now in the daylight, and readjustment was achingly gradual. The air, however, was cooler, if scorched, and her sweated clothes—smelling of sour and yeast and urine, this last from the babies—began to dry.

"We've come out opposite the wild places," Grindle said, pointing across the Hudson. "You can see the Bridge way to the south if you've the good eyes." She sniffed. "Never thought to be this side of the river. Not too harsh the fumes."

Warm water cascaded down the rocks, pooling on the ledge before flowing back into the split cliff they'd emerged from. It was that dripping trickle in the passage that they'd followed, climbing and squeezing through to the outside.

Luck brought the water. The infants had sucked the last of their pink liquid and were dehydrated. Fee herself had begun to feel ill, hearing voices, unsure if Vaulters still chased them or if the shouts echoed in the dark were imagined.

"It's just a short drop," Grindle said of the jagged slope beneath the ledge. "I'll go first and you hand the babes down."

Fee nodded and dipped her fingers in the water, sticking the wet in the newborns' mouths, and while Grindle lowered herself from the jutting rock shelf, Fee dug out the bead stolen from the bound Civ.

She reconnected the two halves, wrapping the thin wire around her head. She'd pulled the Connex-Link apart when the Vaulters entered the tunnel after them so as not to be located, but she was out now and needed find Racine.

"Yah, ready," Grindle called from below.

Fee removed the sling, tied the babies in with a loose knot across the top, and dangled the bundle to Grindle's upstretched arms. Relieved of the weight on her chest, she rolled her shoulders and neck and wiped the damp from under her breasts.

She was just sat to drop herself down when the Connex-Link sputtered, and suddenly she was seeing a tangled landscape of yellow and brown in front of her eyes and hearing feet scuffling in a brush. Racine? "Where are you?" Fee cried. "I'm come outside."

"What do you say?" Grindle called.

Fee waved her quiet. "Identify yourself," a voice demanded through the Connex. "I see the Palisades behind you."

"I'm to join you," she said, hesitatingly, to the voice that didn't sound like Racine's at all.

"This channel is classified. Identify yourself and your location."

No. Not Racine. She ripped the bead from her head, twisting the clear silver gem apart and shoving the pieces into her pocket.

"They see us," she called to Grindle, jumping down with no caution, landing hard on her feet and tumbling through the underbrush past the blue braided woman holding the babies. "We need make moves away. They know where we are."

LEAR

THE WOMAN'S VOICE faded, and as the audio failed, the pixilated visual snapped and disappeared. It wasn't Starly. Lear would recognize her voice.

With so many natives trading for transmitters stolen from newly arrived Civs, the Link's oversaturated channel was useless. But he didn't care about the mystery woman on the cliffs. All that mattered was that he find his asset, and with her, Anthony.

The embedded coordinates of the albino's latest flare put her less than one mile north of his position, and he needed to reach that location before daylight was gone. It would have been faster to continue in the transport, but he'd spent too great an effort, first climbing long, narrow cliff steps from what was once Hoboken, and then, with three hired men costing a Prod, a solar flashlight and a bottle of gin, towing the transport from where it had long been trapped in an unstable crevasse.

No, he wouldn't second-guess his decision to leave the tank hidden back in the thick brush. The detour west around unmapped rivers would have been impossible on foot, but the armored vehicle had taken him as far as he would risk in the unfamiliar terrain and would remain stashed now until his return with Anthony, a victory that would redeem his name with Seth and remove the death sentence Racine's lies had placed him under.

He'd deliver the recovered transport along with the deserter, and Seth would surely reward his loyalty with readmittance to, and promotion in the Project.

He adjusted the mask around his scabbed head and followed the old highway toward thick black smoke rising in the distance.

Starly's flare had warned of an underground explosion. Her group was fleeing the blast, abandoning their search for the Rails. She would update her next location as instructed, but Lear wasn't waiting for a flare that might be days coming. He feared losing their trail—Anthony's trail—and wouldn't give them the chance to get away.

He climbed past remnants of a recent campsite, hiking to a tall barbed gate where smoke rose behind ruins. He scanned for signs of instability from the subterranean caverns, but mosquitoes were swarming and deer grazing in what was once a driveway, and there was no indication of cavern activity at all.

Familiar logos—*GDMP*—reflected stored sunlight through the grass in the deepening dusk and Lear examined the stone building more closely, noting cables and cams across the roofline. A Project substation, he realized, coming around the building to smoke billowing from the ground.

He could smell the rubber burning even through the mask. A plank supporting what looked like trashcans had slipped, spilling molten rubber, but mounds of dirt around the ditch had prevented the fire spreading. He dug with his hands, throwing armfuls of earth and stone into the barrels to stifle the fire beneath the blanket of dirt.

The added weight caused the supporting boards to slip further, and drove the barrels and smoldering rubber crashing into a space that sounded deep and wide according to the echo the fall returned.

Lear pointed his solar light into what he believed to be a cavern entrance, confused why burning cans were set on top, but when he saw the descending stationary escalator through the smoke of the spilled barrels, the reality of the scene became clear.

There had been no subterranean explosion. The fire was staged. Anthony had discovered the passage he'd come to find, and the lying Starly, with no care for her son, was escaped with the traitor and his Resistance.

Lear kicked the remaining planks away, stepped carefully into the pit, adjusted his mask to the highest filter and made his way down the shaft through the smoke and debris.

GRINDLE

THE BABIES WERE asleep, finally, cried to exhaustion but still wheezing. Grindle felt their chests pulling in labored breath as she picked through weeds dried under the cliffs, and she lay a strip torn from her tunic over their heads to shield against the scorched air and keep them cool from the setting sun's last touch.

Fee had continued ahead, climbing a barrier of tumbled rock, and Grindle hurried after her, feet blistered in thin sandals, her more sturdy belongings left on the wagon carting bags brought to the Companion initiative. She hadn't eaten since the meal provided on the journey to the Vault and the babies, too, were hungry, having finished the last of their pink straws a day earlier.

"Oysters," Fee called, and Grindle scrambled up the rocks, bird screeches echoing in the growing dusk. She patted the stirring babies through their bunting, surveying the far side of the ridge. A wide water streamed east from between broken cliffs to empty into the Hudson, its banks host to long beaked birds opening shells on the shore, squabbling and searching for each next morsel.

Fee slid down and the birds scattered, flapping wings with annoyed cries. Grindle followed and stooped to pick an oyster from the pebbles, prying it open with a shard the birds had cast aside. She drank the slippery meat, opening another and another until the pains left her belly and the sun fell behind the cliffs.

Leaning against rocks, Grindle untied the babies, setting the lethargic infants on the flat stone. The boy wheezed and coughed, kicking his pale arms and legs with the effort, and the girl, her wrap dry of void, whimpered without tears, her eyes dull.

Grindle ripped another strip from her tunic, dipping the weave into the river and wringing the cloth over the babies, wetting their skin and raising their flesh in tiny bumps before rewrapping them. "I've gathered seeds for their milk," she said to Fee. "But the waters are salt. One of us needs climb and find fresh for drinking."

"Not before dawn," Fee said, twisting her silver bit as she settled against the ridge, closing her eyes. "Tomorrow we'll think how to cross this oyster river too wide to swim and too deep to wade with the babies. Without them, maybe we'd have success."

Grindle turned from Fee and hugged the infants close, closing her eyes. They slept deep as night spread across the intersection of rivers until she woke with a start to lights over the ridge.

The babies were motionless, so still she couldn't tell if they had breath, and she looked to Fee for help but the dark-haired woman was gone from her sleep place, not anywhere under the silver numbers. Grindle called out, climbing the rocks in search as the lights woken her filled her eyes.

Hairless on the north side of the ridge. Many of them, and Fee in their midst. She'd betrayed them. "No," Grindle cried as Fee pointed and the group moved toward her. She cowered in rocky shadows, afraid for the babies dehydrated in their sling, but a multi-note whistle pierced her terror and she looked out again, more closely—yes, they were bald, but they were stubbled, and they were not of the Vault.

"Don't be feared," a big man called. "It's Tinny. Never Again the Bad times."

"I'm Nia," a woman said, climbing to join her. "We also flee the hairless."

"But how are you here?"

"Fee's Link connected with mine as we sailed south in the dark. She told of the infants and from where you escape."

The woman Nia opened her tunic and the white spirals tattooed across her breasts shone in the light of the numbers. "My newborn left milk in her departure," she said sadly. "Let the babies nurse."

.

SETH

IT WAS FORTY-EIGHT hours since Seth had siphoned the nanobits, preparing the pellets without assistance, exporting the section from the shallow trenches of data grown coiled around nutrient strands, and transferring the contents of the pipette to the syringe. He'd injected the Records under his collarbone and cleared all trace of his work, waiting for the *whispers* to take hold.

His system raced. Palpitations, sweating, mind in a thousand directions. Odd cravings—tobacco, salt, sex. Flashes of data. Images. Comprehension. Already, a *whisper—a* single neuro-ocular event—had solved the Interface connectivity problem.

Specialists had been trying to configure the Heaven Interface into the Vault's brain—the photon servers—and the Touched twins had been working with them to create that connection. All those scientists and not a one with a clue. The blind leading the blind.

Seth's *whisper* had revealed their entire approach incorrect.

The Interface needed to be positioned, not in a server sequence, but chained to the nanos on the Level Thirteen Farm. A specific placement that would initiate the Heaven download.

Seth had ordered the Interface transferred to the Farm, certain now that his secret, self-restoration of Records had been the righteous course and the quickest path to the knowledge required to move forward.

Jittery with *whisper* anxiety, Seth turned to his transparent Panel. "Update," he said, and the Connex lit at his command.

Patrice appeared first, the only sign of her ordeal a deep rash along her neck triggered by the blanket she'd been bound in. "Civs have suspended search in the Rails. We believe the Touched found exit through a collapse in the eastern wall. Teams will monitor the river and shore. We're hopeful they'll find the escaped natives."

He turned his attention next to Marilena's face, her lips swollen from an aerosol sprayed during her confinement. "Speak."

"Racine flared that he's enabled the Water Constriction System to put down a resistance along the east and south."

"Jesus." Racine had no authorization to power up the water electricity. "What about C Team? They were in the East River."

"Charlie was forced to retreat when the charge hit the water, but had already completed the tide diversion into the tunnels. Civs are at subway exits to relocate natives as they're flushed out."

Seth nodded, dismissing the women. "Sabat," he said, as his medical director's peeling face came into focus. "Report."

"I'm onsite. Level Thirty-one remains uncompromised. The data will be shielded." Sabat cleared his throat. "I must again counsel against spending the hours of Heaven restore in Cellblock. The Metas can be difficult. Dangerous, even."

"Regardless," Seth said. "I'll be inside." Though he wouldn't explain to Sabat what he'd done, he had to protect himself and his *whispers* from Field Wipe, just as he needed to protect the Metas.

According to reconstructed logs, the *Humanity Restoration* backup wasn't located in Heaven. He needed Lahara to find where that copy was stored, but until they grabbed her again, or until his whispers informed how to recover Meta-Records directly from the holders, Seth had no choice but to keep these natives safe.

Once he learned where inside the bodies the Meta-Records lay, he'd task Sabat with their removal. Civs would deal with the resultant medical waste.

Rising voices—Metas behind Sabat—interrupted his thoughts. A white-haired man pointed at him through the Link. "Never interrupt your enemy when he's making a mistake," he was telling excited others. "We'll not battle prematurely, lest we teach our art of war, but our time draws close."

"If you were not deluded by data," Seth shouted back, "you'd be honored to be included in this great undertaking. What's your name? You, with your grand ideas, will be the first to return your stolen identity to us."

The man turned—he was albino—and Seth felt chilled at the Meta's pink-eyed stare.

"In our time no one has the conception of what is great," the man said. "It's up to me, Napoleon Bonaparte, to show them." He smiled. "Your words are meaningless. We don't reason with intellectuals. We shoot them."

LAHARA

LAHARA TIGHTENED THE bindings around her leaking milk and leaned against the stairwell, making sure not to close her eyes lest she doze standing, even through her racing heart. She'd only just eluded pursuers, running through one of the warehouse levels to trip alarms in a mayhem that brought the full armed Security Civ force up from their Level Twenty-six station.

"Go," she'd whispered to Rolf through the Connex, and he'd used her diversion to descend undetected past the evacuated guard level.

She was to wait a few moments before following, and although alarms still blared through the warehouse and she expected any moment to be found hiding during the delay, the stairwell was quiet. Perhaps she was safe behind this door she'd sealed with the Prod stolen from Marilena.

She pushed damp hair off her face, fearing to collapse. When had she last slept? Within moments of Grindle's and Fee's entering the Rails and her flight into the core with Rolf and Roman, Civs had poured through Seventeen, voices raised, shouting orders that echoed after them into the open center. With the smell of her babies still on her face and hands, she'd run barefoot, following the brothers up cold, black scaffolding.

She'd clung to the catwalk overlooking whirling levels of machinery as short explosions from below rattled the metal. "We need go back and stop them," she'd cried over the detonations and the noise of the powered equipment. "It's the Rails they blast. There'll be punishments on my babies."

Roman shook his head. "Civs are trying, but your newborns will be brung far away before they make entrance. Fee sealed the passage. They won't be fast to break through."

Roman had been right. It had taken long into that first night to blast the Rails open, but no sooner had he reassured her than a Civ surprised them there on the catwalk, passing with her head down, manipulating a maintenance Panel in her hands.

"Ya ya ya ya ya," Lahara had screamed at the woman in white, baring and clacking her teeth without thinking, a trick of voice used to scare beasts from the fields, and the Civ had looked up, terrified, dropping her Panel and unable to reach her Prod as she stumbled, startled.

Roman had leapt to spray her from the jar he carried, and she'd stilled immediately, allowing Rolf to grab the Panel and drag her away out of sight. "Spray her again and again," Lahara yelled. "Don't let her wake to say we're here."

Fleeing the downed body, they'd hidden in a cramped bay of cables. "Why do we wait?" Lahara asked. "We need go now and make damage to the nanos while all are busy with our escape."

"It's the nutrient tanks below the Farm we'll target," Roman said. "But first we gather information."

He rubbed his head, and where the spiky hair parted, his tattoo was revealed. Same like his brother Reko, Lahara thought, and she calmed to think of him, and her husband, and she nodded in agreement. "You tell me what we're to do, then."

"There are Touched still detained. Hard to feel them, yeah, but when it appeared I wasn't to listen, Seth spoke their location— *Cellblock*. Does it ring a meaning?"

Lahara closed her eyes and pictured the interior of the model she'd explored during her search for the Heaven Interface. "If I can get to the sessions," she said, "I can find Cellblock."

The stolen glass key charms had stopped working but Rolf used the Civ's Panel to access what he called the lock's algorithm, opening the stairwell to Level Fifteen and then turning the door handle on the darkened, familiar laboratory.

It was Roman now directing Lahara's *whisper* session. "Try here," he'd said softly through the belts and panels Patrice had controlled so harshly these past months, and Lahara made easy visit to the model, examining each level until she located Cellblock, a huge fortified center chamber on the deepest Level Thirty-one.

The finding took hours in *whispers* but only minutes in real time, though they remained a long while afterwards as Civs roamed the corridors for night duties. It was then she'd rested, closing her eyes to a blackness that almost replenished. Yes, two days earlier was the last she'd slept any length of time.

Rolf's footsteps faded below as another's echoed overhead. The turn of the stairwell obstructed her view, providing only a glimpse of white cloth between the railings. Lahara tensed, ready to lead the Civ through another chase—away from Rolf—but the unseen staffer exited above without incident.

Rolf had figured the unlock algorithms but had not yet opened the Level Thirty-one door by the time Lahara met him at the bottom of the stairwell. Her Connex tingled and she shifted the bead to see Roman's face like a floating light in her eye.

"I'm still on Fourteen," he whispered. "Civs run like mice trying to sort what happened. They don't know who made the alarms, but they're searching every level."

"And the nutrient tanks?" Lahara asked. They'd been trapped below the Farm for almost two days, unable to get close to the tanks or even leave their hide, each time forced back for Civs on kitchen or water tasks. It wasn't until this morning that the timing of Civs and staff had provided the interlude they'd waited for from their hidey hole, and when the corridor cleared, they'd sped to work their plan, she and Rolf descending, Roman to remaining on Fourteen.

"Done," Roman said. "The tanks are compromised, the nutrients diverted."

"Hurry down," Lahara said. "We won't go in without you."

Lahara dissolved the last bits of protein cracker in her mouth with a water straw given by Roman. Rolf, too, chewed snacks shared by his brother who'd delayed his descent to raid the food boxes. A smart detour as they'd all three been so hungry.

It was cooler on this lowest level, and quiet. No lights on the walls, and the hum heard everywhere in the Vault was here gone. "Cellblock," Lahara said as they stopped at the barred double door.

Rolf tapped his fingers on the Civ's Panel, and where one moment there was silence, in the next Cellblock was unsealed, filling Lahara with a clamor of *whispers* she staggered beneath.

Roman and Rolf, too, were stunned by the strange names come bursting in greeting through the *whispers. Einstein, Jonas Salk, Pliny the Elder, Pope Francis*, and others too jumbled to sort.

"We're to bring you home," Roman said, trying to herd the Touched to the Freight, but the Cellblock group—more in count than the fingers on two hands—were frightened at this unexpected freedom and they pressed into the hall without direction, pushing Lahara away to separate from the twins.

"He who fears being conquered is sure of defeat," a white - haired man shouted, and the group cheered his words.

Lahara, caught in the confusion of the *Newly Touched*, tried to maneuver back to Rolf and Roman, but as she did, strong hands yanked her into an alcove opened quietly along the outer wall.

She twisted to see Sabat looking up and down the height of her. "What have you done?" he rasped. "Where are the babies?"

"Gone to their own home," she said, defiant. "Away and gone."

"Leave us be," Roman shouted, pushing through Touched to reach her. "We won't be detained by any one hairless."

Sabat shook his head. "You have to get inside and conceal yourself among the others. Seth will be joining this group. Cellblock is the only safe place to be."

"No," Roman said. "I've burnt holes in the feed tanks and lines. The nutrients pour out and the nanos dehydrate. There will be no restore and no Field Wipe. We're now only to get home."

"That's a failed plan," Sabat said. "The feed lines self-repair. Backup solution will be already flowing." He shook his head. "The only way to abort is to remove the Heaven Interface from its integration in the Farm."

"You have to help us," Lahara said.

"Impossible. That would be suicide." He raised his Prod and fired into the air as the white-haired man narrowed his lavender eyes. "Back inside," Sabat called. "Every one of you."

ANTHONY

THE LEVEL SEVENTEEN corridor was deserted, mortar and brick and steel fallen where it had been blasted from the entrance, and Anthony led Drake and Starly over the rubble. Elizabeth, some steps ahead, wheeled one of the light handcarts they'd found on the Rails platform. Carts they'd fill with supplies.

"Is my boy brung to this place?" Starly sniffled, hanging onto a second transport. Her pale skin was covered with dirt, eyeliner long cried off and she shivered for a lack of wine. "I don't remember the time took to get here, I'm so confused by the thirst."

Anthony, too, had only vague memory of hiking the Rails. Elizabeth had murmured Lens words, and in formation they'd traveled through the night until they arrived at the platform outside the Vault. There they'd rested a short while in a dark, long-disabled train, before entering the corridor.

"We'll locate your son," Elizabeth told Starly. "But now we're getting medicines for the children, and I need you to stay focused."

"I have my pass code," Anthony said, recalling the encrypted pattern he'd been assigned.

Elizabeth shook her head. "We'll use my father's key. It's not recorded in the system and won't raise alarms."

She tapped a sequence onto a pad set between hor-verts, and an elevator opened right away. "Whatever it takes, Anthony," Elizabeth said as she and Starly rolled their transports in.

A second hor-vert arrived, and Anthony gestured Drake inside, the Touched hesitating only slightly at the strange chamber. "One hour," Anthony called, and both doors shut, his hor-vert ascending to the Farm, Elizabeth's descending to the Warehouse.

Anthony led Drake cautiously into the hallway curving toward the Farm. Lined with pipes and cables and shelves, the corridor was deserted, but voices and light filtered from an office ahead.

They made their way to the lit doorway, keeping close to the wall for security. Dark glass prevented Anthony from seeing anything but shadows crossing inside, and he leaned in to listen.

"The vandals are where?" That was Seth, his deep voice unmistakable.

"I was sprayed. When I woke, they and the Metas were gone," the gravelly-voiced Sabat answered. "I don't know where."

The door opened and as the Vaulters pushed out, Anthony pulled Drake behind a rack. "If I might suggest," Sabat was saying, "suspend Field Wipe and the restore until the situation's in hand."

Seth's face twitched. "The Heaven Interface is fused. Detachment now would destroy the port. We proceed as scheduled."

Anthony leveled his Prod through the shelving, but before he could discharge the current, Drake unsheathed his knife and overturned the unit concealing them, screaming, "Ay-a-ay-a-ay."

"Security to Thirteen," Seth shouted as Anthony scrambled to tackle him, disarming the Vaulter of his Prod and Panel before he could transmit further. Sabat threw his hands in the air, and without a fight, removed his gear.

"Up you go," Anthony said, propelling Seth to where, behind a glass observation wall, an illuminated cube flicked yellow sparks at the nano containers stacked in the Farm.

"Open it."

"Anthony," Seth said, lashless eyes narrow. "I regret not bringing you into the inner circle when Melly died. The transition was made so quickly and you were overlooked. I was wrong. You had concerns. I should have listened."

The man whose leadership he'd fled was crafty, but Anthony was over being manipulated. "I said open it."

"The Farm can't be unsealed." Seth held his stare. "Much has happened since you left. We know more about the world, about the data, about the others. Come back in. You'll be an officer. Top-tier Specialist. I could use your input. Your intelligence."

Of course you could, Anthony thought, shoving his Prod against Seth's chest. The Vaulter only shrugged. "Hurt me or kill me. It won't make a difference."

Anthony swung his Prod away from Seth, sending a full

charged current into the observation window. The glass clouded then cleared, and Anthony turned the laser back on Seth.

"Is this about the Record holder Lahara?" Seth asked, sweat damping his neck. "I can offer protection to her and the Touched she's with. Take me to Thirty-one."

"What's on Thirty-one?" Anthony demanded.

Seth started to answer, but stopped as the ground rumbled beneath their feet. Overhead lights went to brown, and scrolling numbers faded to yellow and orange and to a red almost invisible on the black wall. "Who brought the power down?" he shouted, wrenching himself from Anthony's grasp.

Doors clicked, unlocking along the corridor—the stairwell, labs, anterooms, closets. "Everything's opening," Anthony said, diving to try and grab Seth. "The Farm should be opening, too. Why isn't it opening?"

Dozens of Security Civs spilled from the stairwell, their stark white jackets bright even in the dim light, and as they filled the hall, Seth scrambled away, dodging the current from Anthony's Prod and escaping into a maze of dark labs.

"Fuck," Anthony said, unable to chase after him with the armed Civs approaching.

"Forget him. Use the Connex," Sabat whispered. "They're waiting for instructions."

The clear, flexible, sheet of Seth's that Anthony had stuck in his belt was like an old friend in his hands. Enabling Melly's key, he transmitted a system-wide command.

Immediately a siren blasted the urgent code, a Com voice repeating, *Evacuate, Contamination Alert, Evacuate*, and dark red arrows flashed along the walls and floors to indicate exit paths.

"What did you do?" Sabat asked, eyes wide in horror.

"We're fine," Anthony said, as in unison, the Civs lowered their Prods, raised protective head coverings pulled from their collars, and returned to the stairwell. "Just a faux emergency to get them out of here and out of the Vault."

Sabat spoke quickly. "The Heaven Interface has to be severed from the nano chain, but I swear I don't know how to get through the glass. Seth spoke the truth about Lahara. She was here but escaped with two others. I tried to make them stay. Their only hope was to remain shielded on Thirty-one."

"How much time left?" Anthony asked, examining the Farm through the observation wall. Narrow nutrient lines connected to each stacked container, and larger ducts flowed through the window into the Farm carrying heat and grow gasses.

"One hour minus quarter," Sabat said, pointing to a sequence of numbers below the pulsing cube. "Seth initiated the restore. None of the Specialists were informed in advance and I don't know how he figured the placement. He may have been working with his own Record holder."

"Or he absorbed data himself to access Admin's files," Anthony said, turning to a grinding shriek heard over the evacuation alerts. "And if that's the case, you can bet he's headed to Thirty-one now to shield his own Records."

He motioned Drake and Sabat into the shadows as the grinding sound got louder. "The Freight," he said, and with his back to the wall, he made his way toward it.

The gaping elevator was open, hissing steam. Anthony stepped in front of the dark, idling chamber. "Come out slowly," he said to the shadows at the back, and Starly lunged and shoved her transport onto him, knocking stacked boxes and pouches from the unit.

"I thought you were him," she cried, grabbing Anthony. "Hairless the both of you. He's here now, the one has my boy."

"There were a lot of Civs running in confusion at the power down," Elizabeth said, sorting the spill. "Specialists, too. I don't know who she saw in the dark." She took Starly's hand. "We'll be away before he sees you."

"You found everything?" Anthony asked.

"Yes. All loaded."

"Go on up and secure the provisions," he told them. "I have forty-five minutes still to figure out the Farm."

LAHARA

WHIRLING BLADES DANGLED uncertainly in their hugeness and the wide humming boxes what Roman called *generators* sounded to cough and choke.

Lahara threw one more chair dragged to the catwalk into the Vault core, stepping back at the sparks shot up where it made contact. The first object thrown had triggered the power down, and by the time she and Roman finished dumping metals onto the machinery, entire systems had shuddered silent, and now, the cool air was stopped pumping.

"That should slow the Civs, yeah?" Roman said, leading Lahara to join Napoleon below. "Make a dark confusion."

A metallic voice repeated *Evacuate* and *Contamination* through the corridor as Lahara stepped carefully over two Civs disabled at Napoleon's feet. "What's happened?"

"Hairless fleeing while you worked your sabotage," he said. "They came from chambers into the stairs. These here tried insisting we evacuate to the holding area."

"Nothing from Rolf?" Roman asked, and as Lahara's own Connex remained silent, Napoleon's shaking head was not unexpected. Except for three from Cellblock left with them—Pliny, Jonas and Pope—the rest of Napoleon's group was gone with the yellow-haired twin to Level Five. If Rolf could work numbers in the command center, he might find how to stop the Field Wipe.

"Stay alert," Napoleon said, opening the stairwell, and after a few moments climb they halted in the darkened space between levels Fourteen and Thirteen. The door above had opened, and footsteps were heading right for them.

"What the dangum fux?" the man climbing down shouted as Napoleon grabbed him. "Le' go me. You're not hairless, nor am I."

"Tell who you are," Lahara said, trying to place the razor-balded man who had *whispers* in his eyes. "Quickly."

"Drake of the Mount come with the Resistance," he said. "I know you, Touched One. It's your husband Switch told of the

Field Wipe we've come to stop."

Her throat caught at his words. "We work to stop the same."

"I go now to find hairless Seth, run away like a rat, and force him unseal the Farm. If your efforts are truly as ours, leave me retrieve the Vaulter, and bring yourselves to join Anthony above."

They moved cautiously, unsure who waited at the end of the dark hall, and Lahara stopped, hand to her mouth, to realize it was Sabat—left felled by the sleeping spray—here now with Anthony, pulling down a section of tubing that fed into the Farm.

"We're to help," Roman had called before Prods could be raised, and after brief instructions and positioning of bodies, Lahara found herself between the Vaulter who'd tried to save her and the one who kept her captive, afraid now only that her Prod would slip in her sweated hand.

"On three," Anthony counted off, and the five—Anthony, Lahara, Sabat, Roman, and Napoleon—discharged their currents as one into the pipe that ran through the glass, falling back from the crackling conduit to watch the tube turn hot white in the darkness for the energy coursed through.

A moment passed before the glass wall cleared to show an interior blackened by the combined blast, but despite the char, the Heaven Interface pulsed strong on the platform, its flickering threads of yellow reaching like the tendrils of glowing jellyfish sometimes found washed onto Lahara's fields.

"Again," Anthony shouted, the next attempt no more successful, and he slammed his fist against the window.

"Less than thirty minutes remain," Sabat said, turning to the Touched. "You must secure yourselves in Cellblock."

Roman shook his head. "Not without Rolf and the others."

"There's no time to find them," Sabat said.

"We'll be quick," Lahara promised. "When our people are gathered, the Freight will be just a few moments to Thirty-one."

"No Cellblock," Napoleon whispered. "I and my soldiers are to battle here with the hairless until the very end."

"Succeed or fail," Lahara said, "This will all be over very soon."

It was an eerie climb through the dark, airless stairwell, and Lahara and Roman did so without pause. At Level Five, they peered across the doorway at screens lit even in the power down. There was no sign of Rolf or the Cellblock Touched, and workstations in the open arena were deserted.

Lahara adjusted her Connex as they entered the command center, willing the bead to sputter with Rolf's voice, but the silver spoke only silence.

"Where are they?" she asked, stopping at a wall shining like a window to the outside. She put her hand on the glass and her fingers left brief shimmering marks where they grazed an image so alive that she reached again to the crowds assembled in the sun.

"It's a transmission," Roman said. "Same how we see in the Connex."

"Everyone's on the Bridge," Lahara said, eyeing the solid brick wall at the end, the Vaulters and Civs covered with protective mesh, and the gathering groups of their own people trying to breach the column of armed Civs stretched across the expanse.

"There he is." Roman pointed to Rolf shackled along the Bridge railing with the *Newly Touched*, and although the image transmitted no sound, crowds had mouths shaped like shouting, and Prods in the holding area were discharging currents. "Think on your babies, yeah?" Roman said. "Should you away to Cellblock? It looks hard out there."

"That decision is already made. I'm to finish this."

Multiple stairwells converged at Level One, a twisting of steps that propelled Lahara and Roman into a stream of Civs still evacuating from other corners, and after a short journey down a black corridor they were pushed through the brick and steel wall and onto the Bridge.

Lahara had raised her tunic over her head to cover her hair. Roman too, concealed himself beneath a wide strip of gauze torn from his waistband. The sun warmed her and Lahara cried to breathe the thick air of home, and even through the mesh across her mouth and nose she could smell the flowers and summer berries in the Bridge gardens.

Men and women—familiar faces among them—pressed toward the Vaulters, chanting *Never Again*. A line of Security Civs discharged their Prods into the air, creating a barrier of warning sparks that kept the people from getting too close.

Lahara hid her face as she passed Patrice addressing the growing crowd of hairless. "Do not interact with the natives," the Vaulter directed. "Remain queued until all clear."

Past the far eastern reach of the Bridge, beyond the crowd, portions of the ancient stacked roads that circled Manhattan blazed in brilliant white and green lights visible even in the sunlight, and Lahara rubbed her eyes at the sight.

"That's how I remember the highway," a Civ was saying. "Too bad about the dolphins, though."

"What happened?" another asked.

Lahara leaned in for the answer but heard only, "The power surge—" before Roman led her away across the Bridge to where Rolf and the others were secured.

A quick look around confirmed that none in the evacuation oversaw their captivity, and with short bursts of Prod camouflaged by sun and crowd, Roman melted first Rolf's, and then the others' bindings, whispering to each as he freed them.

Shouts rose as the people surged, the hordes advancing, raised knives and metal clubs flashing. Vaulter Prods felled many in the rush but were not enough to stop those coming onto them.

"Hurry," Lahara cried, though corralling the *Newly Touched* proved impossible, and they remained behind in their disoriented freedom as Lahara and the twins ran back to the Vault.

A shaved, pale woman emerged from the chaos, shouting and pointing from behind a laden wagon. Lahara turned—she recognized Starly from the Theater district even without her long white hair—and as Starly shouted at a hairless man chasing the Touched, Lahara dashed through the shifting crowd.

Roman pushed against the blistering wall at the Bridge's end and Lahara and Rolf followed him down the black corridor past the converging stairs and into the Freight.

"Weapons on the floor," the hairless man—a Vaulter dressed in clothes of the outside—shouted as he caught up, his Prod aimed and ready to fire.

"You recognize me?" he asked, and Lahara nodded. It was Lear, left for dead the day Racine stole her away.

"Your husband threw me in a boat and rowed me to Queens. Dropped me on a shore full of fucking crows." He shook his head. "The traitor, Anthony, did nothing to stop him."

"Please," Roman said, gesturing Lahara to drop her Prod as he did, and moving her and his brother behind him. "We have only minutes to find our way to safety."

Lear kicked the weapons across the chamber. "Bring me quickly enough to Anthony and you may yet have time."

The Prod was sharp between her ribs, but Lahara wouldn't flinch. They made little noise, and as Lear had pushed them to leave the Freight at Level Twelve, there was no warning they were arrived, just soft steps down the stairs and their tiptoe in the dark, a travel covered by voices at the end of the hall.

"Six minutes and you're wiped with the rest," Anthony was saying. "You and your absorbed Records gone."

Lahara winced at his words and recognized Seth's voice in answer. "If I disengage the Interface, the Collect is forever out of reach. I will die first to ensure the survival of the Project."

Lahara heard the fear in Seth's voice—months in the Vault had taught her his tones—and as they came into the light of the sparkling Heaven Interface she caught Anthony's eye.

He had Seth restrained, arms pulled behind his back, Prod at his neck. Without moving her head—so as not to give their positions away—Lahara located Sabat in the corner, Prod raised, and Napoleon, hidden halfway up a scaffold, weapon also wielded.

"Let Seth go," Lear shouted, jamming his Prod into Lahara's side for all to see. Her eyes filled with sudden tears.

"Shoot them," Seth ordered. "Shoot them all."

Lear spun his Prod at Anthony, then hesitated as a loud, hissing and billowing steam filled the hall, and the pale, razor-balded woman that Lahara had seen on the Bridge ran from the Freight, followed by a robed woman and young man.

"He's the hairless has my son," Starly screamed, charging Lear.

"Shoot," Seth shouted. "Whatever's gone before, I know you're loyal to the Project."

Lear turned, Prod back and forth from Anthony to Drake, to Lahara, and now Starly. "I never had your son," he spat, shoving her back. "Your own brother hid the boy for a barrel of wine."

Napoleon made a strange sound, eyes flicking from the pale woman to Lear, and with a second half laugh, half cry, he discharged his Prod, and Lear dropped spasming to the ground.

Starly shrieked, and an expression Lahara couldn't name crossed Napoleon's face, gone in an instant as he settled back, hidden on the scaffold behind clouds of steam, his Prod again at the ready.

"Three minutes," Anthony shouted through the hot vapors to the Touched. "You can still make it down in the Freight."

"Don't leave me here to die," Seth said.

The robed woman turned to Anthony. "I'm so sorry. To keep the Civs from returning, to buy time, I released the steam and disabled the Freight. I didn't know. It'll take too long to build the pressure back."

"Don't be sad, Elizabeth," the young man with her said gently.

Seth squinted. "Melly's Elizabeth? Jesus, you were mourned for drowned. You betrayed us then and now again?"

At his words, the young man moved protectively between Seth and Elizabeth, and Lahara felt him in the current, and even as she was overwhelmed with a sadness that the end had come, that she'd not ever see her babies again, her *whispers* rose to meet those of Jared Hopes.

They stood together at the edge of a water so blue there was no seam between the waves and sky. Jared held a radiant sphere—a miniature alchemic sun—in his hands. Lahara felt his love of the woman Elizabeth, and understood that what he did, he did for no reason but to ease her sadness. More Touched joined them. Napoleon was there, and Rolf, too, came up on the shore, tossing numbers in the water to spread on the horizon. Drake arrived, and Roman, who smiled and told Jared, "Transmute."

Lahara heard Anthony far beyond their *whisper*. "Ninety seconds," he said, and the woman Elizabeth cried, "Jared, don't."

Jared Touched with Alchemy raised his radiant sphere. Lahara took Rolf's hand who took Roman's who took Napoleon's who took Drake's, and on and on a chain of Touched connected, flowing in the undercurrent as the shore and water and sky turned a perfect and wonderful gold around them.

Without warning, Lahara was thrown from the *whisper*, back to the Level Thirteen corridor, still holding Rolf's hand.

The radiant sphere flickered, and as the orb brightened, the Vault began to shimmer and Lahara heard music more beautiful than the piano and voices she'd once heard inside the Midtown Mount, the lyrics rising here in thick layers of harmony—*already done, already done.*

"No," Seth shouted, ripping himself from Anthony's hold and shoving his body against a ridged section of wall. At his push, the observation window slid open and Seth threw himself over the Interface without concern for the energy snaking from its core.

Everything trembled. The floor, ceiling, pipes, ducts, shelving and glass. Stacked nano containers in the sealed Farm. The Interface cube and the numbers blinking beneath it.

Lahara feared a fire was to start for the lightening of the dark and the shine growing to a flame, but the flames were cool and the blaze burned not like a fire but like a change come upon the world.

She leaned closer to the sphere, tethered by hands clutched on either side, and as the corridor grew hotter and wilder, then cooler and calmer, Lahara watched in the radiance what she felt must be the center of Forever, its deep, pure energy rising past the sphere's confines to flood all in its path.

And when the lightening and brightening was done, the Heaven Interface was stilled completely, its sparking tendrils frozen where they snaked, and the Vault, all the Vault, gleamed the purest gold.

Like what King Midas brung, Lahara thought, remembering a

story Reynaud had shared one cold night.

"*Already done*," Jared said, and Elizabeth held him in her arms where he wept for her touch. "*Done*."

Vaulters and Touched dropped Prods that were useless in their gold gleam and stepped out of clothing gold and hard over their bodies. Seth ran his hands over the gold cube of the Heaven Interface, eyes unbelieving.

Starly reached for the father she'd believed left her for the drink, but Napoleon, with no memory of the young woman who shared his white skin and lavender eyes, pulled away, confused, and it was Anthony took Starly's hand instead.

The one called Pope Francis carried Lear who was still stunned with Prod sleep, and Touched and Vaulters and Never Agains—except Seth who remained a long time before removing himself—made their way, naked, in a strange brotherhood, down the gold hall, up thirteen gold levels of gold stairs and through the gold brick wall at the end of the Bridge.

And as Lahara left forever the pure, dead, Golden Vault, free under the numbers 06.10.2257, it was Switch and Marly come running with the others, and the hairless black mare slipping her lead to greet Anthony.

EPILOGUE

DUST BLEW UNDER a sky bright as the SolSat's 10.08.2335, the sun across the plains illuminating not a trace of those who'd left the message. He didn't expect to see them, since so much time had passed, but surely the visitors hadn't ever reached Mexico City, a Vault dark for over two centuries, as were all the rest.

The bald man switched images and the wide desert dissolved, replaced by a city built between the arid hills and warm, green ocean. Seventy-five years ago the settlement had been little more than a trading post risen from the ruins of an even smaller after-event village, and the Awake prior had seen the caravan roads leading to it from the east still burning in the great Overland fires.

The man looked forward to being outside. They would deal with the message left, and the thefts, and respond to the obvious false positive breach alerts broadcasting from the remote nano servers, but soon enough he'd be out assessing the people's need for data, for that was their charge.

To maintain, and restore, by process of vote, the Records of the Global Collect.

Most votes did not pass. A motion to provide a Jesus, or a Mohammed, went unratified twice in the last century, and as religion had still not emerged in this area, he supposed the issue would be raised again this Awake.

He himself planned to propose a release of Records designed to discourage interbreeding—he'd browse the catalog for the correct nano infusion—as according to satellite feeds, pale natives from the high north were traveling south toward his seaside city. No good could come from the mingling of genes and cultures.

In all the years of the Project, Specialists had voted only once—during the previous Awake—to restore. Nature, with her relentless heat and stingy water favors, had forced their intervention, and when the drought-afflicted native they'd chosen found himself back in his struggling village, he had no memory of the time away or the under-collarbone injection.

Two days later, however, he'd begun constructing an irrigation and filtration system, saving his sparse and dying population from extinction.

That history of rescue made the current status of this city even more astounding. The bald man noted, with amazement, that powered vehicles patrolled complex infrastructure and air-pods hovered silently over silver, domed hangars, an almost unbelievable advance of technology, given the time frame.

The man rubbed aloe on his scalp and recalled to his Connex the digitized message left sixty-five years earlier. The means of the messengers' entrance, theft, and retreat were yet unknown, but media had been set to play upon Awake, and the message had transmitted as they left their Cocooning, just hours ago.

"Greetings from Manhattan," one of four robed, hooded visitors said with a warm smile and eyes that crinkled deeply at the corners. "We come to welcome you to your Awake, and invite you to visit our city on the eastern waters. The journey is long, but with precautions, safe. Please accept our gift in exchange for the many medicines and supplies we have removed from your warehouse, and for the gazillion little bits we've delivered to the people. We head now to Mexico with the same invitation and intent, while others cross oceans in multiple, synchronized missions. Peace be with you, Vancouver keepers of the Global Collect. As you come out of Cocooning, this your last, know that the world awaits you, who, for too long, have directed them from your hidey holes."

That was the whole of the nonsensical, vaguely threatening message, and the gift—a radiating sphere—had been left on the communications console.

The bald man was wary, suspicious of their tale of travels and their familiarity with the Vault and Project. Certainly with their odd, breathless speech and dress, the hooded visitors were not Specialists, though they had not claimed to be. Despite his apprehensions, however, the lightning-filled orb intrigued him, and he lifted the sphere, surprised at its unexpected weight.

He would vote to ignore the invitation to the east. No precedent existed for leaving in an extended Awake, and without Admin's guidance they did not have the jurisdiction to do so. As for the theft, he'd recommend new security protocols, confident their inventory would prove, after inspection, sufficient.

The Vaulter was just entering the council room for the first vote of the Awake when the radiating sphere pulsed in his hand. He stopped at its trembling, and as he did, the chamber began to shimmer. Music filled his head, the lyric—*already done*—repeating in thick harmonies, and the Specialists who gathered in committee ran out, afraid, to the corridor.

The surrounding walls and floors were burning, the flames internal. Images transmitted from every level revealed blinding lights spreading cool and hot over the entire Vault, and it took only moments, as the sphere grew louder and then quieter, for the Vault to transmute, forever changed.

Racing to assess damage, the bald man and his compatriots discovered energy gone, systems frozen golden at their core, water and food gleaming pure and untouchable—every corner of every level sterile and golden and dead.

After several incomprehensible days, hungry, thirsty, naked and without a plan, the bald man and the men and women of the Vancouver Vault climbed many golden stairs, forced from their Golden Vault, into new lives, under the sun, in the world of a gazillion freed little bits.

ABOUT THE AUTHOR

CLAUDIA BREVIS is an author, playwright, songwriter and genealogist living in New York City with her husband, surrounded by all her favorite people.

Comments and questions welcome: claudiabrevisnyc@gmail.com

www.claudiabrevis.com
www.twitter.com/cbrevis

Made in the USA
Charleston, SC
28 April 2014